NO HARP
LIKE MY OWN

Marjorie Quarton

COLLINS
8 Grafton Street, London W1
1988

William Collins Sons & Co. Ltd
London · Glasgow · Sydney · Auckland
Toronto · Johannesburg

BRITISH LIBRARY CATALOGUING IN PUBLICATION DATA

Quarton, Marjorie
No harp like my own.
I. Title
823'.914 [F]

ISBN 0 00 223321 5

Typeset in Linotron Trump Medieval by
The Spartan Press Ltd Lymington, Hants
Printed and bound in Great Britain by
William Collins Sons & Co. Ltd, Glasgow

No harp like my own could so cheerily play
And wherever I went was my poor dog Tray.

Thomas Campbell
The Harper

The author would like to thank all those who helped with research for this novel, and particularly members of the Irish Guide Dogs' Association., I dedicate this book to these dedicated people.

MG

.

I WAS LATE FOR DINNER TODAY, or lunch, as Grandmother calls it. Eighty-two she is, and still boss. She's the one with the money, and she keeps us all at home, getting under one another's feet, trying to make some kind of living out of the farm. I wish to God I could get full time work with Terry.

I rode out two of Terry's horses today; the young grey as well as Tankardstown, so I should have hurried. But I stopped as I always do to look back, before turning Dancing Lady's head down Tinker's Lane for the last mile home.

The farm stands in the dead centre of a hundred acres of fertile land. From the T junction where you turn off, you can see the whole place – Cloninch, the Island Meadow. You can see the grey, two-storied house, with the copper beeches in front of it, the new silage yard and milking parlour, the fields with cows and sheep grazing in them. You can see the river flowing right around the boundary like a great horseshoe. The water is deep brown bogwater, and sally trees hang out over it here and there along the banks. There's miles of undrained bog beyond the river, as different from the farm as gravel is from grass. The bog has more colours than a rainbow. When the light catches the dry sedges and the birch trees, it's just as beautiful as the lakes and mountains the travel agencies go on about. You couldn't make a living on it, but that goes for the lakes and mountains as well.

I turned the mare's head for home, and she trotted away down the lane to her stable and her bit of hay like a two-year-old. I was so happy I felt like singing, in spite of the old lady waiting to tell me off like a child when I showed up late.

It was a great day for me when Terry gave me Dancing Lady. Her tendon isn't too bad – no good for racing, or Terry'd have kept her – but it doesn't bother her at exercise. If it wasn't for her and for Terry I'd be gone long ago. The sun was shining, and little sparks of green and red seemed to dance on her black mane. The pattern the veins made on her neck and her ears was as pretty as lace. Her ears twitched all the time; forward as if she could see with them, then back to hear what I was saying to her.

She half stumbled, and I said, 'Pick up your feet, you silly old fool.' Martin Doyle came past with his tractor, and she shied and sidled, tossing her head and wasting time. It went through my mind that Dancing Lady means more to me than my own family. I don't want it that way, but they make it hard for me.

I put the mare in her stable, pulled off her saddle and threw a rug over her as quick as I could, because I didn't want a row with the old lady. The happiness had left me. I'd never once raised my voice to my grandmother, or to any of them, but the temper's there. It's piling up inside me like steam in a boiler. I'm afraid of my temper, and Grandmother knows it, just as she knows everything about everybody. I suppose she's bored, and it amuses her to try to start something. Grandfather never stirs out now, and Mother and Father are afraid to open their mouths. Mike and Brian keep out of her way, and Denis is careful not to vex her, even when she grumbles about Sheila.

I could hear them all at their dinner as I crossed the yard. Old Shep was lying out on the flagstones by the door. He lolled out his tongue, grinning at me. There was nobody in the mobile home; they'd left the radio on and the door open. I sometimes wonder why Denis went to all the expense of buying it when he got married. Neither he nor Sheila ever goes into it except to sleep, and little Sarah's always with Mother.

They were all talking at once when I opened the door; then they all stopped, and looked at me, waiting for Grandmother to say something. Mother was setting out plates round the table; pudding plates, the meat was cleared away. The others were sitting down. They all looked at me, even Brian and Mike who sit with their backs to the door and had to twist right round.

When Grandmother's in a room, you don't notice the other people much. It's not just the funny clothes she wears, there's something about her. She stands out like a pheasant in a hen-run.

She said, 'Late again, Benedict.'

I'd been going to say, 'Sorry I'm late,' but I changed my mind. The room was stifling, and with the cooker and the two big dressers and all the family round the long table, there was hardly room for me to get to my own place, round the far side. I thought I'd take my time washing, and some of them would be finished and go out, or into the sitting room. I went into the scullery and took off my old black sweater and washed in the sink.

There was mud in my hair. It'd take more than Terry to make me wear a helmet for riding work. I washed my whole head and my arms up to the shoulders, to take away the smells of sheep and horses. I love the warm, friendly smell of horses – who ever heard of a horse with bad breath? But it's musty and nasty on your clothes and skin.

'Hurry on, Ben,' my sister-in-law, Sheila, said, with that whiny note in her voice. 'You haven't time for a bath; your dinner's getting cold.'

'Shut the door, Ben, you'll catch your death.' That was Mother.

'Coming.' I left the muddy sweater beside the sink, rolled my shirtsleeves down, and smoothed my wet hair with my hands. They say Grandmother's hair was black like mine once. She didn't have wedding photos, of course, and it's been white as long as I can remember. The looking-glass that Grandfather nailed to the window-shutter was steamed up, but I didn't bother to wipe it. I have to crane my neck to see in it. I'm a head shorter than any other man in the house, and not allowed to forget it.

When I came back into the kitchen, they were all still there. I squeezed round the table, and carved two slices of nearly cold mutton for myself. I made a face at the cool, greasy gravy and the cold cabbage and potatoes. Grandmother won't allow Mother to keep dinner hot for anyone who's late. I cut myself some bread, and sat down.

'What kept you, Ben?' asked Mother. 'You finished the sheep hours ago.'

'I rode out an extra horse at Terry's. A young one – he nearly had me off. Green as a cabbage.' The mutton was leathery and unappetizing. Only unsaleable animals found their way into our freezer.

Grandmother, bolt upright at the head of the table where she always sits, turned her steel-grey eyes on me. I looked straight back at her. Nobody else in our house does that. 'That horse of yours, Benedict,' she said. 'It must cost a great deal to feed. I would have thought that riding was a rich man's occupation.'

I nearly said, we'd all be richer if you weren't boss. If you didn't own the farm and everything on it.

I said, 'She doesn't eat much, Grandmother. Just a bit of hay and a bag or two of nuts. She'll be out in a New Zealand rug as soon as the ewes come in. Anyway, I pay for her keep.'

'Hm. You'll break your neck one of these days.'

I paid no heed to the old threat. I buttered some bread, and reached for the teapot. My gifthorse saves petrol, and Terry pays me. If he didn't, I'd have nothing but pocket-money like my brothers. I knew it was a waste of time arguing. I felt my face turning red with anger, and of course she noticed.

'Some girl telephoned you this morning, Benedict. She said her name was Maura. Why people will not give their full names, I cannot think. Maura.'

'She should've known I'd be out.'

'That would be the young woman who picked you up at the Spring Show, I daresay. She has the manners I would expect.'

I set down my teacup carefully. Stood up. I heard myself

say, 'I don't know why we put up with you. There's grand old people off rotting in homes because their own won't bother with them. You make me sick.'

I was tied in a knot inside. I could have killed her. I was shaking, and had a hard job to keep my voice steady. I knew she was despising the way I talk. Temper brings out the brogue.

I watched her face, with the big nose and the criss cross of wrinkles, turn slowly white. I saw all the other faces, gaping with their mouths open, waiting for the explosion. My parents looked as frightened as if a tiger had walked into the kitchen. My brothers looked scared too, but curious. Sheila was feeding some mashed up food to Sarah and didn't raise her head. Sarah pushed away the spoon and began to cry.

Grandmother got up slowly, glaring at me, resting her brown-blotched hands on the table, either side of her plate. She didn't say anything at all. I slammed my chair in against the table, and walked out of the house.

I was trembling, sweating; my heart pounded. And hell, I was still hungry. I jumped into the little Renault van that Denis bought cheap from Bord Telecom, and stalled it twice before I got it going. Rage made me clumsy.

My grandmother is heartless, powerful, very likely immortal. I can't imagine life without Grandmother. She ran off with Grandfather nearly sixty years ago, and made enemies of two sets of parents. Poor old Grandfather lost his old friends and never made any new ones. She tried to teach him bridge! Grandfather! And she seems so clever in some ways.

While I was thinking, I was driving – fast. I didn't have anywhere in mind, so I went into town. There'd be a pub open, and I'd get chips maybe, or a burger and a bottle of ale. If the pubs were shut, I'd go back to Terry's, and give him a hand bringing in the mares, and have tea with him afterwards. The sheep didn't take up much of my time in January; they were still out, getting a little hay in the racks. We don't lamb until March.

I stopped the van at Browne's Bar. The Odeon is just across

the street. I'd taken Maura to the pictures at the weekend, and she'd said I'd turn into a bloody sheep if I didn't look out. Perhaps she'd rung up to say she was sorry. I didn't much care. The posters were still up for the picture, *Out of Africa*. I'd really liked it – all the wild animals and everything, but the woman's clothes had reminded me of what Grandmother wears year in, year out. Long jacket, floppy blouse, long tweed skirt. I suppose they were the latest thing when she eloped all those years ago, and that was when the clock stopped for her.

There wasn't anyone in the bar except Billy Browne behind the counter. He was reading *The Irish Stockbreeder*. The iron stools have green plastic tops, and the tables look like pink marble, but not very like. It was dark and dusty, and made me wish I'd gone to the chipper instead. I asked for something hot, and Billy said, 'The microwave's on the blink. What are you doing out in your shirtsleeves this time of year? Granny playing up?' I'd come out without my jacket, without even noticing. I said, 'I'm not cold,' but he came round and plugged in the electric fire and knocked down the switch with his toe.

I bought a beer and drank it down in big gulps. I was still boiling with anger. It was true that I wasn't cold. There was a coloured pattern on the tv screen; I might stay and watch the racing.

Billy has a farm as well as a pub; he says he's losing money on both of them. He doesn't talk much, and I was glad of it. The last thing I wanted was a chat. I sat down at the jangly old piano, and banged out a bit of a tune, not really thinking what I was doing.

Billy said, 'Play it properly, Ben, or leave it alone.' So I moved to one of the pink marble tables. I don't like bar stools, my legs are too short – they dangle. Billy passed his paper over to me, folded open at an advert.

SEE BRITAIN'S TOP FLOCKS
VISIT FAMOUS SHEEP FARMS
Three days for £129, including ticket for fatstock
show at Middlegarth, Yorkshire . . .

'Like a coach trip, Ben? See some more sheep. The brother was going across, but he has the flu. Paid an' all. I was thinking of ringing you. Liverpool boat tomorrow night.'

I opened my mouth to say that I couldn't afford it; that I was busy; that I'd have no time to make arrangements.

'Thanks, Billy,' I said. 'I'd like to go.'

One

A biting east wind, straight from Siberia by way of
Scarborough, had replaced the mean, sleety drizzle of the
morning. It swept over the acres of frost-bitten kale, over the
bent shoulders of the huddled group of Irish farmers, and
scoured Charlie Thorpe's meaty face. Charlie stood four
square to the wind, a microphone in his gloveless hand. His
fur-lined parka was unzipped, showing his thick neck and
open shirt. His eyes watered as he talked; he wiped them on
the back of a purplish wrist. He was hatless, and strands of
his grey hair were tugged this way and that by the gale.

Charlie Thorpe was 'the Guvnor' to everyone within five
miles of Middlegarth Farm. He spoke with the authority of a
cabinet minister, totally conversant with his subject. He
was a fluent talker, and needed no notes. His partner and
son-in-law, Ted Wilkes, was just as well informed; but,
unlike Ted, Charlie could hold an audience, even out of
doors in Yorkshire in January. He was talking about sheep.

The journalist or whatever he was muttered something.
Charlie ignored him. He had no patience with people who
walked round farms in spotless new sheepskins, trilbies and
low shoes. He talked on.

'Bring 'em in now, Guvnor, they're freezing.'

Charlie glared at the man from the *Hangleby Tribune*.
'No colder for them than for me,' he said. His words were
amplified across the windswept kale to the shelter-belt
beyond.

'Yes it is. They aren't used to it. They're too cold to listen.'
Andy Pim of the *Tribune* whipped the microphone out of

Charlie's hand and switched it off, winking at the man from *The Irish Stockbreeder*. Only a few farmers in the front row heard Charlie say something about soft buggers not being able to hear because their ears were cowthered up with clothes.

'Right then,' said Ted Wilkes, taking advantage of the pause. 'That disposes of the fodder crops. Let's move on to the pedigree flock, Charlie.'

Charlie shrugged his big shoulders angrily. He turned and stumped into the barn, muttering. He was impatient of interruption. This shed was the one where the pedigree Suffolk ewes and their pampered lambs gorged on concentrates. The barn was large and chilly, but coming into it from outside was like stepping into a warm bath.

Charlie marched over to the pens, and began to talk again. The Irish group listened with interest. Not everyone understood all that he said, but they had soon gathered that what in Ireland is called a 'yo' to rhyme with go, in Yorkshire is a 'yow' to rhyme with cow. The Agricultural Adviser pronounced this word 'ew', to rhyme with stew, but nobody paid any attention to *him*.

The party from County Kildare split up into smaller groups as they moved from pen to pen. They straightened their shoulders, which had been bowed against the onslaught of the wind, and looked about them. Their lovat green anoraks and Hunter boots might almost have been a uniform; only in the matter of headgear was there much variety. Tweed hats were favoured – the sort sold at outrageous prices to tourists surprised by thunderstorms. The two women wore these, and several of the men. There were a few cloth caps, a knitted Aran hat with a pom-pom, and one or two trendy denim affairs, with zipped pockets, possibly intended for spare socks.

Charlie looked them over with a hard, dispassionate stare. They might have been a pen of wethers at a market – a pen he'd decided not to buy. There was only one bare head. It belonged to a broad-shouldered young man he'd noticed right at the start. Only a little feller, thought the Guvnor, but there's ways about him. The bareheaded young man didn't wear gloves either. His hands were workworn, with thick knuckles, but you could tell he washed them. A blocky young man, frowning as he listened. Charlie wondered who he was.

Ben was enjoying himself. He hadn't any particular interest in pedigree stock, because there wasn't enough money at home to buy any, but he liked Charlie's no-nonsense style, and was looking forward to hearing him talk about his commercial flock. He looked down at the pen beside him, where a ewe stood within reach; he scratched her hard black skull, and pulled her ear. 'Well, old girl,' he said, 'that's a fine pair of lambs you have.'

The Guvnor stopped talking. His watery blue eyes focused on Ben. There was a moment's silence. 'Have you anything more to say to that sheep?' he asked. 'If not, we'll get on.'

Ben straightened up, and returned glare for glare. One of the women giggled. Des Walker said, 'Talking to the sheep, Ben? Beginning of the end.' Charlie, broad back turned, was showing how the automatic feeders worked. Nobody interrupted him.

A ram bred at Middlegarth Farm had sired more champions than any other in history. A record price had been refused for him, and he lived in considerably more comfort than the Guvnor himself. The group gathered round while a white-coated man held Middlegarth Northern Hero for all to admire. He was bedded up deep with straw; the wall behind his pen was covered with rosettes – blue, red and tricolour. Charlie had a great deal to say about Middlegarth Northern Hero, also about his remote ancestors. Ben grew bored. He edged out of the group and went back to the ewes, dark-headed and blocky like himself.

'Going for another chat?'

Ben scowled at Des Walker. 'Good listeners, sheep,' he said. But the Guvnor was turning in his direction. Ben walked past the ewes and out of the barn.

17

Ben had noticed a dog kennel close to the door of the barn, in an alley way. Its felt roof was designed for out of doors, but out of doors was too cold. The Guvnor was not a dog lover. He valued Roy as a valuable unit of unpaid labour; reliable, honest, and not in the habit of answering back. The kennel appeared to be empty – everyone had passed it by on the way in, but Ben had seen the movement of the light chain, slithering over the sill. Standing well back, Ben looked into the kennel. Hostile eyes stared back. Roy was not fond of strangers. A tooth gleamed in the shadow as he lifted his lip.

'Hello boy. Come on, Shep. Come here then.'

Roy slowly lifted his head from his paws, pricked his ears. The tooth disappeared from view. Here was someone who was obeyed by dogs. The growl died in his throat.

'Come on Shep. Here, boy.' As a schoolboy, Ben had won small bets with other boys who had been prepared to stake their pocket-money that their dogs wouldn't leave them when Ben called them. They'd always lost.

'Shep . . . Shep . . .' The name was wrong, but this man had to be obeyed. Roy felt the pull of Ben's will, as tangible as the pull of his chain. He stood up, and slowly came to the door of the kennel. He sniffed the stubby hand held out to him, palm down.

Ben had seen dogs like Roy on television and at the local sheepdog trials. Nobody near Cloninch kept a border collie. Old Shep at home was a heavy, lazy dog, fat and idle. Ben could hear the Guvnor's voice through the wall, still discoursing on Middlegarth Northern Hero. He didn't know that the dog, now licking his hand, carried the blood of even more champions than the sheep.

One of the women came looking for Ben – Norah, the pretty one. 'Come on, Ben, we're going over to the other buildings. The old boy's wondering what you're up to.'

'Thanks,' he said, giving Roy a last pat. They walked quickly together, and Ben thought, she's after me. He was used to constant putting down by his grandmother, and often wondered why so many girls should be after him. Having so little to offer, he gave them a wide berth. This Norah now. She had a boyfriend with her, six footer, fine farm of land coming to him. Funny, thought Ben.

'Penny for them, Ben,' said Norah. She had a silly laugh. Ben didn't answer. She took his hand.

'Ah, go on,' he said, took his hand away, put it in his pocket. 'That Trevor of yours could break my neck with one hand.' She laughed again, putting her arm through his. He quickened his pace, and shook her off again. Bloody women, he thought.

Afterwards, they all walked back to the tall brick farmhouse, where the minibus was waiting. The driver had grown bored and cold, and had joined the group of farmers, where he was even more bored but rather warmer. They crunched across the gravelled courtyard, keeping their voices low as they talked. Charlie's bullying and the east wind had dispirited them.

Ted Wilkes, bringing up the rear, hoped that Mandy had tea ready. Charlie knew she would, he had told her to.

Ben was lagging again. There were two stables in the courtyard, with horse's heads looking over the half doors. The light outside the back door shone on the white-blazed face of the nearest. Ben went at once to the horse, and rubbed its face. The horse bent its head in recognition of something it couldn't define. Ben looked over the door, and saw that the horse had been 'roughed off'. It wore a rug, but there was mud in its mane, and it was unshod. It stood with its weight on its right foreleg, the left fetlock was puffy. Interested, Ben stared down, wondering about the leg.

He was alone. Everyone else had gone into the house. The Guvnor turned back, and came with purposeful strides. Nosey little sod. He'd paid to see sheep. He was about to give the young man what he called a bit of straight Yorkshire, but Ben spoke first.

'Has he something in his foot? Is he gravelled?'

'God knows, lad. You tell me. Vet says it's ligaments.'

Charlie looked gloomily over the door. 'You know better than vet, I expect,' he said nastily.

'I'm no vet.' Ben turned away from the door. 'I thought it was hurting him even when he had no weight on it, like an abcess. Can I go in and have a look?'

'No, by lad. If I want another opinion, I'll ask for it.' Charlie turned away before Ben could reply. He was tired. He made up his mind at that moment to put a stop to these capers. He was sick of lecturing busloads of strangers.

Charlie followed the group indoors, and left them to their tea in the kitchen. He went into the front room and dropped into his armchair. He shut his eyes.

'Wake up, Father!' His daughter Mandy was shaking his shoulder. 'They're going. Aren't you coming out to see them off?'

'Suppose I better had.' Charlie felt about for his slippers. Grumbling, he went out to the yard where he stood, a massive figure, under the light at the back door.

The wind had dropped, and it was snowing. The fourteen members of the group piled into the minibus. They were going down to the Turpin Arms in Middlegarth for drinks, then back to their hotel. Charlie Thorpe watched them stonily. There'd be no more. Last to board the bus was the little feller; the one who was talking to a sheep. The first person who'd had anything sensible to suggest about the lame horse. Wasn't he –

'You, lad! You there behind!'

The young man looked round, with his foot on the step. His expression was unfriendly. 'Talking to me?'

'What do they call you, lad?'

'Ben. Benedict Glyn.'

'Ben. Sensible name. Had a goodish dog called Ben. Know a bit about horses, do you?'

'A bit.'

'You drive?'

'I do.'

20

'Endorsements?'

'No.'

'Not looking for a job, are you?'

Ben stopped, holding the door of the minibus. Huge flakes of snow drifted down, settling on his hair. He didn't seem to mind.

'I might be,' he said.

'See you in pub,' said Charlie. He turned on his heel, and disappeared into the house.

His son-in-law was aghast. 'What do we know about him?'

'Nowt. He's right enough, there's ways about him.' Charlie and Ted Wilkes faced each other across the kitchen table. Mandy Wilkes impatiently snatched away the teacups.

'But Guvnor,' said Ted, (nobody but Mandy called Charlie 'father') 'he can't do Peter's work. I mean, Peter was a good lambing shepherd and did the horses as well. How do we know that he's any use with sheep?'

'He'll do. Doesn't chatter. Doesn't mind a bit of snow. See him as we came through back barn second time? Old Roy came out of kennel to him. There's ways about the lad. Any road, if he's no good, he goes. Give over nattering.'

Ted shrugged his shoulders, and picked up the *Farmers' Quest*. Their advertisement had been in two weeks. Still no answers.

Temporary, possibly permanent job offered to energetic young person, capable of lambing 300 crossbred ewes. Able to take charge in head shepherd's absence. Clean driving licence. Knowledge of horses an advantage. Large estate within thirty miles of Leeds. Cultural outlets in village.

That last bit had been Mandy's idea. Considering she was the Guvnor's daughter, she had some funny notions.

By the time Charlie had had tea and changed his clothes, it was snowing hard. Ted and Mandy both refused to go down to the Turpin Arms with him.

'For God's sake make sure the lad realizes it's only temporary,' pleaded Ted. 'Peter might come back in a month.'

'Might he, hell. What good'll he be just out of plaster?'

Ted tried again. 'That's another thing. How do you expect this Irish chap to ride Anagram? Nobody's even tried since he put Peter in hospital. If he was my horse, I'd beef him, Guvnor.'

'He's not your horse,' said Charlie. He shrugged on a heavy overcoat, took his cloth cap from its peg, and marched out.

The Range Rover cruised easily down the snowy lane to Middlegarth village on the Leeds road. Charlie parked it, and forced his way into the crowded bar of the Turpin Arms.

He saw Ben at once, although he was in the farthest corner of the smoky room. He was finishing a pint of the local ale, and looked as though he didn't like it. Beside him, a girl was sipping something greenish and fizzy in a tall glass. On her other side, a big chap, evidently her boyfriend, glowered at them both over a double Scotch.

Charlie pushed his way across the room to the bar. He ordered another pint for Ben, and took it over. Then he turned to Norah. 'What's that you're drinking? Buy you another? Can't drink that rubbish – rot your stocking tops.' He bought a whisky for Norah and a grapefruit juice for himself. Trevor, the boyfriend, he ignored.

Charlie prided himself on his snap decisions and judgment of character. He'd bought Northern Hero's sire on the spur of the moment for a daft price, and what an investment he'd been! He sipped his soft drink, and watched Ben closely as they talked. He was pleased, but not surprised to see that the young man was not disconcerted by his scrutiny.

When Ben was in a room, other people tended to merge into the background. He didn't have to say anything; his vitality was extraordinary. He seemed to displace more than his share of the air around him.

Anagram wouldn't have broken this chap's leg, thought Charlie. The horse was wick as an eel, and Peter must have been dreaming. Idle sod. Serve him right. Good riddance.

Two

—⚬—

Back in the soullessly new hotel in Leeds where the group
was staying, Ben changed out of his black jumper, into his
olive jumper. He had two more at home, but they were too
shabby for anything but work. He took off his denims, and
put on his drab cords. He didn't own a suit. Grandmother had
once offered to have one made for him, as mass producers
don't cater for five feet five men with forty-two inch chests.
Ben had refused, and asked if he might have the cash instead.
He'd finished up with neither.

Jim Riley, who was sharing the room with Ben, hadn't
bothered to change, except for his boots. Ben was taking his
time. He wanted to think about the offered job, he wanted to
be alone. As he tried to consider the implications, he found it
hard to tear his mind away from his fascinating surroundings. He had stayed in farm guesthouses once or twice, but
never in hotels. He was dazzled by the luxury of the wall to
wall curtains, fitted carpet, colour television and built in
furniture. As he thought, he moved about, looking and
touching. He stopped in front of a supermarket reproduction
of Constable's *Haywain*.

It was tempting, this offer; more than tempting. The
Guvnor hadn't mentioned wages, but there'd be a legal
minimum, same as at home. Ben supposed he'd have to go
through some formalities, and hoped they wouldn't be too
complicated. Any wage was better than none. At home, he
got what Grandmother called 'cigarette money', although he
didn't smoke, his keep, a bonus at the end of lambing, and
another when all the lambs were sold. Last year, he'd earned

£250 and his keep. The lambs had fetched over £10,000. All the rest, after expenses, had gone into the new milking parlour. And Ben was only second eldest to Denis, who was married, with one child, and another on the way. Why, Terry had paid Ben almost double for riding work in his spare time. And riding work was Ben's favourite occupation.

Ben sat down on a velvet-covered stool in front of the white painted vanity unit while he thought. He brushed his hair, looking in the mirror. The eyes that looked back at him were as grey as his grandmother's, but warmer. The brows were straight and heavy, the lashes long, thick and black. Ben was ashamed of his eyelashes. Both of his parents had indeterminate sandy colouring. I must be a throw-back, thought Ben.

Eight o'clock. Grandmother would be in her bedroom now. She never sat downstairs after tea. She and Grandfather shared the best bedroom at Cloninch, and that was where the old lady kept the few possessions she had brought with her as a bride. After tea, Grandfather would go to bed and doze on and off; and sometimes listen to the radio, and sometimes pretend to be asleep.

Grandmother would sit erect in her basket chair by the window, reading. She read six books a week, no more, no less. She bicycled to Kilmoon on Tuesday, Thursday and Saturday, to change two books at the Library. If the books were longer than average, she read faster. Short-sighted now, she wore pince nez for reading and for the fine needlework she did downstairs. She never read downstairs or sewed upstairs.

When Ben was a little boy, he used to go into her room and ask to look at the picture, *Young Girl in a Garden*. The pictures in the hotel bedroom had reminded Ben of home, where there were pictures everywhere. The picture with the horse pulling a haycart and the big trees – they had that at Cloninch, in the hall. Then there were holy pictures in the kitchen, and a big framed photo of Arkle and another of Red Rum. But the *Young Girl in a Garden* was in another league

25

altogether. She sat on the grass with her skirts spread round her and her lap full of yellow flowers. Her back was as straight as Grandmother's own. Her dress was green, greener than the grass, and the flowers were just dabs of colour, but you could almost smell them. The girl's face was pale as ivory on a long neck. There were pearls in her red hair. The sun streamed into the picture, but you felt that it had been raining and that the grass was probably damp. For some reason, Grandmother was as nearly pleased as she ever was when Ben told her that the picture was his favourite thing in the whole world. He'd been six years old then.

As Ben grew older, he gave up going into the room, and when he'd painted it just lately, and seen the picture once more, it was like meeting a dear friend again. . .

Then Jim Riley burst into the bedroom, startling Ben, making a lot of noise. Telling him to come down if he wanted anything to eat. Ben jumped up. He'd forgotten all about supper and he was bloody hungry.

Agatha Logan sat perfectly still in her basket chair. Every five minutes, she turned a page. She was reading a life of Marcel Proust. Her other book – tomorrow's – was called *Shoot Me, She Said*. Agatha sighed. She had read three lives of Proust. Working her way along the library shelves, taking one novel and one non-fiction at every visit, the non-fiction section was read first. The library had a limited selection of travel and historical books, but it had six lives of Joyce and four of Shaw. Agatha had read them all, taking them on board with the indiscriminate appetite of a vacuum cleaner. She thirsted for information as some thirst for drink or drugs. But at eighty-two, she could only assimilate three serious books a week if she alternated them with cheap thrillers and light romances. Last week, it had been a history of the '98 Rising, and a novel called *Flames of Desire*.

It was quite dark outside. Agatha laid down her book, took off her pince nez, and stared out into the blackness. She could hear a fox barking out on the bogs, and the sound of rain hissing down on the roof of the new cowshed. She rose stiffly, and drew the faded curtains which had hung there for more than half a century. Michael was sound asleep, had been for hours. He slept more as he grew older, she slept less. Agatha crossed to the big brass bed, tall and severe in her long tweed skirt and pink crêpe de chine blouse with its wide, floppy collar. She looked down at Michael with a curious expression compounded of pity, impatience and affection. Then she returned to her chair and resumed her spectacles and *Proust, Mon Ami*. Her back was as straight as that of the red-haired girl in the picture. The picture which seemed to shine from within. It was carefully hung away from the sunlight.

Agatha found that Proust could not hold her attention; her eyes strayed to the sleeping old man in the bed. She had read Lady Chatterly – naturally – and found it boring and crude. Still, she couldn't help making a parallel in her mind with Michael and Mellors. Fascinating, Michael had been, especially once she had persuaded him to shave every day, even on Mondays. Agatha had made most of the running. She jerked her shoulders, shrugging off uncomfortable memories. Restlessly, she stood up again, and stared at the picture as if she was seeing it for the first time. The girl's fiery hair, loosely twisted into a coil, spilled onto her bare shoulder in a thick, shining ringlet. Almost three dimensional, she turned (or seemed to turn) her long, greenish eyes on Agatha. She smiled, not coyly nor mockingly, but with pure happiness. She was probably about seventeen years old.

'If that picture's so valuable, I wonder you don't sell it.' The voice, coming from the apparently sleeping Michael, would have made most people jump.

'I trust,' said Agatha, 'that my circumstances are not so reduced that I must sell my grandmother.' She laughed shortly, turning away. 'As I am obliged by the terms of my father's will to leave the farm to Denis, I have nothing but this picture within my power to bestow as I like. I do not regret my decision to bequeath it to Benedict.'

'He won't thank you for it,' muttered Michael on a yawn.

He spoke indistinctly without his false teeth. 'Poor old Ben. Needs a farm of land, and gets a picture. Shame – he's a good lad.'

Agatha, whose teeth were her own and excellent, snapped back, 'Even in a recession it must be worth considerably more than Cloninch.'

But Michael had gone to sleep again.

She couldn't go to bed yet – only ten o'clock, she wouldn't sleep – and downstairs the television was on in the sitting room and the radio in the kitchen. One could, of course, simply turn off the television . . . but supposing one of the boys turned it on again? Unlikely, but not worth the risk.

Michael blamed her, she knew, because Benedict had gone to England, and had telephoned earlier that evening to say that he would not return. He had dared to suggest that she was unfair to Benedict and singled him out for criticism. Perhaps she did, but who else was worth her criticism? She had no son of her own, Muriel was her downtrodden daughter. Muriel had married Myles, who hovered between the pub and the greyhound track. Agatha seldom troubled to speak to him. Muriel and Myles could have been mistaken for brother and sister, yet Agatha had been beautiful, and Michael's dark good looks and compelling personality had more than made up for deficiencies beyond his control.

The six grandchildren, of which both daughters were married, were of the same pattern as their parents, except for Benedict. . . . Seven months' child, despaired of by the doctors, he had insisted on continuing to live, against all odds. Of the family, but always apart, he might have been a changeling. Dark, while they were fair, short while they were tall, alert while they were sluggish; he was the only one of the six that Agatha cared a damn about. She hoped and dreamed for him, but could not help him. In her heart of hearts, she cherished a small mad hope that Denis might die. Then by the terms of the will, Ben would inherit. That was why she clung to the farm, instead of taking the obvious step of handing it over to Denis and avoiding death duty.

Agatha began slowly to prepare for bed. Her clothes, made to last, were folded away in tissue paper, her T-bar shoes placed side by side. She put on an ancient handmade silk nightdress, cut on the cross, lace trimmed. Even in January, nothing would have induced her to sleep in viyella or inter-lock. As for hot water bottles, she despised them and all who used them. Fortunately, her circulation was good.

Quietly, she slid into bed beside Michael. Michael, who still, after sixty years married to Agatha, slept in a flannel shirt.

Even in his wildest dreams, Ben had never imagined having a house to go with his job. He had spent the first few days at the farm, under Charlie's cold eye, but now, some sort of un-spoken understanding had come about. Ben knew, although the Guvnor hadn't said so, that he was accepted. He'd been instructed to lunge the brown horse, Anagram, for ten min-utes, and then to ride him in the straw yard. Ben knew that this was the horse which had thrown the absent Peter, but he was surprised when the entire outdoor staff turned out to watch. Charlie had said, 'Careful, lad, he's wackun as a rat,' and gone off in the Range Rover. Ben had disappointed his audience – or rather Anagram had. After an experimental plunge and a buck which was no more than lighthearted, he had settled down, and trotted round as quietly as a riding-school hack.

The same evening, Eric, the head shepherd, had driven Ben up to Peter's cottage with his luggage, an airline bag he'd got in exchange for petrol coupons.

The cottage had many defects, and its two little windows faced due north, but Ben didn't care. He gloried in it. He could do what he liked within its four thick walls. He could do handstands on the stone floor, dance, sing – he wished he'd brought his guitar with him. He beamed round the cold, stuffy kitchen in delight.

The cottage was icy. It was heated by a solid fuel cooker, which had been out since Peter's departure, twelve freezing January days earlier. There wasn't much room to manoeuvre in the cramped kitchen, but Ben was neat and economical in all his movements. Soon the fire was roaring cheerfully, with a tin of stew warming in a saucepan on the hotplate.

Ben drew the curtains, and went to the bedroom, which contained a feather bed and little else. He dropped his bag on the bed and glanced round. There were hooks on the wall, and a pull-out drawer under the bed. The window was set so deeply that the sill provided as much space as the small table. These two rooms were the original cottage. A built on pre-fab room with a tin roof was divided into two, scullery and lavatory. There was a bath under the draining-board, and a hose to fill it.

Ben ate the stew and a tin of beans and a tin of mushy peas. This was all the edible food that Peter had left. Two chops were growing whiskers on a plate. Ben threw them into the fire regretfully. He'd had his midday meal at the farmhouse, and Mandy had given him some eggs which he was saving for breakfast. He hadn't got any bread.

Ben rinsed his teacup and plate. He said aloud, 'I've never been so happy in my life; never.'

There was no television or radio in the cottage, and Ben had nothing to read. It was too early to go to bed. So he put on his gumboots and damp jacket and went out. There was a little frozen snow on the ground, and it was a beautiful starry night. He stood outside wishing he had the little Renault van, or even a bike, although a bike would have been tricky in the snow. From the cottage door, he could see the lights of Middlegarth, half a mile away, down the steep lane. He checked his money – £4. He needed groceries, but supposed he wouldn't be paid until Friday. It was Wednesday.

In Kilmoon, it would have been perfectly possible to buy supplies at 9 pm. Not in Middlegarth. Ben was learning. Disappointed in his search for bread, milk and tea, he went into the Turpin Arms. Conversation died, as the dozen or so occupants of the bar turned and studied him. This didn't bother Ben, he was used to being stared at. He asked for a shandy. Two girls and a man were sitting in the corner, and there was a crowd of men gathered round the darts board.

One of the girls jumped to her feet, and came across to the bar. 'No, it's my turn,' she was saying. As she reached the counter, she became aware of Ben. Or perhaps she came over because she was already aware of him. She looked at him, and he looked back. He moved aside to make room at the bar. She said, 'Hi,' and turned away as he replied. He noticed her hair was pale gold and very smooth. She had a long nose and a short chin, and you couldn't call her pretty.

Ben said, 'Cold night,' to make her turn her head. She did, and he saw her broad forehead, and that she had intelligent eyes and a gentle mouth. She wore long flashing earrings, a big red sweater and black ski pants. He thought he had glimpsed her yesterday up at the farm. She'd been wearing a headscarf and a sheepskin coat, so it was hard to be sure.

'You got Peter's job, eh?' she said, surprising him with her local accent. He'd expected something else, he didn't know why.

'I have,' he said. 'For a while anyway.'

'I was up at the Guvnor's yesterday,' she said, 'seeing about a puppy. They told me you'd been riding Anagram. You want to mind that brute; he'll kill you.'

The other girl at the corner table called out, 'What about those drinks, Dogsbody?'

The girl said, 'Hang on,' counting her change.

'Who's Dogsbody?' enquired Ben.

'Oh, that's me. Silly nickname – I've got another.' She grinned.

'They can't call you Dogsbody,' said Ben angrily. 'I never heard such a thing.'

'A nice girl like me?' She mocked him. 'It's just a joke – don't look so horrified. I help with dogs part time. Guide dogs for the blind.' She picked up the glasses. 'Join us?' she suggested.

Ben shook his head. How could you join anybody with four quid in your pocket? He sipped his drink, his mild interest in the girl, Dogsbody, evaporating, although he knew she was still watching him. He hated thinking about blind people. A world without light seemed to him like a living death. To Ben, a blind man with a dog was a lost soul, wandering through limbo, all hope gone, a drag on himself and everybody else; haunted by the bogies of poverty, dependence, and humiliation.

Ben remembered being terrified as a child by an old blind tramp whose daughter had led him about, begging for him. Ben had never forgotten those milky eyes with their sightless glare. Even now, the horror he had felt hadn't quite left him. He finished his drink, and left.

As he plodded uphill through the snow, Ben felt a twinge of homesickness. He remembered his grandmother years ago, a sprightly seventy-year-old, snatching a shovel from his father, and vigorously digging snow away from the door. He remembered last year, greasing Dancing Lady's hoofs so that the snow wouldn't ball on them, riding uphill round the elbow in Tinker's Lane, and meeting the old lady cycling down. He'd remonstrated with her: 'You might have met something at the turn – you couldn't have avoided it.'

'But I did not meet anything, Benedict.'

He unlocked the warped door of the cottage, and it creaked open. The kitchen was faintly warm, and smelled of tinned stew.

Homesickness evaporated.

The following Sunday, Agatha left Michael still snoring, dressed carefully, added a cameo brooch to her blouse, and descended the stairs for breakfast. She came down cautiously, because the stair carpet was worn right through in the middle of the treads, and one could easily catch a toe in a loose thread. Agatha ate a boiled egg and drank two cups of coffee, then she mounted her bicycle and pedalled off to church.

Agatha attended the Protestant church every Sunday. She rode her bicycle unless the weather was impossible, when she instructed her son-in-law to drive her there. The unusual feature about this dedication was that Agatha was a Roman

Catholic. True, she had not been baptized one. Her grandfather had been a Protestant archdeacon, but she had been obliged to change her religion when she eloped with Michael. Her daughter Muriel had been baptized a Catholic, as had all Agatha's grandchildren.

Agatha had taken instruction from the local priest, and had scandalized him by dismissing the entire Christian faith as poppycock. She had soon ceased to attend Mass. Priests who tried to reclaim her were easily frightened off. After some twenty years, Agatha had gradually resumed the church of her childhood without comment or explanation. She had no faith except in herself, goddess in her own limited universe. She believed that church-going was good discipline. Besides, it was something to do.

Canon Donovan was away. The service was taken by young Tony Robinson, recently ordained. He tried to scuttle into the vestry, unobserved by Agatha who was parking her bicycle by the side door. He was unsuccessful. Callow fool, thought Agatha, as the young man took her proffered hand rather as he might have accepted a loaded gun.

She went inside and knelt, painfully, in the family pew. She stood, and sat, and endured the cold and the choir. She didn't hear the words being said and sung. She was thinking about Ben.

Agatha came back to the present when Major Arnold, a cousin of her own, quavered out a reading from the Apocrypha. (Like her, he was over eighty. Unlike her, he was fragile and wheezy.) Agatha began to listen. The Apocrypha was seldom read from; perhaps Edgar Arnold was going to read the Armistice Day lesson from the Book of Wisdom. This was one of the only passages of Scripture that she approved of. But no; these words were unfamiliar. Some new-fangled idea of the bishop's.

> . . . *The wisdom of the scribe depends on the*
> *opportunity of leisure;*
> *And he who has little business may become wise . . .*

33

Agatha thought of Ben working eighteen hours a day in lambing time. He'll never become wise, she thought.

> . . . *How can he become wise who handles the*
>   *plough,*
> *And whose talk is about bulls?*

Or horses. Or ewes. Poor Benedict.

> . . . *He sets his heart on ploughing furrows*
> *And is careful about fodder for the heifers.*
> *So too is every craftsman and master workman*
> *Who labours by night as well as by day . . .*

Agatha was a light sleeper. She had often heard Ben coming in from the lambing pens at 3 am, and going out again two hours later. It was usually Ben who got up to see to the calving cows too, although the cows were supposed to be the concern of the other brothers.

Agatha stood and sat and stood again through canticles and a second reading, without hearing a word. Then she knelt, her knees protesting, and closed her eyes in simulated prayer. Poor Benedict. What had she done to him? And the farm would never be his, thanks to her father's determination to bypass Michael. Agatha never considered that her life might be nearing its end, and that the *Young Girl in a Garden* might soon be Ben's property. She felt quite capable of living another twenty years. Fifteen anyway. By then, Benedict would be over forty, working as a groom, or as a shepherd.

> . . . *How can he become wise who labours by night*
>   *as well as by day?*

Entirely preoccupied, Agatha knelt through the Creed, a hymn, some prayers, another hymn. . . . That young man was ascending the pulpit. She should be sitting. She sat, searching for her collection. She selected a tenpenny piece,

34

smiling slightly as she remembered her close-fisted father putting a pound note in the plate, and extracting ten shillings change.

During the sermon she shut her eyes again, as it was her habit to sleep openly through the sermon when Tony Robinson was preaching. At once, she saw her picture in her mind's eye. Beautiful thing – she loved it more than any living thing except Benedict. She opened her eyes. 'I shall sell it,' she said aloud, and marched out of the church.

The Misses Bond, who sat near the door, hurried nervously after her. 'Mrs Logan, are you all right?'

'Perfectly all right, thank you, Clare. Oh, good morning, Miriam, yes of course I'm all right. No law obliges me to listen to that young man.'

She collected her bicycle and rode home.

Three

Lesley Peabody woke with a headache; her alarm clock was bleeping insistently. She stretched out a sleepy arm and stopped it. Ten minutes to relax and think about today before she need get up; this was her usual routine. She needed a little while on her own before breakfast, the only meal she shared with Hazel, now shuffling about in the bathroom.

Today, Lesley would visit Henrietta, George Bull, and hopeless, weepy Mrs Betts; then lunch, then the childrens' day centre. A typical day. She wrapped her feet in her long nightie, drawing up her knees. It was chilly, in spite of her radiator. To her annoyance, Lesley couldn't bring her mind to bear on this morning – last night kept getting in the way.

She'd slept badly, the evening at the Turpin Arms had gone sour on her. Her friends Bob and Tina liked to go out for a drink at a country pub after working all day at the Training Centre. Often, they asked Lesley to join them. She had been at school with Mandy Wilkes and the friendship had sur-vived, they often met at the Turpin Arms. Privately, Lesley thought that Mandy's much older husband, Ted, was a bore, but then Mandy hadn't liked Mark either.

Lesley went on thinking about the evening as she dressed. Normally a serene person, she felt edgy and ruffled. She felt she'd made a fool of herself as she remembered the dark young man and Bob's teasing and her own sharp retorts. She had snapped at Tina, 'Don't call me Dogsbody – I don't like it.' And Tina had laughed and said, 'Your young man didn't like it either, did he?' Lesley had flushed with annoyance – 'Oh, shut up, Tina.'

She couldn't get the man out of her mind; his springy, compact build, his vitality, his unreasonable anger. How dare Tina call him 'The Guvnor's funny little Irish under-shepherd'. How dare she! Even if she had immediately added that she fancied him herself.

Lesley said, 'Oh, for God's sake!' out loud. She brushed her hair, fastening it back with a round comb, and braced herself for Hazel's morning face.

Lesley shared her flat in Leeds with Hazel, a moody, swarthy girl who came and went at odd hours. Lesley disliked her quite a lot, but Hazel paid her share, and there seemed to be no valid reason for asking her to go. She ate muesli with her mouth open, but you didn't have to watch.

When Mark had walked out, Lesley had immediately found a tenant. Her job wouldn't pay the rent, so Hazel had taken Mark's place in the flat. His place in Lesley's life was still vacant. Her thoughts skidded about uncharacteristically. She still hadn't given much thought to her morning's work. Whenever she let herself relax, her mind went back to the same thing – 'What about those drinks, Dogsbody?' and the young man's sudden anger.

As Lesley walked into the kitchen, it occurred to her that she might resume her maiden name. Why should she be lumbered with Mark's name? And if she stopped being Peabody, perhaps she'd stop being Dogsbody as well. As for Mark, she paused in the doorway, suddenly knowing that she was finished with him. His return wouldn't mean delight or heartbreak or reconciliation; it would be an embarrassing bore. She wondered, without much interest, if he was still with Charlotte. Probably not. Charlotte would have wanted to marry him, and there'd been no request for a divorce.

Hazel, for once, was up first. She was gloomily stirring a mug of coffee. Thank God, she'd finished her muesli. About twenty, she annoyed Lesley, who was twenty-six, by persisting in calling her Mrs Peabody. She did it now. Like someone boasting of a major achievement she said, 'Morning Mrs Peabody; I laid breakfast.'

'Thanks. And Hazel, look, if you can't get round to Lesley, would you mind calling me by my old name? It's Grant.'

'Right. Mrs or Miss?'

'Hell, I don't know. Mrs I suppose. I hadn't thought.'

'Right.' Hazel stirred and stirred, peering into her mug as if she were telling fortunes. She didn't so much sit at the table, as collapse beside it and spread herself over it.

Lesley thought, if she doesn't stop stirring that stuff in five seconds, I shall throw something. She drank her coffee, ate a piece of toast and made notes. 'Going to have to rush,' she said.

Hazel stirred and slurped. Lesley pushed back her chair hard, and Hazel lifted uninterested eyes. 'You off, Mrs Grant?'

'In a minute.' Lesley moved about tidying things up (Hazel was untidy) and switching things off. 'I might go away for a few days,' she said. 'I'm due a long weekend . . . I don't know.'

Hazel refilled her mug, spooned in sugar, began to stir. 'Right,' she said. 'Have fun.'

Lesley grabbed her diary and rushed out of the room.

Lesley walked the two blocks to Henrietta's flat. Her own was convenient if rather charmless. It occupied the ground floor of what had been a spacious town house; she could have done with a third tenant to help with the rent. She'd gradually converted the big bedroom she'd shared with Mark into a bed-sitting room, leaving Hazel in possession of the even larger living room. She did all her paper-work in the bedroom, had a portable television there, typewriter, telephone and filing cabinet. All her social work was in Leeds. Her work with the Guide Dogs' Association was voluntary.

Since Mark's humiliatingly public affair and departure, Lesley had felt compelled to fill all her waking hours with work. She was highly thought of as a social worker with the blind. Her cool, unsentimental approach was ideal for the exacting tasks involved. It was a measure of her skill that she had been allocated to look after Henrietta.

Poor Henrietta, people said. But that was patronizing, even insulting. She'd had more to lose than most; not only her looks but her high-powered job as foreign correspondent for a national weekly. She was the youngest and the most reckless, and she'd got too close to the scene of action. Lesley had never heard exactly how she got the burns. Henrietta had been out of hospital and back in her flat when they'd first met. Lesley knew Henrietta would be up and dressed, either dictating an article or talking on the telephone. To hear her, nobody would guess there was anything wrong. Lesley rang the bell.

From upstairs, the voice came through the intercom. 'Lesley? Come on up.'

Lesley had stopped minding, she told herself. She spent twenty minutes every day making up Henrietta's face. Trying to make the undamaged lower half of it blend into the upper; masking the scars with heavy makeup. 'You could do this yourself, except perhaps the lipstick,' she said. 'When are you going out?'

'Never. Perhaps after dark, wearing a fencing mask.'

'No, listen. You're getting better every day. All you really need now is cleanser, foundation and makeup. The cleanser's liquid, in a bottle; the foundation's cream in a jar; the makeup's a stick. They're in that order, left to right on the dressing-table. Try it tomorrow, and I'll tell you how it looks.'

'My God, don't do that.'

Lesley arranged the jars and bottles, tissues and cotton-wool. 'You take it off without smearing,' she said. 'I'm sure you could put it on. If you could do your own face, you could fix your hair without waiting for me.'

'Put on my wig, you mean.'

'Don't call it a wig; you know perfectly well it's only a sort of fringe thing. You could pin it on as easily as I can if you'd done your face.' Lesley worked as she talked.

39

'Yes, Nanny,' said Henrietta meekly.

'Your own hair's growing like mad. I'll give you a home perm as soon as there's enough of it if you like.' The skin graft had taken well, but of course it didn't match. Lesley applied lipstick, concentrating on the pretty mouth, perfect teeth and well-shaped chin. The remodelled nose looked what it was – a remodelled nose. Nobody else but the doctor had seen the upper half of the face since Henrietta left hospital.

'I don't want to nag,' said Lesley, creaming Henrietta's throat, 'but you could go out in this cold weather easily, wearing a woolly hat well pulled down. Lots of people wear dark glasses in the snow.'

'You *have* to nag, I suppose. What about my recycled nose?'

'What about it? Oh, never mind – it'll come. But if you wait until June, you might look a bit eccentric. Any washing?'

'On the bed. Oh, Lesley, you know that stuff you put on tape for me to learn, so that I could recognize my groceries? I think I've sent it to the *Illustrated Manchester News*, right in the middle of a piece about race riots.' She laughed, a clear happy sound. 'I'm a clot, aren't I?' she said.

'I hope you learnt it first.' Lesley laughed too as she stuffed clothes into a laundry bag. 'I'm going to the laundrette now. I'll bring this lot back tomorrow. See you then.'

Lesley ran downstairs. She was shocked all over again every time she saw Henrietta, but now the shock wore off in minutes, and always she left the flat feeling encouraged. It was only a matter of time until the other girl would overcome her fear of going out. Already, she had started taking in her milk bottle instead of waiting for Lesley to bring it up. Lesley respected her refusal to allow her boyfriend to see her; she talked to him endlessly on the telephone.

Can she be happy? wondered Lesley. Is it possible? She knew that Henrietta was on the road to a satisfying life. Not ideal, never easy, but satisfying. Never once in three months had Lesley heard the other girl complain. She had made sick jokes and occasionally sworn; that was all. Lesley put the washing in the machine at the laundrette, and paused to make notes about Henrietta in her diary. She was pretty sure that the day would soon arrive when she would no longer be needed.

At the next machine, a dark-haired young man was loading up jerseys and jeans. He was a stranger, but Lesley's thoughts raced back to the Turpin Arms. She hadn't thought about Ben for more than an hour. She pushed him to the back of her mind, and set off on her next call.

Geoff Merchant lunched at his usual place, the Kosy Kitchen. He was pleased with the dog, Pepper. She led him confidently across the little restaurant to an empty table. Geoff told her to lie down, dropped the harness, and went to collect his meal from the self service counter. He was too good a trainer to glance back and make sure that Pepper was staying where he'd left her; he knew she would be. He helped himself to liver and bacon and a cup of tea, and sat down, facing the street.

Geoff, a heavily built man with bristly grey hair and enormous bushy eyebrows, enjoyed his reputation as a brilliant dog-trainer. As a younger man, training dogs for police work, he had felt obscurely dissatisfied. He disliked teaching dogs to attack, and the knowledge that he could train one to attack its own master on command bothered him. Then, after having taken early retirement from the police, he had turned to guide dog training. Geoff had a wife and two daughters. They all knew their place in his scheme of things – next after the dogs and those that used them. As he ate his liver and bacon, his mind was totally occupied with the dog asleep at his feet. Would she or would she not become jealous in family surroundings? On the whole, he thought she might. She had seemed just the dog for young Paul. But Paul had a mother who babied him. A pity. Paul deserved a good dog, and Pepper was one of Geoff's

41

favourites. She was pure German shepherd, not suitable for everyone.

Geoff raised his hand as Lesley came through the door. They often lunched together. To Geoff, she was not an attractive woman, because he didn't think of her in those terms at all. She was simply a hell of a good social worker who never wasted his time and didn't chatter. Even when her husband had left her, she'd hardly missed a day's work. She had grown quieter, smiled less and become even more efficient. She collected a salad at the counter, and came over to his table.

As Lesley spoke, Geoff looked at her sharply. She was more animated than usual. He half hoped the husband hadn't turned up — bound to unsettle her — and dismissed the unworthy thought. 'How's it going?' he asked.

'Fine. I believe Henrietta Lake will venture out soon. She's simply rushing about with her cane. Must be practising.'

'Poor lass. Dreadful business, that. D'you reckon she'll be wanting a dog?'

'No, I don't. You don't know her, Geoff; she's the last person. I haven't said anything about a dog, but I'm sure she wouldn't benefit. George Bull, now, he could do with one any time.'

'He's down for the next course,' said Geoff. 'Did you see him today?'

'Yes. I put his dinner in the oven and set it for him. As soon as he gets the hang of the Braille setting, I won't even have to do that. He's quick.'

'Well, he's a policeman,' said ex-policeman Geoff.

Lesley laughed at him. 'Don't tell me there aren't any slow policemen,' she said, sparkling at him.

Something up, thought Geoff. A man — sure to be. 'What about Mrs Betts?' he asked.

'Hopeless. She can see more than most of my lot, but she does nothing but cry. And if her husband chucks up his job, she'll be ten times worse.'

'Chucks up his job? Madness. Why should he?'

'To look after his wife,' said Lesley. 'She'd let him, too – wants him to, I think.'

They pushed away their plates, sitting at the iron-legged table with its mottled Formica top. 'Where are you off this afternoon?'

'To the Day Centre until four o'clock, then I'm free. I was to take Mrs Leng to the hairdresser's, but she's had to go to hospital. I thought I'd go out to Middlegarth and see how the puppies are getting on.'

'Again? Thought you went Tuesday.'

'I did as it happens,' said Lesley, 'but Bob hasn't seen them yet and he's keen to go. Mandy's picked one out, and Bob's sure to fancy a different one.'

'If Mrs Wilkes has picked a puppy we think unsuitable, we won't take it,' said Geoff. 'You should know that. Tell you what, I'll drop Pepper back at the Centre and come with you.'

'Yes do,' said Lesley – a little too cordially? He wondered if she was making an excuse to visit Middlegarth again. They agreed to meet at the Training Centre, collect Bob and drive out together. Geoff picked up Pepper's harness, and immediately began to imitate the actions of a blind man. Walking slightly ahead and to the left of him, the big dog led the way out of the cafe.

It was quiet at the Training Centre when Lesley drove into the yard behind the square Georgian house which formed the main building. The dogs were mostly out in the runs at the back of their sleeping quarters. There was no residential course in progress. Bob was in the main office, Geoff had taken another dog out, and hadn't yet returned.

Bob, the senior puppy-walking supervisor, was a placid, smiling man in his late thirties, going prematurely bald. His loud, jolly laugh, which went 'ho ho!' like Santa Claus was well known and widely imitated by the kennel staff. Tina, his wife, was in charge of the catering. They lived at the Centre, in what had been a groom's house in the yard. This house was the only place where Lesley felt truly at ease. She

43

could come and go as she liked, provided no course was in progress. By five o'clock Bob had finished for the day, and Tina too, as there would be nobody for tea except the resident staff.

'I don't see much point in looking at those puppies yet,' grumbled Bob.

'Come on,' said Tina, 'it's a drive out.' She dragged him out of his chair. 'Why don't we take Meg with us? Mandy would love to see her again.' So Bob fetched Meg from her kennel.

The only pure-bred Border collie at the centre, although there were a number of Border collie/Labrador crosses, Meg was a big dog for her breed. One ear was pricked, the other bent over at the tip. She had a white-blazed face, with a bright tan spot over each eye. Her coat was fine and silky, shining with health. 'She needs another month to six weeks,' said Bob. 'Geoff thinks she may be over possessive, and he's making very sure. Remember Vim?'

They all remembered Vim, who had mounted guard at his master's door, and refused to let anybody past him. 'In every other way she's a natural,' said Bob, 'but she's still a bit funny if anyone goes near Geoff.'

Geoff arrived with Jinty, a yellow Labrador. 'She's champion,' he said. 'Fastest learner we've got.' He took her away, saying to Lesley, 'I'm looking forward to meeting this puppy of yours. I hear it's irresistible.'

Lesley grinned uncertainly. It was unlike Geoff to joke, but there was an unmistakeable glint in his eye.

An hour later, they pulled up at the back door of Middlegarth Farm House.

The house, built of weathered yellow stone, was as old-fashioned as the farm buildings were modern. The kitchen floor was of worn brick, and hams hung from hooks on the smoke-blackened ceiling. At any given time, there would be a number of people in the kitchen, eating. Mandy offered sandwiches, apple pie and Christmas cake. Lesley's quick glance confirmed that neither of the two men at the table was Ben.

44

There were a thousand ewes at Middlegarth. From Christmas, right through to the beginning of May, it was always lambing time for one of the flocks. There was a floating population of students. Fear of the Guvnor made them clumsy and inarticulate. Few lasted long.

Lesley sat on the window-seat drinking tea, looking down the brightly lighted courtyard towards the double Dutch barn and the rows of sheds. Mandy took Bob to see the puppies. 'One at a time,' she said, 'Old Nell isn't so keen on strangers.' Lesley half listened to the others talking dogs. Somebody was opening the gate at the corner of the barn; a stocky figure, bareheaded. He walked quickly towards the house, whistling a tune she didn't know.

The door opened, and Ben came blinking into the kitchen. 'Did you get that pen-strep?' he asked Mandy, who had reappeared, cuddling a puppy.

All day, while Lesley got on with her work, stray thoughts had intruded, unwelcome and importunate as mosquitoes. Did Ben ever smile? How would he look if he did? Why didn't he smile? True, she hadn't smiled at him, but she'd looked straight at him with smiling eyes. He ought to have responded. Now, seeing her unexpectedly, Ben gave her a wide grin which lit up his whole face.

Mandy went to the cupboard and fetched a bottle and a hypodermic. She and Ben talked for a minute. Lesley swallowed the rest of her tea. Her insides had given a violent lurch when she encountered Ben's smile. Very disconcerting. She hoped she hadn't turned red. Ben went out taking a basin of warm water, a towel, soap and the bottle of penicillin. Lesley watched him going rapidly back along the brick path under the yard lights, carrying the basin, the towel slung over his shoulder. In another week, she thought, it would be two years since Mark left. Far too long to be alone.

The Guvnor, developing his usual winter bout of bronchitis, had heard Ben from the front room where he'd been sitting over the fire. Chesty and irritable, his stubborn refusal to use any remedy except aspirin and extra blankets slowed up his recovery every year. No antibiotic was too expensive for the sheep, but he wouldn't touch anything in capsule form himself. Medicine, he thought, should be liquid, or else plain white tablets. 'Coloured rubbish' was out, and he didn't hold with injections – get typhus or rabies if you weren't careful.

Coughing, he entered the kitchen as Ben left it. 'Don't go out, Father, it's bitter,' said Mandy. 'Just a hard lambing. Ben'll cope.'

'No need to go out,' said Charlie, blowing his nose explosively. 'That lad isn't far off as good as Eric. But he's daft with it. Soft. Know what the little perisher does?' he demanded, turning suddenly on Lesley. 'He sings to sheep. First day he were here I caught him talking to a yow. Thowt he were daft. Now Eric tells me he sings to 'em. Daft as a boathorse.'

'Perhaps they like it,' ventured Lesley. 'I've heard of people playing the radio at milking time; they say cows enjoy music.'

The Guvnor gave her a baleful look to make sure she wasn't daring to tease him. He didn't bother to answer, and sat down by the cooker.

Meg slumbered fitfully under the table where Geoff, her person, had told her to lie. There were a couple of silent young men drinking tea at the table, not fussy about where they put their boots either.

Meg was happy with her person. She had been walked by a family in York who had given her basic training up to a year old, and she had thought they were to be her people always. She had been fair soft about Mr and Mrs Carter and the little 'uns. Especially the little 'uns. Since Meg's trip to the vet's surgery at eight-months-old, she had been indifferent to little 'uns of her own kind. In fact, she'd been annoyed with Geoff when he'd left her lying under the table while he'd gone with the Missus to sort over a nest of mewling pups.

The two youths at the table were hurrying over the last of their tea, now that the noisy man with a cold was there. They got up and clattered out, and Meg sighed with relief. She crossed her front paws and rested her nose on them. The lass who sometimes fed with Geoff was on the window-seat. She'd come with Meg's friends who lived at the place where Meg was learning to take her person for walks. Daft notion. When Meg had left the Carters, she had thought she was being punished for something and sent away. She'd given over worrying once she'd got to know Geoff. She was learning new words every day, and dimly understood that there was some purpose in what she was doing. She didn't care at all for seeing other dogs taking her person for walks; sometimes running him into trees and that. She meant to take such care of Geoff that he'd stop taking other dogs. That would be champion. She dozed off.

Meg woke as the back door opened and the man came in. The man who had gone out with a basin half an hour since. The man you might like to take for walks if you had no person of your own. Meg noticed that all three of the females in the room reacted to him in their different ways. Missus told him to come and warm himself by the fire. Tina pricked her ears, insomuch as a person can, and sat up straight (she'd been laid all her length on the settee,) and the lass at the window watched him like a good dog with a bunch of sheep that might be fettling for breaking away. The man, Ben, noticed Meg and snapped his fingers. She got up, remembered, and lay down again. Geoff had returned and was talking dogs with Missus. Meg lay awake, watching. The kitchen was full of feelings beyond her experience.

In Meg's make up, the herding instinct was missing. Old Nell had been given to Mandy by the Guvnor because, he said, she wasn't worth a cartridge. Her first litter of puppies by old Roy had been unplanned. Meg was the only one of them to take after her mother. The other three, inheriting Roy's genes, were so good that Charlie had allowed Mandy to breed a second litter from Nell.

When Meg saw sheep grazing in a field, the sight left her cold. She hadn't the slightest wish to round them up, or even chase them. She knew, however, that most of her kind were different. She felt that, had she been the sort of dog that works sheep, she would have enjoyed helping the man who was washing his hands at the sink. The three women all looked as if they'd enjoy helping him too. Funny how he didn't seem to notice, thought Meg. She went to sleep again.

'Finished up outside, have you?' Charlie asked Ben.

'I have at last. Nothing but trouble today, but we didn't lose any lambs. I'll be off home now.'

'Stay and have supper with us,' suggested Mandy.

'Thanks, but I'm too dirty. I'd rather get back to the cottage. I left a stew on the range.' Ben went over to Lesley. 'I was rude to you, the other night,' he said. 'I'm sorry. It's none of my business what your friends call you.'

Lesley said, 'You weren't rude; my friends call me Lesley.' She shot a look at Tina, who had started to talk to Geoff with great animation.

'Lesley?' Ben looked surprised. 'Isn't that a man's name?'

'It's spelled differently. Like Francis and Frances. I hope you approve.'

'I do,' said Ben. He did. He approved of what he saw, and wanted badly to know her better. But this one has money, he thought. She was wearing an ink-blue wool dress this time, and the sheepskin coat lying beside her was a beauty. And she had expensive looking suede boots, and a gold necklace and earrings which came from a jewellers, not a chain store. Out of my league, thought Ben, sadly.

He was saving hard, and hadn't got round to buying anything except bare necessities. He lived mainly on bread and potatoes in order to save more. Stew was a treat. The cottage was as bare as ever. He wished violently that he had a car.

'Do you ever come to Leeds?' asked Lesley. 'There's lots of buses.'

Small talk or invitation? He couldn't be sure. 'I was never there,' he said. 'I might go Saturday week. Do some shopping.'

'Why don't we all meet up?' asked Mandy brightly. 'We

could go to that new place, the Hart Royal – they do great bar meals. We haven't been anywhere for weeks. Come with Ted and me, Ben.'

Ben felt Lesley's tension, waiting for his reply. He gave her the chance to say, 'Do come,' but she didn't. She wore rings on almost every finger; thin ones, thick ones, twisted ones. There was a plain one on the fourth finger of her left hand. He counted; she was wearing six rings altogether. So perhaps it wasn't a wedding ring. But it looked like one. Her hand was trembling very slightly.

'Thanks, Mandy,' he said. 'I'll come unless something crops up.'

The Guvnor heaved himself up in his chair. 'Nowt's going to crop up,' he said. 'If it does, it won't be no different than before you came. You go, lad.' Ben noticed that Ted's wishes were as usual not considered.

'Is Leeds a nice place?' asked Ben. This was funny, apparently. They all laughed, even Lesley. She stopped at once, saying, 'It's a big city like a lot of others. Plenty of good shops. Where I live, it's all terraced Victorian houses, with steep little alleyways. I like it.'

The Guvnor said, with a fresh fit of coughing, that Leeds was a mucky shant and he had no use for loin-enders. He hadn't been there for years, he added.

'Lesley's not a loiner,' said Mandy. 'She's from Middle-garth.'

Loin-ender? Ben was bewildered. He took his anorak off the hook and put it on. There was a three-cornered rent in the back of it, mended with insulating tape. 'I'll catch an early bus and get myself summat decent to wear,' he said. 'Or I'll be thrown out of the Hart Royal.' Fresh laughter; he coloured angrily – it was Tina this time.

'"Summat", Ben. You said "summat". We'll make a Yorkshireman of you yet.'

As he rode to Leeds on the bus over a week later, having again refused Mandy's offer of a lift, Ben's mind was taken up with Lesley. She'd been to the farm twice more, she seemed to be visiting Mandy a lot. Both times, they'd exchanged a few commonplaces, both knowing that there would be more than this. Mandy was Lesley's age, but seemed older; perhaps because Ted was years older than she was, perhaps because she was fat. They had no children. She was matchmaking, Ben thought, but why? Why couldn't Lesley find a fellow for herself?

Ben was no fool, but he was puzzled. What did she want? Or rather, on what terms did she want him? He knew little of women, and nothing at all of English women. True, he was pursued by girls at home, but he didn't believe in letting them catch him. There'd been Deirdre, all those years ago, but he'd been a bloody fool then. What a shock when he discovered he was sharing her with half Kilmoon. Obviously, Lesley wasn't another Deirdre; equally obviously, she wanted him.

Love and marriage, in Ben's limited experience, did not go together like a horse and carriage. Even if Lesley wasn't married already, and he suspected that she was, he didn't mean to let a woman support him, and his mind boggled at the thought of a second mobile home in the Cloninch yard. He had guarded against falling in love as a possible prelude to that mobile home. He thought of love as a sort of bonus in marriage; the exception, not the rule. A casual affair, then? Unless he was greatly mistaken, Lesley was not a girl for casual affairs. She had put a distance between Ben and the men he worked with; he felt that they too were surprised.

He was going to have to ask her if she was married, and soon. At least, she didn't seem like a girl who would make a fool of a man – too direct.

Suddenly, he thought of Agatha, always icily remote, except when moved by anger. He wondered what she had been like as a girl, when love for Michael had made her throw family, position and fortune to the winds. If Ben's life went awry, he thought he might be like her some day – that would be terrible. When he was a little boy, she'd had more outlets for her rages. She would dig fiercely in the garden or play difficult pieces on her protesting violin. She still wrote letters to the *Irish Times*, advocating hanging and corporal punishment, followed by letters of complaint because they hadn't been printed. Ben knew there was much of her passion in his own make up, but without the bitterness of the selfish old woman at home.

The bus passed the new roadhouse, the Hart Royal. There was a clump of opulent cars outside. How could he go there in jersey and jeans, even new ones? He saw a bearded man emerge from the building, dressed in a donkey jacket and filthy denims. Craning his neck, Ben saw that the man was unlocking a Porsche. Reassured, he travelled on into the city.

Ben bought a blue sweater, black cords and a sleeveless jacket. They cost less than he expected, so he bought a pair of shoes as well. He put on the new clothes, had the old ones wrapped up, and caught the next bus back to the Hart Royal.

The bar was large, low and lavishly decorated; self-consciously new. The architect hadn't quite been able to decide between functional modern décor and olde worlde Victorian cosiness, so he had tried to combine the two. The bar itself was in the shape of a horseshoe; black, with a laminated top. Some of the chairs in the centre of the lounge were suspended from the ceiling, but along the walls were oak settles. Each of these was bolted to the floor, slightly too far away from the heavy oak tables which were too low to eat off in comfort.

Ben noticed that the clientele was as mixed as the furnishing – some farmers, some tourists, a weirdo in a pink fedora and bellbottoms, two businessmen with their wives.

Lesley was there already, standing at the far end of the horseshoe bar. She hadn't seen him. She was wearing a white dress with a big collar, a gold belt, and earrings, Ben thought, as big as horse-brasses. She was talking to the landlady, an overripe blonde whose low cut-dress appeared to be fashioned out of kitchen foil. A tall man was leaning on the counter beside Lesley and, as far as Ben could tell was trying to chat her up, with asides to the landlady. The two pretty barmaids were taking care to keep their backs to them, serving customers near the door.

Ben saw the man place a large white hand with a signet ring on Lesley's arm. She moved her arm away sharply. The stranger was youngish, fattish, not bad looking, and his clothes suggested a race-meeting. Ben, violently resentful, felt uncertain of himself. What, after all, did he know about Lesley's circle of friends? Too shy to approach them, he ordered a drink and looked hard at Lesley. She turned round at once, and their eyes met and held. She spoke to the landlady, ignored the man and walked over to Ben.

Noting how graceful she was, Ben thought – she walks like a city girl, not used to mud. Bet she's a good dancer. The dim lights glimmered on her smooth pale hair; she looked expensive and assured. Out of my league, Ben thought again, in near panic, but he kept his eyes on hers. He tried to imagine her in his cottage. It was easy.

'Ben, you shouldn't summon me to you like that,' said Lesley.

'I didn't. You came of yourself.'

'You did. You might as well have blown a whistle and shouted, "Here, Lesley!" – Hey! I like your jacket. Casual things suit you, don't they?'

Lesley glanced round to see if the other man had followed her. It was a devil, she thought, when you couldn't wait five minutes for a friend without being pestered. He was watching her. She glared at him and he winked at her and turned away.

'Has that yobbo been annoying you?' demanded Ben.

'Yes, a little. Leave him to Gloria – she'll deal with him. It's good to see you, Ben.'

Ben's face was illuminated by one of his rare smiles and he answered, 'I thought I was going to have to fight for you.'

What was it about Ben, she asked herself. Sex, of course,

but it was much more than that. There was a crackling vitality about him which made the other drinkers at the bar look anaemic and lifeless and cold.

'That man's a right pain,' she said. 'He embarrasses the staff, annoys the customers and never goes far enough to be thrown out – unfortunately.'

'I'll throw him out if you like,' said Ben. She saw by his face and his bunched muscles that he wasn't joking.

'He won't come back when I'm with you,' she said lightly. 'And you'll have to mind your manners, you fire-eater, or you'll be thrown out too.'

'I will not.'

'Oh, Ben, forget him. He isn't worth bothering about.' She changed the subject. 'The Guvnor's poorly,' she said. 'He's stayed in bed all day for the first time in living memory, so Mandy and Ted aren't coming. Just Bob, Tina, you and me.'

'I'm glad,' said Ben. 'I'm no good at parties; I'm not used to them. Could we go out on our own another time? I've no car, but I can bus into Leeds. I've never seen you without a lot of people round; I'd like to have you to myself.'

She guessed that he didn't want to be collected in her car, so she didn't offer. 'I'd like that,' she said.

While they waited for Bob and Tina, Ben asked questions, and Lesley answered – unless she preferred to turn them aside. 'You're inquisitive, aren't you?' she said at last.

'I'm not inquisitive, I'm curious.'

'What's the difference?'

'There's a big difference. I'm taking a short cut to knowing you better. I haven't asked you anything Mandy wouldn't have told me. I'd sooner ask you myself.'

Any minute now, he'd ask if she was married. She didn't want to talk to Ben about Mark, and he was sure to disapprove of divorce. She'd heard they didn't have it in Ireland.

'Are you a Catholic?' she asked. 'Not inquisitive – just curious.'

'A bad one. Protestants don't get called Benedict.'

'Benedict? I imagined you were Benjamin. Benedict's much nicer.'

'Don't call me by it,' he begged. 'Only my grandmother does that – the old devil.'

'Why do you call her an old devil?'

'It's nothing to what my brothers call her; she runs all our lives.' There was a note of reluctant admiration in his voice. He laughed, and said, 'I left home because I had a row with her. The old villain. . . . She kicked up over what my horse cost to keep.'

'Ben, that reminds me, are you still riding that wretched horse, Anagram?'

'When I get time. Don't worry, he's harmless. If I could cure him of shaking his head, he'd be a decent horse.'

Lesley said, 'Listen, Ben, Anagram isn't just a horse you can ride and Peter couldn't. He went over backwards with Peter. I wasn't there, but Eric was, and Ted. They said Anagram screamed out and reared up for no reason – he must have a tile loose. Please don't ride him.' She pictured Ben spreadeagled under the crashing horse so vividly that she caught her breath. 'Please don't,' she repeated.

'I'll watch every move,' said Ben. 'Why does the Guvnor keep them anyway? Nobody else rides them, and Flycatcher isn't much good. He's hardly ever sound.'

'They belong to Stephen, Mandy's brother. He and the Guvnor had a flaming row because Steve was spending time and cash on the horses, so he cleared off to New Zealand last year. Charlie keeps the horses on because he's sure he'll be back; the only son, you see. Ted's a poor substitute but he does as he's told. Steve was too like his Dad.'

Ben said, 'It's me and my grandmother over again, only she's not keeping Dancing Lady and hoping I'll go home; she'd dance on my grave. The mare's gone back to Terry, the man who gave her to me.'

Lesley had her back turned to the man who'd annoyed her earlier. As she wondered aloud what was keeping Bob and

Tina, she heard him shouting unfunny pleasantries to the girls behind the bar. Ben's face told her that he was coming towards them, and she gave him a warning look which turned to one of anger as the man dropped a meaty hand on her shoulder. 'Do you mind?' she said coldly, moving away.

The stranger shouldered in between her and Ben, hiding the shorter man from her view. 'What's it to be, my lovely?' he asked. 'Vodka?'

'Get lost,' said Lesley angrily. 'I'm not drinking with you.'

'That's what you think.' The hand was replaced. 'Vodka for the beautiful lady!' His face was flushed, but he wasn't drunk.

Ben intervened, making an obvious effort to be polite. As always when he was fighting his temper, his accent was more noticeable than usual. 'Please go away,' he said. 'This lady is with me.'

The newcomer looked him up and down offensively. 'Sorry, Paddy,' he said. 'You could have fooled me.'

Ben knocked him down.

The man fell against a table, snatched at one of the swinging chairs and missed, rolled onto his face. He levered himself up slowly onto his hands and knees. Ben picked him by his collar and the seat of his trousers, carried him to the door, and tossed him outside. He landed at the feet of Bob and Tina, arriving late.

Lesley half expected Ben to be asked to leave. Proud and delighted, she went to meet him as he walked back, wiping his hands down the side of his jeans. 'Thank you, Ben, I didn't know there were any knights in shining armour left.' She spoke lightly, hoping in vain to hide her feelings. She needn't have worried about Ben. A group of men raised a cheer, there were shouts of 'Well done, lad!' 'About time he was thrown out!' Bob and Tina were both talking to Ben at once.

The landlady leaned across the counter, resting her foil-wrapped bosom on the bar. 'You can have whatever you like on the house for that,' she said. 'He's been in every night since we opened and we're all dead sick of him.' Her black-edged eyes widened as she saw Ben's slightly grazed hand. 'Let's see that hand of yours, dear. You want a bit of plaster on that. Then you can have anything you like and that's a promise.'

Lesley was annoyed when Ben favoured Gloria with one of his devastating smiles. 'Anything?' he said, allowing her to wipe the blood off his knuckles with a J cloth.

'Ho-ho-ho,' went Bob.

'Shall we order our meal then?' said Lesley. 'It's getting late.' She watched Ben with a sharp twinge of jealousy. Why was he encouraging that flashy piece? He'd thrown the man out for Lesley, not Gloria.

At the mention of food, Ben lost interest in Gloria, and turned his attention to the menu. He asked for steak and chips.

When they'd finished eating, a sing-song started round the piano and they joined the group. 'Sing, Ben, come on.'

'I don't know the songs.' But when the pianist played Loch Lomond, he joined in, singing softly. His voice was strong, unexpectedly deep. He broke off when he saw Lesley looking at him.

Bob and Tina made excuses and left early. Lesley wished they wouldn't be so obvious. 'I mustn't miss the last bus,' said Ben regretfully.

'It's only half past ten,' she said. 'My car's outside – don't worry about the bus. Can't I give you a lift?'

Ben glanced at her doubtfully. She could tell he was sizing up the position. He lived twenty-five miles in the opposite direction. 'Thanks,' he said.

Half an hour later, they went out together. Lesley unlocked the car, Ben beside her was silent. But as always, his stillness was that of a coiled spring; energy seemed to pour from him. Suddenly he said, 'Haven't you a fellow somewhere? You must have.'

'No,' said Lesley carefully. 'No boyfriend.' They got into the car, and she slowly put the key in the ignition, debating with herself.

'What then? What aren't you telling me, Lesley?'

'I've got a husband somewhere. He went off with another woman two years ago.' Silence, almost visible, stretched between them. She had no idea what Ben was thinking. She wondered if she would ever know him properly; he fascinated and puzzled her.

Ben said at last, 'Do you still mind?' She knew he meant, 'Do you still love him?'

'No, I don't now. I did mind – it was hurtful and humiliating.' She pulled out of the car park and into the traffic.

Ben said angrily, 'The bastard. You were well rid of him.' After a moment he added, 'Still, it's an ill wind . . .'

'I know. I'm glad now that he's gone. So should you be.' Lesley was surprised by the anger in Ben's voice. He constantly surprised her. She wondered if he was just furious with Mark or if she had vexed him. She drove carefully and in silence, Ben's presence explosive beside her. Gradually he seemed to relax, and she thanked him again, more warmly, for his strong-arm tactics at the Hart Royal.

'I enjoyed it,' said Ben shortly. 'Any time.'

Lesley pulled up at the cottage. Ben took her hand in his, and she thought wildly, what am I getting myself into? This isn't a bit of fun – it's serious. I could love him. She was sharply aware that Ben had never touched her before. Her heart thumped violently – when had it last done that? Ben said, 'Are you coming in?'

She answered, in a voice that sounded like someone else's, 'Do you want me to stay?' She looked down at his hand holding hers. It was hard to meet his eyes.

'If you don't want to stay, don't come in, because you know very well I'll make you stay,' said Ben. 'I hope you will,' he added more gently.

She got out of the car without a word.

In the cottage it was cold, and Ben made up the fire. It was easier to talk to him when his back was turned. Lesley wondered where her self-confidence had gone. 'Does Mark –

my husband – make a difference to you?' she asked. 'Do you feel righteous about him?'

'He makes a difference – he might come back. I don't know about feeling righteous, I'm disappointed, that's all. Still, I'd sooner you were married to one man than sleeping with half a dozen, and that I know you're not.' Ben slammed the door of the cooker.

'We weren't married in church, if that's any help. I wanted to, but Mark wouldn't.'

'Where I come from, plenty of people would say you hadn't been married at all.' Ben straightened up and turned to take her in his arms, and she knew a moment of joy unlike anything she'd ever experienced. She wanted desperately to say, 'I love you,' but Mark and others had cheapened the words for her. Believing that a girl who valued her independence should never commit herself verbally, she said, 'If you think I'm going to sleep with you Ben, you can think again.'

'I know you are,' said Ben, 'and so do you.' He picked her up and carried her into the bedroom, and for a second she was reminded of him carrying the drunk out of the Hart Royal. 'Why are you laughing?' he asked suspiciously.

'No reason. Just happiness.' You couldn't be coy with a man like Ben, she realized. It had to be yes or no.

'I love you Ben,' she said. 'I'm yours.'

Four

Ben woke with a start. Then he thought he was still dreaming. He had never shared his bed with anyone, except in dreams, since he and Denis were toddlers. Lesley was cuddled against him, breathing quietly. He held her gently – you wake up from dreams.

It was still dark, but with the shimmering darkness that comes with snow. Ben felt stupefied with happiness; the nigglings of doubt were forgotten, he was joyful and relaxed. Last night, he'd been wary. He'd felt he didn't understand Lesley, couldn't entirely trust her. She was outside his experience. His uncertainty had made him nervous; afraid of a rebuff even when reason told him she was all his.

If only she would stay, he thought. But her work was miles away, and she was used to comforts that the cottage couldn't provide. He could hardly expect her to move in and live with him, wonderful though that would be. Perhaps the occasional Saturday. . . . She was waking up, turning to him, murmuring the loving things again. He couldn't take in all that she was saying – surely she didn't mean it, it was too good to be true.

'I love you too,' he said, unhappily aware that he couldn't express himself in words as easily as she could. He was half frightened by her total commitment, her lack of restraint, her obvious delight. He felt he'd been given a dazzling gift and that words were inadequate. He hoped with all his heart that she wouldn't be disappointed in him, get sick of him. He shut his eyes, holding her close, recalling the joy and tenderness of the night.

The alarm clock, a dreadful thing on legs with bells on top of it, jangled violently. Ben, used to it, pushed down the knob and silenced it. Lesley shot upright.

'What the hell?'

'I'm a heavy sleeper,' explained Ben.

'You are an' all. But it's Sunday – what's the time?'

'Six. I'd forgotten. I'm doing an early stint, trying to make a bit more overtime. Another month and there won't be the extra work.' After a minute, as Lesley retreated under the faded patchwork quilt, he slid down beside her, saying, 'You meant all that, didn't you? Things you said to me?'

'Of course I did.' She looked up at him in surprise. 'The first time I saw you, I was sunk. Remember at the Turpin Arms? I didn't know anything about you, not even your name, but I felt we were lovers already.'

'I did too,' said Ben.

'I know. I thought it was just that you're wildly attractive and I was lonely, but I found out different.'

Ben grinned at her and then he sat up and reached for his shirt.

'Oh Ben, don't get up, it's Sunday. Eric will see my car outside; he won't expect you – not if he's any sense.'

'Your car? Oh God, so it is. Don't you mind?'

'Not in the least.'

Ben hesitated. 'I'll have to go this time,' he said. 'I promised the lads I would. It won't happen again.' He pulled the shirt over his head. 'I'm hungry, aren't you? There's rashers and eggs in the kitchen. *Now* why are you laughing?'

He switched on the light, pulled on trousers and jersey and padded barefoot into the other room. The stone floor was scattered with rag rugs, he stepped from one to another. The range hadn't gone out. He filled it with coal, pulled out the damper and opened the draught. Then he started to cook breakfast, moving quickly and neatly in the confined space. He sang softly as he worked.

What luck, what amazing luck! A job, a house, and now a girl who behaved as if she loved him. He had never imagined such a thing. He wondered if the Guvnor would object to Lesley staying with him. Then he remembered the absent husband. What kind of man could have left Lesley for another woman? He must be stark staring mad. Ben filled the teapot, and scooped rashers, eggs, fried bread and tomatoes onto two plates. These he carried into the bedroom.

Lesley ate a piece of fried bread with her fingers. Ben ate all the rest. 'You'd get on well with the Guvnor,' she said. 'He eats cold beef and apple-pie for breakfast. Sometimes, he eats leftover cold cabbage and chips. Mandy can't watch.' She yawned.

Ben chased the last tomato pips. Both plates were clean. 'I have to go now,' he said. 'I'll be back around twelve.' He didn't ask, 'Will you be here?' Lesley was falling asleep. He kissed her, tucked in the quilt round a bare shoulder, switched off the light and went out into the chilly morning.

Funny, he thought, as he trudged along the snowy path towards the lighted sheds, how his own home had dwindled in his mind. He got on well enough with all his family except his grandmother, but she was the only one he ever spared a thought for. He wondered how she and Lesley would get on.

Edward Ryder was not an ambitious man. He sat, chain smoking, in the dark old office where generations of Ryders before him had dealt with the legal problems of Kilmoon. Engraved on the glass door were the words – 'Andrew Ryder & Sons, solicitors. Est. 1806.'

Edward's tall bald forehead and narrow nose and mouth gave him a deceptively ascetic air; he looked as if he might be a scholar or a poet. In fact, he spent most of his time helping people sort out squabbles over land and urging them to make wills. Nobody took a major problem to the dusty chaos of Edward's office – they never had.

Edward's father had retired after coping with the legal procedures that cut off Agatha Logan from her family. The disinheritance, the entail, the wills and codicils, the plots and counter-plots had left John Ryder mentally exhausted.

At last, all was in order. Agatha Vere-Lanigan and the workman, Michael Logan, were married and settled at Cloninch farm, while Agatha's father, Sir Arthur Vere-Lanigan, paid his lawyer's bill remarking, 'Well, Ryder, that's the end of the business. I shall not trouble you again.'

Ever since, the Vere-Lanigan file had lain unopened, gathering dust.

Agatha's father had been dead for forty years. His son had sold Castle Lanigan to pay death duties, and gone with one of his sisters to live in England – a common practice of Irish people who have failed spectacularly at home. Edward lit another cigarette, and marvelled at how the business had worked out. Crazy old Mrs Logan was at least solvent, in spite of the archaic way she ran the farm and her family. Her brother had died almost penniless, his title dying with him. He didn't know if the sisters were alive or not.

There was a tap on the door, and Edward's elderly secretary, Lily, began to say something, but was cut short as Agatha Logan brushed her aside and swept into the room.

'I cannot imagine how you work in all this dust and smoke,' she said. 'It's extremely bad for you. You do still work?'

Edward stood up. Talk of the devil! And the old woman hadn't spoken to him for years. 'Good morning, Mrs Logan,' he said stiffly. 'Sit down. What can I do for you?'

Agatha's derisive glance took in the cobwebs, the papers impaled on spikes, the piles of notes, some clipped together, some not; the curling calendar for the previous year. 'Do you know anything about Tissot?' she demanded.

'– Er,' said Edward, 'What did you say?'

'Tissot. I have a painting by Tissot. You go to Dublin, don't you?'

'Ah, Tissot,' said Edward, who knew nothing about him. 'What have you in mind?' He thought it wiser to ignore the last question.

'I wish to sell the painting which I understand is valuable. When next you go to Dublin, you shall take it with you and have it valued for me.' Agatha was wearing an almost ankle-length Burberry and a brown leather cloche hat which hid all of her white shingled hair. 'I may accompany you,' she added.

'Impossible,' said Edward hastily. 'That is, I couldn't accept the responsibility. It would be a most unwise procedure for me to take your picture to a valuer. You should write, inviting one to your house. You could ask Barney Mangan's advice – he would know about specialists in art valuation. The picture is insured, I take it?' He was trying to see what it was that Mrs Logan had brought into the office with her. It was on the floor beside her. Something large in a case.

Agatha stood up. The grey eyes under the antique hat shrivelled Edward as he too rose to his feet. 'If I wished to ask Mangan to my house, I should have done so,' she said. 'And yes, the painting is insured, but inadequately. The premiums required are ridiculous. You have been most unhelpful. Good day.'

Giving Edward no chance to reply, she marched out of the office, closing the door with an angry snap.

Edward saw that she was carrying a guitar.

Agatha did not pause at Mangan's Auctioneers and Valuers. She had no faith in Barney Mangan, a cheerful villain with a fondness for greyhounds. It was he who encouraged her son-in-law Myles in his gambling. Probably a roundabout way of buying the picture cheaply.

Agatha had bought the guitar at one of Barney's auctions some years earlier. She herself played the violin; had played well at one time. Nowadays, lack of practice and rheumatic fingers kept her away from it except on the rare occasions when her customary chill gave way to passionate rage. Then she would grab her violin and play the *Spanish Gypsy Dance* on it. The dog howled and the family ran for cover.

One of Agatha's few personal possessions was an old HMV gramophone, and a pile of scratched 78 records. When Benedict was a little boy, she used to allow him to wind it up and play his favourite, *Ol' Man River*. As he grew older and his voice broke, he began to sing at his work in a deep baritone, velvety soft, which kept its tunefulness even in the lowest notes. Michael had had the temerity to suggest that the boy might turn his singing to good account, but Agatha had soon put a stop to that. No grandson of hers would be a mountebank, singing for his supper. The operatic stage, possibly, nothing less. Michael said no more, and Ben, sensing friction, had kept quiet. Only the sheep and Dancing Lady heard him sing.

The shop at the corner of Kilmoon Square was called 'Sound and Fury'. It pulsated with sound, and Agatha supplied the fury as she stormed in. 'Turn that thing off,' she commanded. The teenage girl in charge obeyed, looking terrified. 'I want this instrument restrung immediately,' said Agatha, shouting in the sudden hush. The girl stammered something, and a fat man hurried in from the back of the shop. Agatha repeated her wishes, and took the guitar out of its case. It was Spanish, old and scratched. It was the only present she had ever given Benedict. She would have it repaired, and write and tell him. He might be persuaded to return.

'Have it for you Friday,' said the fat man, reaching a hand to a switch. The heavy metal resumed and Agatha left, thin-lipped. Filthy din!

Driving home in the van beside Myles (the guitar had proved impossible for her to carry on her bicycle), Agatha brooded silently. It would require more than a restrung guitar to induce Benedict to come home. She mentally reviewed those of her acquaintances who owned cars, and might be bullied into taking her picture to Dublin. Myles? No. He would get lost or drunk or both. But if she could not turn the painting into money, Benedict would be lost. A temporary under-shepherd, he had told Denis on the telephone. Living in what sounded like the most primitive cabin, and riding two horses, one unsound and the other thought to be dangerous.

Even as Agatha reviewed these things in her mind, she knew that she was not facing up to her biggest worry. Benedict was possessed of the same sort of magnetism that had made her leave everything for Michael. He had the sort of personality that made you turn round when he was behind you. And there was something less superficial than mere charm in his rare smile. Some scheming hussy would snare him and he would be lost for ever. She spoke the words 'scheming hussy!' aloud, with venom. Myles grunted. He was used to her.

Back at Cloninch, Agatha climbed the stairs to her room. She never thought of it as 'our room' always as 'mine'. Coming face to face with the girl in the painting and with Michael, who was sitting on the side of the bed yawning and taking off his socks, she thought it was a pity that it was the picture that had to go. She smiled thinly – the idea of putting Michael up for auction amused her. She didn't speak to him or he to her.

Agatha went to the little rosewood writing table which her mother had given her and sat down. She still had some of the writing paper she had pilfered from her home when she married. It was thick, grey, deckle-edged, the envelopes lined with dark blue tissue paper. The sheets of paper were headed 'Castle Lanigan, Rathfree, Co Kildare,' in dark blue. Agatha selected a sheet, laid it on her leather blotter, dipped a relief nib in the last of the Swan's blue-black ink, and began to write.

Ben arrived at the lighted sheds where the two yawning students were bedding up the lambing pens before going off duty. It was nearly seven o'clock, and the boys had been kept busy since soon after midnight. More than twenty ewes had chosen the small hours to produce.

Ben would be working on his own until late afternoon, but Eric was in the far yard if extra help was needed. Ted never came down to the sheds. He supervised the field work and attended four markets a week. Eric, head shepherd for the past ten years, had resented Ben at first, but now accepted him. Old-fashioned notions he might have, but Ben wasn't hidebound. He was quick to learn new methods and there was nothing Eric could teach him about the care of pregnant ewes and young lambs. Eric, a wiry man in his late forties, was known as 'Rudolf' because his bright red nose suggested a heavy drinker which he was not. He was a dedicated stockman, a confirmed bachelor, humourless, but always fair.

Ben moved quickly and quietly among the sheep. They barely roused as he passed, blinking at him, not bothering to get up, accepting him. The same sheep would all run into the furthest corner of the barn when either of the students, Trevor and Andy, inspected them. Ben went down the alleyway, checking the night's crop of lambs. He turned off an infra-red lamp, wondering how the two boys had failed to notice that the weak lamb lying under it had died. A sharp bleat behind him made him return to the shed. Another ewe was starting to lamb, and he could see that she was going to need help. Taking off his jacket, Ben walked quietly up to the ewe. She got up, rolling her eyes at him, but made no attempt to run away. Quickly, he caught the heavy animal and flipped her down on her side; a matter of knack rather than strength, like a well trained nurse turning a patient in a hospital bed.

Ben knelt by the sheep, gently examining her. As he did so, he softly sang an old spiritual – 'Oh, by and by . . . by and by . . . I'm gonna lay down this heavy load . . .' He delivered the lamb as he did everything, tidily and without fuss. It raised its head almost at once, sneezing and flapping its ears. Ben tipped the ewe back onto her feet and hefted her belly gently with his hands. Another lamb there – maybe two. Number one was a little one. He decided to put her in a big pen, or she might lie on one lamb while she was having another. He worked happily, humming to himself. He wished he owned just a few sheep of his own. He'd never owned an animal except Dancing Lady.

A sudden shuffling and tension among the sheep made him turn round. The Guvnor was standing there. He'd lost some of his high colour, but his collar was open as usual. 'You should be farming,' he said abruptly.

'Thought I was,' said Ben, shaking out straw.

'I'm farming, you're earning wages,' said Charlie. 'You should be giving somebody else orders. Students do just what you say – if they can, the daftheads. So does flaming dog. You should rent a bit o' land in Ireland. You'd do more good, think on.'

'Tired of me?'

'Nay, I don't want rid of you. Trying to advise you.'

'Where I come from,' said Ben, 'landlord's still a dirty word after a hundred years. Leasing's only just starting to come back. Anyway, I couldn't pay the rent.'

'Stay on then. But stop bloody well humming – you're like a hive of bees. Drive anybody mad. Now where are you off?'

'Going to get Roy and go round the big lambs in the back field,' said Ben. He let Roy off his chain, and the two men walked together as far as the gate. Ben sent the dog round the sheep, brought them into the open and began to count them. The Guvnor suddenly called Roy to him. Roy glanced coldly at him, then enquiringly at Ben. Ben, who had lost count and was annoyed, made no sign. Roy decided to ignore Charlie, and continued to work the flock towards Ben.

Charlie grudgingly liked Ben, but this was more than he could stand. 'Keep bloody useless dog then,' he roared. 'Rotten sod wants shooting.' He turned on his heel, and Ben could hear him coughing all the way back to the house.

Ben found the Guvnor hard to understand. He didn't know that Charlie was an unhappy man. In his heart of hearts he knew that his son, Stephen, would never return from New Zealand, and Ted had none of the inborn authority that made the students obey Ben so readily and cheerfully. Roy recognized the quality too. Ben was learning the joy and the saving of labour that a good sheepdog brings, but Roy was not a likeable dog. Suspicious and surly at all times, his heart was given to his work. Ben was merely the means of supplying that work. Roy felt drawn to him, but resisted his instincts. He had seen too many under-shepherds come and go.

As Ben continued his rounds, the dog at his heels, he wondered how long it would be before he fell out with his employer. He didn't want to lose his job, but he was damned if he'd be shouted at by anyone. A few days earlier, Charlie had told him off in front of the students. Ben had been eating his 'lowance, as the mid-morning sandwiches and tea were called, and Charlie had been hunched, wheezing over the fire. Not a good time to tell him that Anagram's head-shaking was getting worse. Charlie had told him he was mutton-fisted, and advised a rubber snaffle, adding, 'Our Stephen never had any bother.' Ben had shut up, but his anger had reduced everyone except Charlie to embarrassed silence.

It wouldn't do to get the sack, thought Ben, he might lose Lesley as well as his job. He must try to control his temper and to keep off tricky subjects.

Ben called Roy to his side, and headed back towards the buildings. He began to hum again and then, softly, to sing.

Ben didn't have Sunday lunch at the farm, although invited. He could see that Lesley's car had gone, but he wanted to be alone with his happiness. He found his cottage warm and tidy, with snowdrops in a mug on the window-sill. There was no note. Agatha's letter lay on the table where he had left it yesterday. Some sort of superstitious misgiving had prevented him from opening it before he set off for Leeds. The writing on the thick grey envelope almost seemed to leap off the paper with its jagged capitals and heavy downstrokes. Ben picked it up and opened it. If the old devil thought she could whistle him back . . .

Dear Benedict,
I have come to a decision. Since you choose to live
elsewhere, I will sell the painting which I had
intended should be yours when I die.

*I must ask you to open a bank account and inform
me when you have done so. A sum of money will be
paid in shortly. I do not know the amount. This
money is to ensure that you do not live in squalor.
I shall be displeased if you squander it on
inessentials.*

*Your loving
Grandmother*

Ben's first thought was, loving? That's a good one. Then it
was borne in on him that she proposed to part with her most
cherished possession on his account. He hadn't told Denis
what a generous wage he was getting, it would have looked
like boasting. But Agatha must be told, and quickly. Hadn't
she realized that someone living in squalor would hesitate to
make telephone calls to Ireland? He would make another at
once. Ben was a poor writer. He dialled, and spoke to Agatha
herself.

'Where are you telephoning from, Benedict?'

'My own house,' replied Ben. He didn't add that the
telephone had been installed so that the shepherd could be
summoned at night, rather than for his personal conveni-
ence. 'Don't sell the painting, Grandmother,' he begged.

But Agatha replied, 'My mind is made up. In these lawless
days, it might easily be stolen.'

Ben knew that Agatha's mind, once made up, stayed made
up so he wasted no more words, merely asking her to bank
the money in Ireland for her own use.

Agatha snorted and hung up. Ben set about preparing a
meal for himself. He remembered a few short weeks before,
how he had told himself he had never been so happy in his
life. That happiness was a shadow of the joy that filled him as
he ate his meal without tasting it. The rest of the day was his
own. He sat by the fire and waited for Lesley.

After a while, he began to have doubts. This husband, he
thought, I wonder if he's really gone for good. Ben no longer
had a conscience about him, because of the way he had

walked out. But would he walk back? And would Lesley decide to return to him? She had said he was a sales rep in Preg-Togs, an upmarket line in maternity wear. Ben had felt out of his depth – how could he compete? When he reached this point in his thoughts, Lesley arrived.

'I've brought a suitcase,' she said. 'You do want me to stay, Ben?'

'You know I do.' He held her gently. She was tense, same as she'd been in the car the night before. 'What's the matter?' he asked.

'Ben, I'm scared. I love you so much, I'm afraid something will happen to spoil it.'

'It won't. I won't let anything happen. Unless your husband comes back . . .'

Lesley said, 'I think it was because I didn't love Mark enough that he went with other girls. Charlotte wasn't the first. But I never understood that until now.'

Later, they sat on the two rickety chairs, making toast at the cooker. Ben's slice fell onto the hot coals and burned to a cinder. He had been watching Lesley's face in the glow of the firelight. She dropped her toast on the floor. 'Save it for Roy,' she said. She reached for Ben's hand and held it tightly. 'I want to stay with you, Ben.'

'I didn't dare hope you would,' said Ben seriously.

Lesley made light of moving in. It meant a long drive to work and back every day, involving an early start. She didn't mind. She set about turning the bleak little house into a welcoming home. Every day, she brought things back from her flat – a lamp, cushions, a duvet, pots and pans. Ben's absence of worldly goods bothered her, but not, apparently, Ben. She was lighthearted, finding everything easy. Mandy, anxious to see the results of her scheming, visited them once. Ben had to sit on the floor. There was less room than in a large caravan.

February came and went, it seemed to Lesley, in a flash. Ben came home with a big bunch of primroses for her. The snow had gone, except from the backs of the hedges, and she'd seen

70

Ben from the window, picking the flowers. Mark had sometimes bought her flowers in the early days, but she couldn't imagine him picking them. She buried her face in their damp coolness. 'My favourite scent – they're beautiful.' She put them in a milk jug. 'I'll get us some more mugs – we've only got two.'

'I like it like that,' said Ben. 'Peter must have done as well. Had he a girl, do you know?'

'I don't think so. Peter didn't stay here if he could help it; he didn't like it. Outside of lambing time, I think he lived in Middlegarth.'

'I don't know how he could.' Ben looked round the room fondly. 'This place is just right. Even without you in it, it's grand.'

Geoff needn't have feared that Lesley's work would suffer. Her happiness infected almost all of the people she visited. She met him at the Kosy Kitchen less often, but when she did she always had progress to report. One day as they sat at one of the pink-mottled tables, she told him she had seen a lawyer about a divorce. 'He didn't think there'd be any problem,' she said. 'And he's traced Mark through his firm. He's living in Bristol.'

Geoff studied her, thinking, as Ben had, that Mark must be raving mad. A great lass, Lesley, and wonderful at her job. She managed to achieve a relationship of mutual confidence and trust with almost all her charges, without allowing herself to be worn out by their emotional difficulties.

'I think your young man would make a good dog-trainer,' he said. 'You can often tell. He's a silent bloke though, isn't he? Nothing to say for himself.'

Lesley said, 'I thought he was rather dour and touchy at first; always on his guard. But that's not the real Ben. He's had a hell of a life in Ireland under his grandmother's thumb; no freedom and expected to do all the work. Of course he was on the defensive. He's quite different now he's happy.'

Meg was lying under the table, wearing her harness. She

was aware that the lass feeding with her person was now the property of the little youth she'd seen in the kitchen at Middlegarth. The one who, with a snap of his fingers had almost, but not quite, made her disobey Geoff and come out from under the table. Her gaze travelled from Geoff's well polished shoes to the pair of long nylon-covered legs at her other side. What had this woman done to deserve a person of her own? Nothing as like as not. And she, Meg, had to share her Geoff with a kennel full of other dogs. Nothing right or fair about it, thought Meg, shutting her eyes firmly.

When Lesley left the cafe, Geoff watched her retreating back, hoping fervently that the new boyfriend wouldn't carry her off to Ireland. She had told Geoff that Ben liked everything about her except her job. She'd have to be pretty far gone to give it up to please him, thought Geoff.

Lesley took the empty milk bottle up to Henrietta's flat again, by mistake.

'You must be in love,' said Henrietta.

'I am,' said Lesley.

She found fresh reserves of patience for dealing with Mrs Betts, and played tirelessly with the children at the Day Centre.

Hazel made no comment on Lesley's absence at first, but after a week suggested that a friend of hers would like to share the flat. Yes, a woman. Yes, she had references. Lesley interviewed Imogen, who had hair like shredded wheat and wore an ankle-length mackintosh and straw sandals. No, said Imogen, she wasn't an art student, she was a social anthropologist. Lesley said, oh, that must be interesting, and accepted a month's rent in advance.

Busier than ever, Ben was usually at work first and home first. If he had time, he would cook a massive meal. His appetite was huge; there were never any leftovers.

Only at night did Lesley allow herself to think ahead. Ben was content to live each day as it came. She had to face the fact that, after two months, she was still more committed than he was. Plainly, he loved her, but not helplessly and totally as she loved him. Her own feelings still frightened her. She and Mark had been together for three years and had no children. Mark didn't want any, and Lesley had no strong feelings about them either way. She would have liked a family, but her life wouldn't be blighted without. Yet the first time Ben had spoken to her, before she even knew his name, she had caught herself thinking about babies.

She had banned the alarm clock, and brought her own battery one, whose discreet bleep didn't rouse Ben. So Lesley woke at first light with the feeling, now familiar, of floating calm. I never knew, she thought. I might have spent my whole life not knowing, but for Ben. She spared a moment's guilty pity for Mark – poor Mark. She tried to recall him, but he had faded from her memory. He was just a man driving away in a company car and not coming back.

Lesley propped herself on an elbow and studied Ben's sleeping face. His dark hair was tousled, his face unfamiliar; the uncertainty and the wary look smoothed out. Those long eyelashes were wasted on a man, she thought. He was serene and vulnerable in sleep, the firm mouth and decided chin relaxed. You wouldn't guess how touchily defensive he could be. She hadn't been altogether truthful to Geoff. She lay down cautiously, resting her head on his broad shoulder.

Obviously, Ben had hang-ups concerning her. She had thought they were religious, but apparently not. Her marriage didn't count, he had said. Then there was the thing about money. She had discovered that Ben thought she was loaded. She'd explained that she had some good clothes which didn't date, but that she wasn't by any means well off. She made her own dresses. Still there was something bothering him. She felt dimly that it was to do with his grandmother, and dismissed the ridiculous thought. She fell asleep.

When she woke again, Ben had got up quietly and was dressing. She watched him pull his jersey over his head, taking pleasure in everything he did, however trivial. She remembered seeing him at the beginning in the Middlegarth yard on a freezing day, bareheaded in his light anorak, while the other men wore padded jackets and caps with earflaps. She had shuddered, thinking, goodness, how cold he must be, and then scolded herself – What am I worrying about him for? That's not part of wanting to go to bed with somebody.

Ben lifted the latch of the heavy old door quietly, and went out. She noticed that he didn't have to bend his head to go through as she did, but his shoulders completely filled the doorway. He'd given up bringing giant meals to her in bed; she heard him preparing his own.

When he left the cottage, she knelt up in bed and watched him going up the path. It was blowing hard – a blustery March morning, a Saturday. Ben never bowed his head against the wind, he walked straight into it. He was still working overtime.

Lesley planned to go to her flat for her sewing machine and some material. She had taken measurements, and meant to surprise Ben with new curtains. The existing ones, cut down from an old pair of Mandy's, were rubbed almost through at the edges, as rotten as cobwebs. She got up, contentedly planning ahead – but only a few days ahead. She hoped as usual that Ben wasn't going to ride Anagram. Mandy had told her that the horse was to be sold to the local branch of the Mounted Police. Some poor copper's going to have a lively ride, thought Lesley.

As Ben walked up the lane to the farm, he could hardly contain his happiness. He hummed to himself as he walked, but when he saw that the Guvnor was there, he stopped.

The bay gelding had gone. Charlie couldn't quite bring himself to get rid of both horses, and the bay, Flycatcher, wasn't saleable, so he'd gone on permanent loan to a neighbour to ride round his farm.

Charlie had been looking over Anagram at Ted's insistence, but couldn't see anything wrong with the horse. How could there be anything wrong with a horse he and Stephen had bought? Logic was no match for Charlie's arrogance.

74

'Nowt wrong with him that regular work won't cure.' Charlie's aggressive greeting didn't disturb Ben. The Guvnor didn't believe in wasting breath on 'good mornings'.

Ben studied the horse, standing, rugs off, in the loose-box. The older student, Trevor, was nervously holding the halter rope. Anagram was a dark brown, with the bumpy forehead which sometimes goes with a sulky temperament. 'Never was owt wrong with him but idleness,' said Charlie.

'You may be right,' said Ben, 'but he's changed since I first rode him. He'd have a go then if you didn't watch him. Now, he rides like an old pensioner up off the grass. And the rubber snaffle hasn't stopped him shaking his head.'

'Don't know what I pay a vet for,' said Charlie nastily.

Ben angrily swung round from his inspection of the horse and faced the Guvnor. 'Don't forget you took me on because I knew what was up with Flycatcher,' he said.

Charlie glared down at Ben from his superior height. 'Happen I did,' he snapped, 'but you don't know what's wrong with this one. Take him out when you've finished in buildings.' He tramped off.

'Bloody old fool,' said Ben. 'He should try riding him himself.'

Trevor pulled off Anagram's halter. 'He doesn't look so clever to me neither,' he said, 'but I'm no horseman.'

'I'll take him handy,' said Ben.

'The Guvnor wasn't suited,' said Trevor, 'but I think you're right. The brute'll be to shoot.' They rugged the horse up and went back to the sheep.

Ben saw Lesley's car go out shortly after he started work. He didn't expect her home to lunch, so he made do with a pile of beef sandwiches, half an apple pie and several mugs of tea in the farmhouse kitchen. He was uneasy with Mandy who was plainly thrilled by the success of her matchmaking efforts. He headed her off when she tried to talk about Lesley.

After his meal, Ben saddled Anagram, noting that the brown hadn't eaten his feed. This was a new development. Oh well, thought Ben, a quiet hack down by the Ings won't hurt him.

75

Riding on Middlegarth farm was boring, because there were sheep everywhere, and miles of electric fencing. You had to stick to the farm roads, and if you met a tractor there wasn't much room to spare between it and the electric fence. Ben preferred to ride down the back lane, past his cottage, to the Leeds road. On the other side of the road was a broad strip of rough grazing, running down to Killington Beck. Known as Killington Ings, this land was only grazed in summer and was a good place for a canter. The road was a busy one; rather than ride straight across, Ben used to take his horse along the grass verge as far as the Turpin Arms, where there was a traffic island.

Ben liked the Ings. The Beck, with its fringe of tall dead reeds and its leaning sally trees, reminded him of Cloninch Bog at home. The Beck would have been called a river in Ireland. It was deep and slow moving. Ben had become used to blackened tree-trunks and dark grey sheep. He'd been told that this was due to smoke from the grimy industrial north.

He picked up the reins, swung himself onto the horse's back. The brown gelding sidled uneasily. Ben shortened the reins, and kicked him forward. The response was lethargic. Anagram switched his tail and plodded off. He shook his head up, down and sideways. Ben thought, this is the last time I ride the devil. Sooner lose my job. Then he thought of the consequences if he did lose his job. Blast the Guvnor – pig-headed, conceited – why couldn't he see sense?

He noticed Lesley's dark blue Fiat turning in off the Leeds road. He followed the car's approach with his eyes, his mind wandering from his listless mount. He rode past the cottage onto the straight part of the lane. It was wide enough to pass a car, riding a horse, too narrow for two cars to pass. There was a shallow ditch on either side, where the last of the snow lingered in the shade. Where he'd picked primroses. As the car came towards him, Ben raised his hand to Lesley in greeting.

76

Then it happened. Anagram stopped dead and backed. He flung his head from side to side. He slid onto his hocks and, with a shrill scream, reared up until he was almost vertical. When he had done the same thing with Peter, he had caught his rider unprepared, and Peter had lost his balance and pulled the horse over backwards on top of him. Ben's reactions were quicker. He dropped the reins and threw his weight forward, wrapping both arms round Anagram's neck. For a long second it seemed as if the horse must topple over backwards, then he righted himself. As his forefeet touched the ground, he stretched out his neck, laid his ears flat back and bolted.

Ben scarcely had time to get back into the saddle and grab the reins. Lesley's car was only yards away; the brute was tearing straight at it. Ben pulled the reins – he might as well have pulled Anagram's tail. He saw Lesley dragging the wheel over, the car on the edge of the ditch. Anagram slammed against the side of it, snapping off the outside mirror with his shoulder and banging Ben's leg painfully. The car crashed into the ditch.

The main road was scarcely a hundred yards away and on it heavy traffic roared to and fro. There was a gate onto the road with a cattle grid. It always stood open. Beside it was a narrower gateway without a grid. Between them was a three feet square pillar of the same yellow stone as the farmhouse. As Anagram raced along the edge of the ditch, out of control, Ben knew he would be wise to throw himself off into the ditch. He dismissed the idea. He must keep trying to turn the horse until the last possible second. There would be an appalling pile up if he galloped onto the road where heavy lorries were coming from both directions.

There wasn't time for weighing alternatives. Ben turned the bolting horse fractionally. Now he was heading for the stone pillar. He galloped straight into it without slackening speed.

Ben had learned how to fall off a runaway horse. He knew how to tuck his head in to avoid a broken neck, how to roll up like a hedgehog to lessen the danger of internal injuries. But there was no time. Automatically, he kept his head down, shielding his face. The bang on the back of his skull knocked him out.

Five

Lesley's head ached vilely, and the plaster on her forehead was pulling the stitches underneath. She made a move to touch it, and saw that her right forearm was encased in a pink elastic bandage. Memory came back unevenly with consciousness. A charging horse, the car heeling over, Ben's face glimpsed, mouth open, as his leg struck the car. The car had rocked perilously, and she had unfastened her seatbelt with some idea of jumping clear, just as it nosedived into the ditch. She had been thrown violently forward – she recalled the pain as her head struck the windscreen, the blood running into her eyes. Semi-conscious, she had heard a dreadful thudding crash, then there was silence. She had tried to shout Ben's name, but no sound came. Then a man's voice had said clearly, 'He's broken his neck.'

Lesley twisted her head on the pillow. 'Ben,' she tried to say. 'Ben.' Her right knee was bandaged too, it was hurting like hell. Fuzzy-brained, she attempted to focus on her surroundings. She was in a large light ward, full of people. The light hurt her eyes and she shut them again. There was a movement beside her, someone was sitting there, reading a book. 'Ben?' She rolled her head sideways. This time, her voice obeyed her.

'No, sorry, it's Mandy. Thank heaven you've come round. I'll call a nurse.' Mandy laid aside the Mills & Boon romance she was reading. Curious reading for the Guvnor's daughter – she lived on them. 'Ben's okay,' she added.

Lesley's head swam as she struggled to sit up. 'What do you mean, Ben's okay?' Her voice rose. 'You're hiding something from me. He's broken his neck – I heard someone say so. Is he dead? He is, isn't he?'

'Take it easy,' Mandy put her arm round Lesley's shoulders. 'Ben's all right, I promise you. Talk about the luck of the Irish . . . He's been sitting with you for ages. I took over while he went to get something to eat; he'll soon be back. Do lie down and let me get a nurse.'

Lesley dropped back wearily against the pillows. 'I don't need a nurse. Thank God he's all right. Something to *eat*? He would. Oh Mandy, I was certain he'd broken his neck – I heard somebody say he had.'

'The horse broke its neck – killed of course. By, you should have heard Father! Poor brute, it had a brain tumour, a huge one. Father knows he made a mistake, so he's cursing everybody into heaps. Trevor's leaving tomorrow.'

Lesley felt her forehead cautiously. 'I seem to be in a mess,' she said. 'Have I got a broken leg?'

'Your kneecap was out of place,' said Mandy. 'It's been put back. You've ever so many stitches in your head – eighteen I think – and a sprained wrist.' She spoke with involuntary relish; Mandy thrived on disaster. 'Thank goodness it wasn't any worse,' she said. 'Ben prevented the horse from galloping onto the main road in among the traffic. It ran slap into the gatepost, and Ben clonked his head. He must have a skull like iron.' She went on to describe the damage to Lesley's car and to speculate about insurance.

Lesley had stopped listening. Ben was coming.

Ben had been knocked out for only a minute or two. He had picked himself up, alarmed by the blood on his clothes and hands, but it came from the horse. There was nothing to be done for Anagram. Ben had wiped his hands with wet grass as he ran back to the car, and had helped to get Lesley out. The back of his head throbbed, there was a bump coming. He had ignored it. His jeans were torn at the knee, he had a long scrape down his shin. The strip of torn material almost tripped him. He bent and ripped it free, noticing that his leg was black and blue. He had driven to Leeds with Charlie, following the ambulance with Lesley inside – neither of them had felt like talking. Ben had gone reluctantly for an X-Ray; there was no fracture. Then he had been taken to the ward where Lesley lay, paper-white and with a dressing covering her forehead. He had stayed with her until his rumbling stomach had reminded him that he was hungry. Chased away by Mandy, he had gone to find a canteen.

When he came back, Mandy withdrew with exaggerated tact. Lesley's shaky smile somehow touched Ben's heart more than anything she could have said or done. He felt he'd been taking her for granted – he never would again. He bent to kiss her, and saw that there were tears in her eyes. She was wearing a sort of white cotton pinny, having no suitcase with her. She asked Ben faintly if he was sure he was all right.

'I'm fine – but you . . . I couldn't do a thing; the horse went crazy.'

She clutched his hand. 'Never mind, love, you're all in one piece, that's all that matters,' she said.

A few minutes later, Ben was turned out of the ward, as the doctor arrived to examine Lesley. He would have to wait until the following afternoon to see her again, he was told. He found Mandy eagerly describing the accident to another visitor, and they drove back to Middlegarth.

Ben missed Lesley more than he would have imagined possible that night. He slept badly, worrying about the cut on her head. Supposing it were to affect her sight? It didn't bear thinking about. He got up early, and reported for work as usual, to the astonishment of Eric and Andy. Trevor had left, as promised. Ben insisted that he didn't want or need a holiday, that the stiffness in his leg was wearing off, but the Guvnor's orders were clear. Ben hung about, his head aching mildly, waiting for the afternoon.

Ben packed Lesley's suitcase, thinking how pretty, how delightfully silky and scented her clothes were. He took his time, enjoying the task. As he shut the case, he allowed himself for the first time to think seriously about marriage.

When he arrived at the hospital, carrying the suitcase, a box of chocolates and a white azalea in a pot, he searched the ward in vain. Lesley had been moved to a private room. The Guvnor had been giving orders concerning her as well.

Lesley, sitting up in bed, still ashy pale, introduced a girl who was eating grapes and spitting the pips into an ashtray. 'My flatmate, Hazel.' Some animation came into Hazel's opaque slate-coloured eyes. She offered Ben some of Lesley's grapes, favouring him with a smile which showed large square teeth.

Ben sat on the bed, waiting for her to go. He had no time for social niceties, and he knew that Lesley disliked her. At last, Hazel got up and slouched out, chewing something out of a paper bag.

'Honestly,' said Lesley, exasperated, 'that woman ought to be grazing in a field. I think she chews the cud. Nice of her to come, but –'

'We won't waste our time talking about her,' said Ben firmly. 'When are they going to let you come home?' He hugged her cautiously. Fear of hurting her made him more tender and considerate than usual; even so she cried out, 'Mind my knee! I'll have to go to the flat, I'm afraid,' she added.

Ben's face darkened. 'Ah no, I'll mind you at the cottage,' he said. 'The Guvnor wants me to take time off.'

'It isn't so easy. I'm to be discharged tomorrow, but I'll have to come back to have these stitches out, and for physiotherapy for my knee. I'm supposed to have my wrist X-rayed again too. I won't be able to drive for a bit – anyway, the car's out of action. Move over, Ben, I'm getting up.'

Lesley got out of bed and tested her knee. 'Goodness, I'm shaky. I'm supposed to walk about, but I can't seem to manage the crutch.'

'That for a story,' said Ben, as she draped her arm round his neck. They both laughed, and he wished acutely that he could take her back with him. He could look after her better than the doctors, he thought. After two turns round the ward, Lesley was glad to climb back into bed. Ben sat down beside the bed and leaned his head over until it was on the pillow beside hers. 'I wish I could get in there with you,' he said.

'So do I. When I get out of here, you can come to the flat.'

'What? With that chewing woman?'

'There's plenty of room. Wait till you see the other one. She wears a mac indoors, down to her heels.'

Ben raised his head and looked out of the window. 'So does my grandmother,' he said. Agatha had suddenly appeared in his mind's eye, grimly pedalling uphill, library books on the carrier. He let go of Lesley's hand, startled by the clarity of the vision.

Lesley said, '*Must* you think about your dreadful old grandmother when you're with me? You always clam up when you do – it isn't healthy.'

Ben bit back a sharp reply; the picture had faded.

It returned to him when he reached home that night, and with it a feeling that he had left something undone. Then he remembered his telephone call to Agatha, and how she had hung up on him. He had done no more about it, and the accident had driven it out of his mind.

Ben found a biro in a jar on the living-room window sill, but he could find nothing to write on except a small notebook of Lesley's. It was too late to go up to the farm, and Ben was determined to write to Agatha at once. He filled seven of the small pages with his painstaking handwriting.

> . . . *Denis got the wrong idea about my job. I have good pay and a nice house. Please don't sell the 'Young Girl', I don't need the money.*
>
> *I wasn't going to say anything yet, but I might get married. It wouldn't be for a long time yet. I like the picture so much, and I think my girlfriend would like it too. So I would sooner have the picture than*

83

the cash when it comes to me which I hope won't be
for a long time . . .

Ben read over what he had written. He could imagine
Agatha snorting, and hurling the letter into the fire. Let her
snort. He had done his best. He finished as he had been taught,
'hoping this finds you in the best of health,' and signed it
'Benedict'.

He posted it first thing in the morning.

On bank holidays when the library was closed, Agatha usually
had her hair cut. This was done by Miss Bond who lived with
her sister in the little house by the Protestant church.

These ladies had hovered on the fringes of Agatha's
existence for a long time. Both over seventy, they were the
only sisters in a large family of sons. They had looked after
their brothers devotedly and, when the last of them had
married, found themselves redundant at fifty-eight and fifty-
nine. One of the brothers had found the house for them (just
the place for dear Clare and Miriam, handy for the church and
shops), and there they had lived, in a strange town for fifteen
years. Neither had ever learned a trade and their incomes
became less adequate every year. But Miss Miriam made all
their clothes, and Miss Clare could cut and wave hair in the
styles of her youth – the Eton crop, the Marcel wave.

There accordingly Agatha had gone with a copy of *Weldon's
Home Journal* dated 1933, and some paper patterns. After
some bullying, she had persuaded Miss Miriam to make her
jackets, blouses and skirts. The pattern had been re-cut many
times, but never altered.

Miss Clare shingled Agatha's springy white hair, tidied her
neck with a pair of clippers, and corrugated the sides of her
coiffure with curling tongs.

Both were nervous of their only customer. Agatha refused
to remove any of her garments for fittings. 'You have my
measurements, Miriam; naturally it will fit. If it does not, you
shall re-make it.' Her payment was prompt and miserly. Miss

Clare was even more nervous, as she had actually to touch Agatha, whose unnecessary commands to 'be careful, woman!' made her hands shake, and caused her to drop things on the floor.

On Easter Monday, Agatha arrived as usual, unannounced. She seated herself in her accustomed place where she could see out onto the street, but was herself hidden by the net curtains. Miss Clare combed and snipped and clipped. Then she offered Agatha a mirror with a hand which shook a little. Agatha favoured her reflection with the same arctic glare which so unnerved the Misses Bond. Miss Clare said nothing. She might be asked if she had lost her tongue, but that was better than one of the blistering snubs which Agatha seemed to enjoy dealing out to those who daren't answer back. She returned the mirror without comment, and sat tight-lipped while the sisters encased her hair in a net, removed the towel from her shoulders and swept up hairs from the floor.

Two men had appeared in Agatha's line of vision, her son-in-law Myles, and the auctioneer Barney Mangan. They stopped in a doorway and conferred together. Myles glanced furtively this way and that. Then he took out his wallet and counted money into Barney's palm. Five notes, Agatha could see, but of what denomination? Pound notes she would have to overlook, so why the guilty looks? Perhaps they were ten or even twenty pound notes. It seemed that Myles had acquired money from somewhere, and now, in all probability, it was to be expended at the dog-track.

Agatha rose slowly to her feet. Still in silence, she handed £1 to Miss Clare. In the same instant, Myles noticed the familiar bicycle outside, and both he and Barney looked at it in horror. Agatha hurried to the door and threw it open. 'Myles,' she said, not loudly, but with withering scorn. 'A word with you, if your business will allow it.'

Myles crossed the road, his expression a mixture of defiance, sulkiness and fear. Barney hurried away, tucking the notes into his pocket and sketching a half wave to

Agatha. She watched Myles coming across the street towards her, and noticed that his jacket was frayed at the cuffs and had a button missing. Her perception seemed heightened, as if she had just had a glass or two of champagne. She stared at Myles, taking in his round shoulders, greying hair and shambling gait. She wondered what to say to him. Perhaps nothing – what was there to say? She might as well order him out of her sight, thereby pleasing him and saving argument.

As these thoughts were passing through her mind, a long shudder ran through Agatha. She felt suddenly piercingly cold, with the chill of the grave. For a moment she tottered, almost falling, trying in vain to speak. Myles reached her in two strides and put his arm round her. 'You're all right – I've got you,' he said. He was a fool, thought Agatha, but good natured. Quarrelling with him was like trying to eat jelly with a knife and fork. For a moment she allowed him to support her, then her eyes strayed to her bicycle. She intended to tell Myles to release her in order that she might ride it home. The deathly chill was ebbing, but no words came.

Agatha thought, I am dying, and I have not yet sold the picture. Benedict . . . She fainted at that moment, but didn't crumple up. She keeled over, all in one piece, like a sunstruck guardsman on parade.

Dr Blake had attended Agatha's daughter for years. Muriel had never been particularly strong, and six children in eight years, followed by a succession of miscarriages, had left her constitution weakened. All the children had been in Dr Blake's care at one time or another, and he had difficulty in remembering which was which – except for Ben, of course. He would never forget the time when he had been called out to attend the premature birth. He hadn't believed that such a small baby could live without benefit of hospital equipment, but Agatha had refused to allow the child to be moved. Dr Blake had come back the next day, expecting to find a dead or dying infant, and had heard Ben's angry yells before he was out of his car. Never had he heard a child bawl quite as loudly as Ben when he was hungry. He liked Ben, and always paused to chat with him when they met – pity he'd emigrated. But whenever he saw Ben, usually on a horse, the doctor remembered the scarlet-faced howling infant which had turned the scales at three pounds.

He had never attended the old lady. She was never ill, so he was surprised when old Miss Bond burst into his surgery.

'Come quickly, Doctor; Mrs Logan's had a stroke.'

Dr Blake lived only yards from the house of the 'Bond-women' as they were nicknamed locally behind their backs. He found Agatha lying on Miss Miriam's bed, while the son-in-law sat beside her. He jumped to his feet – the doctor had never seen him move so fast. 'Thank God you're here,' he said.

Agatha was lying perfectly flat and straight like a crusader's effigy on a tomb. She was quivering with rage. 'There is nothing whatever the matter with me,' she said, speaking clearly but with evident difficulty. 'Go home, Myles,' she added, as if speaking to a dog.

Dr Blake sat down beside her, puffing a little. He was fat and elderly, and he had trotted from his surgery in the wake of Miss Bond, who had run ahead, weakly flapping like a wounded bird. Myles obeyed his mother-in-law with alacrity, making for the door with obvious relief.

'Wait,' said the doctor. 'You'll have to drive Mrs Logan home.'

'Won't she be going to hospital?'

'I doubt it – unless she wishes to go.' Dr Blake knew his Agatha.

'I refuse to go to hospital. I prefer to die a natural death.' Speech was getting easier all the time. Agatha suffered examination without protest, but even the doctor was unnerved when he caught her eye as he applied his stethoscope to her bony chest. Her bleak hostility was worse than the outburst he had expected.

'A mild attack,' he said at last. 'You've been fortunate. But you must have a thorough check-up –'

'No.'

'– and you'll have to take it easy. How old are you?'

'Mind your own business.'

'Be reasonable, Mrs Logan. I know you must be over eighty, and you must be prepared for your own good to slow up a little. For a start, you'll have to give up cycling. This has been a warning which you must heed.'

'Rubbish.'

'Mrs Logan, I would be irresponsible if I didn't insist that you take reasonable care of yourself and –'

'Am I dying, or am I not?'

'No, you –'

Agatha sat up. 'In that case,' she said, 'I will dispense with your no doubt well-intentioned advice.'

Dr Blake was conscious of the two women behind him, oohing and aahing. He felt at a disadvantage. He stood up. 'If you don't take my advice,' he said, 'you must be prepared to take the consequences. Get another opinion if you wish.'

'I always expect to take the consequences of my actions,' said Agatha, her voice vibrant with loathing. 'Kindly leave.'

Dr Blake found Myles outside, loading Agatha's bicycle into the van. 'Can you stop her cycling?' he asked. 'A very mild stroke, but a second would probably be much more serious, perhaps even fatal.'

'I'll try,' said Myles doubtfully, and on the way home, he mentioned it.

Agatha didn't bother to reply. Her mind was with Benedict. If she were to die, Myles and Barney might well dispose of the painting unwisely. She determined to write to Sotheby's, and ask them to send a valuer to Cloninch immediately.

The next time Ben visited Lesley's ward, he found she had been sent home. He hadn't been to the flat before, and was impressed by its size and comfort. Hazel and Imogen were out, Lesley was sitting by the electric fire. She looked thin and tired, and it was the first time Ben had seen the scar on her forehead. She put up her hand to it. 'I'm going to change my hairstyle,' she said. 'Hide it with a fringe.'

'Don't,' said Ben. 'I like your hair the way you wear it, and the mark will soon fade.'

Ben found she was disinclined to talk; usually she did most of the talking. She curled up on the sofa, resting her head against his chest. 'Tell me about yourself, Ben love.'

'I've told you all about me. There isn't much to tell.'

'There must be. I want to know all the little things – it's amazing how little I know. Tell me about your life before we met. I want to know about when you were a little boy, everything that's ever happened to you.' She rubbed her cheek against his hand. 'Go on, tell me.'

'I'm not a great one for talking about myself,' said Ben. 'Why don't we wait until we're back at home for my life story – we have all our lives before us, haven't we?'

There was a pause. Lesley turned her head sharply to look at him. 'What?' she said. 'All our lives? We've got until you finish your job here, isn't that more like it? You're not going to settle in Yorkshire – are you?'

She had turned even paler than before. Ben wondered if she was going to faint. He said comfortingly, 'Don't look so tragic, I'll stay as long as you want me. And you say you can get a divorce, no problem; I thought we might get married. I haven't much money, but I can work, and there's nothing for me at home. You do want to marry me, don't you?'

The door opened, and Hazel came in, bringing a soggy parcel which smelled powerfully of cooking oil.

'Don't you?' repeated Ben, ignoring her.

'Yes,' said Lesley, 'I do.'

The fortnight which Lesley spent in her flat and attending a clinic three days a week, was a busy one for Ben. The Guvnor, seeing him digging his tiny garden, had changed his mind about a holiday. Ben had found himself back at work two days after his fall.

Happiness was too pale a word for Ben's feelings once he

89

knew that Lesley would soon be well again. He went to see her every evening by bus, but he had to catch the last bus home so as to be at work in time. He would get back to the cottage after midnight, still high on happiness. He hung the curtains Lesley had made, scrubbed the stone floor and sang his head off.

They didn't have many hours together. Sometimes they stayed in the flat, but if Hazel or Imogen was there, they walked about the streets instead. Lesley was supposed to exercise her knee, and she enjoyed showing Ben round. Sometimes they went to a small park, sat on one of the benches and talked. They didn't talk about marriage – they shared an illogical feeling that it would be unlucky to do so, but they discussed everything else under the sun.

Lesley gradually found out a lot about Ben's life. He had left Kilmoon Primary School at thirteen years old, and should have followed Denis to the Christian Brothers' in Kildare. But the next two children after Ben were girls, Ben was needed to help with the harvest in the summer holidays, and somehow he had never gone back to school. His sisters had gone to a Convent school, trained for nursing, and were both married, one in Limerick, the other in Cork.

Ben was the only member of the family without a secondary education. It had never bothered him until he grew up and realized that it was idle for him to dream of being a vet with his minimal education, even if his grandmother could have been induced to pay for his training. He had turned to his friend Terry, begging rides in steeplechases, but, in spite of his lack of height, by the time he was twenty he was too heavy. He had resigned himself to unpaid labour at home, and helping Terry school his horses.

Lesley too had a farming background. Her father, a tillage farmer from the other side of Middlegarth, hadn't believed in 'book-learning' for women, who were sure to get married and waste it. Lesley had won scholarships, and saved up the money she earned at holiday jobs. So, when her father was killed by an overturning tractor, only months after her mother's death from leukaemia, and the rented farm was no longer home, she was already earning, and living in lodgings in Leeds. Shortly afterwards, while the shock of her parents' death was still fresh, she had married Mark.

A few days after Ben went back to work, Eric cut his hand when he was paring a sheep's foot. Like Ben, he scorned the hoof clippers provided, preferring to use a razor-sharp clasp knife. The cut, between finger and thumb, turned septic, and he went to his home near Huddersfield to recover.

To Ben's utter astonishment, the Guvnor turned over the pedigree lambs to him. The ram lambs were already being prepared for the summer sales; they were being fed from troughs out of doors. Each one's progress and weight gain was recorded on a chart in the farm office. Ben found himself senior to old Harry who took it well, and to his son, young Harry, who took it badly. Charlie was positively genial. The last student had left, and he had shaken off his cough. He went out to the fields with Ben, hurrying in order to keep up with the younger man's quick, almost jaunty stride.

As they were leaving the yard, Roy came out of his kennel. He greeted Ben with guarded enthusiasm and the Guvnor with civil indifference. Charlie ignored the dog. 'Lambs look well,' he said. 'Contented. That's good. They do you credit, lad.'

'I like them, perhaps that's why,' Ben said. 'Eric has a saying, "Be easy with them, and they'll be easy with you."'

'He's right. Still have a chat with them, do you?'

'I do,' said Ben, glancing up for signs of mockery, but there were none. He walked ahead, humming a tune, but checked himself.

Charlie said, 'Hum away lad, aye, sing if you want.'

Ben knew that the Guvnor, in his own curious way, was admitting that he'd been wrong. This was as close as he was likely to come to an apology, so he said, 'Thanks, Guvnor.' He thought there was something else on Charlie's mind, so he waited in silence. He hadn't long to wait.

'I've nowt against that big daft lass of yours,' said Charlie. 'She hasn't the sense she was born with, but she's a good lass. I meant telling you she'd have to go, but I've had another think. You can stay in cottage as long as you're working here, and she can stay and look after you.'

Ben controlled his annoyance at Charlie's description of Lesley. 'That's good of you,' he said, 'but I have to look after her. I'm not hurt, she is.'

'Nursemaid each other then,' said Charlie. 'It's matterless to me, so sheep don't suffer. Sheep come first – never forget that.' He turned on his heel with his usual abruptness and went away.

Ben watched him go. Then he returned to his work singing under his breath, 'Once I had a bunch of thyme . . . I thought it never would decay . . .' He rubbed his right eye with the back of his hand. Coming into the gloomy buildings from the sunlight, black dots danced in front of him, and a little shower of blue sparks. I must have looked straight at the sun, thought Ben.

That evening, Lesley was hardly limping. She didn't expect to go back to work for at least a week, so they decided it would be a good opportunity for Ben to see more of Yorkshire. They went by bus or coach, or sometimes in Tina's borrowed car, out into the countryside, seeing as many places as possible on the long spring evenings, and returning in time for Ben's bus home.

Sometimes they drove between enormous unfenced fields, where the rippling green barley stretched unbroken for miles; sometimes they went up to the moors. Ben hadn't Lesley's love of the moors; he liked to see how other people lived and worked. Especially, he liked exploring the old villages and market towns. They went up Skipton way, where the road switchbacked between stone-walled fields with old barns in them. Then they went up the narrow lanes of the Dales, where there were bays in the walls to allow traffic to pass. They went to places with quaint names – Agglethorpe, Kettlewell. They went to Scarborough and watched the giant waves thundering against the sea-wall, then along the coast to Robin Hood's Bay, where pieces of the town occasionally slid into the sea. Ben found that more interesting than the neat coastal resorts. They went up onto the high ground near Flamborough where the tops of the stunted trees were blown perfectly flat by the gales that screamed through them.

Ben's eye still wasn't right. He wondered if there was a hayseed in it. He could almost forget the annoyance of the mysterious spots as he took in everything he saw. The last place they went to was Aysgarth Falls. Ben felt a surge of excitement when he heard the roar of the rapids. Lesley had brought her camera, and they took pictures of each other against the background of wild water. It was impossible to talk, and they were both drenched. Ben spent that night at Lesley's flat, getting up at first light to hitchhike back to Middlegarth. They were immensely contented and at ease.

Ben took his day off on Friday that week, so that young Harry could go to the football on Saturday. He rang Lesley up and learned that she would be at the hospital most of the day having final check-ups and her last session with the physiotherapist. So he caught a bus heading the other way, and went to York. He wandered about, looking around him, taking in all the strange sights. He went for a walk along the walls, gazing curiously down on the back gardens below, then he found his way to the Shambles, and joined the throng of tourists. He stopped outside a small dark shop with antique jewellery in the window. An aquamarine ring had caught his eye. It had a slim gold band, and the stone was a delicate oval. Ben thought of Lesley. The colour was exactly right, cool and clear in an uncluttered setting. He went in and bought it. The price startled him, but fortunately he had enough money with him. The jeweller put the ring in a blue leather box lined with cream velvet, and Ben put it in the pocket of his anorak. He treated himself to two pork pies and a pint of beer, and returned to Middlegarth with tenpence in his pocket.

*

On Saturday, Ben collected Lesley's car from the garage, and drove into Leeds to fetch her home. Mandy walked up to the cottage and offered to go too. 'Another time,' said Ben cheerfully. Mandy accepted the snub, as most people accepted what Ben said.

He wasn't a bad driver, but found the heavy traffic alarming because he wasn't altogether familiar with the way. Printed instructions to GET IN LANE bewildered him. He wasn't sure which lane he needed. One or two drivers honked at him. Ben was not mechanically minded and was perfectly happy to allow Lesley to drive when they were together. Also, his eye was worse. He rubbed it, but it made no difference. Black spots like smuts drifted diagonally across his field of vision.

Lesley was standing in her doorway. Her face lit up when she saw him. He pulled up and jumped out of the car shouting, 'We're going home!' One or two passers-by looked startled; Lesley burst out laughing. Ben fingered the leather box in his pocket. He meant to wait for exactly the right moment to give her the ring. 'Think you can drive?' he asked.

'Probably, but I'd rather you drove me home. I've been looking forward to that.'

'Shall we have something to eat first?' Ben said.

'Ben! Oh, all right. But we'll have to go out. I've emptied my fridge.'

They left the car and walked together to the Kosy Kitchen, where they dawdled over an early lunch.

'Is there something wrong with your eye?' asked Lesley. 'You keep rubbing it.'

'I'm seeing spots. It's no harm, just a nuisance.'

'Shouldn't you see the doctor about it? You got a terrific bang on the head after all. It might be delayed concussion.'

'Ah, it's nothing,' said Ben impatiently. He wasn't best pleased a few minutes later when the dog trainer, Geoff, came in, with the collie bitch he'd brought to Middlegarth. Geoff had visited Lesley in hospital. Ben hadn't seen him then and didn't want to see him now. Geoff gave Lesley a rundown on the progress of her cases and Ben took no part in the conversation.

Instead, he made friends with the dog, Meg. She was the picture of health, unlike her sire Roy, whose coat never shone and whose tail was usually tucked between his legs. Geoff noticed that Meg had disobeyed him. She was sitting up, her chin on Ben's lap while he fondled her ears. Geoff sensed Ben's deep antagonism. Searching for a point of contact, he said, 'I hear the old dog has left the Guvnor for you, Ben!'

Ben looked up, smiling reluctantly. 'I don't think the Guvnor minds, unless maybe the hurt to his vanity. Do Border collies make good guides then? I'd've thought they'd be too independent.'

'They often are, and some of them are too possessive or too nervous. We have only half a dozen purebreds; plenty of Border crosses though.'

'I don't like to think of training the working instinct out of a dog,' remarked Ben. 'I think it's terrible.'

Lesley noticed Geoff's expression and broke in hastily. 'I think Meg takes after her mother,' she said. 'The Guvnor told me that old Nell had about as much herding instinct as a broody hen.'

Geoff said aggressively to Ben, 'Don't you think that taking complete charge of a disabled person is more important than picking up a pheasant or bringing the cows home?'

'I suppose it is,' said Ben sulkily. He stopped stroking Meg, who thrust her nose under his hand, begging him to continue. He glanced down at her. 'There's one thing I've wondered,' he said to Geoff. 'How do you transfer a dog you've trained from yourself to somebody who isn't a trainer?'

Geoff said, 'It can be traumatic for the dog, but it generally works out. I never call myself a trainer – I'm an instructor. We breed a quality into our dogs, we call it generosity. When a dog works through generosity rather than self preservation, he'll do anything the instructor tells him to, no matter how fond of him he is. You'd make a good instructor yourself. There's something about you that dogs recognize.'

Ben shrugged his shoulders impatiently and returned to stroking Meg's smooth head.

As they walked back to the car, Lesley said, 'I know you've a thing about my work, Ben, but please don't take it out on Geoff – he's a dear person.'

Ben said he wouldn't, although privately he hoped Geoff wouldn't call at the cottage. He could do with Bob and Tina – they never talked shop when they went out socially, but Geoff was different. His job and his dogs were his life. 'I don't want to put your friends off coming,' he said, 'just don't talk about your work to me. It gives me the creeps.'

Lesley agreed, sounding disappointed. 'It's an important part of my life,' she said, 'and you'd like Geoff if he was anything else but what he is. He's just not into human relationships unless the people are blind, but in some ways he's a little like you.'

Ben wasn't pleased. 'I don't like the man or what he does,' he said. They had reached the car and got in.

Lesley said, 'Look, Ben, before we go any further, it's my job too. You aren't planning to ask me to give it up, are you?'

'I suppose not. It wouldn't be right.'

'I do it well, you know,' said Lesley, 'and I had a long training. I find the work fascinating and very satisfying. I'd hate to change.'

'I'm not that narrow-minded,' said Ben, 'nor that selfish. But you mustn't mind if I don't want to talk about it. That's the way I am. I'm sorry.'

At the cottage, Ben insisted on making a fuss of Lesley, making coffee for her, rebandaging her knee. She laughed at him, but it was plain that she enjoyed it. Later on, Ben asked Lesley why there was never any music at the Turpin Arms. She said it would put the old men off their dominos and the young ones off their darts. 'I like a bit of music,' said Ben.

'Sing me an Irish song, Ben.'

96

Ben struck an attitude and sang with a fine tremolo and an excruciating brogue, 'When Oirish ois are smoilin' . . .'

'No, seriously. Please sing something – sing that song about a bunch of thyme.'

'Ah no,' said Ben. 'I might if I had a guitar or a banjo, or if I was half jarred. Some other time.'

In the morning a letter arrived from Ben's father. It appeared that Agatha had had a slight stroke. Apparently it was nothing serious. There was no mention of Ben's letter to her.

Ben's eye was worse. The sparks and flashes had gone, but the drifting black spots were bigger. It was no longer possible to ignore them. He had managed to forget his fears during the hours of darkness with Lesley in his arms, but when he got up he was afraid. He didn't rub his eye, but kept it almost closed.

It was Sunday. Ben and young Harry took turns with the Sunday morning foddering; today it was Ben's turn. In the yard, the Guvnor informed him that he was five minutes late. Ben's temper was threadbare – he didn't risk an answer.

'Shape yourself,' said Charlie. 'Can't lie in bed all day.'

Ben bit his lip. He loaded meal onto the trailer, and set off to the field with the tractor, followed by the Guvnor's shouted advice to go steady and not pull the guts out of tractor.

Experimentally, Ben put his hand over his good eye. It was like driving through a slanting rain of black coin-sized blobs. He could see very little through them. With his heart beating violently, he pulled up the tractor at the troughs, and jumped down, the sheep mobbing round him, to empty the bag of meal for them. As his feet touched the ground, a jet black curtain descended across his field of vision. The spots stopped drifting, but there was only a narrow slit of vision at the lower edge of his eye. Petrified, he stood stock still, hardly daring to breathe. The curtain descended the rest of the way. Again, he put his hand over his left eye. He could see it, reddish, as the sun found its way between his fingers.

With his right eye he could see nothing at all.

Six

Agatha was feeling unwell. Possibly she would have to give up bicycling after all. Muriel had never learned to drive, Denis was always fussing over that silly little wife of his. As for Myles, when she had tried to shame him into driving her into Kilmoon thrice weekly – no, four times, for there was also church – she had failed. He had fobbed her off with trumped up excuses, so she had been obliged to seek a lift elsewhere. But the driver of the milk-lorry had been insolent; had stated that he was not allowed to carry passengers. Nonsense! She had ignored him and prepared to get into the cab, but had been unable to open the door. The man had laughed, actually laughed at her. He had opened the door and assisted her to climb up. He had said – Agatha preferred to try to forget what he had said. His manner throughout had been offensively familiar. Altogether, the effort had been far greater than that of riding a bicycle.

She had written to a Dublin library which sent its books out by post: wickedly expensive, she would have to limit herself to two a week; a brochure had arrived. She ran her eyes down the pages of a booklet filled with reviews.

'. . . Ms Slope's political awareness is somewhat marred by her unashamed hedonism . . .'

'. . . Joel McTaggart's smouldering ire is tempered by a rare compassion . . .'

'. . . Mike Lambe's limpid narrative is, if anything, enhanced by its innocent obscenities . . .'

Agatha snorted, and hurled the catalogue into the fireplace. She was alone in the sitting-room. Upstairs, Michael was snoring. It was several days now since he had come down. Muriel waited on him. She picked up her needlework and put it down again. She read Benedict's letter for perhaps the twentieth time. Well, she would respect his wishes. She had written to Sotheby's asking them to send a valuer, and, after receiving Benedict's letter had almost immediately written again, saying that she had changed her mind. She who never changed her mind!

It was just as she had thought, and sooner than she expected. The woman, whoever she was, had wasted no time. Agatha did not intend to keep the painting for a scheming hussy to enjoy; she intended to make that perfectly clear in a codicil to her will. The picture was for Benedict himself, to dispose of as he pleased. Idle now to request him to return. His guitar was in her bedroom; she had wasted money on having it restrung for him.

Agatha adjusted her pince-nez and threaded a needle. She was embroidering a white linen table-mat with white silks – very trying to the eyes. Buttonholing round the scalloped edge was easy but time-consuming. Now she was engaged on the motif, a stylized basket of flowers with floating ribbons. Over the years, Agatha had filled a good sized trunk with tablecloths and mats of this kind. They were never used. Her needle flicked in and out of the fine material for only a minute or two, then she laid it aside again.

The restlessness which had affected her since Benedict left was increasing daily. She was bored and constantly irritated. Myles, Denis and Brian had made heavy weather of looking after the ewes in lambing time – Benedict had managed alone. Sheila was expecting a second child, and Agatha considered that, with a little more self-discipline, she could easily conquer her morning sickness. Not having suffered from it herself, Agatha thought it an avoidable weakness in others. But the root of Agatha's unease lay deeper. She was sure that Benedict was in need of her help. He had written and told her that all was well with him, but she was unable to believe it. Something was wrong; terribly wrong.

Muriel came into the room, infuriating Agatha with her trick of sliding round the half-closed door instead of opening it wide. Agatha, not for the first time, wondered about her daughter. If Muriel had been born in hospital, Agatha would have doubted whether she had brought home the right baby. Could this faded, nervy woman be her own flesh and blood? It seemed unlikely, but if she was not, then neither was Benedict . . .

Agatha stood up, a head taller than Muriel, her long putty-coloured linen dress making her seem taller still. 'Now that the rest of my family are dead, I see no reason why I should not visit my sister,' she said aggressively.

'Your sister?'

'My sister Flora. I would not have considered it while my sister Constance was alive – she took my father's part against me. I saw her death in the *Irish Times* recently. Flora lives in Yorkshire, I believe. I have not spoken to her since 1933.'

'In Yorkshire?'

'Muriel, must you repeat every word I say? Have you lost your wits?'

'No, Mother, but –'

'I shall write to her. She and Constance shared a house. I obtained the address from the obituary notice.'

Muriel dared not ask whether her mother intended to travel alone, so she said brightly, 'Yorkshire! Why, you can call on Ben, can't you?'

'I could if I wished to do so,' snapped Agatha.

As Muriel skirted round the door again, leaving it not quite closed – maddening trick – Agatha returned to her embroidery and to thinking about Benedict. She could see him in her mind's eye, scowling at her as he so often did, wearing a sleeveless jacket. A pointless sort of garment, she thought, neither one thing nor the other. She could not recall ever having seen him wear one.

While Ben was doing his Sunday work among the sheep, Lesley, alone in the cottage, found there was very little to occupy her. Ben had left the house scrupulously clean as he always did. She made a stew and put it on the hotplate, then she washed the clothes Ben had been wearing the day before. She scrubbed them in the sink, just as she used to do as a child at home, helping her mother. Her mother had died when Lesley was seventeen years old; she remembered her reddish hair twisted up in a knot and her sturdy arms buried in soapsuds. Her face had gone. The face Lesley conjured up was the pink and white one in her parents' wedding photographs.

She took the washing into the garden and hung it on the line. She smiled at Ben's gardening. She had thought when she saw the freshly dug border that he was planning a flower bed. He had planted three neat rows of cabbages. He wouldn't be back for another hour. She put on a pair of his overalls and washed the car.

Lesley had changed into a clean dress which Ben hadn't seen before and was waiting in the kitchen when he came in. He would be free for the rest of the day and she wondered how they would spend it.

Ben charged up the path and into the cottage, barely greeting her. She glimpsed his savage expression and guessed he'd had a row with the Guvnor – perhaps he'd got the sack. She decided to wait and let him tell her about it in his own good time.

Lesley dished up the lunch early. Ben seemed to have recovered his temper. In fact he was extra affectionate, extra cheerful, positively chatty. He broke off his account of Charlie's ill temper to say, 'Don't give me much of that – I'm not hungry.' Lesley returned the ladle to the pot in astonishment. Ben not hungry?

The table looked welcoming with its blue and white checked cloth and cherry-blossom in a blue jug. It stood against the wall, and usually Lesley sat with her back to the stove, facing the window, with Ben on her left with his back to the door. He sat down at her other side. 'Don't sit that side – I've laid your place over here,' said Lesley.

Ben said, 'There's a draught coming under the door.' It was a bright sunny day and, knowing Ben's total disregard for the weather, Lesley was slightly disturbed. Ben moved to his usual place. 'I'll sit here for today as it's laid,' he said. He finished his sprightly account of the morning, and suggested going to the cinema that evening. Lesley poured tea and pushed the milk-jug towards him, but he ignored it. A moment later, he knocked the jug over with the back of his hand. 'Sorry,' he said, getting up to fetch a dishcloth, 'I didn't notice it.'

'Ben,' said Lesley, 'are you still seeing spots with that eye?'

'No,' said Ben. 'Devil a spot. Which movie would you like to go to? You choose.' He pushed away his plate and refused apple pie.

Lesley hadn't finished eating. As Ben stood up and walked about restlessly, she sat looking at her plate, her own appetite gone. Ben put his hands on her shoulders as she sat there, and kissed the top of her head. 'I don't know what I'd do without you,' he said quietly.

She turned in her chair, looking up at his troubled face. 'You won't have to do without me,' she said.

'I wish I could be sure of it,' said Ben. He turned away and sat down by the fire.

Lesley had loved Ben almost at first sight. But since his fall her feelings had deepened and strengthened; she could no more stop loving him than fly. She could accept that he was not utterly hers as she was his. Nearly, but not quite. Mark had had the power to make her suffer and he had used it. Ben, she knew, had the power to break her heart. She wondered dispassionately if he was aware of this.

At first, she had been sure there was another woman in his life; possibly the reason why he'd left Ireland was an unhappy love affair. Then she'd begun to wonder if, in some odd way, Ben's grandmother had a hold over him. Certainly he seemed to dislike the old woman – and with reason – but Lesley couldn't rid herself of the idea. Ben had been visibly upset when he heard of Agatha's illness, although he said only, 'She'll be okay. She's as tough as old boots.'

Lesley wondered whether Ben had heard something more from Ireland and was concealing it from her. She had never quarrelled with him, but their occasional arguments were always, in one way or another, concerned with his grandmother. She told herself she was having ridiculous fancies, but had to admit she was glad that Agatha was old, ill and elsewhere.

Thank goodness, she thought, Ben's eye was better. She'd been really worried about that. She suggested a drive and Ben agreed. He asked Lesley to drive, but after a few miles, suddenly wanted to change places. Lesley made no objection, and Ben took the wheel. 'That's better,' he said.

'What's wrong with my driving?' Lesley was surprised.

'Nothing,' said Ben. He drove carefully, but faster than usual, turning up the radio. Pop music filled the car. A popular singer announced his more intimate needs to the world in a very loud bellow.

'Do you like that?' shouted Lesley.

'No,' shouted Ben.

She selected a tape they both enjoyed. 'What about this?' she said, holding it out.

'Don't show me,' said Ben. 'Put it on. I haven't an eye to spare.' He was laughing as she slotted the tape into place. It was an old Johnny Cash, and for the first time, Lesley heard Ben sing out freely. 'No, no, no it's not me Babe,' sang Ben. 'It's not me you're looking for . . .' his voice dropped a clear octave . . . ' . . . Babe.' He sounded very cheerful about it.

He drove up to the High Tops above Rosedale, a desolate place, Lesley had always disliked it. When they got out of the car, the wind almost knocked them over. Ben's strange mood of elation continued. He usually chose to drive to a village he hadn't visited before, but not today. He'd wanted to climb up to the white horse at Kilburn, but Lesley said that her knee wouldn't stand it.

Ben climbed onto a wall made of flat slabs of grey stone. He balanced on top of it, gazing back the way they'd come, down the green dale to the village below. A single pine tree grew beside the wall. He leant into the wind, resting one hand on the scaly bark. Lesley wished he'd come back to the car; it was cold up there. But he lingered, silhouetted against the milky sky, his hair whipped about by the wind, a wild look on his face that she'd never seen before. At last he jumped down and they went back to the car, his arm round her shoulders.

Ben was getting to know the moors and dales. He drove all afternoon. They nearly ran out of petrol and filled up in Clitheroe.

Lesley had let him drive where he liked, but now she said, 'Are we going to catch a boat to Ireland? We're heading for Liverpool.' Ben shook his head and started to sing a shanty called *The Leaving of Liverpool*. However, he stopped driving westward.

Instead of going to a movie, he took her to a big roadhouse on the main road. Lesley protested that they weren't tidy enough for such a place. Ben laughed. He had laughed more in a few hours than in all the weeks she had known him. There was a group, and dancing, so they danced. It was a rock number, and Ben threw himself about, guying the antics of some of the other dancers. Lesley's knee was aching, so she contented herself with twitching her hips, and occasionally twirling round with her weight on the good leg. She twirled, and there was nobody to catch her hand – she'd lost Ben. He emerged from among the dancers. 'Where did you get to?'

'Nowhere,' said Lesley. 'You lost me.'

'I'll take care not to lose you again,' said Ben. The music changed to a slow number, and she linked her hands behind his neck while he held her closely. 'This is how I like to dance,' said Ben. 'Close as butter on bread, as we say at home.' To the tune of the dance, he sang, 'You are the butter, darling, I am the bread.'

Lesley chuckled. 'You should be up there with the group,' she said. 'You're good.'

They had supper, but Ben still wasn't hungry. He ate a small piece of pie and drank whisky instead of his usual beer. 'Anyone you want me to throw out, say the word,' he said, looking about him with a brooding stare. Lesley was half frightened. She was relieved when he allowed her to drive home.

That night, there seemed to be something desperate in Ben's love-making. They were so well suited, so perfectly attuned to one another that there had never been any need for reassurance. Never before had Ben asked, 'Was it good? Do I make you happy? You're sure?' There was no need.

Lesley said, 'Ben, you're all I ever dreamed of and more. Better than anything I ever imagined.' She kissed his eyes. He recoiled as if she had hit him. 'Darling, what's the trouble? You must tell me.'

But he said, 'Nothing,' and pulled her close to him again. It was early morning before she fell into a fitful sleep, troubled with dreams. She was a light sleeper and usually woke first. Ben, once settled, would sleep like a baby until morning. But when she woke from an uneasy doze, he was awake, lying on his back, his wide open eyes staring at the ceiling.

Geoff was tired. The last few days before the start of a residential course were always tiring, and he'd had an argument with the Director of Training, Michael Jones. This was unheard of; generally the two were in perfect accord. It concerned Meg, the Border collie. Geoff had spent a testing week with the dogs which were to be allocated. He had taken them into Leeds in batches, and had worked them in heavy traffic and in pedestrian shopping centres. He had allowed each one in turn to lead him through an area where a mysterious gas leak had caused the Corporation to dig holes at intervals all along the road, and to leave parked machinery and barriers in unexpected places. All had done well. Meg had remained in her run.

The director was a tall thin man, nearing sixty. His voice, clipped and brusque, was deceptive; he was seldom put out. He praised Geoff and the dogs warmly, then asked, 'You mean to keep Meg back for the next course, then? I think you're wrong.'

Geoff spoke in the tone which dogs and kennel staff alike respected. 'I know I'm right,' he said. 'She's not an easy one. She has more brains than any of them – maybe she's too brainy. If we place her badly, we'll have a blind person in trouble and a brilliant dog spoiled.'

Michael Jones said, 'I've seen her working a dozen times; I can't see any problem.'

Geoff was exasperated. He had been a professional trainer of police dogs, and had come to guide dog instruction as an apprentice. He had trained police dogs to a peak of performance which his replacement would never attain. He said, 'Somewhere out there, a blind person is waiting for a dog. Not any dog, a special one. Meg will be perfect for somebody young and quick, probably a woman; best of all, someone who's had a Border collie before. By the time we start the next course, she'll be as good as I can make her.'

Michael shrugged his shoulders. 'Have it your own way then.' In theory he had the final word, but he bowed to Geoff's experience.

Meg was bored. Still, if her person knew she was bored and did nothing about it, there'd be a reason. She stood quietly in her run, watching him. It had diamond-link wire mesh on the front, and metal posts. Some of the dogs, seeing Geoff and Michael, stood on their hind legs, their front paws against the mesh, frantically wagging their tails, whining for attention. Some barked.

Meg fitted the end of her nose into one of the lozenges of wire. She considered that the other dogs had more hair than wit. They'd been out all over except for her. It was Meg's turn. She hadn't done anything wrong – not for long enough. Bingo had made a mullock of leading Geoff off a bus – he'd nearly fallen all his length. Why then was Meg left behind and not Bingo?

Meg's long feathery tail swung gently to and fro as she listened to the two men talking. She wondered what they were fratching about. It was something to do with her – her name was mentioned twice, but still she wasn't taken out. She didn't count walks with Lucy, the kennel maid. Lucy came out just then and started to fetch the dogs in and feed them. Geoff went away, and Pepper set up a howl. Sally and Bingo joined in, noses to the sky. Meg never howled. She wished the other dogs would give over wowing.

There was change in the air that evening; all the dogs felt it. It wasn't a matter of sight or scent, it was a sort of electric prickling, not unlike the messages which travelled through Geoff's hand and the harness to the dog he was teaching.

That evening, Geoff stayed out for his tea. His wife and daughters were visiting friends. So he headed from habit for the Kosy Kitchen, for once without a dog. Approaching the cafe, he met Lesley with a companion; a girl. He knew she had returned to work that day, and was relieved to see her without the young man. Lesley was too good for Ben, thought Geoff, and she looked strained and tired. The ugly scar across her forehead hadn't faded, and he wondered why she didn't change her hairstyle and hide it. Geoff liked the way Lesley dressed, but he deplored her earrings. This time she was wearing square black and white ones which creaked and swung like inn-signs.

The girl with Lesley had a mop of red-brown curls which hid much of her face. She wore wrap-around dark glasses and carried a cane. Lesley introduced Henrietta Lake. Geoff, of course, knew her history, but had never met her.

'Lesley's persuaded me out,' she said. 'It's my birthday – a not very well preserved twenty-three.' She didn't add that her boyfriend had given her a new stereo and it was being installed in her flat.

'Your birthday? Many happy returns,' said Geoff. 'Wouldn't you like to go to a proper restaurant? I'll treat you both.'

'No thanks – I might meet someone I used to know. This place smells all right; what's it called?'

'I can't smell anything,' said Geoff.

'You haven't got a new nose.'

'It's called the Kosy Kitchen,' put in Lesley, seeing Geoff at a loss.

'Good God. With two Ks? Perhaps we'd better go somewhere else,' said Henrietta.

'Oh come on. There's only this or the chipper open so early.' Lesley put her fingers lightly on the other girl's arm, steering her through the door and towards a table. Henrietta moved confidently, her head held high.

Geoff went to collect food for all three, noting that there was indeed a tense look on Lesley's face. That ruddy boyfriend, he thought. I suppose they've quarrelled. Of the two girls, Henrietta looked the happier. 'How's your young man getting on with Charlie Thorpe?' he asked.

'Fine,' said Lesley. 'Eric's back – the head shepherd, you know – and he's teaching Ben how to clip the show lambs.' Turning to Henrietta, she went on, 'They clip their backs flat, right down to the backbone in the middle, and leave the wool long at the sides. Then when the back wool grows up and the colour matches, the sheep looks quite square. It's something of an art, and Ben's pretty good at it already.'

Henrietta said, 'It sounds more like yew hedges than sheep to me. Isn't it called topiary work?'

Lesley laughed. 'Try asking the Guvnor and tell me what he says. He'd have a fit.'

Geoff was noting Henrietta's alertness. His eyes strayed to her hands, locating and breaking a bread bun. He was thinking about Meg. Surely the two would be a good match. Her manner towards Geoff was light and bantering, almost flirtatious; she had a pretty voice too. He couldn't laugh at her occasional jokes at her own expense, although Lesley did.

He thought her too flippant. 'Why *dark* glasses?' she was saying. 'Why not silver or gold for special occasions? Much more cheerful.' The steadying influence of having a dog to care for would do her good, he thought.

Geoff said, 'It's great that you're going on with your journalism, Henrietta. I've read some of your pieces in the *Post* – great stuff. But don't you feel you'd have more freedom with a guide dog? I have a particular dog in mind.'

Henrietta stopped eating. 'Who, me? A dog? It's easy to tell you don't know me. I've an appalling temper and no patience, and I live in an upstairs flat.' Her carefree laughter made some of the other diners turn their heads. 'Heavens,' she said. 'Poor dog. Is it one you've got a grudge against? I might throw it out of the window.'

There was a shocked silence. This was more than Geoff could take. 'I don't think that's funny,' he said.

'No,' said Henrietta contritely. 'It isn't in the least funny. It wouldn't be funny for the dog either, or for anyone who happened to be underneath. I'm sorry, Geoff. Just take it that I'm not a suitable person for a guide dog.'

'Evidently not.' Geoff thought, she doesn't know what she's saying; I must make allowances. Stiffly, he added, 'My dogs are too important to me perhaps.'

'Perhaps you have a blind spot about them,' suggested Henrietta sweetly.

Lesley hastily said it was time to go. She wanted to get back to Middlegarth, she said.

Back to the young man, more like, thought Geoff, heartily wishing that Ben would return to Ireland – alone. He comes here, hi-jacks my best voluntary worker, then he makes her unhappy. Perhaps not so much unhappy as uneasy. He sat on at the table when they'd gone, thinking about it.

Ben and Lesley had shared a companionable breakfast as usual. Both were tired. Ben noticed that she had laid his place on her right. He felt ashamed of himself. Doing his level best to reassure her, he ate a bowl of cereal and, with difficulty, a plate of bacon and eggs. Normally this would have been followed by several slices of bread and marmalade and washed down with four cups of tea, but today he had refused bread, saying he had to be at work early. But instead of going, he had helped to wash up, cleaned the flues and shaken the soot round his cabbages. Still he lingered.

'I suppose I'd better be going, or the Guvnor will play hell,' he said regretfully at last.

'He will. It's almost your usual time. I'll be off myself in ten minutes.'

Still Ben had hung about. He took Lesley's hand in his, and turned the rings round and round. 'Such a lot of rings – why do you wear so many?'

'I don't know. I seem to collect them.'

Ben thought about the aquamarine in its leather box. He longed to give it to her there and then, but fear held him back. He knew he could get by with one eye, but supposing the trouble, whatever it was, spread to the other?

'Dearest Ben, I *must* go. We'll both get the boot. Oh . . .' she emerged breathlessly from a violent embrace. 'We're not parting for ever, bless you. See you later.' She jumped into the car and drove away. He watched until it had joined the stream of morning traffic on the main road below.

As the day wore on, Ben's mood had improved. It was amazing how quickly you could get used to the loss of an eye. He had tended anyway, to use his left eye more than his right. It was the stronger of the two.

The work of a shepherd in late spring was comparatively light. The foddering took only a short time morning and evening. There were days when the calm routine gave way to long hours of dosing or shearing or dipping, otherwise it was mainly a matter of checking that all was well. Ben had nothing to do with the marketing of fat lambs.

The Guvnor had bought some cattle and turned them out in Killington Ings. Ben walked down to count them. He was nervous as he crossed the busy road, but once he had reached the low-lying pasture and was walking among the Charolais bullocks, confidence returned to him. He went to check the watering place in the beck and saw a trout under the overhanging bank. Browny-grey against grey-brown water and brown earth, only the slight movement of its tail gave it away. About two pounds, Ben judged. He wondered if anyone fished in the beck.

The willow trees were in leaf now, and a gentle breeze rippled through them and ruffled the surface of the deep water. As Ben watched the trout, peace flooded back to him and the roar of traffic blurred in his ears as he remembered Cloninch Bog . . . Would Lesley like it?

The bullocks, crowding up behind him, staring and snuffling, put an end to his reverie. He recrossed the road, looking both ways, then sprinting, and returned to the yard. The Guvnor was waiting, not patiently.

'Where'd you get to then? Thowt you'd gitten lost. Sharpen your ideas up lad, or you and me'll have to part.'

Ben had learned that Charlie's threats were no more than that. He set off for the North meadow to take up an electric fence and close the field for hay. He took the tractor and trailer, with Roy sitting at his feet in the cab, and found that the task took no longer than it normally would have done.

As he worked, rolling up the wire and pulling up the stakes, Roy followed. Generally, he stayed in the tractor cab unless he was needed. Today, he was at Ben's heels, not underfoot, but always within a yard of him. When Ben stood still, Roy lay down. When Ben moved on, the old dog followed him.

'That's that,' said Ben aloud, hoisting the last of the wire onto the trailer. 'Up you go, old dog.' Roy obeyed, jumping into the cab ahead of Ben. But instead of lying down, he put a paw on Ben's knee, looking up searchingly into his face. Ben looked down at the wary light-brown eyes, and read concern in them. 'You know, don't you?' he said. 'It's no good trying to hide anything from you.' Roy retreated to the corner of the cab, and Ben drove back to the yard.

Ben was soothed by his work among the sheep, and

delighted when Eric lent him a fishing rod. He failed to catch the trout, but brought home three small and bony perch. Lesley gave a good imitation of surprise and delight. Ben knew that she was worried about him, and puzzled too. He cursed himself for a selfish clod, and resolved that he would tell her about his eye – but not yet.

For more than a fortnight, Ben got on with his work cheerfully, and Lesley began to wonder whether she'd been stupid to worry about him. She'd known he was moody from the start; he wasn't moody now. He was sweet-tempered and loving, going out of his way to please her. He was eating more normally, and amused her with stories about his life in Ireland.

Lesley wondered why she wasn't happier. She and Ben seemed to have everything going for them, his oddities had vanished. But there was something preventing perfect harmony.

One day, Lesley came home from work and told Ben, 'I met Charlotte in Leeds. You know – the girl who went off with Mark.'

'I hope she doesn't want to give him back.'

Lesley laughed. 'She can't do that; he's ditched her too. He's shacked up with some rich widow now, somewhere in Scotland. I've got his address. Oh, Ben, it was awful – I felt quite sorry for her. She was always pretty wet, but I think she loved him more than I did. Anyway, she cried and cried and said she'd wrecked my life and Mark had wrecked both our lives. It took two large gins to calm her down. I can get a divorce any time. Mark's planning to marry his widow.'

Ben was down on his knees, fixing a board onto the bottom of the door. He looked up sideways at her. 'That's good,' he said. 'Except for the widow.'

'Ben – we can get married. I – I thought you'd be glad.'

He stood up and put his arms round her, holding her tightly. 'I think of you as my wife already,' he said. 'You *are*

113

my wife. Is there a big rush about making it legal?' He kissed her mouth and the scar on her forehead.

Lesley drew back a little, looking into his eyes. 'I know, love, I feel I'm your wife too. But somehow I don't feel as if you were my husband. Don't you want a proper wedding? You suggested it, not me.'

Ben's gaze narrowed suddenly as he looked at her. 'Orange blossom, champagne and six bridesmaids,' he said in a hard, light voice she'd never heard before.

'Don't be so bloody selfish,' said Lesley, firing up and twisting free of him. 'I don't know what's the matter with you sometimes.'

'No, you don't, do you,' said Ben slowly. He stared at her with deepening horror, his face turning livid under its deep tan, his arms falling to his sides.

'I'm going to have to tell you,' he said.

Seven

Sweat stood on Ben's forehead. His heart knocked against his ribs. He stood in frozen horror. Lesley was wearing a light blue cotton dress. As he'd looked up from mending the door, he'd thought how fresh and pretty she'd looked and had jumped up to hug her. Now he stepped back, releasing her, the words she was saying making no sense. He saw the blue dress through drifting black spots, like a snow shower seen on a negative. Emotions crowded in on him so fast that they cancelled each other out – he felt nothing at all.

A memory flashed through his mind. His friend Terry staring at his hand after losing two fingers in a chaff cutter. 'I didn't feel a thing,' Terry had said in astonishment.

A few minutes earlier, as he fitted the new piece of wood on the bottom of the door, Ben had been thinking it was high time he saw a doctor – he'd been stupid to delay. Perhaps even now something could be done about his right eye, and he wanted reassurance about the left one. He wanted to get married as soon as Lesley's divorce came through, but only if his sight was in no danger. He sensed her need for a secure foundation for a life free of Mark; free of the flat with its memories of Mark; free to have children.

Ben could have pinpointed the exact moment when he began to love Lesley. It was when she had given him a brave, lop-sided grin in hospital after the accident. Ben, who thought he was in love already, had experienced the real thing for the first time. And he had been worried in case the blow to her head might affect her sight.

'I'm going blind,' he said.

Lesley's face seemed to shrink behind the rain of black snowflakes. She took a deep breath and asked, 'Is it those spots again?'

He nodded. 'This is worse than the other,' he said. 'Much quicker. The right one hardly bothered me at first.' His voice was expressionless. He might have been discussing a sick sheep.

'You mean this is your *left* eye? What about the other?' He could just see her frightened eyes through the spinning black globules.

'The right one's gone,' he said. 'You asked me if I was seeing spots the day we drove all that way and went dancing. I wasn't seeing anything.'

'Darling, don't panic. There's nearly always something that can be done nowadays.' He sensed her own panic and thought dully, this is how she's been trained to talk.

'Your retina must be detaching. Oh God, Ben, why didn't you tell me? Why didn't you see a doctor?' There was anguish in her voice, but she controlled it. 'Listen. You musn't make any sudden movement. Go slowly to the bed and lie down on your back while I ring the doctor. Don't rub your eye; keep as still as you possibly can. Please, darling.'

Ben obeyed, his legs moving like lead weights. He sat on the side of the bed and pulled of his shoes. He could hear Lesley speaking urgently on the telephone. As the second shoe came off with a slight jerk, he became aware of a thin sliver of jet black at the topmost edge of his left eye. He lay down on his back and shut his eyes.

Lesley came back and knelt on the floor beside him. He found her hand – it was icy and trembling. He could find nothing to say to her; he supposed what he felt was despair. It seemed more like an impossible weariness. It was almost too much trouble to listen to what Lesley was saying.

'I phoned the hospital where I used to work,' she said. 'They've got one of the best men in Yorkshire there – Dr Stroud. They're sending an ambulance, less than an hour,

116

they said. They repair retinas all the time; I'm sure they can mend it. Is there any pain?'

'No,' said Ben. 'It doesn't hurt, it never has. But the shutter's coming down. Now, while I'm speaking to you.'

She gripped his hands and went on talking, trying to reassure both of them. She seemed to be telling him how lucky he was to have somebody who understood about eyes on the premises. Lucky? The black rain thickened, and the curtain descended, cutting off the last of his perception of light. He struggled to fight off panic, unable to speak. And instead of Lesley's horrified face he saw the blind tramp at Kilmoon fair. The picture was all too clear; the old man's daughter pointing to his eyes with one worn, dusty hand, while the other clutched his ragged sleeve. The old man carried a biscuit tin with a few pence in it.

The girl's practised begger's whine, 'A copper for the blind man and I'll say a prayer for you,' was clearer in his ears than Lesley's voice.

The hours that followed were pure nightmare. Ben had never in his life suffered from anything more serious than a cold in the head or a few bruises after a fall. He had feared to be left in the dark, but the blackness had gone. Instead, he knew the colourless gloom experienced behind closed lids in daylight. Sometimes the no-colour nothingness was prickled with tiny sparks.

Ben wasn't cheered by the reassurances coming from all sides. He couldn't believe that anything so final could be cured. He thought, what will become of me? His future stretched ahead, an endless grey vista, perhaps fifty years or more. He'd have to leave the cottage, go home to his family, an object of pity, a financial burden. The idea of continuing to live with Lesley he dismissed out of hand. He heard a man's voice saying, 'Providential for him – you know all the ropes . . .' He heard Lesley's subdued answer. There was no way he would leg-shackle the woman he loved like that.

He tried to move his head, but something was holding it

steadily in one position, pressing gently from both sides. Some kind of frame. He supposed he was in a hospital – smell of antiseptic, slap of soft shoes, feeling of height and space. He had been lifted on and off a stretcher, driven somewhere, wheeled somewhere. He heard Lesley say, 'I have to leave you now, love. You'll be all right, you're in good hands. I'll come back later.'

A man's voice said, 'Whatever you do, don't move. I'm putting drops in your eyes. Try not to jerk away or blink.' The drops were cold, and stung. He was left, possibly alone.

Later, a woman's voice asked questions about his identity and state of health. Then, after another warning to keep still, he was given the first injection in all his twenty-seven years. It hurt less than he expected. He thought inconsequently that he'd wasted sympathy on the thousands of sheep he'd inoculated over the years. He began to feel calm and uncaring. After a time, he slept.

Lesley went back to the cottage for the night. She packed Ben's belongings, so as to take them to her flat. The cottage went with the job; she couldn't see the hard-headed Guvnor allowing her to keep it warm for Ben. He was sure to be in hospital for a week; probably for much longer.

Next day, she talked to Dr Stroud, whose lectures she had attended when she was learning her job.

'But my dear girl,' said the doctor, 'if you're living with this man, why on earth didn't you persuade him to get help? His right eye is likely to be beyond repair; we've a good chance of saving the other one – better than fifty-fifty. But there was no need to lose either. Didn't you realize the danger of delay?'

'I didn't know anything about it,' said Lesley. 'He didn't tell me. Scared, I think.' She knew Dr Stroud thought her careless and unobservant. Ben was to have an operation in three days' time. Meanwhile, tests were being carried out on him.

She wondered about the family in Ireland. Probably his mother had a right to know, but she didn't mean to bring his relatives over unless Ben wanted them to come. She asked him, and he said he didn't want anybody. He was brighter today, buoyed up by accounts of successful operations on conditions exactly like his own. After a time he added, 'I think you should let my grandmother know.'

'But Ben, she'll tell the others.'

'She won't. Not if I don't want her to.'

'Won't it be a shock, at her age?'

'It'll be a bigger one if this op doesn't work and she finds out when I go home with a white stick. She'd die of shock and come and haunt you.' The words were light, but he gripped Lesley's fingers painfully as he spoke.

She said, 'Oh, all right then. I'll ring her when I go home.'

A flustered female voice answered the telephone. Ben's mother, Lesley supposed. It seemed dreadful not to tell her. She asked for Mrs Logan, giving her name as Lesley Grant. Evidently Ben hadn't told his mother her name; there was no flicker of recognition.

There was a long delay, and Lesley could hear two voices arguing, one insisting feebly that the other, more distant one should come to the 'phone. At last, a chilly voice said, 'Yes?'

'Lesley Grant speaking. Are you Ben's grandmother?'

'Benedict Glyn is my grandson, yes. Who are you?'

'I'm his fiancée,' said Lesley bravely, wondering if she was. 'I'm afraid Ben's had an accident. He was most anxious that you should be told, but not the rest of the family.'

'Very sensible of him.' The voice would have cut glass, thought Lesley. 'I suppose he has fallen off a horse again. I have warned him frequently, to no avail. Go away, Muriel. And shut the door behind you.'

Lesley cautiously tried to explain matters, softening the details in deference to Agatha's age.

'Am I to understand that Benedict has gone blind?' There was no quaver in the uncompromising tones, but there was unmistakeable shock.

Lesley said that the operation should restore the sight of one eye, and might be partially successful on the other.

'Balderdash,' said Agatha. 'Either one can see, or one can not.' She replaced the receiver, leaving Lesley staring helplessly at the telephone for a minute before she hung up.

'Heartless old bitch,' said Lesley aloud, sounding almost as venomous as Agatha herself. What message could she possibly give Ben?

When she visited him next day, Lesley told Ben that Agatha had sounded upset. But Ben didn't want to talk today. She had been warned not to kiss him, but he carried her hand to his lips and kissed it. His eyes were bandaged, and he had three days' black stubble on his jaw. Even the movement of shaving him could be dangerous. Lesley had also been warned not to make him laugh. Laugh?

She had seen some gruesome sights when she was learning about diseases of the eye and considered herself shockproof, but she couldn't look at Ben. Some patients wanted sympathy, some shouted and swore, some were resigned, but Ben. . . . What was he doing, bandaged and helpless in a darkened room? It was all wrong. Similes came to Lesley's mind – a felled oak, a wrecked ship. He would laugh at that, but he mustn't laugh. Speech had to be rationed.

As she drove to her flat after work, she felt so weary that she could hardly find the energy to write up her report for the day. She hadn't told Hazel why she was there. She'd think Lesley and Ben had split up. Let her. It was a relief to find that both Hazel and Imogen had gone out. The living-room looked as if it had been hit by a tornado. Lesley trailed through it, had a bath and went to bed. She hoped that Ben's grandmother wouldn't tell the rest of the family. Probably Ben hadn't expected any message.

The old woman's razor-edged voice haunted her dreams.

Everything at Cloninch was in Agatha's name. All cheques were made payable to her and cashed by her. She employed an accountant, to whom she took her receipts and bank statements at intervals, in a laundry bag. She drew whatever cash she considered necessary for the household, and paid

Denis a regular allowance. She cashed Michael's pension, and payed it into a savings account in Ben's name. Ben was unaware of this, and if Michael knew, he made no comment.

Myles and Denis had sold a pen of calves at the mart a few days before Benedict's young woman telephoned. The cheque had arrived that morning. Agatha had no trouble in persuading Myles to drive her to Kilmoon that day – she never had when there was a cheque to pay in. He would receive commission, which his mother-in-law thought of as his pocket-money.

As usual, he waited for her outside the bank. She carried an old pigskin handbag, cracked and stiff with age, initialled in silver. Myles never went into the bank himself – he had some remnants of pride. It was ten minutes before Agatha reappeared. She looked abstracted, unlike her usual self, but once in the van, she began to speak with confident authority.

'Myles, I shall be travelling to Yorkshire on Monday. Muriel may have told you that I wish to visit my sister.'

'But Mother, the doctor –'

Agatha talked on and over the interruption. 'I have asked Edward Ryder to drive me to the airport. He raised some ridiculous objections, however, he values my custom. He has agreed. I have decided to sell my picture immediately. You had better take it to Morgan's Sales Rooms in Dame Street. I am told that is the best place. I have made arrangements for you to take it there the day after tomorrow. You will be expected.'

'But Mother, the silage –'

Agatha turned her head and looked him up and down. Myles felt like a fieldmouse being considered by a sparrowhawk. 'The silage,' she said, 'can go to the devil.'

Agatha climbed the stairs slowly, using the banister rail. She was pleased to find that Michael was asleep. The room was frowsty; the red-haired girl more than ever out of place. Agatha opened the window and sat down to read the letter she had received from Morgan's Fine Arts. The first letter had doubted the authenticity of the Tissot, although the writer hadn't seen it – simpleton! Most of Tissot's models, said this person, were painted lounging in their drawing rooms. He wanted to see the painting. For answer, Agatha had sent him a copy of the receipt for the money paid to the artist by her grandfather.

The second letter was conciliatory and eager by turns. The commission alone would be enormous. If the picture was in good condition it could be worth six figures. The writer spoke of insurance, of security measures, of publicity. Agatha crumpled the letter and threw it into the wastepaper basket.

She had no faith at all in Benedict's recovery. The young woman would not have telephoned had she really been confident of a successful outcome. She had sounded tense and strained. Possibly she was fond of Benedict. The boy had considerable charm. Perhaps she imagined herself to be in love with him. She would soon change her mind if the operation did not succeed. Agatha was determined that, if Benedict could not see the *Young Girl in a Garden*, neither should this Grant woman. She did not sound like a scheming hussy, but one could never tell.

Agatha climbed carefully onto a chair, and fetched down a dusty gladstone bag from the top of the wardrobe. It trailed cobwebs, and spiders raced for cover under the dressing-table. She coughed as she dusted it off with one of Michael's socks. She placed two changes of underwear in it, night attire, washing things and clean blouses. Michael snored on. Then she went to Benedict's room and looked round. It was small, and as bare as a monk's cell. She looked in the cupboard, but he appeared to have left nothing behind except his working clothes.

She went back to her own bedroom and checked the cash she had drawn from the bank. Seven hundred pounds. She had heard that it was illegal to take any quantity of money out of the country. Agatha smiled grimly to herself. Once the notes were pinned inside her camisole, it would take an intrepid customs man to remove them.

She sat down by the window and picked up her library book; *The Human Eye: an Everyday Miracle.*

Edward Ryder's office was in even more confusion than usual. He had bought a computer, and was trying to learn how to use it with marked lack of success. Several piles of documents had been moved from his desk to the floor to make room for it, and long coils of paper were everywhere. One of them wound itself round Edward's ankle as he gathered the papers he needed for the court case in Dublin. He kicked at it irritably, but it pursued him out of the room. His secretary followed him with last minute reminders. Edward hardly answered. He was cursing himself for a fool.

Old Mrs Logan seemed to know everything. She had known that Sean More was taking the case about his farm to the High Court, and when it was sitting, and that Edward would be obliged to attend. He had been unfortunate enough to encounter her in the library (he'd thought she'd given up coming into town), and had at once become engrossed in a book. But Agatha had marched over to him, had told him that he was a bad colour and should take more exercise. Before he could think of an answer which combined diplomacy and dismissal, she had asked him if he didn't find the Dublin train inconveniently early. Unsuspecting, he had replied that he was driving there before lunch on Monday. He would be staying overnight for the hearing.

'In that case,' Agatha had said, 'you may take me to Dublin Airport. I wish to be there by half past two.'

When Edward had made a number of ill-prepared excuses, she had reminded him that he was her man of business (for want of a better term, she said), and had threatened to take her custom elsewhere.

So the next day Edward, who was a bachelor and lived over his office, left hasty instructions with his secretary and set off for Cloninch in his fairly new grey Austin.

He had been prepared to find the old woman in her Burberry and her cloche hat, had steeled himself for the journey and for the looks he would get at the airport – please God he wouldn't meet any other clients. He was not prepared for the gladstone bag or the guitar. He got out of the car and opened the door for Agatha, thinking that she looked ill; pinched about the mouth. Hope she doesn't die on me. He put the bag and the guitar in its case into the boot.

Edward started the car, remarking, 'It's a long time, fifty-four years; but I'm sure your sister is looking forward to your visit.'

'Unlikely,' said Agatha. 'She knows nothing about it.'

'Oh,' was all that Edward could find to say. He tried again. 'Your husband will miss you. Does he go out at all now?'

Agatha said, 'I did not tell him of my plans. He might have raised some objection. He sleeps far too much – a sad waste of time.' As she spoke, she bent forward to adjust the laces of her ghillie shoes. This movement produced a strange crackling and rustling. It seemed to come from the region of her midriff.

After that, conversation languished. Edward turned on the radio. Agatha extended a gnarled hand and turned it off. Edward had spent half a lifetime settling disputes about trifles. He prided himself on his patience and understanding. He suppressed a childish wish to turn up the volume and tell Agatha she could put up with it or walk. One knew the old girl was eccentric, but really. . . .

Edward's habitual speed was a steady fifty-five miles an hour. He tore along at seventy, fidgeting at the traffic lights. 'Reckless driving does not become you, Edward,' said Agatha.

Edward shut his teeth hard, and didn't answer or speak until he had deposited her at 'Departures'. Then his innate good nature made him park his car, carry her peculiar luggage and follow her into the building. She was checking in as if she flew to England every day. He said, 'Have a pleasant journey, Mrs Logan.'

She turned her head. 'Journeys are never pleasant; I have successfully avoided them for half a century,' she said. Then she added, 'It was good of you to bring me here. Thank you.'

More astonished than by anything that had gone before, Edward said, 'I'll meet you when you come back if you like.'

Agatha was watching the revolving belt bearing her gladstone bag and Benedict's guitar out of sight. The girl at the desk was trying not to exchange glances with her neighbour. Agatha froze both with one glare.

'Possibly I shall not return,' she said.

Agatha was tired. She hoped she had hidden this from Edward. Poor man, he had done his best. At the desk she had been more nearly flustered than she could remember. She had never flown before, and she had been the object of rude surmise from two uniformed girls. She had found the flight boring but not alarming. At Yeadon, a busybody in uniform had queried the guitar. The name of a student from Toledo was painted on its stained canvas cover, but what of that? There was only one flight a day to Leeds, and she had been fortunate to find a seat vacant. It had not occurred to her to book one.

Early that morning, Agatha had telephoned Benedict's cottage. Three times she had tried without success, and she had forgotten to ask the Grant woman where Benedict might be found. A fourth attempt drew an answer from a female voice, another one, with a more pronounced accent and far less address, Agatha thought. Mrs Amanda Wilkes had supplied the name of the Waterloo Street Hospital. There would be an omnibus to take her into the city, and, presumably taxis. Benedict was awaiting surgery.

Agatha had said that she was flying to Leeds that day, and rung off. It appeared that Mrs Wilkes was the daughter of Benedict's employer. A ninny, thought Agatha, and overwrought.

She was not prepared to find Benedict's young woman waiting at the airport. Not a painted Jezebel, but a tall, pale girl who might have been attractive but for an unsightly scar on her forehead. She looked as if she needed a good square meal and a night's sleep. At all events she was not a fool like

125

the other. She wasted no time in chit-chat, but drove straight to the hospital.

As they crawled through heavy traffic, the girl explained that she had been living with Benedict almost since his arrival. Agatha greeted this admission in stony silence. The girl flushed and said something about a divorce. Agatha said that her grandson had not informed her that he was living in sin with a married woman. 'I blame his mother,' she said. 'His upbringing was sadly neglected.'

The young woman said angrily that it was their own affair.

'Precisely so,' said Agatha.

Benedict's mistress then made a visible effort to control her temper. Her name, she claimed, was Peabody, although she preferred Grant. Diffidently, she asked Agatha to call her Lesley. Was she deliberately trying to be confusing? She said that Benedict had a great respect and admiration for his grandmother; that she had hoped that Agatha would be broad-minded.

Agatha explained, patiently she thought, that she had been broad-minded as a girl, but had outgrown it.

At the hospital, Agatha was again obliged to wait, while Lesley (stupid name) disappeared. Two flappers in the waiting room peeped rudely at her round the magazines they were pretending to read. They appeared to find her laughable.

Agatha returned to the entrance, where there was a long mirror, to check on her appearance. There was nothing remotely amusing about it, she decided. The linen hat she had worn every summer since the cloche returned to fashion in the 'sixties was well pulled down: her Burberry was shabby, but in no way an object for mirth. There were no ladders in her stockings or smuts on her nose. She returned to the waiting room.

After a prolonged wait, she went out into the corridor and accosted a nurse, demanding to see Benedict Glyn.

'I'm afraid you must wait a bit longer, Mrs Glyn,' said the nurse, a saucy piece if ever Agatha had seen one.

'Mrs Logan,' corrected Agatha. She recalled that she had

given her relationship to Benedict as 'mother'. Exceedingly careless. She must be overtired. She sat down, choosing an upright chair with its back to the wall. The flappers had gone. She accepted a cup of tea – it would not do to fall asleep.

After a while, she noticed that Lesley had returned. Perhaps she was not a bad lot after all. She thought Agatha was asleep, and the despair on her face was plain to see.

Agatha felt a long icy tremor pass through her. She sat, bolt upright, her eyes closed, her hands tightly clasped in her lap. The tremor passed. Willpower, she thought, conquers most things.

The Guvnor had been the last person at Middlegarth to hear about Ben. He had gone to a sheep-breeders' meeting in York, followed by a lengthy dinner and lengthier speeches. He'd come home late, gone straight up to bed, and was last down to breakfast the next morning.

He hadn't believed Mandy when she'd greeted him with the words, 'Father, Ben's gone blind.' She had turned away in tears, sniffing and hiccuping into a tissue.

Charlie had waited in angry silence for her to control her sobs. He had observed his daughter, her back turned, getting the milk out of the fridge. 'Give over; you're making my teeth ache,' he said.

Mandy's mousy hair was fastened back with a rubber band. She wore a too tight pink T shirt, solid fat bulged above and below her bra; her bottom was broad in a spotted skirt; she had sturdy bare legs and large feet in Scholl sandals. Her appearance didn't match up with hysterical nonsense. She turned to him, her face damp and scarlet, her hair in wisps. She stopped crying.

'Where did you hear that rubbish?' Charlie had asked. 'Lad were right enough yesterday teatime. Found him looking on scrapheap for summat to mend door. That's what I like about him. He doesn't come whining and begging if owt's wrong; he gets on and puts it right. Don't know when

I've taken such a liking to a lad. Reckon him and Lesley'll make a match of it?' He gulped tea and reached for the carving knife.

'Father, it's *true*. Ben went to Leeds by ambulance after you'd gone to York. He's in Waterloo Street – Ted's been to see him. He's stone blind.'

'Why in hell didn't you tell me as well as Ted?' Charlie had jumped up, violently pushing back the table. 'Why am I the last to hear owt that's going off round here? You tell that lapdog of a husband of yours and you don't tell me. It's a bugger, is that. By God, my lass, you're a rum 'un, you are an' all.' He had banged out of the house and gone to find Ted, leaving Mandy weeping into the teacups.

Charlie was of the opinion that a cheque, if it was big enough, was a cure for most human ills. Nobody was going to call the Guvnor careful, not where anyone he liked was concerned. If he didn't like you, you could die of starvation before he would put his hand in his pocket. He did like Ben, so he went straight to Leeds, taking his cheque book.

Ben was already in a private room, so there wasn't much that Charlie could do. Dr Stroud listened to him patiently and told him that nothing further could be done for Ben for several days. He had been sedated to keep him quiet. Would Mr Thorpe please keep his voice down?

The next day and the next, the story was the same. Charlie contented himself with telephone calls when he found he couldn't bulldoze his way into Ben's room.

At the farm, Ted imported a tow-headed student called Gideon. The Guvnor ignored him. The men did their work in gloomy silence and Roy stayed in his kennel. Lesley had packed up and left the cottage. When Ted suggested that Gideon might move into it, Charlie cursed him for several minutes. Ted, used to it, didn't add fuel to the fire by answering back. Charlie always finished his tirades with the words, 'Don't make me say summat I'll be sorry for.' So far, Ted had never managed to do this.

Early the following week, the Guvnor could stand it no

longer. The hospital staff would say only that Ben was comfortable, which he didn't believe, and he suspected that Mandy was half enjoying the situation. She was one of those who would be first on the scene at a fire or a road accident. Her kindness and capable help were real enough, but Charlie was beginning to think that she thrived on the misfortunes of others. He got out the Range Rover and drove to Leeds without telling her he was going.

The Guvnor's simple plan was to find the eye doctor and ask him why the flaming hell he didn't operate on Ben and get it over with. He was sure that there was a conspiracy of silence, and he meant to see that something was done, and quickly.

The woman at the desk called out, 'Yes?' as he was about to march straight through the reception area. Charlie stopped unwillingly. He summed her up mentally as a not-mucher. All dolled up and good for nowt, he thought, as he told her his business. While he was talking, Lesley went past, but he didn't notice her. He was directed to the waiting room.

The room was large, with chairs set around the walls. There was nobody there except an old woman who looked so ill and so odd that Charlie hesitated, taking her to be a mental patient.

'Good evening,' he said politely, wondering if the old boiler was violent.

'And who might you be?' enquired Agatha.

Eight

Lesley had worked at Waterloo Road for a year, caring for the newly blind, before she started social work in patients' own homes. She knew something about surgery for retinal detachment. She was aware that, once the retina was separated from its blood supply, it would die for lack of oxygen in a short time. She had little hope for Ben's right eye.

She knew that, unless the vital part of the retina, the macula, was detached, surgery was usually successful. She knew too that a reattached retina took as long to become secure as a set limb. There was no chance that, after the operation, Ben's sight would be immediately restored. He would be kept immobilized for days, perhaps for weeks.

It was a pretty thought – the sufferer, his eyes unbandaged, looking up ecstatically at his beloved – but it was a fairytale. First came the waiting.

She wondered how she would endure it.

Mrs Betts, the most trying of the people Lesley cared for, had lost her sight in the same way, after having been mugged. The attack had broken her nerve, and she had willingly remained comatose for weeks. This had helped her chances of recovery. She had had two operations and now had navigational vision: she could easily have cared for herself. Lesley knew that Mrs Betts was more in need of a psychiatrist than a social worker, but hadn't been able to convince her superiors.

Ben had done just about everything he could to endanger his sight. He had caught sheep, jumped off tractors . . . He had refused to take care because he would not accept what had happened.

For hours that Monday he had been out of his ward. The hospital had the most sophisticated machines for scanning. Gone were the days when a surgeon would shine a light into the eye and make a sketch.

Lesley had been hanging about at the hospital waiting for news ever since collecting Ben's awesome grandmother. Thank God the old terror was asleep in the waiting room. Lesley wondered what was to be done with her; she didn't intend to go home without some word of Ben's condition.

She'd had a bad day. After a restless night, she'd had to endure first sulks then open quarrelling from Hazel and Imogen over breakfast. Finally, Imogen had gathered her few belongings and left, shouting abuse of a kind seldom heard in that genteel Victorian backwater. Lesley told Hazel not to import anyone else, and fled to the hospital, hoping for a glimpse of Ben before she went to work. She was told that he had gone for further tests and that the operation was planned for the following morning. 'Ben's granny is coming to see him, isn't that nice?' said the nurse. 'She's flying over from Ireland today.'

Fortunately, Monday was Lesley's afternoon at the childrens' day centre. She had been able to persuade another girl to change days with her. Ben's granny. How cosy it sounded.

Lesley didn't intend to offer Mrs Logan a bed for the night. She was still smarting after their exchanges on the way from the airport. She supposed she'd have to take the old fright to a hotel.

As she went towards the waiting-room, she heard the Guvnor's familiar voice. He was loudly proclaiming his dislike of 'niggers and Jews and suchlike'. Approximately half of the hospital staff were black; Dr Stroud was a Jew. Lesley cringed, looking nervously over her shoulder. She heard Charlie add that if he had his way, all nancy-boys would be locked up – soon cure 'em. Who on earth could he be talking to? She opened the waiting-room door in time to hear Agatha's reply.

'I am fully in agreement with you, Mr Thorpe. A most refreshing viewpoint in these decadent days. Another cup of tea?'

'Aye, go on then.'

Charlie and Agatha were sitting together at a small table. She was pouring out tea. Charlie was smiling broadly, and Agatha's austere features had relaxed into a grim near-smile. When she saw Lesley, she made a quick movement to rise, asking, 'How is he?' but swayed as she stood.

Charlie grabbed the teapot, and he and Lesley caught hold of her arms. They exchanged glances. 'I'm afraid I haven't any more news,' said Lesley.

'A good night's sleep, Mrs Logan, and you'll be like a new catched 'un,' said Charlie encouragingly.

'I doubt it,' said Agatha. 'I have not yet engaged any accommodation.'

'Take you back to farm,' said Charlie. 'Less than an hour in Range Rover. Plenty of room.'

'I should prefer to be closer to Benedict,' said Agatha. Her voice was faint – a mere thread, but a steel thread. 'I have travelled a long way at great personal inconvenience to be near him. I have brought his guitar with me.'

Lesley thought, she cares. Almost as much as I do, in her own dried up way. She said, 'I'll put you up if you like, Mrs Logan. I'm only ten minutes from here. Do come.'

Agatha appeared to consider. 'Very well, I will,' she said.

At Cloninch, everybody was blaming everybody else because Agatha had gone without leaving a forwarding address. They all knew she was going to see her sister, nobody knew where she lived except that it was in Yorkshire. Agatha had left unobserved, an hour earlier than the time she had mentioned to Muriel. Michael, cross-examined, had admitted that he had noticed that she was packing. Why hadn't he said anything? He replied that he couldn't be bothered.

In the evening, Edward telephoned from his Dublin hotel to tell Muriel that he had seen her mother safely onto the plane. He was answered by Myles, whose first question was, 'Had she got seven hundred quid on her?'

'I have no idea,' Edward had said crushingly. 'It was none of my business. She would hardly carry so much.'

'Oh, wouldn't she,' said Myles bitterly.

The family, knowing nothing about Ben's state, didn't dream that Agatha was staying in Leeds. They presumed she was with her sister. They presumed she would come back when it suited her. Probably soon; they were certain to quarrel. In the meantime, there was a shortage of ready cash.

The silage was ready to cut, but even in her absence, Agatha's word was law. Myles took the *Young Girl in a Garden* down from the bedroom wall, wrapped it in a fairly clean piece of sacking, and put it in the back of the van. He lived only an hour's drive from Dublin, but his visits there were mostly to the greyhound track, or the RDS showground at Ballsbridge. He had never once driven into the city centre. The idea made him nervous. Fear of his mother-in-law prevented him from asking Denis to go in his place, so he asked Barney Mangan, Auctioneer & Valuer to go with him and direct him. Barney dismissed Morgan Fine Arts as a crowd of cute hoors, and said he wasn't speaking to them. This could be taken to mean that he owed the firm money.

Myles set off on his own. He followed the airport signs, knowing they would lead him to the river where he could get his bearings. He recognized the great grey shape of Houston Station with gratitude, and the one-way signs with alarm. He would have to cross the Liffey here, and he had somehow got himself onto the wrong side of the road. Bloody system, thought Myles; be back in Phoenix Park if I'm not careful. He began to nudge his way to the right, and was astride the white line when he reached the busy intersection.

Half way across, the van sputtered and almost stalled. Innocent victim of a reckless postman for a number of years, it was unreliable; needing coaxing and humouring. Myles barely caught a glimpse of the Hiace van coming up on his right. Big and battered, it was crammed to the doors with yellow-haired tinkers. It caught the back right hand corner of the Renault, peeling off paint, grating along its side, furrowing the metal, causing the picture to bound in the air. Myles could hear the furious shouts of the driver recede as he accelerated.

Safely on the Quays, he drove slowly, hugging the kerb, searching for a handkerchief to mop his forehead. And to reach Dame Street, he would have to cross the bloody river again. Christ!

After a while, he noticed the friendly frontage of a pub on his left. The Crock of Gold. He hadn't meant to stop, but he felt that he needed a drink as never before. It wouldn't take long. He drove round the block, and found a vacant site, filled with cars. One of them was pulling out. He slid into the space and got out. He wished the steering would lock. Never mind; it would only take a minute to swallow a brandy. He locked the doors, and hoped he wouldn't be caught with all his rear lights broken.

The pub was allegedly closed for the afternoon, but Myles went unerringly to a side door and knocked. A young woman let him in, and he found his way to the lounge bar which was in semi-darkness.

'Myles, you old devil! Where were you since? I didn't see you these ages.' The voice came from a corner where a hugely fat man in a pinstriped suit was relaxing in front of an army of empty glasses. 'What'll you have?'

'Dan! Am I glad to see you. This one's on me. Any chance of a lift to Dame Street?' Myles knocked on the deserted counter with a coin.

'No, let me.' Dan heaved himself up, lurched to the counter and banged on it with his fist. 'Yeah, I'll give you a lift. What's wrong with you Myles? Run over somebody? You're shaking.'

'I'm all right,' said Myles. 'All I need is a drink.'

'The barman's having a rest for himself, the bloody cripple,' said Dan, ringing the bell. 'The devil is standing in him.'

The barman appeared, yawning, and they had a drink, and another. Myles said uneasily, 'I musn't stay long. I have a picture to deliver. Belongs to the mother-in-law.'

Dan knew all about mothers-in-law. He knew a number of jokes about them, and he told them all. 'Same again,' he shouted.

'I hope the old van's all right,' said Myles, going to the window. 'I can't see it from here; I left it out the back.'

Dan laughed. 'Old van? Safe as houses. The thieves around here are educated; they only bother with BMWs and Mercs. Posh cars. Don't you worry; take your time boy.'

They took their time. 'It's past four,' said Myles. 'What about that lift?' They finished their drinks and went to the site. The van had gone.

The Garda was unimpressed. 'Renault 4 van,' he said, writing. 'Year of registration 1976. Ex *An Post*. Colour chocolate. Dented right rear. Rear lights broken. . . . What kind of a picture? Oil painting, gilt frame. Woman sitting on the ground holding a bunch of flowers. Right. Leave it with us. No problem.'

Myles badly needed another whisky. He had yet to face Morgan Fine Arts. He remembered watching Pascal Morgan, head of the firm, on tv. Even when wreathed in smiles you could tell he was a man to be reckoned with. He was large and dark and very smooth. His grooming was immaculate; so was his diction. But when, two whiskies later, Myles phoned him, the façade slipped.

'Jesus!' cried Pascal Morgan. 'You left a Tissot in an old van on a derelict site? You're a bright one, aren't you? You should be in Grangegorman.'

'Here, steady,' said Myles. 'I've lost my van too.'

Mr Morgan spoke slowly, with scornful emphasis. 'Your van,' he said, 'might be worth a grand, though from what you say, I doubt it. The picture's worth a small fortune. Get the crime squad onto it at once, if you haven't already.'

'The crime squad?' said Myles, astonished. 'Even if the picture was worth a grand as well, they'd hardly bother.'

Pascal Morgan seemed to be about to have a fit. 'Have you any notion of the value of that picture?' he asked.

'I think my mother-in-law had it insured for eight hundred pounds,' said Myles. 'She'll slaughter me,' he added aside to Dan.

'So she should,' said Pascal Morgan, overhearing. 'The last Tissot sold at public auction fetched a quarter of a million.'

Ben knew that he was more or less permanently sedated. Drugged, he thought, the humiliation of it. Night melted into day, into night. Another day must be nearly over. The day after his operation. There was no difference. He was still bandaged, still immobilized. He felt nothing as positive as despair. Only discomfort, itching in inaccessible places, boredom, profound unhappiness. He slept a great deal.

'Lesley, are you there?'

'Yes love, I'm here.'

'Look, don't feel you have to stick around. There's no need. I'll be okay.'

'I want to be here. I've been at work all day.'

'As long as you're not making yourself miserable. Have you heard anything about the operation? They haven't told me.'

'No, nothing,' said Lesley. 'I don't suppose they know themselves yet. Ben, your grandmother's here. She stayed at my place last night; she'd like to talk to you. I'll go away now, and come back later.'

He felt the touch of her fingers on his shoulder, heard the tap of her shoes, then nothing. He would never see again, he thought. Never see Lesley again. He felt he might cope with it if he could talk to her, touch her, make love to her. But she wouldn't want him, would she? Oh, she'd pretend she did, perhaps even convince both of them for a time. Then one day he would sense her true feelings, know that he was pitied. Loved as a mother loved her retarded child. He would rather die than accept that.

Slow footsteps: a voice. 'Well, Benedict, this is a sad state of affairs.'

Ben said, 'Lesley told me you were here – I never dreamed you'd come. Is mother with you?'

'No. I did not inform your mother. If you can be cured, she will be spared needless worry; if not, I imagine she will come here.'

Ben heard her seat herself, give a small sigh. He heard the rasp of her stockings as she crossed her legs, the sound of her breathing – light and quick. There was also a muffled crackling sound that he couldn't identify. 'I'm not going home,' he said suddenly.

'I did not suppose you would. I was incensed when I discovered that you had taken a mistress, but she seems to be a capable young woman, and is obviously besotted. Doubtless, you would be well advised to remain with her.'

'I couldn't do that. I want a wife, not a nurse.'

Agatha ignored this. 'I have always disliked horses,' she said, 'and have warned you repeatedly that you would injure yourself. Your great-grandfather was brought home on a gate.'

Ben felt the quiver of a smile. If he had expected any softening in Agatha, he would be disappointed. 'How long do you mean to stay?' he asked her.

'I shall remain here until you recover your sight,' said Agatha, 'and when you do, you will oblige me by shaving off that beard. I cannot endure bearded men.'

A flip-flop of soft soled shoes and a woman's voice saying, 'You must go now, Mrs Logan. Time for Ben's injection.' There was a brief, bitter argument, cut off by the entrance of a third person, a doctor. Ben heard Agatha's feet as she left the room, protesting all the way.

He was used to injections now. He said, 'You'll make an addict of me.' Then came the welcome drowsiness, then sleep.

Dr Stroud was a slight, olive-skinned man with clever brown eyes. He was sitting beside Ben's bed. Ben's bandages were off, his head no longer immobilized. His feelings were impossible to guess. The room was gloomy; it was daylight, but the window faced north. The doctor shone a bright light into Ben's right eye. Ben gave no sign. Dr Stroud grunted, and directed the light at the other eye.

'There's a light somewhere,' said Ben.

'A bright one?'

'No. A kind of paleness – hardly anything.'

'Any difference now?'

'It's gone . . . it's back again.'

'Can you see anything else? Anything at all?'

'No.'

Dr Stroud sat back and considered Ben. He had never seen him standing up, so he judged him by his powerful physique. A fine big chap, he thought. He knew Ben was registered as a farm labourer, but would have guessed it anyway. Ben's short square hands had calloused palms, and the brown of his sunburned arms and throat contrasted with the milky skin of his shoulders, upper arms and smooth chest. He didn't believe in parting with his shirt when he was working.

To Dr Stroud, he seemed an unlikely mate for Lesley Grant, whom he remembered as a bright, rather sensitive girl, who might have trained to be a doctor herself if her circumstances had allowed it. A vulnerable girl, unfortunately, he thought, and not over blessed with a sense of humour. It was to be hoped that Ben would understand that he was not the only one needing help.

He said, 'The news isn't too good, Ben. There's nothing to be done about your right eye, and the left – well, it's doubtful if we can do much more. We re-attached the retina, but it detached again almost at once. There's only a slight chance that further surgery will help. Trouble is, the macula's been off – do you understand?' The doctor knew he was dealing with a man of limited education but quick intelligence. He had tried to explain his condition to Ben earlier, but he had shown no interest, probably due to a combination of sedation and shock.

'I don't understand anything,' said Ben flatly. 'I don't even know exactly what a retina is.'

Dr Stroud sat back, putting the ends of his fingers together. 'The seat of vision is at the back of your brain,' he said. 'Think of your brain as a computer which won't work unless it's fed with information. The retina is part of your brain and gathers information in the form of a picture. It photographs the information through the lens in your eye, and the optic nerve passes it back to the brain. The brain interprets the photograph, and stores the information in the memory – like a computer again.'

'The camera's broken, you mean?'

'Something like that. The retina is the film, not the camera itself. It takes colour photos and develops them ten times every second as long as your eyes are open. An eye without a retina is like a camera whose film has slipped. But don't forget that's only a fraction of what your brain does. You taste, feel, smell, hear – all your senses pass messages back to your brain in their various ways.'

'Aren't you going to have another crack at loading the camera? Lesley said you re-attached retinas all the time.'

Dr Stroud wished he knew Ben better. It was hard to judge a man he'd never met in a normal frame of mind; Ben was still in a state of shock. Perhaps a harsher approach would have been more suitable, then again, the true verdict might turn natural incredulity to depression and withdrawal – perhaps even suicide. The doctor knew there was virtually no hope for Ben's sight, but he softened the verdict.

'We may be able to do something further,' he said. 'It depends. As you are, there's no disfigurement. If we persist in trying to patch you up, there may be.'

Ben's hands clenched. With his first sign of animation, he asked, 'No disfigurement? You're sure of that?'

'Certain. Ben, I wish you'd gone to your doctor sooner. In a case like yours, speedy action is a must. Boxers sometimes detach a retina after a violent blow to the head, but they're caught in time, they don't lose their sight. I can't understand why you did nothing.'

Ben considered. 'It goes back a long way,' he said. 'I used to have nightmares about a blind man when I was a little lad. Nothing frightened me so much.' He thought about it, his fingers pleating the sheet. At last he went on, 'It isn't so very different from cancer. My aunt, my father's sister, was afraid to go to the doctor when she found a lump in her breast. It was only the size of a pea when she noticed it. She died of cancer, and they say she could easily have been saved. But she had this dread of cancer – she saw her mother die of it.'

'Understandable, I suppose, but a dreadful waste. Well, Ben, I must hand you over to some very capable people who will help you to cope with your condition until you leave here. Let's hope that in the future, some means will be devised for grafting a new retina. Medicine advances all the time, and there is almost always some hope, however slight, for the unsighted.' Dr Stroud felt that he had done his best to let Ben down lightly. He got up and left, saying 'Goodbye' from the door.

Ben sat up in bed, staring in the direction the voice had come from. 'You lying bastard,' he yelled. 'I'm blind. "Unsighted" – Christ, what a word! I'm blind, man. Blind.'

To the surprise of both, Lesley and Agatha had formed a sort of alliance. Friendship was definitely not the word for it. Lesley's charitable idea of giving the poor old thing a bed for a night or two had not worked out as she had planned. Agatha had settled herself firmly into the room vacated by Imogen, had unpacked, and the next day had summoned a taxi to take her to the hospital. There, she had been allowed only a few minutes with Ben, after which she had returned to the flat.

On the second day, she went through the same routine. When Lesley got back from work, she found Agatha reading a paper by the window. They exchanged looks which told that there was no further news of Ben.

Lesley prepared a meal, and they ate sparingly. Agatha said

nothing; Lesley made a few polite remarks. After a while, she said, 'I wonder where Hazel's got to.'

'I was obliged to complain about her table manners,' said Agatha. 'She was then extremely uncivil to me. She has gone to seek accommodation elsewhere. Doubtless, she will return to collect her belongings.'

'Doubtless,' agreed Lesley. 'You didn't tell her to go, did you?'

'Certainly not. She suggested it herself, and in the crudest of terms.'

'She owes me a month's rent,' said Lesley.

'What is a month's rent when it is compared with freedom from vexation and with privacy?' demanded Agatha.

Lesley said, 'I'm obliged to keep this flat until my husband shows up. It's expensive, so I share it. I've been living in a cottage of Mr Thorpe's since Ben and I set up house together. I moved out the day you came. I agree that Hazel's a pain – I just wish she'd paid.'

Agatha stood up, pushing herself out of her chair with both hands. 'I appear to have been thoughtless,' she said. She went into her bedroom.

Lesley wished that she and Ben's grandmother could share their grief. She supposed they did in a way, but there wasn't much comfort in it. Even in a few days, she could see a difference in Agatha. Outwardly she was unchanged – perhaps a little less active, but the hurt in those cold eyes was plain to see. And with every hour they were together, Lesley became more convinced that Ben was Agatha over again.

Ben had told her about Agatha's elopement and disinheritance. He had said that those events had unhinged her. What would the trauma of blindness do to Ben? She shuddered. For in Agatha's bitterness she could see traces of Ben's passion; in her tantrums and spite, there were echoes of Ben's aggression. She thought that the basically sweet nature that Ben took pains to conceal from most people, might exist locked up inside his grandmother's steel armour.

Agatha came out of the bedroom. 'I have been at fault,' she

said, adding untruthfully, 'I never hesitate to admit a fault in myself.' She placed five Irish ten pound notes on the table between them. They were warm, crumpled, and smelled of talcum powder.

'But Mrs Logan, I can't take –'

'Don't be a fool, girl. If you do not need the money now, you may rest assured that you will when you have Benedict to care for. I am convinced that you are the best person to look after him. You may consider it a months' rent in advance. Take it.'

The last words were an order. Lesley did as she was told.

That evening, Agatha watched Lesley leaving the flat with real regret. She no longer thought of her as Benedict's concubine . . . a pretty word, she thought, it sounds like a climbing plant. What was the matter with her today? Her thoughts were tangled, and she was not always able to find the word she needed.

She had talked to Lesley today – *really* talked for the first time. Lesley insisted that there was hope for Ben's sight. Agatha knew somehow that there was none. She had known for several days.

Lesley had gone to spend the evening with a blind girl named Henrietta who had, she said, been given a music centre. Lesley had explained that this was not a shop like *Sound and Fury*, but a – what *had* she said? Not a gramophone nor yet a wireless. It was all most confusing. She was a good-hearted girl, this Lesley. She had left a pie in the oven for Agatha's supper, and an evening paper on the table.

As Agatha picked up the paper, she shivered, although the flat was warm. The cold tremors were getting more frequent. Difficult to ignore. She remembered having her hair cut, the icy shudder, the feeling as if her head were stuffed with cotton wool, Miss Clare running for the doctor. She had put Dr Blake's words out of her mind, but they returned now. 'A mild attack . . . another could be far more serious, even fatal.'

Agatha went to Lesley's desk and found writing paper and

142

envelopes. How she hated those stupid modern pens which ruined your writing and couldn't be refilled! And of course there was no ink. She found a green felt pen and began to write. That was better. Good thick lines; you could read it.

To whom it may concern: If I should die, I may as well be buried or burned here whichever is the cheaper. I deplore the practice of ferrying corpses here and there. Morbid. I want no religious service unless it is required by law.

My grandson, Benedict Glyn, who by the terms of my will is to receive my unencumbered property, may also have my wedding ring. He may give my rosewood writing-table to Mrs Lesley Peabody (or Grant) if they marry. Not otherwise on any account. The wedding ring will save him unnecessary expense.

My daughter Muriel may have my clothes.

To my husband Michael I consider I have already given more than enough.

Somebody should inform my sister, Miss Flora Vere-Lanigan, of my death. She lives in Harrogate; I have forgotten the address. . . .

Agatha read the letter through, wrote 'To be opened in the event of my death' on the envelope, and propped it up against an ornament. She opened the paper and sat down at the desk again.

As she sat in the wing chair, Agatha found that her thoughts were straying back to her childhood. She must be getting feeble. Her thoughts were not allowed to stray. There was a barrier in her mind as effective and as unpleasant as the Berlin Wall, and there her reflections were encouraged to stop and go back no further. Somewhere in the early 'thirties, about the time Muriel was born.

But now her thoughts, out of control, were rushing back to her girlhood. She and her sisters had been virtual prisoners at Castle Lanigan, while their brother had gone to an English public school. Constance had married a visiting master of hounds from Yorkshire; Flora had seemed content to spend all her time in the garden. But Agatha, apart from her music, for she sang, and played the piano and the violin, had no outlet for her stormy personality. Her sisters read and talked about romance. Agatha dreamed of a grand passion – the world well lost for love.

Walton Carmichael was a divorcé, ten years older than she. He had served all through the Great War, as it was still called, and his wife had gone off with another man while he was abroad. He was living alone in a mansion near Castle Lanigan. Agatha did her best to turn a mild flirtation into a grand passion, but she had picked the wrong man. It had slowly dawned on her that Walton preferred to be alone. She took it as a personal insult and tried to quarrel with him, but there wasn't enough passion left in him even to quarrel.

'My dear,' he had said, 'I wish you weren't so quarrelsome. It's very wearing. You're more than an attractive girl – you're spectacular, but you are also selfish and spoilt. I have married one spoilt, selfish woman already; that's enough for anybody.'

Even now, the memory of his words had power to wound.

There had followed years of boredom. She was given a niggardly dress allowance; there was nothing that she wanted to do. She was twenty-seven when, at harvest time, her eye fell on an amazingly handsome young man pitching sheaves up onto the ricks. As the load grew lower, Michael Logan had to throw the sheaves higher. Agatha watched fascinated as each one landed neatly at the feet of old John Joseph who was building the rick.

The cart empty, Michael jumped down and saw Miss Agatha watching him. He smiled at her – a brilliant smile which lighted his sunburned face. Poor devil, from that moment, his fate was sealed.

144

Agatha knew she had made a mistake before she and Michael had been married a week. She had been thrilled by the runaway match, careless of her father's rage. Michael's main concern had been to run as fast and as far as possible. Their combined savings took them only to a comfortless terrace house in Dublin, where disillusionment set in.

Apart from her music, Agatha's only accomplishment had been fine needlework. She couldn't mend or darn, she couldn't cook. She had ignored her pregnancy until it became impossible to ignore any longer. Then she had fixed her hopes on a son – a little boy with Michael's looks and her own iron determination. She and Michael had moved to Cloninch with its five-bedroomed farmhouse and its hundred fertile acres. Her little boy would start his career as a farmer. But he would not be satisfied to plod along. No, he would excell in everything he did, and be all that she had hoped Michael would be. He would fulfil her dreams.

When Muriel had been born, something in Agatha had snapped. She would have no more children, she would run the farm (and Michael) herself, she would ignore the passage of time. She would exist independently, and never allow anything or anyone to touch her emotions again.

She had succeeded. A fleeting picture of Benedict came to her mind. She amended her thoughts – she had almost succeeded.

She sat back, feeling very tired, and began to glance through the paper.

It was almost midnight when Lesley let herself into the flat. An acrid smell met her at the door. She ran to the stove, and opened the oven door. Black smoked poured out. Agatha had forgotten the pie, and it was burned to a cinder. Lesley hurried to the dustbin with it, coughing. Then she saw that Agatha was sitting at the writing desk, her back turned, in the wing chair that had belonged to Mark. Couldn't she smell the smoke?

Lesley thought Agatha must have fallen asleep. She picked

up the newspaper from the floor, pausing as a headline caught her eye.

'Art Treasure Dumped in Field. Valued at £250,000.'

'Wake up, Mrs Logan,' she said, gently shaking her shoulder.

Agatha's head was propped in the angle of the wing back. Her hands rested on the arms of the chair. On her face was an expression of fury.

She was dead.

Nine

There was a first day of term feeling at the Leeds Training Centre. The first day of a new residential course had ended, and the students had gone to bed. There were ten of them, six men and four women, ranging in age from seventeen to fifty; each facing the four weeks ahead hopefully. Some doubted their ability to work with a dog, some were quietly confident, others nervous. They had little in common besides their blindness, coming from all walks of life – a policeman, a schoolboy, a hairdresser, a company director.

Leeds had the newest centre in England, and it was still unfinished. Extra kennels were being built in what had been the orchard of the old house. Outdoor runs were shaded by the old fruit trees. The existing kennels were converted stables in the courtyard, where there was an impressive archway and a brass bell which had once summoned farmhands to their dinner.

The city of Leeds had sprawled westwards, almost encircling the old Manor Farm. Housing estates had sprung up in its outlying meadows, and a new road bisected the original home farm. The house stood facing down a slight slope, its back to the city. Flowering chestnut trees, pink and white, lined the short drive.

'You might think you were in the country if you were wearing ear-plugs,' said Michael Jones, the director, to Geoff. They were standing on the steps, taking a breather after a long hard day.

'Mm,' said Geoff, not paying much attention. He was the most senior of the three instructors, and his literal mind had no room for fanciful ideas. They were not in the country; why pretend they were? The ten students and ten dogs occupied all his waking thoughts. He could hear the kennel maids shutting the dogs up for the night, for there were fifty in training in addition to the ten which had been allocated. There was a daytime staff of forty, plus part time and voluntary workers.

Bob joined Michael and Geoff on the steps; he had spent the day catching up on paperwork, while the other puppy walking supervisor, Jessica, had been out all day on routine calls.

'How's that Border collie pup doing, Bob?' asked Geoff. 'Brother of Meg's.'

'No problems so far,' said Bob. 'The Carters have walked three Borders now; I don't expect any trouble if Max is as steady as his sister.'

'They're so damned active mentally,' said Geoff. 'They're harder to keep out of mischief than Labs. Still, I wouldn't look any further than Meg if I needed a guide myself.'

'I'll bear it in mind,' said Michael dryly. 'Well, I think I'm for an early bed.' As he went across the hall, he turned his head to say, 'You wouldn't be keeping Meg for yourself, Geoff, just in case?' He didn't wait for an answer.

Geoff said to Bob, 'It's a good job I did keep that bitch on, in spite of Michael. We could easily have Ben Glyn on the next course, and she'd be just the dog for him. I hear the news isn't good.'

'Yes, a bad job, that. Tina was talking to Lesley about him. Poor lass, she simply adores him. It's a heaven sent coincidence for him though, isn't it?'

'Don't know.' Geoff stared into the gathering darkness. 'I suppose it is. He can be a touchy little sod, can Ben; he's not as simple a character as I thought. If he'd settle for a dog, it might be the saving of him.'

'Ho ho,' laughed Bob. 'Instead of Lesley? He's blind, man, not insane. 'Night Geoff.' He went off to his house in the yard, pausing to look in at some of the dogs. Two had come in from their walk that day, had their routine baths and veterinary examination, had been weighed and recorded in the files. They were whimpering miserably, missing the families they'd been with since they were six weeks old. It was surprising how quickly the new dogs adjusted, though, thought Bob. A matter of days.

Meg was lying in her kennel, her nose as usual resting on her crossed forepaws. She raised one ear and rolled an eye upward when she saw Bob, but didn't get up.

Bob found Tina watching a movie on tv. Her job, catering for sixty to seventy people, was quite as arduous as his, but she worked regular hours. Bob might be called out at any time. He poured them a whisky apiece, and they drank in companionable silence. By midnight, they were sound asleep in bed.

They were woken by the bedside phone at 1 am. 'Bloody hell,' said Bob. 'You answer it, Tina. If it's a puppy walker with a crisis, tell him I'm dead.'

Tina, who knew that Bob wouldn't think twice about going out, picked up the phone reluctantly. 'Yes? *What?* Good lord! Yes, of course you can. . . . Do you want us to come for you? Sure? See you then.'

She jumped out of bed. 'It's Lesley. She came home an hour ago, and found Ben's grandmother dead in her chair. The doctor's been, and the old lady's been taken away, but Lesley couldn't face sleeping there tonight. I said she could come here.'

'You did right. Funny that – Lesley's tough, and it's not as if she'd liked Mrs Logan. She said she was a terrifying old crone with a heart of flint.'

'She isn't as tough as you think,' said Tina.

Lesley had gone to bed in her flat when the ambulance had taken Agatha away, but the feeling that she was being watched had been too much for her. It was as if the old woman was still there. Even when Agatha had been laid on the bed with her eyes closed, Lesley had been conscious of her cold scrutiny.

When the doctor had examined Agatha's body, he had found more than five hundred pounds fastened to her underwear with safety pins. Lesley had found and read the letter. The doctor knew her well, and told her to take care of the money for funeral expenses. He eased the wedding ring off the knotted finger and put it on the table. 'You'd better take care of this too,' he said. 'Had she any relations besides Ben?'

Lesley had said she'd notify them, and tell Ben in the morning. In Tina's pretty chintzy bedroom, she could shake off the presence of those fierce hooded eyes, but she couldn't sleep. She lay with aching throat and dry, burning eyes, wondering how she would break the news to Ben.

'I'm due a week's holiday,' she said at breakfast, 'So I'm taking it now. And thank you for everything.'

Afterwards, she looked up Miss Flora Vere-Lanigan in a Harrogate directory, and left a message with her daily help.

Lesley put the cash and the wedding ring in the bank for safe keeping, returned to the flat and packed Agatha's clothes in the gladstone bag. Her feelings of regret surprised her. She sat on the floor on her heels with a cameo brooch in her hands, wondering what to do with it.

— You may as well keep it. It is of little value.

Lesley started, and dropped the brooch. She picked it up, pinned it to the neck of a blouse and returned both to the bag. She mustn't start imagining things.

At the hospital, Ben was absent from his room. A pimply young house doctor told her that he'd turned violent, put his fist through a pane of glass and was having it stitched. She sat down and put her head in her hands.

Presently, two men came to repair the glass, and she moved to the corridor.

Lesley looked up and saw Ben walking towards her, a nurse leading him by the arm. He walked with his head high, and she was reminded of the way he used to march straight into the wind on the moors. His right hand and wrist were bandaged. He still exuded vitality, and on his face was an expression of rage. She didn't speak, knowing that he would hate to know that he was watched. As he passed, his grey eyes met hers coldly, fiercely. It was almost impossible to believe that he couldn't see her. She waited until he was back in his room, where the workmen were departing.

'Wouldn't like to annoy you, mate,' said one. 'That's double glazed.'

The nurse guided Ben to a chair. He was dressed in jersey and trousers, but was barefooted. 'Throwing his shoes about,' the nurse mouthed at Lesley.

'What? Who's there? Lesley?'

The nurse whispered, 'Got it into his head there's something wrong with his granny.'

Lesley pushed past her. 'I'm here, Ben.' She announced herself as she'd been trained to do, staying still so that Ben would be spared talking to the place where he thought she was, and being answered from somewhere else.

'Tell me,' said Ben. 'For God's sake tell me. They don't know and they won't try to find out. Is she ill? Is she dead?'

'She's dead, Ben. She had a stroke last night at my place. The doctor thought she must have died at once – she was still sitting in her chair – oh, I'm sorry, love. I was – not fond of her exactly, but we got on. She loved you, Ben.'

'She didn't love anybody,' said Ben in a low voice, 'but I can't imagine life without her.'

The whole family came from Ireland for the funeral. They respected Agatha's wishes in so far as they didn't take her body back to Ireland, but they insisted on a conventional funeral service. Not cremation.

'She was a good Catholic,' sobbed Muriel.

'Was she hell as like,' said the Guvnor aside to Mandy. 'She was a ruddy heathen. She'd a good head on her though. Sensible.'

They were waiting for the hearse to arrive at St John's Hospital, the Glyns all together like a flock of cornered sheep.

They'd been waiting for years for Agatha to die. Now that she had, the lynchpin was gone. They didn't know where to turn or what to do without her tyrannical rule. Ben was still not allowed out, to Lesley's relief. Of Agatha's sister there was no sign.

Lesley, neat in a charcoal suit and her most restrained earrings, stood despondently, waiting. She hated to see Agatha's wishes ignored. She had nearly quarrelled with Mandy, whose exclamations, 'Isn't it awful? Did you ever? Oh, the poor old thing and all alone too,' had almost driven her to screaming point. As she waited, she thought about Mandy, and how friendship can become a habit. She had turned to the other girl when her father had died, and Mandy's kindness had helped her to get started on a new life. But even then, there'd been that vicarious thrill, that feeding on misfortune.

A taxi drew up, and a large, fat old woman scrambled out of it. She shut her coat in the door, freed it and dropped her handbag. It opened, and loose change rolled on the ground. Lesley bent to help pick it up.

'Are you Miss Vere-Lanigan?' she asked.

In a welter of half finished sentences, the old woman said she was. She straightened up, and Lesley had a chance to study her. Wildly untidy, she wore a battered black straw hat on her longish grey curling hair. She seemed to have thrown on the first garments that came handy; a flowered cotton skirt, a blue cardigan over a pink jumper over a red blouse. Gold chains of different lengths and thicknesses swung from her neck. She had covered it all up with a shapeless black coat, flapping open, shorter than her skirt. A perfect shell pink rose was pinned to the coat. Her broad face was pink under layers of powder. Lipstick of a cruel shade of cyclamen was slashed across her mouth, and had seeped into the tiny vertical lines which time had etched above and below her lips.

'I'm Lesley Grant,' said Lesley. 'I'm so sorry about your sister. She was staying with me when she died.' Could this old haybag be related to the corpse on the bier? she thought. Yes, because Flora had Agatha's craggy nose, which sat incongruously on her round powdery face.

At this point, Flora burst into torrents of tears. She flung herself at Lesley, who took a hasty step back, but was obliged to submit to being kissed on both cheeks. The kisses left damp pink smears. Flora rummaged for a handkerchief, gasping.

Lesley wiped her own face with a tissue and glanced at the Glyn family. But they had shied away from Flora like frightened horses – all their backs were turned. She was relieved when the hearse arrived.

At the graveside, Lesley managed to interpose the Guvnor's solid bulk between herself and Flora. Standing still, she looked like an old woman in a cartoon. Her massive body and legs tapered down to tiny ankles and feet.

As they walked back to the waiting cars, Flora cried out, 'You were the only one who cared about her!' and again enfolded Lesley in a damp, powdery, scented hug. Then she turned to Mandy, who showed an unusual turn of speed and fled.

Lesley had a light headed feeling of unreality. The funeral seemed too bogus to be sad.

– A vulgar charade. Hypocrites.

She couldn't remember Agatha saying that, but for a moment, the scornful voice sounded clearer than the priest's.

Then they all went to see Ben. Myles, Muriel, Denis, Brian and Mike. Sheila had stayed at Cloninch to look after old Michael and little Sarah.

Mandy insisted on going along too, but the Guvnor refused. Instead, he took Lesley to a cafe and ordered a pot of strong tea and beef sandwiches. Flora agreed to join them, then changed her mind and decided to go and see her great-nephew. Lesley and Charlie tried hard to stop her, but Flora showed some of Agatha's mettle. She won by showing signs of weeping over Charlie (Lesley was still strategically keeping him between herself and Flora). Charlie told her sharply to give over. 'You'll make yourself badly,' he said, and almost lifted her into the waiting taxi.

The tea was hot and reasonably strong. The Guvnor tore the teabags open with a fork to help it along.

'I been thinking, lass,' he said. 'Ben isn't forced to get his sight back, is he?'

'No,' said Lesley. 'I don't believe he will.' She swallowed a mouthful of tea, and looked at her plate.

'What about cottage then? D'you reckon he could make out living there? He can have it for nowt – aye, and you can stop with him, same as before.'

Lesley looked up. 'It's a wonderful offer,' she said. 'I think it would be perfect for Ben. As for me, we'll have to wait and see what he wants.'

'Oh aye? He wants you, doesn't he? Fair soft about you. You want to get shut of that Peabody – I never thowt anything to him – then you can get wed.'

'I wish it was that simple. Thank you anyway. Ben should stay in the place he knows; he's had a shock to recover from, a double shock. His reactions are extreme. He alternates between aggression and dull acceptance. He's miles from any sort of adjustment.'

'You what?' said Charlie. 'You've had too much schooling, I reckon. You wrap things up, so I can't make head nor tail of them. Lad's gone blind; he wants his own home and the woman he's used to. Isn't that what you mean?'

Lesley gave him a shaky grin. 'Something like that,' she said.

Charlie went to the hospital when he judged that Ben's family would have left it. He was wrong.

Ben was in the same dim room, standing with his back to the wall and his arms folded. The angry look had given way to an expression of bewilderment. His parents, his brothers, Flora and Mandy were all talking at once, suggesting cups of tea, tranquillizers, a drink, a rest. They crowded round him, speaking loudly as if he were deaf, their voices determinedly kind and patient. Ben turned his head from side to side, baffled.

Charlie was reminded suddenly of a day at York market. He'd been watching a little Angus bull in a pen. It had stood with lowered head, pawing the ground, turning this way and that, as the buyers crowded round, discussing in loud voices its probable weight and value.

He heard Muriel say, 'You musn't worry any more, Ben. We'll take you back to Ireland right away. We'll look after you properly, won't we, Myles? You musn't be unhappy any more.'

Ben turned his head in her direction. He said, 'Where would I live? Who'd pay? What would I do? I don't want to go back. I know my way round the cottage; maybe the Guvnor'll let me stay until I get the hang of things.'

Muriel turned to Mandy. 'We can't let him stay here,' she said. 'His place now is at home with his family. We'll cheer him up – we won't let him be miserable.'

Charlie stormed into the group, his temper, always fragile, snapping. 'What's gitten into you?' he shouted. 'Why shouldn't he be miserable? Be a bloody rum lad if he weren't, wouldn't he? Any road, he's a right to his own feelings.' He turned on Myles, who backed away. 'Let him be can't you, you daft sods! I'd like to throw the whole boiling of you out into street. He's gone blind – of course he's unhappy! Let him get over it his own way; you make him worse nor what he is with your wowing and genning. Moving him around, messing him about – you make me sick!'

There was a stunned silence. Ben looked gratefully in the direction of the shouting.

Mandy nervously put her hand on Charlie's arm. 'Don't worry, father,' she said. 'We understand Ben, really we do.'

Charlie shook her off as a ward sister bore down on him. 'What's all this noise? Kindly keep your voice down,' hissed the nurse.

Charlie, his face crimson, glared at her, then he turned back to the others who were standing gaping. Speaking softly, he said, 'Aye, you may well stay stood there gawping. You don't understand nowt about him. I've had my say; if you've owt to say to me, say it.'

Nobody had anything to say to him. One by one, they sidled past him and out of the room.

'Have they all gone?' asked Ben.

'Aye, they've gone. How do you come to have such a set of clodpolls for a family? The old 'un was worth the lot of them, she was that.' He saw that Ben was smiling.

Ben had heard the Guvnor shouting through a fog of bewilderment and misery. Ever since he'd lost his temper with the house doctor at the time of Agatha's death, he had been living in a sort of blank. He could hardly remember striking out in impotent rage and hitting glass, although his bandaged hand still throbbed. He could hardly remember the reason, except that it concerned Agatha. But he *had* struck out, and then hurled a shoe after the disappearing footsteps.

He was furious because he'd been told off by an unidentified voice, because he hadn't been allowed to go to Agatha's funeral, because he couldn't be sure he was alone. He'd been glad when he'd been told that his mother was there, then puzzled by the medley of voices. No one, not even his mother, touched him. He had felt like an animal at the zoo. He was being offered some sort of cushioned existence as a monkey might be offered a banana; the familiar voices loud with nervous self-consciousness.

The Guvnor's angry shouts brought instant silence. Then there was a half protest from his father, a stifled whimper from his mother. . . . Where was Lesley? Whose was the fat, motherly voice which burbled about a garden of scented flowers grown especially for the blind? He felt the room emptying, the space round him being vacated.

'I scattered 'em,' said Charlie. 'Numbskulls.'

'Mother didn't mean any harm,' said Ben defensively. Then he felt himself grinning. 'Thanks,' he said. 'Why were they bullying me like that, I wonder? I thought they'd be pleased that I was being looked after here.'

'Blood's thicker nor water,' pronounced Charlie. 'How's the hand? Savage devil, aren't you? We'll be glad to see you back in cottage.'

'I'll be glad to get out of here,' said Ben. 'And I mean to do everything for myself right from the start. I've been scared stiff for the past weeks. Thought I'd be helpless and penniless, maybe weaving raffia mats, but I've been getting around in here pretty well.'

'Pretty well? You're black and blue, lad.'

'Yeah, well, I sort of went berserk. I thought I was on my own, started talking to myself. Then I heard breathing, and there was a man, a doctor I suppose, sitting there. I didn't really know what I was doing. I chased him out, and I went all round the walls to make sure there weren't any more of them. I walked my face into a door, then I fell over something and got a few bruises. I'd lock myself in, but there's no key.' He added regretfully, 'I don't see that I can come back to your cottage. It goes with the job.'

'You'll have to if you aren't off back to Ireland. Or would you sooner stop in Leeds at Lesley's place?'

'I can't do that.'

'You aren't going to ditch poor lass, are you?'

'I wouldn't put it like that,' said Ben. 'There's a chance I might get back the sight of one eye. When I do – if I do, we'll get married.'

He sensed Charlie's angry incredulity. 'You're a fool if you wait,' he said. 'Her husband's back in Leeds; Mandy saw him. I don't say Lesley'll go back to him – she's not as left to herself as that – but he'll be here for divorce. Don't wait too long.' He said goodbye, clapping Ben unexpectedly on the shoulder. The door banged.

'Guvnor?' said Ben. There was no answer. He left the window where he'd been standing since his family arrived and, hands extended, made for the door with a rush. He was incapable of taking things slowly and learning every detail of the little room. The bed was in his path — it skated away. Some piece of furniture without castors grated on the vinyl floor. He grabbed the iron frame of the bed and stood listening. Then he threw himself down on the bed which suddenly seemed to be the most desirable place in the world. He dragged at the covers, kicking his way between the tidy sheets. He was back in the limbo of the first days.

When a nurse brought his supper, he refused to sit up and eat. But when she threatened to feed him, he reached for the plate.

When he had been immobilized, he had been fed from a spoon. As long as he had been told, 'This is mince, or potato or whatever it was, he had swallowed the food, even enjoying it. But sometimes a nurse in a hurry would feed him a mouthful of some unspecified substance. This always made him gag, unable to force it down. Hunger was preferable.

The nurse said brightly, 'I hear you're leaving us tomorrow.'

'Am I?' said Ben. 'I didn't know.'

'Yes, you're going to live in the country — Middlegarth — lucky you. Lesley Peabody's a lovely person.'

'Would you please go away,' said Ben. 'I want to undress.'

'Sure you can manage?'

'Just clear off will you, like a good girl.' He got up and checked every inch of the room to make sure she'd gone. Then he stripped off his clothes and dropped them on the floor. He made a short and futile search for his pyjamas. He bent down to find his shirt where he had dropped it and hit his forehead on his locker. He located his underpants and put them on. He plunged back into bed.

As sleep evaded him, Ben found that there was nothing he could bear to think about, so he tried to make his mind a blank. He could remember what people looked like, but when he tried to examine them in his mind's eye, their likenesses slid away. Their voices were clear enough.

– I trust you will play your guitar, Benedict. I have brought it at considerable inconvenience.

'I shall never forgive myself – never,' said Flora.

I shall go mad, thought Lesley. She had heard Charlie's routing the Job's comforters from Ben's room. She had seen the Glyn family leave, and Flora, who had decided that perhaps she loved them all, throwing her arms round those who were too slow to avoid her.

She had seen Ben's elder brother supporting his weeping mother, Myles on her other side, the younger boys glancing back nervously in case Charlie was following. She had backed into a doorway when Mandy hurried by, sniffing. But when Flora trotted towards her, she had felt guiltily obliged to help. The Irish family, she knew, was booked into a hotel, but she had thought Ben might expect her to do something about Flora.

They sat in the waiting room where Agatha and Charlie had talked. Flora clutched Lesley's hand like a child and repeated that she wouldn't forgive herself ever.

Lesley patted the fat hand, whose fingers bore almost as many rings as her own. 'Please don't worry, Miss Vere-Lanigan. I'm sure you've nothing to blame yourself for.'

'I'm eighty years old, alone and bereft,' said Flora with a tragic smile. 'I deserve it, I suppose.'

Hell, thought Lesley, she's enjoying herself. 'Mrs Logan wasn't an easy person,' she said.

Flora stared. 'Agatha?' she said. 'I'm not talking about Agatha. I'm talking about my painting. Agatha kept it in Ireland, but I know our dear mother would have wished me to have it.'

Lesley said, 'Do you mean the *Young Girl in a Garden*? Mrs Logan left it to Ben in her will.'

For answer, Flora went off into peals of laughter. 'There's poetic justice for you,' she said. Lesley wondered if she should call a doctor or slap her face.

'Shall I call a taxi to take you to your hotel?' she asked.

Flora stopped laughing as suddenly as she'd begun. 'Oh my goodness,' she cried. She plunged into her oversized handbag, scooping out a mass of papers and crumpled hankies. 'I've left my purse and my cheque book at home,' she said, 'and I haven't booked in anywhere.'

Lesley took a deep breath and said, as calmly as she could, 'I can put you up for the night, but you'll be on your own – I'm going out myself. I won't be in until late. You can get some money in the morning when the banks open, and I'll put you on the Harrogate bus.' She evaded Flora's grateful embrace, and led the way rapidly to the car park.

Lesley's flat was tidy, but felt unlived-in. She had stayed at the Training Centre for three nights, and was glad in a way not to be going home alone.

Flora, who had quietened down, asked for a mug of cocoa. She sat down in the wing chair and opened the paper.

'That's Thursday's,' said Lesley. 'I haven't bought a paper since Mrs Logan died. I haven't even read that one.'

Flora was staring at the page. 'I suppose that was what finally killed her,' she said.

Lesley put down the cocoa. Bonkers, she thought. 'What did?' she said.

Flora pointed. *Art Treasure Dumped in Field*. Lesley had noticed the headline when she found the paper beside Agatha's body. She bent over to look.

> *Valued at in excess of a quarter million, the painting by fashionable Victorian artist James Tissot was in the back of a van stolen from the rear of the 'Crock of Gold' licensed premises on Thomond Quay last Monday.*
>
> *Discovered by schoolchildren, the canvas had been almost destroyed by a herd of cows, the property of Mr Thomas Mullins, 71, who also owns the land.*

The van has not been recovered, and it would appear
that the painting, which was wrapped in sacking,
was thrown over the hedge by the thieves.

'I had no notion it was worth all that,' said Myles
Glyn, 56, farmer, of Cloninch in Co Kildare. . . . The
painting had been insured for a mere £800, but the
premium is believed not to have been renewed. Mrs
Agatha Logan, 82, owner of the picture, is at present
unavailable for comment.

There was a photograph of Myles, looking sheepish;
holding in one hand the splintered frame, in the other a
tattered object which might have been anything.
'Owner of the picture!' cried Flora. 'The audacity of it.'
'Do you know if Ben was told about this?' Lesley asked.
'I don't know . . . I don't think . . . Does it matter?'
'If the painting was left to Ben, it matters quite a lot.'
'Oh nonsense, dear. It was mine.'
Lesley bit her lip. She showed Flora her bedroom, lent her a
nightdress, and went out.

There was no light in the upstairs flat, but Lesley could hear
the stereo. Henrietta's taste ran to country and western, even
the soppy, little boy lost sort. She also liked early rock
numbers and, surprisingly, chamber music. She greeted
Lesley affectionately, and turned down the sound. Her
movements were totally assured now, and Lesley visited her
only twice a week to do her shopping.
'I've come for sympathy and understanding,' said Lesley.
'Role reversal. Are you on?'
'You sound as if you needed it. Yes, I'll be a Dutch aunt, if
there is such a thing. Are you going to tell me you've
quarrelled with Ben and beg for advice?'
'No,' said Lesley. 'Much more serious than that. It's the
sort of coincidence you read about in trashy books. He's gone
blind. You're the only person I know who won't give me a lot

161

of baloney about grit and stamina and courage. Me being so capable and Ben being so brave. You *know*.' She added with a forced laugh, 'If you put it in an article, I'll never speak to you again.'

'I wouldn't blame you. Lesley, I'm shattered – what can I say? I've been so happy for you and Ben.'

'I wish I thought he'd make out as well as you do.'

'You're joking. Owen's stuck by me for two years, he phones me twice a day and he's given me this stereo, but I still can't make my mind up to let him see me like this. If I don't decide soon, he'll stop wanting to see me. Serve me right if he did.'

'He won't,' said Lesley.

'I'm not so sure. I think perhaps we should say goodbye.' Henrietta leaned back in her chair, thinking. 'I'd get by,' she said, 'probably better than Owen. I'm tough – a thin-skinned reporter isn't much use. Probably I'm tougher than Ben, and from what you say he hasn't many resources. Thank God he's got you.'

'Yes, well. He has and he hasn't. I'm not sure that I'm the person to help him; I don't feel that I've enough patience. His mad great-aunt is staying in my flat by the way.'

'Oh, *that's* why you're here. Did you say you were short of patience? You don't know what you're talking about.'

They listened to music and talked until late. At last Lesley said, 'I suppose I'd better go. Miss Vere-Lanigan might burn the house down. Nothing would surprise me.'

'Not Flora Vere-Lanigan?'

'Yes, from Harrogate. Why?'

'She's a celebrity. Used to grow roses, and there's a rose named "Flora" after her. I interviewed her once. Crazy old bag but rather amusing. And she says she owns Ben's picture? I scent a story.'

'That new nose of yours will get you into trouble,' said Lesley. 'Goodnight, and thank you. You should cheer people up professionally.'

'No thanks. I aim to shock you, amaze you, and make you buy the paper.'

When Lesley got home, she found a wilting rose on her pillow and a note which read, 'Bless you, dear. Sweet dreams.'

She dreamed about Agatha.

Ten

Geoff was too busy to call and see Ben. He was working at the Centre all day and every day, often staying overnight. He phoned the cottage at Middlegarth twice, but there was no answer.

One evening, a week after Agatha's funeral, he called at Lesley's flat. She opened the door, looking haggard in shirt and slacks. He thought there was something missing, and realized he'd never seen her without earrings before.

'Come in, Geoff; I'm delighted to see you,' she said. She sounded extravagantly pleased. Geoff followed her into the living room, where an untidily dressed old woman was sorting through a boxful of papers. She looked up, and Geoff was startled by her garish makeup. She beamed at him, and Lesley introduced them, saying, 'This is Geoff Merchant, who instructs at the Training Centre, Aunt Flora;' and to Geoff, 'Miss Vere-Lanigan is Ben's great-aunt.'

Lesley, knowing Geoff's preferences, offered to make a pot of tea, but Flora asked for, and downed, a large gin and French. While Lesley was making the tea, Flora talked to Geoff, hardly pausing for breath.

'Poor dear Lesley,' she said, 'I felt I had a positive duty to stay for a little while and take care of her. You know all about the tragedy? Two young lives blighted at one stroke. . . Never mind, our dear Father knows best.' In response to Geoff's surprised look, she added, 'I refer of course to our Heavenly Father.'

Geoff muttered something non-committal, while Flora rummaged in the box, and extracted a bundle of brown, curling photographs. 'Perhaps you knew my sister? No? Here's a snapshot. Ravishingly pretty, wasn't she?'

Geoff, perched uneasily on the edge of a chair, looked obediently. He had not seen Agatha, but even if he had, he couldn't have recognized the strikingly handsome raven-haired young woman in the photograph. She was holding a violin, but not as if she intended to play it; more as if she planned to break it over somebody's head. She wore a string of beads to below the waist, and a slave bangle above the elbow. The skimpy little dress with its flounced hem above the knee looked utterly incongruous. Geoff was far from being an imaginative man, but he was suddenly reminded of a Christmas party he had been obliged to attend. Well-fed pin-striped businessmen talking earnestly together, wearing paper hats.

He'd lost track of Flora's chatter. Anyway, he didn't understand it. Sitwellian, neo-Bohemian, pre-Raphaelite – what was she talking about? Surely not Ben's grandmother, described to him by Lesley. He was relieved when she returned with the tea.

Flora launched into the story of the stolen picture, drank two cups of tea and suddenly began to weep. Lesley, looking resigned, silently handed her a full box of mansize Kleenex, and Flora dragged out a handful, dropping several on the floor. Lesley's eyes met Geoff's above Flora's bent head.

'What about a walk out, Lesley?' said Geoff. 'It's still light – lovely evening.'

Lesley jumped up and, hardly giving Geoff time to say goodbye to Flora, hurried him out into the street.

'I should think you need a change of scene,' said Geoff.

'I do, badly. And I want to talk to you please; it's important.'

They went to a cafe which was almost deserted, and Geoff ordered more tea. 'Why did you ask the old lady to stay?' he asked.

'I didn't. Well, only overnight. In a way she's company; she takes my mind off Ben. She's a perfect nuisance and appallingly emotional, but she's very kind and I feel obliged to do something for her.'

'*She's* very kind! You let people take advantage of your good nature, Lesley.'

'Oh I don't know, she's entertaining in her own peculiar way, and she buys her own gin. Her old home in Ireland has been turned into a hotel. Years ago, but there was a picture of it in the paper when the painting was stolen, and she howled like a banshee when she saw it.'

'Where's Ben then? I thought he was going back to Middlegarth last week; then I thought he might be with you.'

'He's still in hospital, having treatment. Apparently he's still in shock. They say he was getting better, although he was pretty abusive to the staff. Then, when he heard about his grandmother, he regressed. He was back in bed and hardly speaking when I had to tell him about the picture being stolen. He didn't seem to care.'

'Poor chap, he couldn't see it anyway.'

'No,' said Lesley, 'but it was worth a fortune and the insurance had run out. I wonder what else can go wrong for him.'

'Once he gets discharged from hospital he should manage. He couldn't have anyone better than you to look after him. Hope it happens before old auntie drives you round the bend.'

Lesley didn't smile. 'That's what I wanted to talk to you about,' she said. 'I don't think he wants me.'

'Oh come now. I can't believe he said that.'

'If I try to carry on where we left off, I'll mess things up worse than they are now. I think he should have a dog.'

'You aren't usually in a hurry for people to get a dog.'

'No. But Ben's so fit; so active and quick. Losing his freedom's going to hit him harder than losing his sight in the long run. You're the expert, but my opinion for what it's worth is that he should have a guide dog, and the sooner the better. He's good with dogs too.'

Geoff considered, drinking his tea. 'I think you're wrong,' he said. 'As he is now I don't believe he'd benefit. Too funny tempered.'

'You're worried about the dog.'

Geoff nodded. 'Of course. He might waste it. But you can see to anything he needs before you go to work, and again when you come home in the evenings. We can send a Mobility Officer to assess him for a dog in a week or two.'

'But Geoff, you don't understand. I'm sure he doesn't want me to stay with him. I mean, the cottage is tiny; there's just the one bed.'

Geoff stirred his tea, embarrassed. 'He'll get over it,' he said. 'Probably just a phase in his adjustment. Why not stay at the farm for a bit? You could still look after Ben.'

Lesley looked up. 'No,' she said in a low voice, 'I couldn't. Mandy gloats over Ben – oh, not openly, but she's having the time of her life. It's disgusting. Listen, Geoff, I'd do anything for Ben, but this isn't on. Not when we've lived together, talked about getting married. I love him too much.'

Geoff's bushy eyebrows came down as he frowned. He wouldn't meet Lesley's eyes. He had never once been involved in such a conversation. His relationship with his own wife was, and always had been, friendly and reticent rather than passionate.

He said, 'Well, my dear, you've got a choice. Either ask the boss to allocate him another social worker or bully him into having you back. Surely you can handle it. You're not a daft lass, seventeen years old. You've been married, and there's been one other bloke that I know of. Can't you cope?'

'No,' said Lesley. 'I've never gone overboard for anyone like this before. I can't manage it. I can't cope with my feelings – they're coping with me. Please persuade him to have a dog. A nice undemanding dog that'll settle for a pat on the head and a tin of Pedigree Chum.'

'Hey up,' said Geoff. 'Don't you start crying. Auntie's enough for one evening. I'll talk to Ben as soon as I can. Try and talk sense into that thick head of his, although mind you, I reckon he'd come round in time anyway.'

'I'm not crying; I never do. Don't talk to him about me, talk to him about a dog. What about Meg?'

'She'd be perfect for him – if he treats her right,' said Geoff. 'But if you're wrong – if he wastes her . . .'

'. . . you'll never forgive me,' finished Lesley. 'I'll risk it.'

Geoff found Ben alone. He was neatly dressed and had had his hair cut. The black beard was gone, making him look younger. It had given his jaw a squareness it did not possess and added to his aggressive appearance. He had been in the cottage for a week now, and the anger seemed to have gone out of him. He was sitting with his guitar on the table beside him, staring at the door.

Geoff knew that Ben disliked him. One could not be disliked by Ben without noticing. He had put it down to jealousy over his association with Lesley until she had explained about Ben's childhood fears. Geoff had been sorry, seeing much to like in Ben, not least his authority over dogs.

'It's Geoff,' he said. 'May I come in?'

'Geoff. Come in; sit down. Thought it was that bloody Mandy. She isn't with you, is she?'

'No, luckily. What's she been doing?'

Ben's hands clutched the edge of the table. 'Nothing,' he said, and he repeated as if he'd learned it by heart, 'I shouldn't talk like that. She's Charlie's daughter after all. Very kind, very sympathetic, very understanding.'

'I thought the shepherd was looking after you,' said Geoff.

'Eric? He is. Grand fellow. I gave out to him when I was in bad form, and he said he couldn't very well leave me to die, much as he'd like to.' Ben laughed shortly.

'And you liked him for that?'

'I like him for being honest. Funny, isn't it, how much easier it is to tell if a person's genuine if you can't see him.'

Geoff said, 'When I was training, I was blindfolded for three days and nights. It should give one an idea, but it doesn't.

You know you can take the blindfold off. I came to talk to you about a guide dog.' He got out his cigarettes. 'Smoke?'

'No thanks, I never have. Good job – I might set myself on fire.'

'Some blind people smoke, but it helps if you don't. Has Lesley talked to you about a dog?'

'She mentioned it,' said Ben sulkily. 'I don't want one. I can manage without.'

Geoff said, as if he hadn't heard, 'The way you walk is perfect. You hold up your head, and you walk quickly. People who have been blind for some time, finding their way around on their own, often start poking their heads forward, shuffling their feet and staring. It can get to be a habit. It wouldn't suit you to be like that, Ben.'

'A dog wouldn't suit me either. It would be like a leper's bell; like a label round my neck. "Blind. Be kind to him."'

'I didn't think you'd take that attitude,' said Geoff. 'The dog is a sign that you're independent of human help, not a badge of dependence. What does Lesley think about it?'

Ben stood up. 'Leave Lesley out of it,' he said loudly. 'She's not going to waste any more of her life – not if I can help it.'

'I'd let her be the judge of that if I were you. Lesley knows her job. She wouldn't let you get over dependent; she'd encourage you to help yourself.'

'Help myself?' shouted Ben. 'I can't. I can't read or write or drive a car. I can't even tell if I'm properly dressed. Better if I'd split my skull that time. What's left for me to do? Beg?'

'Calm yourself down, Ben. There are plenty of skills to be learned nowadays, and in the meantime you can look after Meg, feed her and groom her, and get yourself some exercise taking her out.' Geoff stood up. 'She's that collie, you know; bred at Middlegarth. I'll give you until the end of the week – three days – to think about it, then she'll go to somebody else.'

'I don't want a dog,' said Ben sullenly.

Geoff went to the door. 'I bet you were a rotten little sod when you were four years old,' he said. 'Think about it.'

*

Ben listened to Geoff's car going away, then listened again, trying to detect approaching footsteps. There were none. He had learned to recognize the flip-flapping of Mandy's sandals at a hundred yards, there was nowhere to hide except the loo, and if he locked the house door, she would tap on the window. He couldn't hear the Guvnor's heavy tread either, or Eric's firm gumbooted stride. He must be alone. He shut the door, picked up his guitar and tuned it. Then he began to strum a tune he'd heard on the radio. It was a catchy song, *I Want to Wake up with You*, but it reminded him painfully of Lesley. He tried something less sentimental, an old pop song, *Garden of Eden*.

As he played, gaining enthusiasm and confidence with every note, he began to sing the words. But then he remembered another garden; mown grass, tumbled flowers and a girl with red hair. He stopped playing, and tried to concentrate on bringing the picture – his picture – into focus in his mind's eye. It was there, yet not there. Tantalizingly, he knew every brushstroke in memory, but it refused to be held still and examined. He played six notes down the scale in a minor key.

'Young girl in a gar-den,' sang Ben.

The familiar sound of Lesley's car made him start guiltily, as if caught out. He laid the guitar aside and waited for her.

Lesley was the only person whose presence never irked Ben. Her voice betrayed nothing except affection – no irritation, no sorrow, no pity. He wondered if it came naturally or if she had to work at it.

She said, 'I've only come for a few minutes; I brought you some food. Mandy tells me you're getting tired of mince.'

'I am. She thinks I have to be fed like an invalid.' He heard her moving about. 'What are you doing?'

'Picking up your socks. You'll never sort yourself out if you chuck your things down when you undress.' Her voice came from low down as she stooped for something; close. He could smell her skin and her hair.

Off his guard, he said, 'I'd rather undress you,' lunging with his arms, spinning round. Where was she?

She came to him saying, in a carefully light voice, 'Do. I wish you would.'

But there was a catch in her cool voice. If he could have seen her, he might not have been so sensitive to her tone. For one moment his resolve left him; his arms went round her, he didn't think he could bear to let her go. Then he forced himself to turn away saying, 'It won't do. You know it won't.'

She didn't hold onto him, or press her body against his. He thought she was standing very still, just behind him. She said, 'Why won't it do, love? I know you want me.'

'Of course I want you. But it's all wrong for you. Almost obscene.'

'Silly. Blind people get married, have lovers. They often marry one another.'

'That's different.' Ben deliberately made his voice impatient.

She was facing him again. She said angrily, 'Am I supposed to stick around while you find a blind woman to take to bed?'

'Shut up.' Ben's impatience was real now. Anger helped; he made no effort to check it. 'You know very well what I mean.'

She said, 'I can't stay on any other terms. I'll talk to the Technical Officer, get somebody else.'

'I don't want somebody else,' Ben said violently. 'And for Christ's sweet sake don't suggest a guide dog.' He found the chair and sat down.

He heard her go to the door; she seemed to hesitate. She was coming back. He made up his mind not to relent again.

Lesley felt ill. Her head ached, her throat hurt; she felt drugged and sluggish.

All her training and experience pointed the same way. Never, never allow yourself to become emotionally involved. Be friendly with your cases, care about them, have compassion, even affection for them. Never express pity, but always show that you care. But love? Love was out. Especially first love, as agonizingly hopeless as any schoolgirl crush, but adult and lasting. She couldn't let him go; she doubted if she could stay on his terms – it would destroy her.

She said conversationally, 'You wouldn't believe it if you saw it on tv. You lose your sight, and here you are with a fully trained social worker, readymade on the premises.'

Ben sat with his head lowered. He said, 'You must go back to Leeds. To your work there.' The anger had gone. There was no emotion at all in his voice.

Lesley's instinct told her to go to him and put her arms round him. She knew that if she did she would be repulsed, and that if she were repulsed she would cry. She tried again, controlling her voice with a fierce effort. 'My place is with you – we both know that. I won't abandon my work in Leeds, but you come first. I – I need you, Ben.' She wondered what had happened to her pride.

Ben laughed loudly, without a trace of mirth.

'Don't laugh like that, Ben. Please don't.'

'Sorry. Thought you were trying to be funny.'

This new mood was much harder to take than anger. She took a step towards him and stopped. She remembered a day when she was about twelve, when she and her father had found a cat caught in a snare. They had both been bitten and scratched as they tried to free it. At last, her father had pulled up the stake and the cat, snarling, the wire still round its neck, had run away to die somewhere else. She hadn't thought about it for a long time.

She wanted to tell Ben that she had real friends who had once been despairing patients. Friends whose laughter was true and genuine, like Henrietta's. She found she couldn't say anything at all.

Ben spoke for her. 'Don't bother to tell me about all the blind people out there, singing and dancing and holding down

172

highly paid jobs,' he said, 'because I don't want to know.'

'You will,' she managed to say, 'one day.'

He didn't answer.

Lesley said, 'You laughed when I said I needed you, but it's true. I can't help it if you don't believe me.'

'I don't believe you.' Ben stared past her. 'I wish I was dead,' he whispered.

Lesley had heard these words so often that they had lost much of their power to shock. She would like to have told him, everybody says that – it doesn't last. Life is still sweet, but she didn't trust her voice. This was plain stupid. She must go away, for a time at least.

She pretended she hadn't heard him whisper. With an effort, she said, 'I've left the food on the table. There's scones, pork pies, sausage rolls and apples. Eric and Mandy will see to you until I can arrange something else. I'm not the person to do it. I'm going now.'

She went out and sat in her car, where she found that the desperate urge to burst into tears had gone. Instead, she was suddenly overcome by a cramping pain under her ribs. She gasped, and pressed her hands against her body, holding her breath. Slowly the pain faded, receding like a wave on shingle, leaving her giddy and faint.

She drove to the farm, left a message for Mandy who was out, and went home to Leeds.

Ben stayed where he was, his hands gripping the arms of the chair. The strain of sitting still, of not holding out his arms to Lesley and begging her to stay with him, had left him feeling ill. He had been brutal, he knew, but the slightest weakening would have been fatal. He would have been done for, and so would she.

At least she hadn't cried. Her low-pitched voice had been clear and steady – no hint of a tremor. Perhaps, secretly, she was glad to be rid of him. One day, he thought, she would thank him for his ruthlessness. He hadn't meant to say he wished he were dead – he was glad she hadn't heard – but at that moment it had been true. Life without Lesley, without sight, without love, without work, couldn't possibly be worth living.

He sat listening. Why hadn't she driven away? Then he heard the engine start, and the car was driven up to the farm, then back, past his door without stopping and down to the Leeds road.

To Ben's annoyance, Lesley's mention of food had taken root and reminded him that he was hungry. He ran his hand across the table and discovered the plastic bags. The pastries were homemade, so were the scones, which were split and buttered. Hating himself, he got up, located the electric kettle which was full, and switched it on. He could have found the teabags in his sleep.

His tidy habits and knowledge of his surroundings helped him now, as he made tea in a mug. Every move took him twice as long as formerly; he was careful, and managed not to scald himself. His hands bore the blisters of earlier scalds, and the scar left by his encounter with the hospital window.

When he had finished his tea, he took the empty mug to the sink, found the pedal bin with his toe, dropped the teabag in, and rinsed the mug. In a way, he felt pleased with his achievement. A lifetime of congratulating himself on a successfully made cup of tea?

Ben stood by the table, wishing fiercely that Lesley would come back. Not to stay – he would never allow her to do that – but to give him a chance to say he was sorry. She must be used to black moods, perhaps she would understand. Thoughtfully, he ate another pork pie.

The telephone rang. He dived towards the sound and fell painfully over the chair he had just pushed back. Forgetting that Lesley must still be on the road, he was sure she was on the line. He plunged to his feet and found the receiver, lifting it with a clatter. The moment he was sure that the voice was not Lesley's, he slammed it down.

He felt his way into the other room, and lay down on the

bed. He discovered that eyes which could not see could shed tears.

It wasn't in Ben's nature to give himself up to self pity for long. He soon found that he was thinking of Agatha and how, already ill, she had come to him. Such dedication deserved recognition. He got up and found his guitar.

Ben had never taken music lessons, but he had a good ear and a natural feeling for music. The little melody was putting itself together in his head, and words to go with it. In his mind, he was looking into the garden of the picture. And as he looked, the girl jumped to her feet; he caught a glimpse of her smile, then she was gone. But as he added line to line, he thought that perhaps the song was about the lost Lesley, or Agatha, or even his lost sight. Maybe it was about all three. He wondered if he would be able to remember the words. He'd ask Lesley to write – but no; she'd gone.

Putting the guitar down among the plastic bags on the table, he went outside. For the first few days, he had feared to go even a few yards from his door. His surroundings seemed suddenly to have become hostile: a sort of enemy territory where obstacles lay in wait to trip him, where he could wander endlessly in circles; an alien, frightening place. He was getting his bearings by degrees, but was still disinclined to stray far from the safe haven of home.

It was warm, with a gentle breeze. He felt his way round the cottage until he reached the bare back wall where he was invisible from farmhouse and road alike. Mandy wouldn't look for him there, and Eric would shout. He sat down on the ground with his back against the sun-warmed stone. For a time he juggled with the words of his song, changing a phrase here and there, then the black sea of depression engulfed him again. He put his arms round his knees, and wondered how to set about returning to Ireland. It was unfair to Lesley and to the Guvnor to stay where he was.

There was a movement close to him, and his sharpened

senses told him that he was watched. He was going to say, 'Who is it?' when he became aware of the smell of an elderly dog, not over clean. 'Roy?' he said.

He felt a hard, narrow skull pushed against his knee, and a hot dry nose in his hand. Roy was not a dog that licked people's faces. His present behaviour was demonstrative by his own standards. He whined.

Ben rubbed the head, and the base of the scruffy ears with their matted locks of hair. What a mess the dog was in. He might trim him with nail scissors, he thought. Roy whined again, and Ben felt a paw placed hesitantly on his instep. It was cold and wet, with overgrown toenails. It smelt of silage.

'Off you go, Roy,' he said. 'Run away home.'

He felt Roy stiffen. The paw and the nose were removed at once, but the smell of dog was still there beside him.

'Ah, go home,' said Ben. 'Go on. You're no use to me – you're the wrong sort of dog. Get away.' Even as he reached out to push the dog away, he sensed Roy's bewilderment, and relented. 'Silly old fool,' he said. 'Hurt your feelings, have I? Come here then.'

But Roy had gone. Ben heard the scatter of gravel as he galloped away.

Roy was not the sort of dog to inspire love in human hearts, but Ben was as fond of him as the dog would allow. He was angry with himself for driving Roy away. Ben could have recalled him as easily as he could have recalled Lesley; self contempt prevented him. If he couldn't reasonably be angry with others, he would be angry with himself. Why should dog or man – or woman – put up with his moods? But when Roy had gone, he felt deserted.

Alone, but without privacy, thought Ben. He had escaped the crowded, impoverished captivity of family life at Cloninch, and tasted a sort of freedom. Now he was a prisoner, with no freedom at all.

Ben's dour reflections were interrupted by a skittering noise, growing louder, accompanied by panting, bleating, and the sharp reek of sheep on a warm day. Eric must be taking the ewes to fresh pasture, Ben thought. Roy's ears, sharper than his, must have picked up the sound of the whistle which Eric carried, hung round his neck.

The patter of small hoofs stopped, came on, stopped again. Ben scrambled to his feet, hands held out. He sensed the flock's retreat. Then the sheep closed in again, all round him, closer and closer. One of them squeezed between him and the wall at his back. Ben toppled forward, saving himself from falling by putting both hands on a woolly back. The back jerked away and his hands met the ground as his chin struck a hard object – a sheep's head? For a frightening moment, he sprawled on the ground as the startled animals piled round him; sharp hoofs treading on the backs of his hands and the calves of his legs.

Ben thought wryly that even the most determined suicide would prefer not to be trampled to death by sheep – surely the ultimate humiliation. He shouted and swore, but still the stifling invisible bodies crowded in, heaving and jostling.

Suddenly, Ben realized what was happening. Roy, driven away for no fault that he could understand, was doing something which he was certain would please Ben and take away his evil mood. Who could fail to be cheered by a beautiful flock of sheep? He must have brought a hundred or more from the back of the farm buildings. Just as Mandy, snubbed, had rushed home and fetched him a dish of mince, Roy had fetched him a flock of sheep. But there was a world of difference between Mandy's indulgent nannying and Roy's grudging affection.

Pushing the hard unseen heads away, Ben shouted, 'That'll do, Roy, that'll do!'

Answering immediately to the universal command to cease work, the dog came straight round the flock to Ben's side. Ben heard the sheep wheel, and race away into the distance. Roy, uncertain of his welcome, kept out of reach; Ben could hear him panting.

He held out his hand, and received a brief nudge from the

hot nose. 'Thanks, Roy,' he said. 'That was just what I needed. I'll get that daughter of yours to keep me out of trouble. No human being would put up with me.'

He went indoors, locked the door, drew the curtains (against Mandy), and set about the major operation of having a bath.

Eleven

On the last evening of the residential course, Geoff decided to leave the students to their supper, and make do with a cup of tea later. Usually he enjoyed the last evening of a course, so different from the first. It was satisfying listening to the friendly talk of a group of people who had been given fresh hope, partly due to his own efforts. And this time there were no failures. Geoff would be visiting the six men and four women in their homes regularly, and in ten days' time there'd be another batch arriving. He felt suddenly unbearably tired.

Geoff stood under an apple tree smoking, and watching the dogs in their runs. These were the dogs for the next course, whose training was nearing completion. Geoff often said that he had no favourites, either among his dogs or his students. He let Meg out of her run.

Meg was not given to displays of affection. A working dog, like her father Roy, she despised effusively friendly dogs. She knew she had a purpose, though she didn't yet know what it could be. She was devoted to Geoff, but would never wriggle, waggle or slaver as some of the young dogs did. She had needed no lessons to restrain her from jumping up, and from getting under her handler's feet.

Geoff had been in Leeds all of the long, hot summer day, along with the other instructors, the students and their dogs. It was grand to be away from the din, the exhaust fumes and the stress. He put on Meg's harness, and let her lead him along the obstacle course which was set up in the garden. A series of planks were leaning against poles of varying heights.

Meg, leading Geoff under or round these obstacles, knew his height to a centimetre and never made a mistake. Geoff knew that she would quickly learn Ben's height too, although he was six inches shorter than Geoff. Even more surprising was the quickness of the dogs to adapt to the height of someone much taller than the instructor. George Bull was six feet four, but Pepper had never run his face into anything.

Geoff had to hurry in order to keep up with Meg. She was so active, so swift in her reactions that she would be all wrong for an elderly person, or anyone slow in the uptake. She had needed more work than any other dog, not because she was stupid or disobedient, but because her active brain could easily have led her into mischief. She was probably the most intelligent dog at the centre, but too much initiative was as bad as not enough. Obedience was more important. Before handing her over to Ben, Geoff would work Meg in the traffic of Leeds wearing a blindfold; he knew he wouldn't have any problems.

Because Meg had been held back, Geoff had to be careful not to overtrain her. He sensed her impatience with him, just as she sensed his approval or displeasure, through the harness. Meg knew quite well that Geoff wasn't blind – all the dogs at the centre knew who was blind and who was not. They didn't trouble to get out of the way of a sighted person.

Geoff had cut a few corners in order to get Ben accepted for the next course. He had had to overcome opposition from director Michael Jones but the rest was easy. Ben's association with Lesley and his ability with working dogs were both in his favour; so was his youth and activity. Living alone, there was no problem with family jealousy and over protectiveness, while Eric would notice at once if there was anything wrong with Meg.

When Geoff had shut Meg up in her sleeping quarters, he went to the office and checked her individual score sheet once more. Each dog was assessed for hearing and body sensitivity, for nervousness and for various forms of aggression, for concentration, willingness and initiative. Meg had top scoring for everything except protective aggression, but for that, Geoff had been obliged to knock off two points. However, the last time he had been to see Ben he had taken Meg with him, and she had been only slightly uneasy when Ben's always simmering temper had begun to show.

Dogs bred at the centre from selected stock seldom had this over possessive instinct. The failure rate in 'bought in' dogs was far higher.

'It isn't Meg that worries me, it's Ben,' Geoff said aloud.

Ben angrily refused when Mandy offered to read his letter to him. He put it at the bottom of the air-line bag he'd brought from Ireland. So when Geoff came to collect his application form for a dog, it wasn't filled in. Ben said he would have let the Guvnor open his letters, but he was away at a ram sale in Scotland.

Most of the questions were straightforward, like any other application form. Then came questions like, Do you like dogs? Have you facilities for keeping one? Can you take part in a four week training course at any time?

Ben answered yes to all these questions. He was in an odd mood – elated, excited even, but with a weary note in his voice. Geoff suspected that he was sleeping badly, due to idleness and boredom. He seemed unable to keep still, and was much more talkative than usual.

'I've been thinking a lot,' he said. 'I haven't had anything else to do. I mean to fight this thing every inch of the way. Did you know there's a chance that I might be able to see again one day? When that happens, I want to be able to pick up where I left off. There must be things I can do – I won't be pitied for ever.'

Geoff said, 'You're not pitied now by anyone who matters – not in a patronizing sense. And of course there are things you can do. But take it easy, there's plenty of time.'

Geoff was familiar with this urge to fight back; it was called over-compensation. Ben's suppressed rage came from a desperate fear of being beaten by a destructive force he could neither attack nor understand. A man used to working ten hours a day on the land, and who never sat idly in his spare time, he was determined to break the invisible enemy by sheer bloody-mindedness. If he could maintain his outlook, he might well achieve more blind than sighted – he had never been ambitious – but his chances of happiness looked slim. Lesley's chance of happiness with him looked even slimmer. Geoff had no faith in a miracle cure, and thought the doctor should have been frank with Ben. False hopes were a poor basis for a well adjusted future.

'How do you mean to fight?' he asked. 'It's easier to go along with your condition and come to terms with it by degrees. The dog will give you mobility and independence; after a time you'll be surprised at how much you can do.' He noticed that Ben's astonishing vitality did not seem to be diminished; he was still a personality rather than merely a person. He would never be ignored.

Ben said, 'I'm not made like that. I can't wait for things to happen to me. If I can't make them happen, I might as well settle for singing for my supper at the Turpin Arms.'

'You could do worse,' said Geoff.

That day, a van drove up to the farm. On the side of it was painted in elaborate lettering; THE BED OF ROSES HARROGATE, and underneath, JUSTIN AND DAISY BEALE.

The driver unloaded a dozen flowering roses in pots, an enormous bouquet of carnations and mignonette, and a rooted sweetbriar with a card which read, 'To be planted in Benedict's garden.' There was nobody about, so he left these things outside the back door, where they were discovered by the Guvnor returning from Scotland.

Mandy, who had met Charlie at the station, buried her nose in the flowers, sniffing rapturously. 'Poor Ben will have to come and enjoy them here,' she said, as she took them into the kitchen.

'Enjoy his dinner, more like,' said Charlie. 'Shift yourself, lass, it's past twelve.' He picked up the sweetbriar in its sacking wraps, and turned the card over. On the back was written in purple ink, 'It's the wrong time of year. Bushes and half standards follow in the autumn. See you soon. Blessings, Auntie Flora.

'I suppose I could plant the briar in Ben's garden,' said Mandy doubtfully. 'It smells lovely.'

Charlie threw it down. 'You do have some notions,' he said scornfully. 'Eric found him fast in barbed wire last week. Put it on fire.'

'But Father, there's nothing in Ben's garden but cabbages.'

'Sheep's eaten cabbages,' said Charlie.

Lesley was having problems with all her charges except Henrietta. She was short-tempered, impatient and inclined to lapses of memory. Mrs Betts complained to the Technical Officer, who warned Lesley to keep her private life separate from her work.

Flora had gone home to Harrogate for the Royal Yorkshire show, where she was a patron in the rose section, but to Lesley's amazement, she returned at the end of the week, bringing a suitcase, a hamper and a wilting sheaf of roses.

'Poor darlings, I hadn't the heart to throw them away,' she said.

'There isn't much left to throw,' said Lesley. 'I followed the trail of petals all the way from the bus stop. It was like a paperchase.' She scooped up a handful off the carpet.

'Aren't you pleased to see me, dear?' Flora's face quivered.

'It isn't that,' said Lesley hastily, 'I'm expecting somebody. It's a business thing; that's why I'm not at work. I ought to have the place tidy.'

'Somebody nice, I hope.'

'I used to think so,' said Lesley. 'He's my husband. He'll soon be my ex-husband.'

Lesley was obliged to meet Mark, in order to discuss the lease of the flat. She had been dreading the meeting, and could have done without Flora, she thought. But, as three o'clock approached, she began to be glad that she wasn't alone.

The encounter was an anti-climax. There was no emotion, no resentment. She could hardly believe she'd been married to this man for three years. Good-looking Mark had put on weight, and had bags under his eyes. He obviously expected recriminations; when they didn't come, he was affable and impersonal.

Their divorce was almost complete and Mark, although he didn't mention it, was poised to marry the rich widow.

Lesley had taken trouble with her appearance, fearing that Mark might blame his desertion for her loss of weight and her pallor. She had had her hair permed for the first time in years, and set in a tumble of curls and waves, hiding the scar and most of her forehead. Her earrings, long wriggling gold snakes this time, were almost hidden too. She wore a gaily patterned dress and sealing-wax red lipstick. She could see that Mark hardly recognized her.

The lease of the flat was sold. Lesley agreed to move out before the end of the month. They had been talking in the kitchen because Flora was in the sitting-room. Mark told Lesley she could keep any furniture she liked, and she replied that she wouldn't need much. She had enough of her own to furnish a smaller flat.

'What about the dinner table?' asked Mark. (The widow dined off Hepplewhite and sat on Chippendale.)

'Much too big,' said Lesley. 'If you're keen for me to keep something, I'd like the wing chair.'

Mark had forgotten the chair, and agreed willingly. Flora was sitting on it, wearing a tent-like dress made of orange and green cretonne. Lesley introduced her as a guest and saw Mark's amused disbelief. Sick of Flora as she was, Lesley hastened to defend her. Surely Mark must have heard of her – such a well known personality, a real friend in need. Ben's great-aunt. Ben? Ben and I hope to get married eventually.

'You seem to have fallen on your feet,' said Mark.

184

'Oh yes. Born under a lucky star.'

'What does this Ben do for a living?'

'He's a farmer,' said Lesley recklessly.

When Mark left, she realized that she'd probably thrown away financial support, but rather than tell him that Ben was blind, she would have lived on bread and water. She said to Flora, 'I'm moving out of here soon. I'm looking for something much smaller, probably just a bedsit.'

'Come and live with me, dear. I'm sure you'd fit in . . . Daisy Beale's quite reasonable once you get to know her . . . funny little ways . . . none of us is perfect.'

'It's very kind of you, Aunt Flora, but I'd be too far away from my work and from Ben.'

'But my dear – *plenty* of work at the "Bed of Roses" . . . Benedict can come too. Have you heard of Brother Sebastian? Some amazing cures . . . did wonders for Daisy's knees.'

'But –'

'No buts, dear . . . Is there any gin left? Just a teeny one then.' Flora leaned back in the chair and laid down her needlework.

'That's where your sister always sat,' said Lesley. 'It's Mark's chair, but I've asked him for it because I think of it as your sister's. Sometimes I imagine she's still sitting there, keeping an eye on things.'

Flora laughed so that her chins wobbled. 'Really, my dear, it's lucky that you didn't have her here for ever. So rude, foistering herself on you . . . no manners. If Agatha wanted anything, she got it. Not Walton Carmichael of course. . . She threw herself at his head; I can't *tell* you, dear – she was considered fast, you know. He told her she was, let me think – beautiful, bad-tempered and bookish . . . something like that.'

'And was she?' asked Lesley, fascinated.

'I suppose so . . . she was always a little odd. Girls were boyish then . . . no bosoms, slangy. Agatha hated parties . . . bored. We all were, but I loved my garden. I wish you could have seen it. . .'

'Go on about Mrs Logan,' prompted Lesley.

'Oh, my dear, the scandal! Michael was splendid – a veritable Apollo, but one *didn't* . . . We read Mary Webb, Lawrence too, under the bedclothes. Noble savages . . . merry peasants . . . But Michael was just an ordinary man. She said he ravished her, but Constance and I – is there any more in the bottle? Thank you – we thought she suggested marriage, having first seduced him.'

'I thought she was rather prim and proper,' said Lesley. 'She didn't approve of Ben and me.'

Flora tilted her glass. 'Of course not. She used to be amoral . . . Bohemian . . . cushions on the floor and all that. Splendid young man . . . soon tired of him, couldn't bear to see others in love. She went quite the other way . . . quite the other way. . . .'

Flora had drawn the wing chair up to the table. In front of her was a pile of tapestry wool in every conceivable shade of pink and green. An immense piece of canvas, sprouting patches of flowers and leaves in gros point, trailed across her lap and onto the floor. Flora knocked back her gin and tonic and beamed at Lesley. 'Was Agatha very like me in her old age?' she asked.

'Not a bit,' said Lesley faintly. 'And I mean it about living with you Aunt Flora. I'll have to stay in Leeds, thank you all the same.'

'I *am* disappointed. . . .' The ready tears began to trickle down Flora's cheeks and drip on the tapestry. She dabbed at them with a tissue. 'If your mind is made up,' she said, 'you shall have this wall hanging for your new home . . . now, don't say no. Oh, if only Benedict would consent to pray with Brother Sebastian! You don't think? I was afraid not. . . .' She sighed, and stretched her fat braceleted arms wide. 'I *feel* that his sight can be restored,' she said intensely.

The next day, Lesley took a two roomed flat in the street where Henrietta lived, and started to move her belongings there. She helped Flora to pack, and again put her on the Harrogate bus, with promises to write.

Lesley hadn't been to see Ben again. She had phoned Geoff, and told him that she wouldn't be going to the cottage any more. Geoff told her that Ben had just been accepted for a residential course. 'We never see you at the centre nowadays,' he said.

'No,' said Lesley, 'and you aren't going to. I'm thinking of moving right away. Taking up some other kind of social work. Geoff, I bought Ben a mini tape recorder. Henrietta uses one all the time; but somehow I've never got round to giving it to him. Would you?'

'It would come better from you,' said Geoff, scenting a reconciliation. 'Take it to him when he gets back from the course. They're great things, I use one myself.'

Lesley packed the little recorder, wondering if she might post it to Ben. But the thought of Mandy teaching him how to use it was too much for her.

Mandy had phoned about the flowers that Flora had sent. The sweetbriar had completely disappeared, she said, and the Guvnor had put the bouquet in the back room because the scent put him off his food.

'I'm reading a super book called *Invisible Dawn*,' said Mandy. 'A real weepie. The hero's just like Ben – so brave and cheerful. And of course he gets the girl in the end.'

Lesley had hung up saying merely, ''Bye. See you.'

Ben's residential course was to start in late July. He had learned to manage very well for himself in the cottage. Mandy did his shopping and washed his clothes, and he needed no other help. He got up when Eric called him on his way to work, dressed, shaved, and prepared simple meals. He listened to the transistor that Lesley had given him, and walked about incessantly outside. On the narrow path at the back of the cottage, he sometimes jogged to and fro, fifteen paces each way, keeping himself fit for some purpose he hadn't yet worked out. He did this when Mandy had gone down to Middlegarth. He could hear her change gear as she turned in off the road, and he would be sitting in the kitchen when she bounced in, bringing goodwill and groceries.

He played his guitar only when he was certain that she had gone out.

Various wellwishers had assured Ben that he would develop a sixth sense. As he had suspected, this was nonsense, but the four senses left to him had sharpened immeasurably. He found he could orientate himself easily now. He knew where the barbed wire was, and had a fresh crop of scars to prove it. The traffic on the Leeds road behind his home and the farmyard noises in front of it were about half a mile apart. The area between was bordered on both sides by farm roads, edged with shallow ditches. Ben fell into these ditches fairly often – nothing would induce him to use a stick – but he learned to sense where he was with some accuracy.

Down at the farm, the smells of sheep, silage, diesel oil, grain and chemicals were enough to guide him round the buildings. His nose had learned to separate the smells in an almost uncanny way. He got some shocks from electric fences at first, but never walked into the same one twice. Eric treated him exactly as if he could see, and the other men kept out of his way.

Ben had been eager to start the course, but as the time approached he became unhappy about it. By nature he was a loner. He could be contented by himself, and happy with somebody he liked, but large gatherings had always bothered him. In Ireland, only lack of cash and opportunity had kept him at home; he had been a solitary, sardined into a crowd. He thought the course would be like school. During his brief years at school he had been a natural leader, but how could the blind lead the blind? At this point in his thoughts, he fell into a ditch, and laughed aloud at himself as he climbed out. The shock of loss was wearing off.

It was Charlie who drove Ben to the Training Centre. Although he had rushed to Ben's defence after Agatha's funeral, he had found the young man's continuing blindness so upsetting that for a time he had hardly visited him. Then he had taken to calling every evening for a short time. He talked with a sort of false jollity which Ben found intensely annoying, but before he left, he usually said in his normal voice, 'By, it's a bad job, is this,' and departed muttering to himself.

Charlie came down to the cottage the night before the course in a gloomy mood. 'By, it's a bad job, is this,' he said, for perhaps the twentieth time. 'Don't start ruffling up; it's a right bad job, choose how.' As Ben made an impatient movement, he added, 'Don't you move, lad, I'll mash tea.'

Ben said, 'I've been blind for three months now. Can't you give it a rest?'

'What are you on about?' demanded Charlie.

'You told my family I wanted time to be sorry for myself. You were right and I'm grateful. But now I've had enough sympathy. It makes me so bloody miserable I feel like lying in bed all day. It slows me up; stops me trying to get around and make the best of it.'

There was silence as the Guvnor digested this. Ben wondered if he'd said too much. At last Charlie said slowly, 'Aye, you're in the right of it. If you don't find your feet soon, you'll be like a youngster too long in playpen, or dog tied up all the time. Let him off chain and he'll stop in kennel as like as not. Well, get on then, mash tea. I'm dry if you're not.'

Ben mashed it.

At Leeds, Ben's first impressions were so confused that afterwards he could remember only the barking of dogs, and Geoff's familiar voice among a babble of unfamiliar ones. He heard somebody laugh, a loud, jolly laugh, 'Ho-ho-ho,' but couldn't place it.

Geoff said, 'Ben, you remember Bob, don't you?' and he wondered how he could have forgotten.

It was Geoff who took Ben along a corridor, showing him the lounge on the right (first door), the dining room second on the left, the two telephones near the door; the lavatories at the end of the passage with the laundry room close by. Ben felt shut in and bewildered. He only half attended.

They went upstairs – thirteen steps – and turned left. Three doors and eight paces from the landing, Geoff stopped. 'This is your room,' he said. 'You share with Dave Leyburn whose dog has had to be put down. He's about your age – been blind since he was fifteen or so.'

Ben hadn't thought about sharing a room. Geoff explained that he'd deliberately been put in a room with someone who'd had a guide dog before, as Dave could help Ben with advice. Ben hardly listened. He thought of the course as a battle to be fought and won, and he wanted to fight it, as far as possible, alone.

'Where's my dog?' he asked.

'You don't get your dog until you've been here for a day or two,' said Geoff. 'We have to be sure that you suit one another, and we want to see how you get round without one. Dave hasn't arrived yet. Wait in here until you hear a bell, then come down for lunch.' He explained the layout of the room and went away.

This was Ben's first time in a strange room since he had left hospital. He found that he had made more progress than he would have thought possible. He knew where the window was by the current of air from its open top. He could tell which surfaces were hard and which soft or upholstered by the way that sounds bounced back or were absorbed. He made a thorough investigation, then sat down on the bed. He tried to remember what Geoff had told him. 'Walk on the right – your dog will be on the left. Stop at the top and bottom of the stairs, as your dog will have been trained to do. Knock before you open a door, and never leave it half open for someone else to run into.' There was a lot more he'd forgotten.

Bitterly he resented having to attend this course, or rather the reason for it. The childish 'It isn't fair' came to his mind. He clenched his fists, digging his nails into his palms; the familiar boiling resentment was near the surface. He choked it down, wishing he were back at home. The effort of training with a dog suddenly seemed beyond him.

There was a tap on the door, and a plaintive voice said, 'Anyone here?' Slow footsteps approached.

'I'm here,' said Ben. 'Ben Glyn.'

'Dave Leyburn,' said the complaining voice. 'I hoped for a room of my own.'

'So did I,' said Ben. There was a hostile silence.

Dave was first to speak. 'I'm studying advanced relaxation therapy,' he said. 'I need to concentrate.'

It was a young voice; nasal and unattractive. Ben imagined the owner sandy haired, with buck teeth and a prominent Adam's apple. 'It sounds easy enough,' said Ben, 'as long as your bed's comfortable.'

'There's no need to make fun of what you don't understand.' The voice came from a lower level, and the bed creaked. 'I worked with computers, and the stress caused psychosomatic problems. I suppose when I get a new dog, they'll pressurize me back to work.' He sighed heavily.

Ben didn't know whether he should congratulate or sympathize when Dave added that he had restricted peripheral vision. He didn't care enough to enquire further. He decided there were worse things than being blind and lonely. A month with Dave Leyburn, for example.

They were summoned to lunch, and Ben made rapidly and unerringly for the door. 'Coming?' he said. There was no reply, so he shut it behind him and paced eight strides along the passage, keeping to the right. Thirteen steps – he rattled down them, wondering if he needed a dog after all.

A woman's voice said, 'Look out!' as he walked into a group of three or four, stepping heavily on somebody's foot. A hand grasped his arm, and the same female voice said angrily, 'Here, look where you're going!'

'Can't,' said Ben. 'That's why I'm here.'

'Student, are you? You'll kill somebody. Don't you know there are nine others here, some of them elderly? Lucky for you Mr Jones didn't see you, or Geoff Merchant.'

The voice was harsh, so Ben imagined a plain, middle-aged woman. Later, it occurred to him that this judgment was unreasonable. It also happened to be wrong.

'Sophy Fryton. Instructor. Not yours, I'm glad to say.' The woman led him along with a hard grip on his arm. 'Here's the dining room. Sit down, here's your chair, and stay sitting down. The students have quite enough to cope with on their first day without someone charging about like a bull in a china shop.' She was gone.

Ben felt the other students moving about, heard the clatter of plates. Somebody brought him food, told him what it was and how it was arranged on his plate. Meat at twelve o'clock, potato at twenty to, vegetable at twenty past. Could he manage? Ben said he could.

This was back to school but worse. He'd meant to learn faster than anyone else, to be the star pupil. Now he was deflated, ticked off by a prefect, and a girl at that.

It was a good lunch. He ate it all.

Twelve

Cloninch without Agatha had at first all the scurrying panic of a kicked ant's nest. There were bills and reminders and solicitors' letters to be dealt with. There were impatient creditors and sarcastic bank managers. There were thin-lipped money-lenders. Myles passed them on to Denis, and Denis passed them back to Myles.

For all the years Agatha had reigned at Cloninch, she had been assumed to be the owner of an entailed fortune which would, at her death, be passed on to her family. It was one of those assumptions which become legend until disproved. There was nothing. And the men and women who had allowed Agatha to deprive them of their very identities, idled and bickered for weeks until obliged by debt to sort themselves out and deal with the situation.

Denis sold all the sheep – with profound relief – and let some of the surplus grass for silage. This paid the more pressing bills. Mike and Brian both got work in Kilmoon, Brian at the creamery, Mike at a garage. Denis saw to the cows, with limited help from Myles, whose interest in dog racing had flagged.

Sheila, without Agatha's spiteful presence, lost her sickly whine and helped Muriel. For Muriel was the only member of the household who regretted Agatha. Ben's blindness and Agatha's death together were more than she could take; she moped about with red eyes.

Old Michael lay on the big brass bed on the left side, except for the short time every evening when he got up and sat by the window while Muriel made the bed and hoovered and tidied and complained. He made no comment when the bad news was told to him. He appeared equally unconcerned about Agatha, Ben and the picture.

When Muriel came back from Yorkshire, she noticed that he now lay in the dead centre of the bed, where his head rested on Agatha's pillows as well as his own. As she helped him to the basket chair, put a dressing-gown round his shoulders and guided his feet into slippers, she gave him a mournful account of all that had happened. She thought he hadn't understood, he spoke so seldom. There seemed to be little understanding left in that noble-looking skull. She couldn't remember when Michael's hair had been black, or even grey; it seemed to have been white for ever. The white hair on his chest was like the wild cotton that grew on the bog.

Muriel was an even-tempered woman: had she not been, she would never have survived Agatha. But as she helped the old man back to bed, propped him up and met his vague stare, she suddenly cried out, 'You might say *something*!'

'Nothing to say,' mumbled Michael. He seldom bothered to wear his teeth.

'Nothing to say! You might say "thank you" sometimes.' Muriel dragged the sheets over her father and rushed to the door. She stumbled downstairs, wiping her eyes.

Muriel was now the joint owner of Cloninch with Denis. There were papers to be signed, fees to be paid. Myles, like Michael was excluded. If Denis had no son, everything would go to Ben eventually. Denis didn't intend this to happen, not if it took him and Sheila twenty years to produce a boy.

Myles, Muriel and Denis went to Edward Ryder's office, and spent two hours there. Myles and Denis sat patiently while Edward fussily sorted the yellowed pages of foolscap, written all over in brownish ink, bearing important looking stamps and seals, clamped together with a great brass clip.

Muriel came no further than the outer office, where she turned over the pages of the *Irish Business Man* for 1981 without seeing them. She felt strangely isolated. Sometimes Edward asked her to sign a document, and she did so without reading it. She needed Agatha's whiplash tongue to motivate her – without it she was nothing: a useful household item like the washing machine or the cooker. She knuckled her eyes like a child.

When they got home, they found Michael sitting in the kitchen. He wore his shirt and trousers, but his white, blue-veined feet were bare.

'Where are my bloody boots?' he said.

When Brian and Mike got back from work that evening, Michael, fully dressed and wearing his teeth, was sitting in Agatha's chair at the head of the table.

With Michael out of the way, Muriel thought she would collect her mother's clothes and see what was to be done with them. Agatha had wanted her to have them; she wouldn't give them away. So she spread out the garments on the bed and looked at them hopelessly. They were pathetically few in number, beautifully kept, totally useless. And, as they emerged from the wardrobe, something of Agatha herself seemed to come with them. As Muriel sighed and folded them up, she felt that she was beadily watched.

Muriel laid aside a black crêpe de chine evening dress, heavy with thousands of jet beads. It was the only one her mother had brought from her old home. Perhaps the Heritage Society would like it. She left it on the bed, along with the violin. Everything else went back into the cupboard. She pulled out the trunk from under the bed. The embroidered tablecloths and mats would keep her supplied with wedding presents for the rest of her life. There were dressing-table runners too – out of date, thought Muriel, redundant on her glass-topped modern furniture. Poor mother . . . Impatiently, she wiped at the tears which were never far away.

She considered a white linen runner, delicately embroidered with ears of corn. She could remember her mother ironing it when it was finished, and adding it to her hoard. A shame to waste it; it might make an altar cloth. . . . A great idea! Father Mulcahy would be delighted.

195

A menacing chill suddenly gripped Muriel. Her very tears seemed to freeze unshed. The moment passed. She put the embroidery back in the trunk, the trunk back under the bed. She scrambled to her feet.

– Fool!

Oh dear, thought Muriel, why can't I remember the nice things Mother said to me – there must have been *some*.

Brian and Mike between them filled a tape with news for Ben. They felt guilty about the meeting in the Leeds hospital, each wishing he could have talked to Ben alone. So they took turns with the tape, talking to Ben as if he'd been there. They told him that Grandfather was up, sitting in the Old One's chair and bossing Dad about, that he had taken all Grandmother's funny old dresses and burned them when Mother was out, that Sheila was as pregnant as hell and in a shocking temper, that Denis had been robbed all ends up when he sold the sheep, that old Shep had been run over by the milk lorry at last, that Dad had won £100 in the National Lottery.

They asked Muriel to contribute, but she shook her head, so they said that Mam was in great form and asking for Ben. Then they took the tape to Billy Browne's pub, and all the lads had a turn with it.

'I hope he doesn't get his girlfriend to play it for him,' said Brian.

Finally, they went to Terry's place, and he talked until the tape ran out, about horses. Dancing Lady was almost sure to be in foal, the grey had won at Leopardstown, he'd bought a new filly – a flyer. While he was talking, two young horses galloped up the field, the sound of their hooves drowning his voice as they passed.

'Blank that bit out,' said Mike. 'It'll upset him.'

'I will not; he'll like it,' said Terry, so they left it in.

They sent the tape with a blank one for a reply to Middlegarth Farm.

'They haven't any labels – I wonder what's on them,' said Mandy.

196

The Guvnor put them in his pocket. 'Go on wondering,' he said.

As the first day of Ben's course progressed, his sense of claustrophobia increased. After lunch, Geoff lectured the whole group in the lounge. He wasn't a fluent speaker, although he knew exactly what he wanted to say. He had a habit of saying, 'Now then!' at the beginning of every sentence, and Ben found himself waiting for it, clenching his fists.

Ben was sitting between the limp silence which was Dave Leyburn and somebody large who was eating peppermints. There were two women behind him who whispered together and were shushed, somebody in front of him whose eagerness was as obvious as Dave's disinterest. He didn't know if it was a man or a woman.

Ben felt lost – a traveller in a seething foreign city, an outsider who had strayed into a board meeting. He didn't belong, he wanted to go home to the cottage – he checked his thoughts firmly. He wondered if blindness would draw these differing people together into a common group with similar aims and ambitions. He decided it was unlikely. A minority group like the 'Jews and Blacks' so hated by the Guvnor, they would always be lumped together by some. The Blind. Ben was determined to go his own way, to ask nobody for help; he concentrated hard on the lecture.

'Now then!' said Geoff.

After the talk, Geoff and Sophy (the head girl, thought Ben) took the students, two at a time, to the dogs' quarters. They were shown the way to the room where the dogs were groomed, and told something about their care and feeding. They met the kennel-maids, and Ben was introduced to Lucy, who had looked after Meg throughout her training. Lucy's voice was rather like Lesley's, so Ben imagined her tall, fair and with a natural elegance.

'Have you any questions, Ben?' asked Geoff.

'When do I get this damned dog?'

197

'I've told you; when you're ready to work with her. Anything else?'

'What does that girl – Lucy – look like?'

'I meant relevant questions,' said Geoff, patiently. 'Since you ask, she's plump, dark haired, round face, wears sweatshirts and jeans. Satisfied?'

'No,' said Ben.

Later in the evening, they were asked who would like to go out. Some had friends in the neighbourhood, some opted for the pub, a few wanted to go to the pictures.

'What's the good of going to the pictures if you can't see?' asked an impatient voice.

'It's not so different to a play on radio,' said Sophy briskly.

Ben didn't go out. He worried about making his money last. He wondered where he would get any more. He went to his room and thought about it. He'd been there for some minutes before a slight sound told him that Dave was there too.

'Where are you?' asked Ben.

'In the shit, same as you,' said Dave, 'but in this holiday home, our gaolers like to pretend that blindness is just a minor inconvenience.'

His voice came from just behind Ben, who spun round. 'Why don't you keep to your own side of the room,' he said. 'Get on with your relaxation?'

Dave went on speaking as if he hadn't heard. 'My mother made me put my name down for another dog,' he said. 'I don't want one. If there's anything good about being blind, which I doubt, it's that you aren't criticized for not working.' A hand brushed Ben's face. 'I can see – a little . . . small guy, aren't you?'

'I'm big enough to break your jaw if you don't get away,' said Ben savagely.

There was a scuffle, and Dave's voice came from the door. 'I know about you. You attacked a man at the Hart Royal and had to be thrown out. Something to do with a woman; you were drunk. I heard the staff talking. I'm not going to be shut up for a month with you.'

198

Ben rushed at the door, but Dave had gone through it.

Later, Geoff knocked and came in. 'Ben, what have you been doing? Dave says you attacked him.'

'I didn't, but I will sooner or later. He stroked my face. Let me go home, Geoff. Forget the dog. I'm sorry I've wasted your time.'

'I don't think you were altogether to blame,' said Geoff. 'I wouldn't have put you two together if I'd known Dave. He did his first course at Nottingham, before this place was opened – they have single rooms there. He told me he liked to "learn people's faces by touch", so I was relieved to find him all in one piece. For God's sake, don't be so violent.'

'I'm sorry, Geoff. I just can't stand people creeping about behind me.'

Geoff said, 'As it happens, we have an odd number of men, and Dave wants a room to himself, so he's getting it. I'm putting our youngest student, Paul Gates, with you. I don't think you *could* quarrel with Paul.'

'I don't quarrel!' yelled Ben.

'Ben,' said Geoff, 'I've liked you since the first time we met. But if there's any more trouble with you, I will personally hand you over to Sophy and that's a promise. Get it into that thick head of yours that you don't have to take on the world single handed because you've lost your sight. It happens to thousands.'

Ben heard him leave the room, heard the door close. He had been wrong about Geoff, he knew. A great fellow, just as Lesley had said. Lesley. He tried all the time to keep her out of his thoughts, but it was impossible.

Meg watched the class coming out on their second day from her run. She had become accustomed to seeing her Geoff training people as well as other dogs. Two days earlier, he had put on a pair of black glasses and made her take him for a walk in the middle of Leeds. Afterwards he had done the same with Cindy and Sailor. He had praised all three, but the note in his voice told Meg that she was his favourite although the words were the same for all. 'Good girl – or boy. What a clever girl. Well done.' His words warmed and cheered her. She wanted nothing more than to do whatever Geoff asked of her for the rest of her life.

Meg watched the group of students, ten of them, talking eagerly together. Lucy and Karen, another of the kennel-maids, stopped in their work of hosing down the night kennels to watch. Lucy said, 'The little guy in the black jumper's dead sexy, isn't he?' They talked about the men on the course and about their own boyfriends. Meg liked Lucy, and tolerated Karen. When Geoff was about, they ceased to exist for her.

Geoff, Sophy and James, the junior instructor, were talking to the class, demonstrating the dog harness. Each student had the construction of the harness explained to him and was told how to hold the handle in his left hand, along with the dog's lead. Most of them had some knowledge of this already; Meg could sense their unspoken impatience, their eagerness to get on with the lesson.

Geoff was going to do his dog imitation. Meg found this somehow embarrassing, almost as if he'd dropped on all fours, or lapped from a dish. The exercise, called a 'handle walk' taught the students without the risk of bewildering and upsetting the dogs. The instructor was the 'dog'. As Geoff put the harness in the hands of the broad-shouldered man with the dark curly hair, Meg suddenly knew who he was.

Here was the man that Meg had thought would be good to work for. But he already owned the woman Lesley. Couldn't she lead him about? Apparently not. The man Ben took hold of the handle and charged straight at Geoff's broad back. Meg felt the fine hairs on her shoulders prickle as her Geoff staggered, but he merely laughed and said, 'Try again. You're getting a collie, not a greyhound.'

They walked to and fro on the mown grass, and Meg heard Ben giving Geoff the commands she knew. Only the basic ones – 'Forward, straight on, stop, down, stay.' They practised the direction commands, Geoff told Ben to try to imitate his voice and they both laughed at his efforts. Then Geoff left Ben, and moved on to a young boy with spiky hair, whose anxiety was such that he stood apparently unable to move at all. Meg watched Geoff patiently leading the boy, Paul, step by step, with many pauses for explanation, until the two walked confidently, Paul holding the handle, and giving the commands in a firm voice.

Meg would have torn out the throat of anyone who tried to hurt Geoff. The difficulty was to learn the difference between hurting and helping. But she had learned, slowly and painfully that she must not be possessive, or try to prevent people from touching her person. She had learned it through trust in his teaching. Her wish to please him by her obedience was now stronger than her instinct to defend him.

Meg paced up and down. It was quite unnecessary for that giggly woman in pink to cling to his arm like that.

Ben and Paul got on well from the start. Paul, eighteen years old, had been blind from birth. His mother hadn't wanted him to have a dog, she was afraid of letting him out of her sight. Geoff had considered giving him Meg at one time, but feared a jealous reaction between the dog and the over protective mother. Paul was a bright lad, and was to start an Open University course in the autumn. He was surprised when Ben told him that he didn't want to learn Braille.

'Life would be much easier for you,' said Paul, 'and you'd learn it in no time.'

'I had a job learning to read and write ordinary letters,' said Ben. 'I didn't read much beside the paper, or write unless I had to. Why learn Braille when I may be able to see again?'

He and Paul set mental problems for one another to pass the time. Both found them hard, as Paul's were pure mathematics, the terms often unfamiliar to Ben. Ben's problems were different. 'How many sheep would you need to yield

£4,500 worth of wool, with fleeces averaging seven pounds at 61½p per pound?'

Geoff, overhearing them, was amused and pleased.

On the second evening, after tea, Geoff took most of the students to a local hotel, where the management was used to people from the centre, and they settled down to enjoy themselves.

Ben, drinking a shandy and making it last, amused himself by isolating the different voices, trying to place them, trying to visualize their owners. He was getting to know his fellow students and, although he hadn't made friends, he was on easy terms with several. He was getting good at picking out a single voice in a group, and hearing what it alone said – a thing he could never have done before. He listened for Geoff, and heard him greeting somebody who had just come in. He said, 'You'll see a big difference in him already.'

'It's a bad job,' was the reply. 'Poor lad. A bad job.'

'Guvnor!' Ben got up, carefully setting down his drink. He knew better now than to charge towards the voice – Mrs Seamer was somewhere about. It was her foot he'd stepped on when he'd arrived first.

'Eh, Ben lad, I'm pleased to see you.' Ben's hand was crushed, his shoulder thumped. 'Where's dog, then?'

'It's great to see you,' said Ben, without noticing his own words. 'No dog yet. They say we're not ready for them.'

'If you ask me, they think more to dogs than folks.' The overloud jolly note was back in Charlie's voice; Ben felt his discomfort acutely. 'Brought something for you; from Ireland.'

A small flat object was pressed into his hand.

'A tape?' he hazarded.

'Aye. Summat o' that. Mandy reckoned you'd be able to get someone to play it for you.'

'I can play it myself. Paul's got a cassette recorder. What is it?'

'There's nowt on label; just your name. Mandy was all for playing it, but I soon stopped that.'

They sat down, and Charlie's voice gradually lost its false heartiness. Ben thought he was more at ease when they were side by side on a settee than when facing each other on two chairs. Charlie didn't have to look at him.

'Seen Lesley lately?' Ben asked, with extreme carelessness.

'Nay, more's the pity. She doesn't come to farm, not since her and Mandy fell out. I hear she's moved house.'

'Still in Leeds?'

'Reckon so. Ask Geoff, why don't you. I told you not to let her go. She's shut of that Peabody now – divorced.'

'Remember me to her if you see her,' said Ben, choosing the formal words with care.

Charlie didn't stay long. He'd been at a wool-grower's meeting and had to go home, he said, but Ben knew he was bothered and embarrassed by the other students. Ben stood up as Charlie did, half sorry, half relieved that he was going so soon.

'It'll be grand to have you back at Middlegarth,' said Charlie.

'Thanks. When I get there, I'll find out what kind of work I can do,' said Ben. 'Geoff says I'll be able to go by bus once I've got a dog, and there are jobs going in the factories. I won't live on your charity.'

'Aye, that you won't,' agreed Charlie. 'Ask anyone round Middlegarth if Charlie Thorpe's a charitable man. They'll tell you he'd skin a louse for its pelt.' His hearty laugh was genuine this time, not the forced 'ha ha' that Ben dreaded hearing.

Ben braced himself for the buffet on the shoulder, and offered his hand to be crushed.

'Soon as you can earn any brass, I'll be after you for rent.'

Ben guessed at the wink which went with this promise. Through the closing doors, he heard faintly, 'A bad job . . .'

Somebody started haltingly to play the piano, and Paul said, 'Sing us a song, Ben.'

'No. I'm no good.'

'He is.' Paul had turned to speak to somebody else. 'You should hear him in the bath. Come on Ben, what's the one about a girl in a garden?'

'Just a ballad,' said Ben. He found himself drawn into a group, and was reminded with a stab of pain of how he had sung *Loch Lomond* until he had seen Lesley watching him.

'Can you play the piano, Ben?'

'No. The guitar, a little.'

'Here – here's a guitar.' Voices began to sing *Ilkley Moor*. Ben reluctantly strummed a few chords. The guitar was a cheap, clumsy instrument.

A more practised hand began to play the jangling old piano, and, to everyone's astonishment, Geoff sang a verse of *Amazing Grace*. He sat down to shouts of 'Encore!'

'I think that's plenty,' said Geoff. 'What about you, Mrs Seamer? Didn't somebody tell me you belonged to some big choir in Huddersfield?'

Mrs Seamer asked for a note, and said diffidently, 'Is that an A flat?'

'It's the nearest I can get to one on this piano.'

Ben recognized Dave Leyburn's bored voice. He set the guitar aside while Mrs Seamer quaveringly sang *Scarboro' Fair* and Dave played variations on the melody for several minutes with professional ease. Then he tired, and Ben heard his chair scrape back.

Other voices urged, 'Sing to us, Ben!'

'What used you to sing to the Guvnor's old ewes, Ben?' asked Geoff.

Ben laughed, and strummed his guitar. '"O by and by, by and by – I'm gonna lay down this heavy load . . ." Might have been written for them.'

There was laughter and calls for more. Ben was shy of singing in public – Agatha had seen to that – Mountebank! He could almost hear her say it. But an audience he couldn't see wasn't nearly so alarming.

Mrs Seamer said, 'I love the old spirituals – do you know any more?' Almost before he knew it, he was playing and singing, 'Michael row the boat ashore,' while the room resounded to Hallelujahs.

He began to enjoy himself, to be warmed by the

enthusiasm of his companions, until he found he was singing alone.

'Everybody's gonna have a wonderful time up there . . .'

He said, 'I think that's enough from me,' and refused to sing any more.

He was sorry when it was time to go home.

The twice-daily handle walks continued. Ben's interest increased as he began to understand the business of training student and dog separately. He stopped asking for his dog. He and Geoff practised kerb drill in Willow Close, a quiet housing estate where the class had gone by bus. Geoff stopped at the kerb until Ben told him to go on; Ben knew whether to step up or down by the angle of the harness he held.

'That's twice you've stepped on my tail,' grumbled Geoff. 'You say "Down" and step forward. Use your head, Ben.'

Ben's eagerness slowed up his progress. His new sense of purpose cheered him – he was getting somewhere at last. He behaved like a nearly happy man.

Geoff's doubts were allayed. He had a problem student or two, but not Ben. Ben's tendency to push Geoff along, his wild hand signals and incautious speed could all be cured. His confidence was being built up hourly, his only need was to relax. 'It's not a race,' Geoff said. 'You don't have to prove anything.'

On the third day, he charted the students' progress on paper, and made some reassessments, but it never occurred to him to give Ben a different dog. As he had known from the start, Meg might have been made for Ben. Ben asked Geoff how he matched man and dog.

'I could tell you a dozen ways,' said Geoff, 'and quote all sorts of facts and figures, but it's mainly instinct and experience.'

All day long, classes and lectures took place. It was tiring, even for the physically fit, because of the mental strain. Ben found Paul less anxious to exercise his brain in his spare time. They slept like logs at night.

Ben played his tape while Paul obligingly went out of the room. 'Are you going to tape a message home?' he asked when he came back. 'I'll clear off again while you do.'

'Don't bother,' said Ben, 'it'll wait.' But while Paul was in the shower, Ben put on the blank tape and hummed the melody he'd been working on. Then he recited the lyric and finally sang a verse. He stood for a few moments, thinking, sang a line of the second verse. He played it back with the volume down. Then he rewound the tape and recorded the beginning of a 'letter' home over the song. From time to time he added to this, but he thought it was so dull that he never posted it.

Ben no longer thought of blindness as an ongoing tragedy; mainly because he was living with a group of people who were mostly adjusting to life without sight, and also because he expected Meg to return his lost freedom to him. His brothers' familiar tones had given him a shock. They might have been trying to amuse a backward child. It wasn't what they said, it was their bright, encouraging voices. The lads at Billy Browne's and Terry, after expressing sympathy, had spoken naturally, pointing up the contrast.

Ben was beginning to see in perspective. He was still convinced he'd been right to send Lesley away, although the loss of her was more painful than the loss of his sight. But he knew that, if he'd let her stay, it wouldn't have worked. His true tragedy was his inability to accept her love.

All the least likeable facets of Ben's character, the pride, temper and suspicion, had been emphasized by his blindness. He couldn't recognize selfless devotion for the rare gift it was, suspecting always that he was pitied. He sensed dimly that he would have to work the aggression out of his system, but how, he couldn't imagine.

Geoff enjoyed the build up of tension during the first week of a course. A few of the students were happy enough to train with the instructors, still reluctant to trust life and limb to a dog, but most were growing impatient. Ben was frustrated almost beyond bearing by the delay. All the students would get their dogs on the same day.

The day came when almost a week had passed. It was a day which was looked forward to by the instructors nearly as much as the students. Geoff assembled the ten, and told each the name, breed and description of his dog. As his eyes travelled from one eager face to another, he thought of the first lecture of the course, only five days earlier. Then, those faces had shown anxiety, puzzlement, even fear. Especially he remembered Ben, tense and frowning, arms folded in what Lesley used to call his 'Napoleon pose'. Today, he still looked tense, but the frown had gone. Nobody was scowling except Dave Leyburn, who sat, slumped and bored, plaiting and unplaiting a piece of string.

Dave was getting Sailor, a large, patient dog, part retriever, whose previous owner had recovered his sight. Geoff was prepared to bet that the dog would be found unsuitable. Dave had decided on his future lifestyle, and it didn't include mobility.

'Paul,' said Geoff, 'your dog is called Max. He's a black Labrador, two years old, with a smooth coat. He's black all over, and you'll have to look lively with him. He's a fast walker, and he's very quick and intelligent.' As Geoff described Max, he saw Paul's long serious face break into a huge grin. Geoff never tired of seeing worried faces break into smiles when their owners first had their dogs described to them. It was one of the compensations which made the punishing hours, hard slog and responsibility worthwhile. And Ben's smile was worth waiting for.

'Ben, your dog Meg is a Border collie bitch. She's medium coated, with one ear pricked and the other bent over at the tip. She's a tricolour – black, white and tan, with a white collar, legs and tail tip. Oh, and she has a white stripe down her face. She's almost two years old.'

The smile came. Geoff had once thought that, to be whole hearted, the person would need to be able to see – to smile with his eyes. He had found out long ago that he was wrong.

The three instructors all found themselves beaming back at Ben, and so did Bob who was standing by the door.

'Is she like Roy?' asked Ben.

'Very like him to look at – I think you saw her once – but she's more generous and outgoing by far.'

'I wish I could have had Roy,' said Ben. 'His daughter's the next best thing.'

'You're joking. He'd have guided you round flocks of sheep, and bitten anyone who tried to help you.' Geoff passed on to Mrs Seamer, whose frail looks belied her. Three guide dogs had lived out their useful lives with her and been retired.

The instructors issued the now chattering students with slip chains, leads and grooming equipment. Then Geoff told them to go to their rooms where their dogs would be brought to them.

Ben and Paul's room was the third on the corridor, so Geoff had handed over four dogs to their new owners when he reached it. As he passed the first two doors with Paul's dog, Max, he could hear a variety of sounds from the rooms. Dogs were whining and panting, while the students' voices were raised in excitement as they exclaimed to the dogs and to one another. He could hear Judy Walker sobbing, but he was used to tears from students of both sexes. Tears of happiness and relief.

Ben was in his favourite place, standing with his back to the window, but Paul was sitting on the edge of his chair. The big dog went straight to him, Paul reached out, overbalanced, and they rolled on the ground in a heap; Paul protesting half-heartedly as Max licked his face. Geoff looked on until both were settled, Paul on the chair, Max sitting on the floor at his feet. He had to tell the dog to 'Stay' or it would have followed him out of the room.

'Sit down, Ben,' he said. 'It'll be easier for both of you.' He looked again at Paul, tousled, delighted, his arm round Max – a boy and his dog. How easy to sentimentalize, to think of the dog as a migically clever protector rather than a professionally trained partner and liberator. Geoff was sure that Max would save Paul from the natural over-protectiveness of his parents, would give him freedom and literally make a new man of him. He wasn't quite so sure about Ben.

As Geoff made his next trip up the stairs, with Meg sedate at his side, he wondered how he would get out of the room without her. He would order her to stay of course, but Meg was *his*. She had been his throughout her training; she was special. They had a bond which was more than the usual trainer/dog relationship. He knocked, and opened the door. 'Here's Meg, at last,' he said. 'Call her by name.'

'Meg?' Ben spoke quietly, seeking her by the sound of her paws. Meg left Geoff's side and went to Ben without a backward glance. There was no need to say 'Stay'. As Ben stretched out his hand, Meg lowered her smooth head, pressing it against his palm. She sat down with her back to Geoff. She half turned her head, rolled an eye in his direction. She rested her chin on Ben's knee.

With a pang remarkably like jealousy, Geoff closed the door.

Thirteen

Lesley had been allocated a fresh case to look after; a teenage boy who had been blinded in a street fight. He lived in a new housing estate in the suburbs – so new that the houses were still going up, and the gardens were littered with broken bricks and rubble.

It wasn't going to be a long assignment, as it was more important to advise Ron's mother than to help the boy himself. Lesley was glad. Mrs Watson kept up a furious tirade against the gang who had blinded her son, never pausing for breath or to listen to Lesley; Ron was bitter and silent. Lesley hated the job. A few months earlier, she would have seen it as a challenge to her patience and ingenuity, now it was a depressing chore. She had used up all her holiday time – there would be no let up. She drove away from the brightly painted little house with Mrs Watson's outraged cries ringing in her ears.

As Lesley drove round the central area, with its fountain and its embryo flower beds, she saw the familiar minibus from the Training Centre turning into the estate, with Geoff driving it. Bob was following, driving a small pick-up van with two bicycles in the back.

Lesley stopped her car beside a rustic sign which said 'Willow Close' in old English lettering. Her heart thumped, her hands sweated on the wheel.

Lesley knew to the day how far the course had progressed. This was the third week; the students would soon be going home. The minibus, bicycles and pick-up were to be used as traffic hazards, the bricks and uncovered drains as natural hazards. She clutched the steering wheel convulsively as she waited for Ben.

Meg was first off the bus, followed by Ben. Both exuded confidence. The other students and their dogs came behind, some hesitant, some clumsy, some quietly assured. Lesley saw that Geoff had noticed her. He raised his hand silently, and she nodded. Then he began to explain to the group how to deal with traffic in open places, with cars on narrow lanes and with reckless cyclists.

Ben's hair was an inch or two longer than usual and he had lost some of his tan, otherwise he hadn't changed in appearance. He looked, not happy, but determined. Meg might have been working for years. She was cool, capable, and never made the semblance of a mistake. She had matured in the last months, a beautifully proportioned animal, whose coat glowed with health, all her attention on the job she was doing. This was no sloppy dog, but a no-nonsense guide with a well developed sense of responsibility and, Lesley supposed, the canine equivalent of a social conscience.

Meg led Ben within ten yards of Lesley's car, waited as Bob cycled out of a side alley and swerved across her path, walked on. She and Ben walked quickly. Ben's head was held high; his hand on the harness sensitive but firm as if he'd been riding a horse with a light mouth.

Unreasoning rage filled Lesley. He's mine – mine. How dare he take that dog home and leave me out . . . throw me out? If only she could go on being angry with him, the rest would be easy. She would be free of him for ever. Free to – well free, anyway.

Ben would be interviewed by the Technical Officer, checked up on and visited by Geoff. With a quick mind, he'd have no trouble in getting a good job. Not in Leeds – please God not in Leeds. A job in York. There would be no reason why they should ever meet again. She could ring up the Guvnor and ask him how Ben was getting on in his job in York. After a time, there'd be no reason even to do that.

Meg had seen her. The dog turned her head and studied Lesley as she led Ben round a young willow tree tethered to a stake. Lesley could hear Ben's firm commands as he imitated Geoff's gruff tones. He gave the flattened Yorkshire 'U' in 'Hup-up' as they reached the kerb.

Blast him, blast him, with his self confidence and his clever dog. Who but a besotted fool would hanker for a blind man who didn't want her when there were plenty who both saw and wanted . . .

Lesley discovered that these reasonable thoughts, presenting themselves in her mind had no more reality than a bad tv movie. The sort you watch because you can't be bothered to turn it off. Because you don't want to read or go out or go to bed. Because your book bores you, there's nobody you want to see, nothing to go out for, your bed is cold. And she'd let herself be reduced to this pitiable state by Ben, now practising crossing the road while Sophy, grimly pedalling, shot out of turnings. Meg stopped and started and turned; Ben said, 'Well done, Meg, clever girl.'

Lesley consulted her notebook, wrenched her car round and drove home. It was lunchtime and she didn't feel like going to a cafe. She didn't feel like eating at home either, so she walked down to Henrietta's place. When she rang, Henrietta's voice came joyfully, 'Come on up; surprise.'

Lesley wasn't surprised, she'd seen it coming for weeks. Owen was there.

'I've been such a fool, Lesley,' said Henrietta. 'Such a bloody fool. Ring up your Ben and tell him what a fool he is.' She stretched out a hand, and Owen took it and held it tightly.

'Do stay,' they both said, while they were plainly longing for her to go away.

'I can't,' said Lesley. 'I'm taking a class of children from the day centre to the swimming pool this afternoon. Another time. I can't tell you how happy I am for you.' She kissed them both and left, while they urged her to come round whenever she liked.

Lesley knew she wouldn't. She remembered what Flora had said about Agatha. 'She couldn't bear to see anyone else in love.'

She had chosen her new, small flat because it was near Henrietta's, now she would be more alone than ever. She was too unhappy to care where she lived as long as the roof didn't leak. Her low-ceilinged living-room was painted slate grey, picked out with salmon pink. She hardly saw the hideous colours. If anything, she liked them because they matched her mood. She made no attempt to make a home. She ate sparingly, slept fitfully, and got on with her work.

Sometimes, letters arrived from Flora. They were written on pink lavender scented paper, so encrusted with flower designs that there was little room to write anything. She thought they might have been amusing if she had been capable of being amused. She also received a number of pamphlets from Brother Sebastian. They bore Ben's name and were marked 'Please forward'. Lesley didn't.

It was Saturday evening. The next week would be Ben's last at the centre. Lesley pushed him firmly to the back of her mind, and opened a tin of spaghetti. She had grown careless of what she ate, or when, or where. Guiltily, she thought she should invite Henrietta and Owen to supper. As she turned off the gas, the bell rang. Lesley started, splashed the sauce, burned her fingers and swore. If I get any jumpier, I'll have to resign, she thought, opening the door. Henrietta and Owen were there.

'Come in,' said Lesley, with forced enthusiasm. 'Lovely to see you.'

'Spaghetti,' said Henrietta, sniffing. 'Is there any left?'

'I haven't started. I can open another tin or make something else. What would you like?'

Owen, tall, stooping, with floppy dark hair and thick glasses, led Henrietta to the sofa, his arm round her shoulders. 'Don't bother about food,' he said, 'we came to see you. We don't want to put you out.'

'Do her good,' said Henrietta. 'She deserted a poor blind girl who needed her gentle pity and understanding.'

'Oh do shut up,' said Lesley, not quite joking. 'I've never seen anyone less in need of pity. I've got some cold chicken – we'll have that. If Owen sees his poor blind girl winding spaghetti round her neck, he might change his mind.'

'But it would slither down my front and he could fish it out. He'd enjoy that.'

Lesley's spontaneous giggle was her first for some time.

'I'd hate it,' said Owen. 'Don't flatter yourself.'

They ate chicken and cheese. Owen had brought a bottle of wine. 'We mean to get married as soon as I can get it organized,' he said. 'You'll come, won't you? We're not asking anyone else except parents.'

'A pity we have to ask them,' said Henrietta. 'I warn you, our mothers will weep like fountains. Bring plenty of Kleenex. Bring old Flora too if you like – she'd love it.'

'I draw the line at Flora,' said Lesley. 'How did you talk Henrietta into this, Owen? I could do with a few hints.'

'I had to stop her bullying me. It's bad for her to get away with it. She was using her disability as an excuse to refuse to make an honest man of me. When cajolery failed, I tried threats. Caveman stuff.'

'Brute.'

'I suppose,' said Henrietta thoughtfully, 'I could write a touching little piece under a false name.'

'No you couldn't,' said Owen. 'You will come to our wedding, Lesley, won't you?'

'Yes, of course. I wouldn't miss it for anything.'

As the evening passed, Lesley felt that some of their happiness was rubbing off on her. Although she could hardly bear to look at them, she was sorry when they went, but that night, she cried herself to sleep. For weeks, she had choked back tears whenever they threatened to spill over, feeling that if she began to cry there was no good reason why she should ever stop. Though red-eyed and headachey in the morning, she felt a great release of tension. She washed her face in cold water and remembered gratefully that it was Sunday. Over a late breakfast, she came to a decision.

When Lesley had drunk three cups of coffee, she drove to Middlegarth at illegal speed. Her purpose was to patch up her quarrel with Mandy.

The Guvnor was almost as restless as Lesley. He called one of the new students a sloven lubber and the other a shuffle-arsed bastard. Both left, threatening reprisals, never to return. He bullied Mandy, snarled at Eric, and threatened at intervals to shoot old Roy. The last three knew him too well to be intimidated.

The ram show and sales were beginning, and Ted and Eric spent hours washing and trimming the thirty rams which were going to be shown. They haltered them and led them about; they trained them to stand posed to the best advantage for the judges, heads up, legs planted squarely.

Some of the classes were for groups of three, and, as Charlie hadn't seemed interested, Eric asked Ted to decide how they should be divided. They spent the morning weighing and comparing, and finally picked out four groups of three.

At this point, Charlie appeared and said, 'Being clever, eh? Take second tup from left out. He's ten pounds lighter than t'others.'

'I know he is,' said Ted. 'But he's the nearest in make and shape. There isn't another to match those two.'

'Well, he doesn't bloody match. Take him out.'

They took him out.

After tea, Ted told Charlie that he and Mandy were leaving. The Guvnor was thunderstruck. 'You can't leave,' he said.

Ted had been steeling himself for days; he met the hard blue eyes firmly. 'You don't want us,' he said. 'You treat Mandy like dirt, and me like one of your students. They've left: we're leaving.'

'How d'you think you're going to live? Have you gone wrong in your heads? You'll be half-partners soon as I'm sixty-five – only another two years.'

'You can keep it,' said Ted. 'I'll look for a job as a farm manager. A job with a house going with it. I'm sick of being the lad around here. I'm not standing another two years of it.'

Ted's nerve gave out at that point. He marched out of the house, slamming the door. Then he doubled round to the front door. Running back to tell Mandy what a clever lad he's been, thought Charlie, hearing him go.

Let 'em go. Let 'em all go. They'd be glad to come back by spring. Charlie banged his fist on the table making the crockery jump. He sat down heavily, and thought about Stephen, and catching the next ship to New Zealand. Charlie had kept his horses, but he had known from the start that Stephen had gone for good. He wished more than he'd ever wished anything that he'd listened to Ben about Anagram. If he had, Ben wouldn't be blind, but living in the cottage with Lesley. Ted could go to hell.

The Guvnor had never been known to admit that he might be wrong, but he was going to spend the rest of his life knowing that, because of his arrogance, Ben would not be able to see.

He went to the door and bellowed, 'Mandy! Mandy! Bloody hell, have I got to wait all day?'

Mandy appeared at a run. 'Yes, father?'

'About flaming well time. Were you asleep? Tell that gawphead of yours he can forget about leaving.'

Mandy stood her ground. 'He means it,' she said.

'*You* mean it, more like. Ted never meant owt in his life. I maybe was a bit hasty. Tell him he can mix sodding tups any road he likes, and show 'em too, but don't blame me if it's the first time we don't bring any prizes home to Middlegarth.'

'Oh Father, thank you, he'll be so pleased.' Mandy knew that Charlie considered he had made a handsome apology. 'We didn't want to go, but you were so mean to Ted . . . And Father, Lesley came round yesterday and said she was ever so sorry she was rude to me, so I said it was quite okay. That's nice, isn't it?'

'Oh aye? Ben's due back next week, isn't he? Hope he's in better humour than when he left, or he'll set dog on her.'

'Father! He wouldn't dream of it – he and Lesley were made for each other.' She sighed dreamily. 'Shall I mash you some fresh tea?'

'No!' roared Charlie. Then he remembered he had vowed to be patient and tolerant in future. 'No, ta,' he said patiently.

Mandy considered asking him if he was feeling all right, and wisely thought better of it. She hurried away to report to Ted.

Nothing more was said about leaving.

Charlie went to the market the next day. When he came home, he saw Lesley's car outside Ben's cottage. He went in and discovered her cleaning the cooker, while Mandy polished the windows.

'Mandy, go and find Ted,' said Charlie. 'Tell him stir hisself; Broughton's want forty wether lambs eleven o'clock tomorrow. And while you're on, you might as well get tea. Give us a shout when it's ready.'

Mandy, her brief rebellion over, obeyed without question.

'Now then, Lesley, what's to do? Ben seen sense yet?'

'No, Guvnor, I don't think so. I'm just helping Mandy to clean up the place for him, then I'll go away.'

Charlie looked at her pale face critically. 'You could do with feeding up,' he said. 'And why in hell did you get your hair frizzled up? Better the way it was. You look like a stranger.'

Lesley smiled faintly. 'I thought a change would cheer me up,' she said.

'It's good to tell it hasn't. Face as long as a wet fortnight.'

Lesley returned to the cooker. 'I'll finish this job, if you'll excuse me,' she said politely.

Charlie watched her, his thick red hands resting on the table. 'Tell you what,' he said, 'I'll fetch Ben home myself, and you can come along o' me. Break the ice like, me being there. Talk about dog. Talk about weather if you must. Then I'll leave you both here, and you can get him his tea. If you can't carry on from there, sod isn't worth bothering with.'

He saw the colour rise into Lesley's face, and recede, leaving it whiter than before. He knew he was witnessing suffering which it was beyond him to understand.

'May I think about it?' Lesley said.

'Aye, but think sense if you can. This last month'll have changed lad. Maybe he'll have seen sense hisself. Went down to see him early on; he was asking about you.'

'What did he say?'

'Nowt much. He's same as you. You two want your heads jowling together. Knock sense into you.'

As Ben's course neared its end, he thought more and more about his homecoming. He had indeed become Geoff's star pupil, and he and Meg were perfect partners. To start with, he'd been in too much of a hurry. He'd fallen over Meg, and sometimes stepped on her paws or her tail. She had not been unnerved as Geoff had feared she would be. She had treated Ben with exasperated patience, as if he had been a stupid and uncooperative puppy, had looked after herself as well as him, had ignored his commands when they were obviously wrong. Ben had learned quickly, and formed a strong bond with her.

Almost as important, Ben was no longer a solitary outcast, but a member of his group. His constant striving to achieve more than he was able prevented him from being happy, but he now saw life in proportion and no longer felt like the only blind man in a seeing world.

Ben's last meal at the centre was in complete contrast to his first. The students crowded, chattering, into the dining-room, their dogs leading the way; then they sat in their usual places, while the dogs lay quietly under the table. Meg liked to lie with her chin on Ben's instep. The talk was lively and general – the last day of term this time. Sophy was almost flirtatious.

Ben was the only one of the ten who was unsure what he was going home to. The cottage, yes, but beyond that he knew nothing. He felt energy build up in him as they waited to be collected and taken home; the bottled up energy which had so often led to fits of temper. All the things he used to do to work it off were now beyond him. It was no good wishing he could gallop a horse over fences, he couldn't even work to exhaustion on the land.

To occupy his mind, he practised once again with Meg all the basic obedience work. He couldn't keep still, so he went right round the outside of the building, dodging obstacles with ease. It came so easily now, that his mind was left free for thoughts which he would have preferred not to think. He had thrown away his chance of living with Lesley, and he was beginning to realize he had made a mistake. Four of the students were married to sighted people. Ben had questioned them cautiously, but they didn't seem to share his hang-ups.

Ben decided that he would achieve something remarkable – he didn't yet know what – and when Lesley congratulated him . . . if she did . . . provided she hadn't found somebody else . . .

'Ben.' It was Geoff's voice. 'The Guvnor's come for you.'

Ben, saying goodbyes all round, kept an ear cocked for Charlie's voice saying that it was a bad job. But what he heard was the Guvnor saying that he never would've believed it and that you could have knocked him down with a feather.

'By lad, Ben, it's good to see you.' The thump on the shoulder made Meg edge closer to Ben. 'Awd bitch bite? She better hadn't. Come on then.'

'Leave him to the dog, Mr Thorpe,' said Geoff. 'Don't ever take hold of Ben's left arm when he's with Meg, and if you want to thump his shoulder, thump the right one.' To Ben he said, 'I'll be round to see you soon. You'll be all right, both of you.'

Ben sat beside the Guvnor in the Range Rover with Meg at his feet. Charlie said that he couldn't have believed it, that Mandy wouldn't half look, that Eric wouldn't half look, that farm hadn't been same without Ben. He didn't mention Lesley, but then, why should he?

'You haven't seen Lesley about, have you?' asked Ben.

'I have that. Up to this morning, I thowt she were coming along o' me to bring you home, but she couldn't make it. Phoned Mandy at last moment. Didn't talk to her myself. Happen she'll be coming round to see you.'

'Happen she won't,' said Ben glumly.

Ben listened to the traffic as they drove, automatically gauging its speed, direction and weight. His ears had learned to pinpoint different sounds, just as his eyes had once focussed on whatever he wanted to look at. His nose registered diesel oil, plastic, boot polish, tweed, tobacco, his own smell and Meg's. There were dozens of fainter scents from outside. Straw – somebody was combining – petrol, tar, grass. It occurred to Ben that half the things he could hear or smell were invisible anyway.

Ben smoothed Meg's head, trying to relax. It was plain stupid to imagine that Lesley would be at Middlegarth to meet him. He'd told her to go away and she'd gone; why should she come back to be snubbed again?

He felt the Range Rover swing in off the main road, and heard chippings crunch under its wheels.

'That's it then,' said Charlie. 'We've gitten home.'

Ben had tea at the farm. Eric greeted him as if he'd been on holiday, told him how the sheep were getting on and that there was a new vaccine for footrot. Mandy exclaimed over Meg, going down on her knees to pat and cuddle. Meg endured politely. Ben could sense her boredom.

'How's old Roy?' asked Ben, and knew the answer before it came.

'Dead,' said Charlie. 'Poor old dog missed you, I reckon. He used to hang about cottage, then he wandered out on road. Never knew him to do it before. Eric found him, dead as a nit. I bought a new dog two days since. Longton's breed. Cost a bundle.'

Ben said nothing. Mandy assured him that Roy couldn't

have known a thing about it. Meg moved closer to him; automatically, he caressed her.

'He was getting on,' said Charlie. 'Ten, maybe twelve. Decent dog – always was. Don't take on, lad; it's only a dog when you've finished.'

'I'd like to go home now,' said Ben.

'I'll take you,' cried Mandy.

'Meg will take me,' said Ben firmly, 'thanks all the same.'

Somebody, Eric? put the key in his hand. He shook Mandy's eager hand off his left arm fairly gently, and left the house. He could have found his way home easily enough without Meg. He put the key in the lock without fumbling, went in, sat down and took off Meg's harness.

It was ridiculous to be so affected by the death of an old, not very likeable dog. He slumped in his chair, remembering how Roy had sensed his misery and brought him a flock of sheep. He buried his fingers in Meg's ruff, twisting a lock of hair until she whined.

He'd left the door open. 'Here's your case, Ben. You left it in the Range Rover,' said Mandy's voice. 'Cheer up, don't look so down. It'll all come out in the wash.'

He didn't answer and presumably she went.

Later, Charlie came in and told him there was nothing so bad it couldn't be worse, that it would all be the same in a hundred years, and that it would have been worse if it had been Ben under a lorry on the Leeds road. Ben agreed, to save argument.

When Charlie had gone, he unpacked, fed Meg, let her out, remembered the Leeds road and called her in again. He spent ten minutes grooming her with the brush and pin-comb he'd brought from the Centre. He considered ringing Lesley up – hers was the only phone number he could remember. What business was so urgent that it had kept her from coming to meet him at the last moment, he wondered. In this mood, he didn't feel like risking a rebuff; he would have preferred to talk to Geoff.

He went to bed early.

Lena Danby, Technical Officer, called on Ben next day. She asked him a great many questions.

'Is there anything useful I can do?' asked Ben. 'I haven't had much education.'

'There are dozens of things you can do; it depends on you. If you want an interesting job with a decent wage though, you'll have to learn Braille.'

'How long would it take?'

'Not more than three months, usually. Then you could use computers, typewriters – all sorts of things.'

'I'd better learn to weave baskets,' said Ben.

'Why not? I didn't mean that you should spend three months just learning Braille. I thought, at your age, you might fancy a more active occupation, especially now that you've got a dog. What about music? Somebody said you played the guitar.'

'I don't play well. It's there somewhere – can you see it?'

'No. I'm blind.'

'*You're* blind?' Ben was staggered.

'It's a help in assessing people. I can't see you, but I may know more about you than if I could. Let's find that guitar.'

Ben found it. 'I sing better than I play,' he said.

'Sing then.'

Ben demurred, but after a weak protest, he began to sing with more confidence than usual, because nobody was watching or sympathizing.

Why is she waiting alone out there
In the empty garden?
The sun's rays spark on her shining hair,
The grass is wet but she doesn't care.
She is waiting for somebody – not for me.
Whose is the face her green eyes see
In the sunny garden?

'Sorry. I'm not much good.'

222

'Yes you are. Love the song – what is it? I've never heard it before. Do go on.'

But Ben wouldn't. When she'd gone, he tried another verse.

Where have you gone to, girl of mine,
Gone from the garden?
I was only away for a minute or less
And I caught just a glimpse of your long green dress
And the edge of a smile like sun in the rain,
And now I'm alone, alone again
In the shadowy garden.

Ben tried again to recall the garden in Agatha's picture, but it was all muddled. Lesley was sitting on the grass in her ink-blue dress and the earrings like little silver fans, with the sun on her fair head. But he'd sent Lesley away.

When I slept I dreamed you were in my arms –
Spring in the garden.
I held your body close to my own –
Don't vanish, my love, and leave me alone.
But you slide away like a falling tear,
The rain pours down and my arms hold air.
Night in the garden.

The song was coming into shape. The words weren't quite right, but the sense was what he intended and he knew the melody was good. It had pathos, but strength too, and none of the Saturday-night-at-closing-time sentiment which spoiled so many romantic ballads.

He had never tried to compose a tune before, and now, already, another was forming in his mind; a cheerful thing with a good beat to it. He forgot the ever-present Mandy, and began to improvise, sitting on the corner of the table, one foot on the floor, the other swinging in time to the music, his back to the door.

*

Meg wished that Ben would stop singing and playing. She could put up with it but she didn't like it. She wished he'd left her outside, where there were interesting smells, including that of another dog. Although trained to disregard other dogs and smells of all kinds when at work, when her harness was removed she was off duty. She sat close to the door, squinting through a crack.

Ben didn't hear the car pull up, he was making too much noise, he didn't hear the tap on the door. Meg swallowed the growl which rose to her throat. The woman Lesley was not wanted there, had no business to be there. She had given Ben away to Geoff who had passed him on to Meg. He was Meg's person now, and she had no intention of giving him back.

The door opened. The woman was happy, laughing. She spoke to Ben in a warm, loving voice. Apparently she liked to hear him sing. Ben jumped off the table, spun round. The strap of the guitar caught on the shutter, the guitar clattered to the floor.

Meg sensed that Ben was angry because he hated to be approached from behind, but she could sense his delight as well. Geoff had spent a year and a half training Meg not to show protective aggression or jealousy. She tucked in her tail, and with her ears flattened to her head, pushed open the bedroom door with her nose and crawled under the bed. She lay there, sulking.

Meg could hear their voices rising and falling, two people who wanted to be together. Ben had forgotten about Meg. He would remember her when the woman had gone away.

Meg couldn't see much from her place under the bed, but enough. The woman bent to pick up the guitar and put it aside, then she was hidden as Ben's back hid her from Meg's view. Ben's voice meant many things to Meg; like all guide dogs she had a wide vocabulary of words and phrases, but it was the tone of voice that told her most. Ben had been angry because he was startled; now he didn't care. There was a note in his voice which Meg knew well. He sometimes used it when he spoke to her . . . not often. She could see the woman's hands – her arms were round Ben. One hand with spread fingers caressed the back of his neck.

Meg backed further under the bed. The coverlet hid them from her view.

Afterwards, Ben couldn't be sure how the quarrel started. He loathed being watched, and hadn't wanted Lesley to hear the song until it was finished. But she'd only just arrived, he should have known she wouldn't spy on him. Then he forgot everything but the joy of her presence, her voice, her scent. He knew what she looked like, and when she spoke he could see her in memory. He had always loved to smooth the hair back from her forehead as he kissed her – its silkiness gave him special pleasure. His hand touched her face . . . 'Darling, how thin you are!' Then his fingers tangled in a mass of curls, right down to her eyebrows.

'What the hell have you done to your hair?'

'Had it permed. One of those long shaggy perms. It hides that scar and I felt like a change.'

Ben felt shocked out of all proportion. He held the bunch of curls in his hand, not silky but springy. 'You've put something on it,' he said. 'Some disgusting spray.'

'I haven't. It's only setting lotion. Please don't be cross when we've just found each other again. A new hairstyle's a cure for depression.'

'It isn't a cure for mine,' snapped Ben. 'Can't you do it the way it was before?'

'Not possible. It'll have to grow out. It'll take weeks.'

'How could you?' Ben let her go. 'I don't know what you look like now. Why did you have to change?'

'I haven't changed,' Lesley's voice rose. 'You've changed – I never have. You're being childish, I wish I'd stayed away.'

And that was only the beginning. Like any quarrel between people in love, it was bitterer and nastier than if either of them had cared less. Ben was abusive, Lesley spiteful. Meg padded out of the bedroom and stood in front of Ben.

Lesley, losing her temper for the first time in years, suddenly realized that she might be throwing away her last chance of staying with Ben. She said, 'I'm sorry, darling, I didn't mean it, forgive me,' but it was too late.

Ben said, 'I'm sorry too, but what chance have we got? Half an hour together and we're fighting. I told you before to leave me alone.' He stepped back, caught his foot in the chair leg and nearly fell. Lesley grabbed his arm, Ben dragged it away. Meg, goaded beyond endurance, growled.

'That dog should know better than to growl,' said Lesley. 'Over-protective and jealous. Has she bitten Mandy yet?'

'How dare you find fault with Meg!'

'Oh, she's perfect, is she? Give her a kick in the ribs and she'll come crawling back and lick your feet. Okay, if that's what you want –'

'Lesley, wait –'

'Here, I brought you a pocket recorder. I'm sure Mandy will show you how to use it.' A hard object was banged down on the table. 'You have my phone number and Geoff's. I'll be there if you learn to control your foul temper, but I won't play second fiddle to your sodding dog.'

The door slammed.

Ben found that he was shaking so violently that he couldn't control his hands. When he had sent Lesley away before, he had been reduced to tears of self-pity, frustration and loneliness. But at least he had believed he was right. This time he was wrong. He had been selfish, cruel, childish – everything Lesley had said was true. He didn't blame her – he had started the row.

He dropped into the larger of the two chairs, exhausted. Somebody had mended the rip in the upholstery. A cold nose was pressed into his trembling hand. He thought of Roy. In that black moment, he felt responsible for everything that had happened since he left Ireland. If he hadn't quarrelled with Agatha, he wouldn't be blind, Agatha herself would probably still be alive, the picture hanging in her bedroom.

Lesley would be happy with somebody else, Roy would never have wandered onto the main road.

'I think we'll go for a walk, Meg,' he said.

Ben's fingers shook so that he was clumsy adjusting the harness, but he managed at last. Meg waited while he fumbled with the key and locked the door. He lifted the handle of the harness from Meg's back and told her to turn left. She led him down the farm lane towards the traffic noises, stopped. He'd forgotten the cattle grid.

'Left, Meg, good girl. Stop.' He opened the hand gate and they went through. Meg stopped at the edge of the road.

Ben considered. He didn't want to go to the village where he would meet people he knew, and this was a stupid place to try to cross the road.

'Turn left, Meg.' They walked along the road at a brisk pace for about half a mile, then Ben heard the screech of brakes as a bus overtook them and drew up. He raised his arm saying to Meg, 'Onto the bus, girl.' She led him along its side – smell of hot metal and oil – stopped.

'Hup-up . . .' Three steps. He took a seat, felt in his pocket, held out a dozen coins, some of them the thick ones which were pounds. A hand selected some of them as a voice asked, 'All the way?'

'All the way,' said Ben.

Fourteen

———— ❧ ————

'I've had a row with Ben,' said Lesley.

'You what?' Charlie looked up from the *Yorkshire Post*.

'We quarrelled. I know it was stupid. And now he's disappeared.'

'Well, that beats hen-racing. You two were in that house quarter of an hour at most and you fell out. What about?'

'Nothing much. It was a straightforward slanging match. We were a couple of idiots. I think it was mainly stress.'

'Stress? Bugger that. It were daftness.'

Lesley walked about the kitchen restlessly. 'I wanted to say I was sorry,' she said. 'So I went down to the Turpin Arms and rang him up. There was no answer, so I went back to the cottage and he'd gone out and locked up. He hasn't been up the yard – I asked Eric. You haven't seen him, have you?'

'Nay. He'll have taken dog out.'

'But where? If he'd been on the road, I'd have seen him. He's vanished.'

Charlie crackled his paper impatiently. 'Gone down to Ings and drowned hisself, like as not,' he said. 'Daft enough for owt.' He turned to the factory report.

Lesley went back to the cottage where she'd left her car. Sometimes, even now, she felt that she didn't know Ben very well. She was sure he wasn't the type to kill himself, certainly not because of a silly quarrel, but he was in a temper and might easily have gone to the Ings, once a favourite place, to cool down in privacy. The beck was deep, with treacherous banks, and she didn't know how well he could swim. Meg would know better than to take him close to the edge, but theirs was a very new partnership – it was no place to go walking.

She crossed the road and walked up to the field gate. There were sheep in the pasture, they didn't seem to have been disturbed, but she wasn't convinced. She hurried down to the beck and along its reedy banks. A pair of mallard flying up almost under her feet made her jump, she laddered her tights and got burrs in her skirt.

There was no sign of Ben or Meg.

Mandy and Ted were away. Lesley drove home slowly. It was stupid to be so worried. Even at the height of their quarrel, common sense had told her, this isn't the end, we can sort this one out; it might even clear the air. She thought Ben knew it too. Anyway, if he was going to jump in the beck he'd have done it long ago, before he got Meg. Not his sort of thing at all, thought Lesley. Still, months of mental strain did funny things to the most normal. She was bitterly ashamed of herself, and badly wanted to tell him so.

When she got home, she washed her hair, dragging out the curls, combed it back and plaited it in two pigtails. Ends of the fringe escaped and coiled up like springs. She pulled them straight and clamped them down with hairslides.

She rang the centre and asked for Geoff, but he wasn't there. He wasn't at home either. She determined to find him, wherever he was.

It was late afternoon. Ben will come home when he gets hungry, thought Lesley.

Ben found the swaying of the bus soothing. It seemed to be full, because, after two more stops, it hurtled along, mile after mile. There was somebody between him and the window – a woman. He wondered whether in the old days, he would have known blindfolded the sex of the person beside him.

Ben had got onto the bus because he wanted to be alone. True, it seemed to be full, but he had learned that in England there wasn't much fraternizing on public transport. He

229

wouldn't have boarded an Irish bus in search of solitude. He and Meg would have been the centre of attention and would have been the centre of a chattering group when they got off.

Always, he would have to assume that he was not alone. He found this one of the hardest things he had to bear. He was certain that Mandy spied on him, and hoped fervently that the Guvnor would catch her at it. He found a sort of privacy rocking along in this crowded bus going he didn't know where. His unreasoning guilt had gone, and his anger was now all directed against himself. Why, why quarrel with Lesley? He loved her, he wanted her, he had shouted at her and kept a row going when he could have stopped it. He was learning more about her now that he couldn't see her. Her voice held shades of meaning which once would have passed him by. He would have seen her angry face and no more.

Ben knew she would come back. He had a curious feeling of triumph. There had been no pity in her today. You don't yell at someone you pity, you don't call him a selfish, pig-headed bastard. But he was sure that it wouldn't solve everything to make it up, to kiss and be friends. He simply wasn't ready to share his life with Lesley again – not yet. He needed time to think things out, to adjust to living with Meg and his new independence. He still felt a compulsion to prove himself in some way. He wished he could talk to Dr Stroud again, find out what his chances of sight were.

'Give you a hand, lad?' The bus was emptying – had emptied. Lost in his thoughts, Ben had sat on.

'I'm okay,' he said, jumping up. 'Out, Meg.' A hand clutched his elbow as Meg led him down the steps.

'Where are we?' Ben asked the owner of the hand.

'Runcie Sands. The seaside. Didn't you know? Come on then, I'll take you down to beach.' It was a man, elderly, with ill-fitting dentures.

'That's all right. My dog'll find it.'

'No trouble,' said the man, taking a firm grip on Ben's arm. 'It's a poor look-out if we can't help one another.'

Ben heard the sea, hissing on the sand about fifty yards

away. 'Please let go of my arm,' he said, his voice tight with controlled annoyance.

'It isn't a bit o' trouble to walk you down. Never know when you might fall over this or that; dog can't do it all, can it? Now, you wait here, lad, don't move. I'll get you a deck chair, be back in two shakes. Don't want to go nearer when tide's on turn.'

The man's feet receded, crunching pebbles. Ben listened like a hunted animal. 'Turn left, Meg, hurry. Walk on, quick, good girl.'

Meg turned left, guessed the meaning of the rest, hurried. Almost running, Ben followed. The sea was on the right now, voices of children playing.

'Straight on, Meg.' Ben walked on ribbed sand. He lifted his feet high, it was easy to catch a toe or trip over one of the large smooth stones. He imagined himself falling flat, being helped up and gently scolded by the man with the clacking teeth. This sand would be submerged at high tide. He wondered if it was coming in or going out.

The voices dropped behind. Meg stopped. 'Straight on, Meg.' But she veered to the left, and Ben knew that there was a high solid mass in his path. A cliff? A beached ship? A breakwater? Meg led him onto loose stones, he slipped and tripped. She bore left again, not waiting to be told, and there was a path underfoot. It felt like asphalt, smooth under the worn runners on his feet. The childrens' voices were fainter, he heard the cry of gulls.

'Straight on, Meg.' Damn it, he was hungry. He had smelled chips down there, but the deck chair man had driven him away. The path climbed and twisted. Meg walked purposefully ahead, happier now, with a well defined path under her feet. After a while, the metalled surface gave way to dirt, the path became a track, long grass, or perhaps sea thrift brushed Ben's legs.

'Straight on, Meg.' She had to walk directly in front of him now instead of to the left; the path had become a narrow cutting, carved by sheep. They reached high ground – a strong

231

wind struck them suddenly. The track began to twist down-ward, narrowing until it was lost in the clumps and tussocks of grass. A damn silly place for a blind man to go walking, he knew. Meg stopped.

They must have come the best part of a mile. Ben sat down, and Meg leaned against his knees. There was higher ground behind and ahead. They were out of the wind; the crash of waves was close below. Ben thought he heard a distant hail. Yes, somebody a long way off was shouting at the top of his voice. Ben didn't pause to consider that it might be anybody, shouting for any of a hundred reasons that didn't concern him. He jumped to his feet. Why couldn't he be left in peace for five minutes?

'Straight on, Meg.' She went forward a few yards, stopped. There was some sort of fence on the left. Barbed wire, sod it. 'Straight on – get on, lass.' Meg stood her ground, firmly ignoring the wrong command as she had been trained to do. Ben had been trained too. In a case like this, trust the dog. Check carefully before attempting to go any further. 'Shift, can't you?' Meg sat down. Ben stepped forward, trod on her tail, withdrew his left foot and took a long step forward with his right.

As he fell, Ben let go of Meg's harness and dropped sheer. There was no bank to roll down, no ledges to grab at, even if he could have seen them. He dropped flat on his stomach on the water, winding himself. A mouthful of salt water roused his survival instincts and he began to swim, probably in a circle, he thought.

Ben could swim moderately well. All four brothers used to strip, and plunge into the deep, cold, dangerous river at Cloninch after work on a hot day. But the river was nowhere more than sixty feet wide – he had never swum further than from one side to the other. The sea was more buoyant and much warmer. He supposed he could keep afloat for some time. But he couldn't protect himself from bangs on rocks he couldn't see. He wondered how long it took to drown.

Ben felt the nearness of a cold, dank wall of rock before he reached it. Then his face and hands were thumped and scrubbed against the stone. The sea wasn't rough, probably this was a small cove where the waves were forced in through a bottle-neck of rocks. This must be the cliff he'd fallen from – he could hear Meg barking up there somewhere. The rock was as slippery as ice; no shellfish here, no fingerhold. Meg wasn't so very far above him – six feet? Ten? Too far, anyway. The sea picked Ben up and threw him carelessly against the high, wet wall of rock. Then it dragged him back and ducked him. Automatically, he began to swim again, hopefully along the cliff side. Meg's barks grew hysterical – he guessed that she couldn't see him any more. Where was he going, anyway?

Self pity began to return, bringing with it a kind of warped comfort. Why bother to swim? Agatha gone, Lesley driven away. Blind. Helpless.

A small wave ducked him like a cold hand on the back of his neck playfully pushing him under. It receded, taking him out into the open with it, and banged him agonisingly against something sharp and large. He reached out, and hooked his right arm round a slimy, limpet-encrusted lump of rock. He spat out water and shook his head.

Self pity had evaporated. Pain turned it to anger. A picture came to his memory with sudden vividness. Agatha at the head of the table having breakfast. Muriel had come into the room, white-faced, big with bad news.

'Gossiping with the postman, Muriel?'

Muriel had told them that the postman had found Timmy O'Moyne hanged in his own cowshed. Timmy was known to be in debt, and his wife had left him.

'Oh, the poor soul!' Muriel had wailed.

Agatha had buttered another piece of toast, then she had delivered her verdict.

Ben's wild laughter was lost among the sea noises – the waves, the gulls, the wind. For a moment, he thought he heard her voice.

– Weakling. Probably inbred.

Meg stopped barking. She was standing on the extreme cliff edge, overlooking a small bay with a rock in the middle of it. Ben was clinging to the rock and, for some reason, laughing. Beyond the headland, on the right, lay sand and safety.

Meg had to make a conscious decision, training against instinct. Two conflicting happenings urged her to two different courses of action. On one hand, her Ben, her own person, for whom she was responsible, had fallen into the sea and, if no help came, he would drown. Instinct told her to go to him and stay beside him as long as there was life in him. Whether or not she drowned with him was beside the point and didn't enter her mind.

On the other hand, Meg was on duty and in harness. If Ben had once called her, her plain duty would have been to go to the recall, whatever mess he had got himself into. Otherwise, she should obey her training, and remain at the spot where her last command had been given, right or wrong. She could bark to attract attention, she had barked herself hoarse. The sea drowned her voice, the wind carried it away.

Ben didn't call her. He didn't shout or scream for help. She had heard him under the cliff edge, out of sight, swearing and choking, and now he was laughing like a madman.

It was a fair drop — about twice Ben's height. Nothing, if she hadn't been in harness. The cliff edge overhung the spot where Ben had sworn and choked a few minutes before. She could hear the breakers echoing under the edge. There was no way of bringing Ben up to where she stood, but if she swam — tried to swim — towards that headland, she might be able to tow him within sight of the cheerful seaside crowd round the point.

She hesitated, her paws at the very edge. The wiry, silvery grass was as smooth as glass, the cliff eroded by centuries of salt wind and water.

Meg jumped.

Ben didn't hear the splash. He was concentrating on his piece of rock. He had almost been dragged from it by a big wave and carried out to sea, but he had clung to it like a barnacle. Before the next wave, he had worked his way round to the landward side of it, keeping his handhold, and had wedged a knee into a hollow on its inhospitable surface. If the tide was coming in, he would soon know, and he would have to let himself be carried out into the open sea and hope to be seen – some hope!

He'd noticed that Meg had stopped barking without much interest. Thank God he hadn't pulled her in with him. The thought of Meg drowning as a result of his own carelessness was unbearable. Then, suddenly, she was there beside him, panting and paddling, her body rising and falling on the waves. His hand closed on the handle of her harness. 'Oh, Meg, Meg, you bloody fool!' But Meg responded to his tone, not his words. She was trying to drag him away from the rock; trying to swim out to sea with him.

Ben pulled her back, caught hold of her collar, got his left arm round her. He hoisted her up as high as he could, and she, seeing what he intended, scrabbled her way upwards until her front paws were hooked over his left shoulder, her head level with his own.

Every few seconds, a wave washed right over both of them. In one of the intervals, Ben said to Meg, 'I think the tide's going out,' and in the next, 'I hope I'm right.'

Ben felt stinging pain all over him as the salt found a dozen cuts. His right elbow and knee were numb with bruises, his fingernails broken as he hung on. Yes, the tide was going out all right – only about one wave in seven was breaking over their heads.

After a long fifteen minutes, Ben was able to look for a handhold further down the rock. He felt his shirt ripping as he inched his way down. The waves hit him chest high. Meg anxiously licked his ear.

'We've got a chance, Meg. Don't worry, I won't let you drown – nobody's going to drown today.'

Down, down. There was ground under Ben's feet at last. Pebbles shifting and sucking, seaweed and blessed sand. He stayed where he was, growing very cold, until the water was only thigh deep. Then, carrying Meg, who would still have been well out of her depth, Ben waded painfully to the cliff, guided by the sound of the waves receding on the shingle. The water was just above his knees when he reached the cliff, turned left and began to work his way along it. The dog was unbelievably heavy in his arms – her thirty-five pounds felt like a hundred.

Meg struggled to be put down. She could manage now, the water was only just above Ben's ankles. He fell into a small rocky pool which he supposed she must have seen, and she fell with him, underneath him.

They scrambled out, and Ben wondered how much he had hurt her. He sorted out harness and lead. 'Carry on, Meg. Back to the bus. Clever girl.'

It took them half an hour to round the point. Again and again, Ben fell, as the smooth wet stones slid about. One of his shoes was gone, the sole torn from the other. In places, he was shuffling through piles of loose pebbles, then there would be a patch of smooth wet sand, then they were paddling through tepid shallow water. Meg stopped twice to shake herself thoroughly, otherwise she didn't delay. Some-times she steered him round something, a rock? A pool? Mostly, she kept on over going which would have tested a man with the use of his eyes.

Ben fell twice more, tripping over the sole of his shoe – he wrenched it off – then catching his foot in a mass of seaweed which was heaving nastily in shallow lukewarm water. Once, he trod on something small, soft and alive. Now that he was, he supposed, out of danger, his thoughts were all of Lesley. He might have drowned – almost had – leaving her nothing but rejection and hard words to remember.

'Lesley,' he said aloud. Meg walked faster, and didn't bother to go round a patch of weed which might easily have crabs in it.

As they rounded the point, away from the eastward facing cliffs, no warmth from the sun greeted them. It must be evening. The bathers had gone too. The smell of frying chips was still there. Ben headed for it.

'It's been a long time since breakfast, Meg,' he said.

'Double fish and chips please, salt, no vinegar,' said Ben, and added in dismay, 'Oh God, no money either.' For his pocket had gone, torn right out. Furtively he checked that he was decent. He found another large rent in the seat of his jeans.

'We're closed,' said a woman's voice, then, 'Hold on, though – Fred, come here . . . One minute, love, get you something in a tick.'

The man and woman in the van talked together, was he going to have to make do with a bit of bread? Thoughts of food and Lesley jostled for first place in his mind. He was very cold. He took off what was left of his shirt, wrung the water out of it and towelled his head with it. Then he tied it round his middle. Gratefully he heard a tremendous sizzling begin. Fred and his wife were preparing supper.

'I can't pay –' he began.

'On the house.' Fred was beside him. He spoke in the loud, jolly voice Ben had grown accustomed to. 'Want something for dog, then? He looks as if he could do with it.'

'I was going to give her half my chips and ask for some milk for her.'

'I'll get him some chips for himself – cool 'em down like. Fancy a guide dog getting you into such a pickle. Why, I thought they were almost human.'

Ben defended Meg hotly. Fred didn't believe him, he was sure.

'Want a lift?' said Fred. 'We're for home too.'

'Where to?'

'Goole.'

'Where's that?'

There was a pause. Ben had displayed an unbelieveable depth of ignorance. 'Is it anywhere near Middlegarth?' he asked. 'Leeds road?'

'No, sorry about that. It's t'other road. Hull way.'

The fish and chips came, not in paper but on a dish. Fred put another dish on the ground for Meg. 'He's not hungry, your dog isn't. Funny that.'

Phil Monk had gone to Bridlington that day to watch the Duchess of York bestow her name and her blessing on the new Maritime Museum. He had searched in vain for anything to say about the event that every other reporter there wouldn't have said too, got bored, phoned the evening paper, had a drink, and had finally driven up the coast, putting in time. He had a dinner to cover in Leeds, but that wasn't for hours yet.

At Runcie Sands, Phil met a talkative elderly man who seemed the type to know everything interesting – if there was anything interesting – about the place. The village, a few hundred yards from the beach, was unpopular because the bathing was dangerous. Coaches came there, but only after they had deposited most of their passengers at Bridlington. The man accepted a beer at the Three Jolly Tars, and Phil wished he'd gone straight to Leeds. The old devil's teeth clacked like castanets.

'One of those guide dogs he had. I told him wait, because it stood to reason dog couldn't fetch him chair, could it? Got chair – he'd gone, just like that. Well, I thought, he's lost his manners along of his sight, poor chap. I mean, I'm not one to bear a grudge; for all you and me know, poor sod's gone and drowned. Put me in mind of –'

'When was this? Where did you see him last?'

'Two hours since, maybe more. I'm from Bridlington, me, come to see my sister. That's my bus out there, it's the last 'un; goes in ten minutes. I mean, he's not on it, is he? I mean, where's he got to? It's not fair on folks, blind men running about losing themselves. I'm broad-minded, but what I always say is –'

'Absolutely,' murmured Phil. 'Well, Mr Green, it's been nice meeting you, but you don't want to miss that bus, do you?' He firmly saw Mr Green onto the bus, then returned for another drink, wondering if there was a story. . . . But no. Somebody would have noticed a blind man and his dog drowning, even at Runcie Sands. He looked idly out of the window, and saw in the distance the group by the chip-van which was still parked on the beach.

He took a number of pictures. God bless the telefoto lens. . . . He went nearer, intrigued by Ben's appearance. Good-looking chap – or would be when he was cleaned up – and packed with personality. Get him in the foreground, the bloke from the van was much taller. The dog was lying down, licking its paws, and the blind chap had his shirt off, knotted round his waist. His jeans were in ribbons – he was probably trying to hide a bare backside. His face and chest were streaked with blood, dirt and weed.

Phil was old enough to have enjoyed the vintage Hollywood movies of the forties. This chap reminded him of the young Spencer Tracy, except that his hair was black.

Phil had been a journalist for thirty years. He didn't put on a special voice for anybody. 'You look as if you could do with a lift home,' he said.

The young man gave him a smile which illuminated his stern features. There'll be a girl somewhere, thought Phil. Probably half a dozen.

'I'm catching a bus.'

'You're out of luck. The last one's just gone. Where are you going?'

'A village called Middlegarth.'

'That's a bit of luck. I'm going to Leeds, and it's on my road. Good pub there, isn't there? Turpin Arms.' Phil noticed that the guide dog was hurt. It got up stiffly and stood on three legs; it had a cut over one eye. 'Lovely dog that – mind if I take his photo?'

'I don't, but she must be all to hell; we've been half drowned. It's "she" not "he". She's called Meg. I'm called Ben.'

Phil didn't worry about the damage that the wet, sandy, bloody pair were doing to the upholstery of his nearly new car. He drove slowly and, without ever seeming to pry, learned a great deal about Ben.

'Put me down at the bus shelter, please,' said Ben. 'It's this side of a notice saying "Middlegarth Farm". There's a sign with a picture of a sheep on it.'

'Just passed it,' said Phil. 'I'll go on and turn at the roundabout, then you'll be on the right side of the road. Can't I drive you to your door?'

'No thanks. I'd sooner walk up.'

'Want to get cleaned up before the girlfriend sees you? Don't blame you. And poor old Meg's going to need a vet.'

Five minutes later, Phil was at the telephone in the Turpin Arms. 'Lorraine? Phil. Get me the news desk – quick.'

Ben followed Meg at her slow pace up the path to the cottage. He put his hand under the tub of hydrangeas Lesley had bought, feeling for the key. It wasn't there. She'd come back! She was there in the house, waiting for him! He charged through the door.

'What the bloody hell have you been doing to that dog?' demanded Geoff.

Fifteen

———— ❧ ————

Ben had been seen boarding the bus for the coast at noon, and Geoff had been waiting for half an hour to meet the last one. Lesley, who had tracked Geoff down in the Kosy Kitchen, had so obviously been afraid for Ben's safety that she had almost persuaded Geoff. He had calmed her fears and promised to meet the last bus when it reached the stop outside Middlegarth. When it arrived without Ben, he began to be really worried and questioned the conductor.

The conductor remembered Ben well, and said he'd got off at Runcie Sands. 'That's as far as we go,' he had said. 'I had to tell him when to get off. Godforsaken spot, end of the line. Some families go there to picnic, but the tiderip and the quicksands keep the swimmers away.'

'Is there a pub there, or a guesthouse?'

'Just the pub where we stop. The Three Jolly Tars.'

By this time, Geoff was almost as frightened as Lesley. He drove to the cottage, found the key and went in. There was a pocket recorder on the table and he switched it on, thinking Ben might have left a message. Lesley's voice recited telephone numbers. Meg's belongings were unpacked and tidily laid out, there was a mug with some tea in it on the table. Geoff picked up the telephone and asked Enquiries for the number of the Three Jolly Tars. If he drew blank, it would have to be the police.

He was dialling when he heard Ben looking for the key under the tub of hydrangeas.

Geoff's temper never got the better of him, he was too good a dog trainer for that, but he seldom had to tell off the same person twice. As for his dogs, they were never punished, they were 'corrected'. They too, hardly ever had to be corrected twice. When he saw Meg, her fur clotted with dry blood, limping into the kitchen, he told Ben, not mincing his words, exactly what he thought of him.

'You frightened Lesley out of her wits, and let down your friends who got you the best dog I've ever worked with. Have you ever given a thought to what our dogs cost to rear and train? Did you think about the two years of work and care that have made Meg what she is? Don't you know how many people there are waiting for a dog who would look after it properly? I thought you'd learned to behave like a responsible man. It seems I was wrong.'

Geoff looked up from inspecting Meg's swollen paw, and for the first time saw the extent of Ben's injuries. Ben pushed past him and took down a jacket from a hook on the back of the door. He put it on, and bent to pull at his remaining shoe. It was reduced to tatters of canvas, held in place by wet, knotted laces. He felt in his pockets.

'Have you got a knife?' he asked, ignoring Geoff's reproaches. 'There's one in my sleeveless jacket, but I can't remember where I left it.'

'It's on the back of the chair,' said Geoff, feeling in the pockets. He found the knife and also a small leather box of the sort that jewellers use for rings. Hm, thought Geoff.

He cut Ben's shoelaces, and filled a basin with water. Ben put on the electric kettle, while Geoff went to his van for his first aid kit. Then Geoff gently bathed Meg's cuts and sores, kneeling beside her on the floor.

'I don't think she's broken anything,' he said. 'But she'll have to go to the vet. I know a good chap who won't mind me calling so late. I wouldn't like to take her to the Centre like this – she can stay at my place. What about you? Shall I clean up those cuts for you?'

'Thanks. And Geoff, I'm as sorry about Meg as you are.'

As Geoff washed and refilled the basin, adding fresh disinfectant, he said, 'I should have seen to you first, Ben.

Sorry about that.' He began to bathe Ben's cuts with as much care as Meg's (no more). But when he'd washed away the blood and saw the deep dirty grazes and the black bruises, he stopped and said, 'I'll get you to bed, Ben. It's the doctor for you.'

'I'm all right. I'll be fine.' Ben allowed Geoff to help him reluctantly. Suddenly he said, 'Do you really think I tried to drown both of us on purpose? Does Lesley think I did?'

'We didn't know what to think. And you aren't helping much.'

'I fell into the sea. Meg jumped in after me off a cliff. She tried to rescue me, but I'd got hold of a rock and the tide was going out. In the end, I supposed I rescued her. We saved each other.'

'She jumped off a cliff? With her harness on? I don't believe it.'

'Right then, don't. That's what happened.' Ben got into bed. 'Good night,' he said.

'I'm going for a doctor, Ben. Dr Richards from Hangleby.'

'I don't need a doctor.'

'Do you want tetanus and pneumonia and Mandy to nurse you?'

Ben smiled reluctantly. 'You win. But if I have to have a doctor, get me the one who came when the Guvnor had pleurisy. Boozy old lad, but I liked him.'

'Dr Strang? I don't think he has any patients left besides the Guvnor. I doubt if he'd come. Are you sure you want him?'

'I am. And he lives in Middlegarth, so he won't have far to come.'

'He lives in the Turpin Arms,' said Geoff. 'I'll get down there while he can still stand.'

Dr Strang had met Geoff Merchant before and liked him, and he liked Charlie Thorpe. The list of people he liked was short. He had met Ben once, had heard a fair amount about him from Charlie, and was secretly pleased to be sought out. He was usually sent for only when nobody else was available.

He finished his drink and asked Geoff to drive him to the cottage. 'Charlie Thorpe'll run me home,' he said. He waited outside Ben's door while Geoff lifted the dog into his van and drove off in the direction of Leeds.

Dr Strang was about seventy, short, red-faced and fat, with thin little legs which didn't look strong enough to carry him. He was completely bald, and his mouth was set in a downward turn of surliness. He lived in the village, alone except for a ginger tom cat. He was a steady drinker who was never drunk, and his temper was vile.

He banged on the bedroom door and stumped in. Ben was brushing his hair by the window.

'Get back to bed, and let's have a look at you,' ordered the doctor. He added, 'Don't expect soft soap and a bedside manner, my lad, because you won't get them from Albert Strang.' He shook his head testily at the multi-coloured bruises appearing all over Ben, then he examined him thoroughly, taking no particular pains not to hurt him. He dealt with each injury in turn, showing neither surprise nor sympathy. He gave Ben an anti-tet, a shot of penicillin and a prescription. This being as much as he was prepared to do for anybody, he was about to leave, but had enough humanity to help Ben into his pyjamas first.

'Why did you do it?' he asked abruptly.

'If Geoff told you I tried to drown myself, I didn't.'

Dr Strang sat down on the bed. 'You deserved to drown – chasing about on the top of a cliff like a lunatic. What's driving you, I wonder? Charlie told me a bit about you.'

'I need to do *something*,' said Ben, 'and I don't know what. It's sending me mad. If only I knew if I was going to be able to see again one day.'

'What, with totally detached retinas six months back? No chance, lad.'

'But the eye doctor said –'

'Medical science is wonderful? New cures every year?

Don't tell me, I've heard them all. That's called letting you down lightly. By the time you've found out it's all moonshine, you're supposed to have found something or somebody worth living for.' He laughed shortly. 'Doesn't work of course.'

'It'd be rough having to give up hope,' said Ben. 'That's what's kept me going.'

Doctor Strang looked down at the man in the bed, wondering whether he would bother to try to help him. It was a long time since he'd bothered much about anybody.

He made up his mind, and tramped into the kitchen where he looked in the cupboard. 'Haven't you got anything to drink in the house?' he shouted.

'No. Been away. Make some tea.'

'Tea!' The doctor's tone expressed unspeakable scorn. He felt inside his coat and produced a small flask. Using Ben's two mugs, he helped himself liberally, and tipped up the flask to pour a very small tot for Ben. 'Brandy,' he said, putting the mug in Ben's hand. 'Can't drink tea – rot your guts. Now, tell me what you mean to do with yourself for the next year or two. Any plans? Any ambitions?'

'How can I have? I suppose I'll mark time and wait for a miracle. If it doesn't happen, I'll think again.'

'What about that girl of yours? Lesley something. Is she waiting for a miracle too?'

'I don't expect her to wait indefinitely,' muttered Ben.

Dr Strang said roughly, 'Miracles don't happen. If you don't stop hoping for one, you'll mark time for the rest of your life.'

'You want me to live without hope? I'd be better dead.'

'I'll tell you this, lad. You'll never lead a full life while you're chasing rainbows. It isn't possible.' Ben didn't answer, so Dr Strang went on, 'I'll tell you what your life will be like. You'll be same as some silly devil wrecking his life over a woman he hopes will leave her husband and marry him instead. He knows in his heart she never will. Oh, she may say she will – when the children leave school, when her old mother dies; this year, next year, sometime – but he knows bloody well she won't. A life like that isn't worth living. Don't do it. Be free.'

He got up. 'I'll see you tomorrow,' he said.

'I'll think about what you've said,' said Ben wearily. 'It sounds like cold comfort, though.'

Dr Strang stopped at the door while he thought. The single electric bulb shone down on Ben's bruised puffy face mercilessly. The doctor could feel the strength of the younger man's personality, even when he was hurt and exhausted. What sort of person was he? No ordinary shepherd, that was certain. There was a brilliance and forcefulness in him that touched some answering chord in the grumpy old doctor. He thought of his own youth; wasted chances, lost opportunities.

'Ben,' he said. 'I'll tell you something that may help you.'

'You've just told me I haven't any hope.'

'I did no such thing. I told you there was no hope for your sight. That's not the same at all. Until you accept that, there's no hope for you as a man.'

'What were you going to tell me?' Ben's voice was friendlier. He was interested. He moved over in the bed so that the doctor could sit down on it again. The old man seemed to be searching for words. He turned an empty mug round and round in his hands, leaning forward, staring at the floor. At last he spoke in a low voice.

'My wife left me and the boy years back. We didn't hit it off – my fault I daresay. Our son Keith – anyone ever tell you this?'

'No. I don't know anything about you except that the Guvnor thinks the world of you.'

'More fool him. Keith was sixteen when it happened. Some virus – they can cure these things now, but that was thirty years back. He was ill, paralysed, for six months. When he died, I felt like any father losing his only son. . . .'

'I didn't know; I'm sorry,' said Ben.

Dr Strang sat up straight and, turning to Ben, resumed his usual rough tones. 'Listen. As long as Keith was alive – if being alive is the right term for what he was, there was hope. I lived

246

on it, same as you're doing. When he died, and this is the point, hoping for a miracle was over. I had to start living again. I'd been no good to anyone, couldn't practise – couldn't keep off the bottle. But when Keith was dead and buried, I got back on the tracks again.

'Oh, I was younger then, had some strength of purpose left, some zest for life. Couldn't face it now. My sister lived with me, she depended on me, poor soul – you need that. I've nothing now, just my cat, randy old devil . . . I'm fond of Mog . . .' His voice trailed off. 'Think about it, lad,' he said, almost kindly. 'You've a girl fair silly about you, so I've heard, and if you don't feel the same about her, make no mistake, there'll be others.'

Ben protested indignantly.

'Ah, it's like that, is it?' Dr Strang's grim chuckle was seldom heard. 'Give it time. Don't rush yourself – look after your dog instead.' He stood up. 'That's that, then. Can't stay all night. Remember the saying about one door closing and another opening.'

'What if it doesn't?' asked Ben.

Dr Strang turned as he went out. 'Kick the bugger down,' he said. 'Start living.'

The bedroom door shut. 'Wait! Dr Strang –' The outer door banged. Ben climbed stiffly out of bed. In the distance he could hear the little old man's footsteps half way up to the farmhouse.

Ben knew that he had been thrown a lifeline.

Sixteen

———— ❧ ————

Lesley looked at her watch. She got up and twitched a curtain straight, sat down. At the best of times, the flat was unfriendly – it seemed somehow to resent Lesley's presence. Now, in her anxiety and waiting, its ugly walls seemed to be closing in on her, to be positively hostile. She longed to go out, go away, but Geoff had promised to let her know if Ben was found.

She turned on the television, looked at her watch again – what could have happened? She watched the local news, and sighed with relief when there was no account of bodies washed up; no bad news at all, for once. She had seen it all in her mind, just as it would appear on the screen: the small, silent crowd, the policeman, the ambulance, the covered stretcher, the local correspondent using his hollow-toned death-voice. She switched the set off. Why hadn't Geoff telephoned?

'Too worried about the bloody dog, I suppose,' she said aloud. Was no news good news? Probably not. She was standing by the telephone, wondering whether to try Geoff's number or not, when it rang.

Startled, Lesley snatched the receiver, clumsy in her haste – it clattered on the stand. 'Geoff?' But it was Ben himself.

She found it hard at first to make sense of what he was saying. Relief seemed to cloud her brain, blocking out understanding. She wiped her eyes with the back of her hand – 'Oh Ben love, I've been so scared, I thought you were dead.'

Ben said he hadn't meant to frighten her – she thought – his words were still half scrambled in her mind. Then the fog cleared and he was thanking her for her present.

'Present? What present? Oh, the little recorder; I'd forgotten it. Did you find my number on it?'

'It's the only one I can remember by myself, except for the Guvnor's,' he said.

Lesley grew calmer. The man at the other end of the line sounded like her own Ben, not the furious, driven stranger she'd quarrelled with.

'Tell me what happened,' she said.

Ben told his story quickly, as if he wanted to get on to something more important. He had more to say about Meg than about himself. Lesley stifled the urge to say, 'Never mind about Meg, I only want to hear about you.' She exclaimed in astonishment when he told her that Dr Strang had attended him.

'That old soak? What was Geoff thinking of? He should have seen that you had a proper doctor.'

Ben said, 'Thank God he didn't. Now listen; this is what he told me.'

Lesley listened obediently. When Ben had finished, she said, 'I thought the surgeon was wrong about you. He was sure you were too shocked to stand the truth.'

'You mean you knew all the time? Why didn't you say anything?'

'I was like you. Hoping for the impossible – not admitting what I knew was true, even to myself. I'm sorry, Ben.'

She waited anxiously for an outburst, but he said, 'We spend our time apologizing when we aren't fighting. It's not going to be like that any more. When I get a real life worked out you'll be in it – if you still want to be.'

'You know I do.'

'Will you wait a bit longer then?'

'I'll be here,' said Lesley. Disappointment hit her like a bucketful of cold water.

He said, 'I've treated you rotten and I couldn't help it and didn't know why. The old doctor knew. He said I was afraid of being poor and idle.'

'I've never known you to be afraid of anything,' said Lesley.

'He was half right,' said Ben. 'I'm used to being poor, but without any work, I wouldn't be fit to live with. I can't adapt or adjust – whatever it is they tell me to do. With Meg's help, I have to fight this thing –'

'What about me?' demanded Lesley, the words out before she could stop them.

Ben seemed not to have heard. 'When I ask you to come back, you're going to be proud of me, I promise you that,' he said.

There was more, she couldn't take it all in. She'd imagined him dead, and he was alive, excited, exalted almost. He finished on a less arrogant note. 'I have to find a way to work off these black moods or we'll never be happy. Please try to understand.'

'I'll try,' said Lesley flatly.

Later still, she had another call. Geoff explained that he'd been so concerned about Meg that he'd forgotten to phone. He sounded tired and cross.

'Forget it,' said Lesley.

She overslept after a wakeful night, skipped breakfast and went straight to her first assignment. Mrs Hammond lived alone and still had to be helped to dress. Lesley's work no longer absorbed her. Even as she coped efficiently, with her usual patience and show of cheerfulness, her mind was elsewhere. She felt she was wasting her time away from Ben. She tried to phone Mandy for news of him, but there was no reply.

She left Mrs Hammond having breakfast while she ran down to the corner to do some shopping for her. Waiting for her change, she glanced absently at the *Leeds Morning Echo* on the counter.

The picture occupied a two column square in the middle of the front page. The story took up the bottom half of the two columns.

BLIND SHEPHERD BENEDICT GLYN IN CLIFF
FALL RESCUE: *'I Couldn't Let Meg Drown,' says Ben.*

Ben's bare torso was romantically battered, his expression remote but pleased. Phil had chopped off the print short of the dish of fish and chips in his hands. Inset was a picture of Meg, one eye half closed, one swollen paw raised, her fur spikily on end.

Lesley bought the paper and read it in the shop. The article, written in terms that made her cringe, was factual – obviously the reporter had talked to Ben himself. The Guvnor and Geoff were mentioned by name; there was no reference to her.

She got through the rest of the day's work automatically and, on her way home, saw a headline in an evening paper –

MEG: LEADING LADY

She stopped. Yes, it was in all three papers. The others were divided in opinion.

GUIDE DOG PLUNGES TO RESCUE OF
BLIND MASTER

BLIND MAN'S LEAP FROM CLIFF TO RESCUE
DOG FROM SEA

She bought them all.

About to turn the key in her door, she found that she couldn't face the empty flat. She walked back down the street, the papers under her arm. If Ben could fight, so could she. She would read the reports to Henrietta, and they would laugh together over them. Henrietta had fought disfigurement as well as blindness successfully; her own troubles were nothing by comparison.

Something of Dr Strang's philosophy struck her. Henrietta had never had any hope of restored sight – perhaps the cranky old devil had known what he was talking about after all. She and Owen were to be married the following week.

Owen let Lesley in. He was all welcoming smiles and so was Henrietta, but they both had a slightly shamefaced air. A tall grey-haired man who, although tidily dressed, had a somehow rumpled look about him, was standing by the window drinking whisky.

Owen introduced Phil Monk.

It was lucky for Phil that Lesley had made up her mind to treat the articles about Ben as a joke. Impossible to hide from him who she was – he guessed at once. For a time, she hardly dared speak to him, fearing she might feature in a sequel – I Still Love Him, Says Social Worker Girlfriend. She shuddered. She kept quiet, and let the others do the talking. Owen opened a bottle of wine, and another. Henrietta, spurning assistance, got a casserole out of the oven.

'Lots for you, Lesley. Do stay – you must.'

Lesley sat beside Phil who exerted his considerable charm to win her over. By degrees she relaxed, glad of an opportunity to talk about Ben to somebody who had obviously been impressed by him.

'Pity he's such an outdoor type,' said Phil. 'The best jobs for blind people are in offices – the best paid, I mean. Has he any other skills, hobbies even, that he might turn to account?'

'He can sing,' said Lesley.

Phil smiled pityingly, infuriating her. 'I'm sure he can,' he said.

'No, but I mean, *really* sing. Well enough to earn a living by it.'

'My dear girl, have you any idea what that entails? He'd have to be good – bloody good – and he'd need a sighted agent who'd want his whack. And he'd need capital behind him.'

'He *is* bloody good.' Lesley disregarded the rest of the speech. She was getting angry. Let him write it down and publish it – it was true. 'Have you heard the Dalesmen?' she enquired. 'Big Harry and the Dalesmen? They sing and play at the Hart Royal on Saturday nights. There isn't one of them in the same street as Ben. He plays well enough to get by, too.'

'Well enough isn't good enough,' said Phil. 'What's his line then, pop?'

'He can sing anything,' said Lesley. 'Ballads mostly. If he's heard a tune once he can play it, and he's composing a song, or was. I don't know much about it, I'm afraid.'

'He might be able to earn a few pounds playing in the pub,' said Phil kindly, 'but don't bet on it. It's a hard nut to crack, that world. Even if you can see.'

'I thought that was one thing blind people did before Braille and guide dogs,' said Henrietta. 'Blind harpers and singers and fiddlers. The old stories are full of them.'

'Audiences weren't so selective before radio and tv,' said Phil. 'They were thrilled when the blind harper arrived with his faithful dog Tray, even if he did sing flat. They didn't know any better.'

Lesley set down her glass carefully. 'Will you promise me one thing,' she said. 'If ever you see Ben again, persuade him to sing something. I don't care what it is, *Pop goes the Weasel* – anything.'

'All right, I'll do that.' Phil turned up the charm full volume. 'I'm sure he sings beautifully. Just don't expect him to make it big. It's a hard cruel world, you know.'

'I know,' said Lesley.

Phil was freelance. He did some reporting for the local daily, and often a 'human interest' story as well. He also wrote regularly for a variety of magazines. An assignment in Scotland kept him away from home for the next few days.

He had been meaning to visit Ben ever since meeting Lesley. He'd been intrigued by him at the time of his accident, and it was nice having a story handed to you on a plate. Now he was wondering if there was another story in Ben. The *Hangleby Tribune* had dished him up a week late:

ONE MAN AND HIS DOG IN DEATH RACE
AGAINST RUNCIE'S DREADED TIDE RIP!

Phil had learned a great deal about Ben's past; now he was curious about his future. On this subject, talking to Ben himself, he had come up against a brick wall. Ben had said he hoped to get his sight back, but seemed to have no idea what he would do if it didn't happen. Once he had said, 'I've enough energy to turn a mill, and nothing to do.'

The phrase had stuck in Phil's mind, and Lesley had given him more to think of. (Attractive girl, he thought, it says a lot for Ben that she still wants him.) Let other reporters copy and embellish the sea rescue, Phil meant to find out if Ben's energy could be harnessed and channelled.

He went first to the Turpin Arms, in search of secondhand news. Young Darren Waters from the *Star* was there, gulping beer. Phil joined him and they talked about everything and anything except Ben. But, as Phil was leaving, Darren said, 'I wish you joy if you're after your blind shepherd for another story.'

'Why? Dog bite you?'

'No. You can kick a dog. Have you met the man's boss? Go on then, off you go, you'll like him. Grand chap, salt of the earth, backbone of England – Christ!' He buried his face in another pint.

Phil left his car on the road (for a quick getaway), and walked up to the cottage. Ben wasn't a pretty sight. His purple and black bruises had turned green and yellow, his lip was cracked, his feet swollen in sandals. He was walking about outside his door, giving quiet instructions to Meg who appeared to have recovered. Phil stopped to watch, but Meg saw and Ben heard him in that instant.

Ben turned quickly, his face lighting up with that extraordinary smile. Phil had half forgotten it. Even with a lopsided, discoloured face, it was quite something, he thought.

When Phil spoke, the smile faded, was replaced by a wooden expression. Ben had been expecting somebody else – Lesley perhaps. But he accepted Phil's story about being worried over him, and his sympathetic enquiries about Meg.

Meg inched herself closer to Ben. If she remembered Phil, she wasn't admitting it. Ben, probably only because Phil had helped him, invited him in. They sat down, and Phil's eye fell on the guitar. Talk about that later, he thought.

He said, 'I've met quite a few blind people in my time, mostly much older than you. But there's a girl, Henrietta Lake, that I admire enormously; lost her sight in a terrorist attack. She's getting married soon, to a chap called Owen Reed. They're both newspaper people.'

'I haven't met her,' said Ben as he unbuckled Meg's harness. 'I've heard a lot about her though. My girlfriend looked after her for nearly a year.'

Phil decided not to mention that he'd met Lesley – not yet. Plainly, all was not as it should be there. Play it by ear, he thought. He told Ben more than Lesley had about Henrietta's courage in tackling a double affliction. Lesley had been afraid of seeming to criticise Ben.

'Extraordinary girl,' said Phil. 'She used to be too serious for my taste, wrote articles that were far too deep for the likes of you and me. Now, with only the time she spent in hospital between, she's re-emerged as a most talented comic writer. Does a piece for an up-market women's mag – upped their circulation by I don't know what. She keeps up her political reporting too, but an article's always a bit low-powered without an eyewitness. You should meet her.'

'Lesley's told me about her,' said Ben, 'but mostly funny things she's said. I didn't know about the terrorist attack.' His voice was much friendlier. He hung Meg's harness on a nail on the back of the door without seeming to feel for it. 'Would you like a beer?' he asked. 'Or a cup of tea? There's food if you look around.'

Phil refused. He was looking around all the time. A relief to be able to do so unseen – well, sort of. Meg's eyes, watchful, coldly enquiring, followed his every movement.

'Do you play that guitar?' he asked.

'A little. I wish I'd learned it properly, it's good to sing to.'

'You can get computerized sheet music in Braille.'

'I never learned to read music at all,' said Ben. 'I can play for a sing-song and that's about it. I used to play the piano in the pub at home sometimes, where I knew everybody. Here, I mostly say I can't. There's always somebody there can do it better.'

'Why don't you ask Sid Walker at the Turpin Arms to take you on – lunchtime, say? If you're good enough, that is. He can but say no.' Phil was already writing in his mind the heart-warming little piece which would help to launch Ben. He could see that the younger man was taken by the idea, rejecting it reluctantly.

'Too near home,' he said. 'I'm living in Mr Thorpe's cottage, on his charity. He'd hit the roof if I did that – and offer me money instead which would be worse.'

'Get on a bus and go to Leeds then. Try one of those posh road-houses. There wouldn't be a fortune in it, but if they like you, there might be a modest living. If you're shy, get a song down on tape.' Phil had been making notes, but he saw that Ben had heard the faint scratch of pen on paper, so he stopped.

'There's a place called the Hart Royal,' began Ben.

'Perfect. Somewhere like that. You try it.'

'I've recorded a song already,' said Ben, 'but the quality isn't good. Listen to it and tell me if you think it's worth offering. I don't want to go making a fool of myself.' He handed a pocket recorder to Phil. 'It's on there,' he said.

Phil's hopes for Ben had risen, and he regretted having been so dismissive with Lesley. He had heard plenty of only mildly talented singers performing in pubs. And now that Ben was recovering from his hammering in the sea, his personality was more evident than before. Personality was as necessary as ability if a singer was to distract the chatterers and the serious drinkers in a place like the Hart Royal. He hoped Ben could sing in tune. He switched on the tape.

– What is she doing alone out there . . .

'You're right about the quality,' said Phil when it was over, 'but any fool could tell you've a good voice – more than good.

256

Not my kind of song, but it's something. Have you a copy I could look at?'

'No. I made it up lately.'

'You what? The lyric or the tune?'

'Both. Is it any good? I know loads of old favourites I could sing instead.'

'It's good. Just the right amount of pathos, but not sugary. Forget the recording – here's your guitar. Sing it to me.'

Ben twanged the strings. 'I can't,' he said. 'Not here like this. I sang some of it for a woman, but she was blind. I need a crowd, or to be on my own.'

'Do you propose to hire a crowd? Or blindfold the customers? What if the bar's empty? Come on now; sing it. Then I'll give you an opinion.'

Ben, starting almost inaudibly, got into his stride halfway through the second verse. His right arm seemed to be bothering him, he barely sketched an accompaniment. The deep, soft voice had perfect pitch and was without tuba-like effects at the bottom of the register.

'You sing like a black man,' said Phil.

'Is that a compliment?'

'Yes.' Absently, Phil rested his hand on Meg's head. She moved, politely but decidedly, out of reach. He wasn't thinking about her. 'Enough energy to turn a mill –' he'd need it all. Phil meant to see that Ben sang to an audience before long, before the local people had forgotten the newspaper story. Even without that, he was good enough to earn his living, but there was nothing like a good boost to start with. Ben and his song would find their way into the local papers, and Phil Monk would be around, making capital out of him.

'Ben,' he said, 'the pub's okay for starters, but I'd like to see you on a stage.'

'I'd look a right fool, a little fellow like me,' objected Ben.

'You're thick as a brick if you pass up the chance – I might be able to help. Anyway, what about Prince? What about Bruce Springsteen? Nobody's going up there with a foot rule. . .'

He had lost Ben's attention. 'Here comes the Guvnor,' he said.

Phil got ready to deflect any attempt to throw him out with diplomacy. He needn't have bothered; Charlie ignored him.

'If you want tea, it's on table,' he said to Ben. '. . . Starving hisself,' he muttered audibly to no one in particular.

Phil said, 'I was going to ask Ben if he'd like to come out for a drink with me. Would you, Ben?'

'Aye, he would that, looking like a scarecrow,' Charlie answered for him. He and Ben grimaced at each other, and the clash of their personalities was a live thing, charging the air.

Phil felt urgently that Ben must not be permanently under an obligation to Charlie Thorpe. The older man, however well-meaning, fatherly even, would overwhelm him, make him toe the line out of gratitude. It occurred to Phil that he no longer saw Ben as a possible source of extra income and nothing else. He had a blazing talent which must not be wasted, but he was also a man in need of help.

Getting altruistic in my old age, thought Phil.

'If you're set on going out, you could've come to York along 'o me,' said Charlie.

'I could,' said Ben mildly, 'but you didn't ask me. Thanks, Phil, I could do with a drink.'

'Don't go getting lost now, I'll be expecting you back. You know what doctor said.' Getting no answer, Charlie went on, 'If you need some brass –'

The colour rushed up Ben's face. 'I'll beg for it,' he said savagely, 'on the street corner in Middlegarth.'

Charlie turned angrily on Phil, acknowledging him for the first time. 'This is your doing,' he said. 'Lad were right enough before your lot started messing him about. Go on then, the pair of you. Get going.'

Phil was ready with a high voltage smile and tactful disclaimers, but Charlie didn't wait to hear. He'd gone.

Phil smoked a cigarette while Ben changed his shirt and eased a pair of socks over his feet. Meg watched sympathetically. She licked his toes, with a sidelong glance at Phil.

'I'm still lame,' said Ben, 'but it's both feet so it doesn't show.' He ran his hand along the shelf over the range where there were two tins marked 'tea' and 'coffee'. He took a five pound note and some silver out of the coffee tin. Then he put on Meg's harness.

'Bring your guitar – here, I've got it.'

'What, play for my drink? No thanks.'

Phil put it back in the corner. 'All right. I thought we'd go to the Hart Royal. I know old Tony Garrowby fairly well. Good chance to start something going without Big Daddy breathing down your neck.'

'He's the best in the world,' said Ben. 'I don't know why I went for him like that.'

Phil said, 'You can have him. I'll take him as read.'

As they drove, he questioned Ben about the inspiration for his song. Stories everywhere you look, he thought, trying to memorize this one. Why, he'd seen the report in the *Yorkshire Post* back in the spring. A picture worth a fortune and not insured. Easy to look it up. That would be a piece for *Art for Art's Sake*. Maybe two pieces.

'What do you say to a steak, Ben?'

'Great. I'm starving.'

So they ate steaks and Phil, on the pretext of paying, went to sell his wares to Tony Garrowby.

Afterwards, they went to the bar, and Ben renewed acquaintance with Gloria, the gaudy blonde lady behind the horseshoe bar. She remembered him at once, took in the guide dog with one horrified glance, recovered quickly, and began to tell everyone in earshot that here was the chap who'd thrown out 'That yobbo from Tadcaster way.'

Ben could have got paralytic on free drink, but he stayed sober, while consuming more than his usual modest ration of beer and exchanging badinage with Gloria.

Phil watched him curiously. He noticed that some of the drinkers were over friendly, causing Meg to sit up straight with her ears laid back, a sign that she was resisting an urge to growl. Others slid away and grouped in corners, where they discussed him among themselves in low tones.

It was Friday evening, people were coming in on their way back from work, their pay packets intact. Noise and smoke filled the room. Phil decided to wait a bit longer and then suggest a song to somebody else. Tony Garrowby's reactions had been poor. He was by no means sure that a blind singer would go down well with the customers.

Meg was feeling miserable. Driving in the car was all right, although she mistrusted Ben's new friend, but she hated the brightly lit low-ceilinged place they had come to. She would have liked Ben to have stayed at home where she could have him to herself. She'd lost some of her confidence that day at Runcie Sands, and ever since then, Ben had been jumpy and strange.

For two days, he'd had to stay in bed, while Geoff looked after Meg; then she'd returned, to find him somehow different. He was short-tempered and carefree by turns. His arm and his feet hurt him, but he couldn't keep still. He often talked to Meg, but she couldn't make out what he wanted – apart from the woman, Lesley. Yet, when Meg had been sulking under the bed, he'd shouted at the woman as though he hated her. Perhaps he was a little bit mad? Mad or not, he was Meg's person, to be loved and cared for.

Whenever Lesley's name was mentioned, Meg made a point of showing Ben extra affection. She was not demonstrative by nature, but a reminder could do no harm. Geoff, unlike Ben, never changed, but Geoff had given her away to Ben. He was forgiven, but no longer wholly trusted.

Ben was drinking beer and laughing with a fat golden-haired woman. Fortunately the bar was between them – Lesley was bad, thought Meg, but this one wouldn't do at all. She had difficulty in swallowing a growl; it gave her hiccups. A number of people patted her head and called her 'Good boy' or 'Awd lad'. They were more to be pitied than blamed.

The place got fuller and noisier every instant. Somebody began to play the piano. Ben made jokes, and some people laughed. Meg sensed that there were others who felt uncomfortably that he shouldn't joke. Disapproval and embarrassment mixed with the laughter and the tinkle of glasses.

Phil led Ben towards the piano – officious, Meg could have done it if asked. She was deeply unhappy, sensing his uncertainty. He didn't want to sing, but he was going to. Meg didn't want anyone to sing. Her ears were highly sensitive and she had no way of keeping the noise out. She flattened one of them against Ben's leg, and felt that he was trembling.

Phil wanted Ben to sing the song he often sang at home, it wasn't as bad as some, but he wouldn't. He wouldn't play either, because of his bad arm. He sang a song that everybody seemed to know – or think they knew. More songs were called for – he knew them all. People crowded round and demanded this tune or that; there were glasses all over the piano. Somebody asked Ben for an Irish song and shouted at the others, 'Belt up, you noisy lot!' He sang a song called *Four Country Roads*; it was bearable. Anyway, Meg's left ear was becoming accustomed to the noise. There was clapping and shouts for more. As Meg endured, she felt Ben relax and start to enjoy himself. The uncaring crowd of strangers was achieving what neither Meg nor Lesley could.

The applause was going to Ben's head. He sang out, and forgot all the worries and fears which Meg tried in vain to share with him. For the moment he was happy. Meg tried to be happy with him, but instinct told her that nothing would ever be quite the same again.

Ben was tired and his feet hurt. But he felt like a man who has found an oil well on his farm – over the moon, with reservations. He had made a discovery which would affect his whole life, but he was entering unknown territory in the dark – sentimental rubbish, he told himself, seeming to hear a distant echo of Agatha's voice.

Ben knew that he couldn't have sung as well if he could

have seen his audience. Their invisibility made them into an anonymous mass. He couldn't be upset by the faces of those who were tone-deaf, anti-Irish or plain bored. The warmth and positive reaction of the others worked on him like strong drink – without the disadvantages. He felt as if he'd drunk a bottle of champagne instead of six halves of light ale.

Once, he asked where Phil was, and was told he'd been buying up the phone for the last half hour. He had come back; Ben heard him ask if he might take some photos. What ever for? Phil put a handkerchief in Ben's hand, told him his cracked lip was bleeding. 'That would be laying it on too thick,' he said.

Ben mopped his chin impatiently, wondering what he was talking about. Shortly afterwards, they left. People made way for Meg to lead him out. Ben had almost forgotten her, although her warm body, pressed against his leg, had helped his confidence at first.

Back in Phil's car, Ben could hardly speak because of jawbreaking yawns. 'I'm taking you miles out of your way,' he managed to say. 'I could easily have caught the bus.'

'You're worth more than a gallon of petrol to me,' said Phil, sounding as if he was dead serious. Ben had been engrossed with his own problems lately – he'd never asked Phil what he did for a living. It seemed a bit late to ask now, so he didn't.

'You were right to save your song for a different audience,' said Phil.

'I didn't. I was too shy to sing it.'

'I'm not sure what Tony Garrowby will decide. He'll ring you. He thinks, as I do, that your future will be as a singer, but you distract his customers from buying drinks. On the other hand, long term, you should bring in extra customers as the Dalesmen do. He talked of giving you a trial run, two evenings a week for four weeks. I'd keep that song in reserve if I were you.'

'Will he pay?' Ben struggled with another yawn.

'Of course. Probably not very much, but it'll be cash and you'll get a free meal and drinks – I'd watch those.'

'I could get drunk on coke if I was in good form,' said Ben. He fell suddenly asleep.

When he woke, some sort of commotion was going on and Meg was sitting on his lap.

'What's up?' he said.

'We're home,' said Phil. 'I tried to shake you awake and the damn dog thought I was attacking you. Too well trained to bite – she just showed her teeth. I'd rather argue with a shark.'

'Down, girl.' Ben, still half asleep, tried to find words to thank Phil. 'You've started me off,' he said. 'It's up to me to keep going . . .' He yawned hugely.

'Don't go to sleep again. There's a light on in your house – I see somebody moving. Oh, Jesus, it's your Guvnor. Off you go, Ben, I'm not facing him twice in one day.'

Ben heard the horn toot, and the car drove away.

Seventeen

Ben's engagement with the Hart Royal ended early in November. Enormously popular with some, his presence sent others to the White Rose, a couple of miles up the road. Also, as Tony Garrowby had feared, the crowd which gathered round the piano often forgot to order any more drinks. Ben hadn't worried. He'd been asked to sing at the Cock and Lion at Hangleby three times a week. It was a cosy, old-fashioned pub, much nearer home, and the customers were mostly country people; middle-aged couples, enjoying a drink or two after tea. They, the women especially, took Ben to their hearts. He sang old favourites and requests.

Ben was asked to sing at the Hangleby Christmas concert, and agreed readily. The Boy Scouts' Hall in Hangleby, about half way between Middlegarth and Leeds, was a dingy spot. There was olive green high-gloss paint on the walls, a good many faded flags drooping in corners and a small stage at the end. A concert was held there every Christmas, consisting of a popular group eked out with local talent, and sometimes a guest artist if funds would run to one and he could be persuaded to go. Ben was amazed to find that this was the slot he was to fill.

Ben was fairly into his stride now, walking briskly down to the bus stop with Meg, anticipation giving a spring to his step. At the Cock and Lion, he would sing and play quietly while the customers were thin on the ground, then he would demolish a large meal. After that, he would sing until closing time, sometimes accompanied; sometimes not, and catch the last bus home.

Practice was improving his playing, both on guitar and piano, and he sang from the heart, buoyed up by the response he received.

Even Meg, surly to start with, was now part of the act. Ben sensed that she was proud of him, eager to show him off, like a mother with a precocious tot.

The coffee tin on the shelf over the range was almost full. Ben was saving up.

Sometimes he wondered why he'd been so readily accepted, but he didn't dwell on it. He was busy tinkering with his song which he hadn't yet sung in public, and was completing another.

Lesley was constantly in his thoughts, but he was discovering that he needn't accept poverty and humiliation. He need never depend on man or woman. If only she would wait, Lesley's time would come. He couldn't and wouldn't approach her until he was making enough money to support both of them if need be. In the meantime, he feared he might lose her to someone else before he was established.

Mandy had said something about the 'marvellous publicity' Ben had had, but he never took Mandy's remarks over seriously. The Guvnor knew better than to tell him about the coverage he'd been getting in the press, and had warned Eric to keep quiet.

Mandy was a nuisance. He had to be civil to her because she kept the cottage clean and did his laundry, but she constantly hung about chattering, especially when he had a half-formed idea taking shape in his head. Meg wasn't at all jealous of Mandy, seeing her as a mild irritant rather than a threat.

The day before the concert, Mandy, who had brought Ben his mid morning 'lowance of sandwiches and pie, asked him to go with her to buy a suit. 'You can't sing in a concert in a jumper and jeans,' she said.

Ben argued that he didn't want or need a suit, that he looked all wrong in one and that he was too short and too broad to buy one off the peg. He could have done with some new shoes, but he didn't intend to go shopping with Mandy. She stood behind him, watching him, a maddening habit.

'Ben,' she said, 'I've got some bad news. Bad for you, that is.'

Ben spun round, his heart pounding. Lesley! 'What do you mean?' he asked roughly.

'We're going, Ted and me. We nearly went months since. Well, Father's a right pain at times, isn't he? Anyway, Ted's got a job down in Suffolk, and we're off after Christmas.'

Relief almost robbed Ben of speech, but he managed to say he was sorry without much conviction, adding guiltily, 'You've been very good to me, Mandy.'

'Well, one does what one can; that's what we're here for, isn't it? And Ben, when we've gone, I'm going to miss you a lot.' He backed away as he felt her come closer in the tiny kitchen.

'I'm going to drink this before it gets cold,' he said, arming himself with a mug of tea. To his alarm, his free hand was caught and clutched.

'Ben,' said Mandy, 'you're a very special person, you know. We all feel sure you'll rise superior to your misfortune, and I do hope you'll be able to persuade Lesley to come and look after you when I'm gone. It might take a while, but I'm certain she'll come round in the end.'

Ben freed his hand, found and bit into a sandwich. It was rudely done, but speech just then would have been far ruder. 'Hungry,' he mumbled through bread, butter and beef.

'And when she hears we're going,' Mandy went on unstoppably, 'she'll know you need someone beside Meg to take care of you.'

Ben swallowed. 'Mandy,' he said, 'I have a fierce headache. I think I'll lie down for a while and finish this after. I'll see you tomorrow.'

He felt her breath on his face as she offered to fetch him some aspirin. He caught her by the shoulders, turned her round, pushed her through the outside door and shut it. He turned the key in the lock.

Charlie banged on Ben's door soon afterwards. 'Thought I'd find you in bed,' he said. 'What's been saying to our Mandy, then? She isn't half taking on.'

Ben sighed. 'I didn't say much,' he said. 'Told her I'd a headache to get rid of her. Tell her I didn't mean it – no, you'd better not . . . Hell, I don't know what to say. I was bloody rude.'

Charlie sat down. He'd got a heartfelt apology from Ben over his outburst the night he first sang at the Hart Royal. Since then, they'd been on better terms than ever before. Charlie said, 'You don't reckon nowt to Mandy, do you?'

'I –'

'Don't know as I blame you, lad, although she's my own flesh and blood – supposed to be. Me, I think they got sucklings mixed in hospital. Ted's off, did she tell you? He might pass down south, but he'd never do for Yorkshire.'

'What'll you do for help?' asked Ben.

'Dunno. Married couple, I reckon. Mind you, there's a chance my son might come home from New Zealand. He's gitten wed out there to a lass from up Hexham way. He couldn't abide Ted. Him and the wife might come home now.' There was a long silence, as Ben, who'd heard Eric's version of this story, decided not to comment. At last Charlie said, 'I've never been to hear you sing in pub, lad.'

'I know. I'm not surprised.'

'Forget all that. Thowt as how I might go to concert and take you along o' me. T'other lot can come by bus or stay at home. And I think – don't fly out at me now – you could do with a new outfit.'

Ben burst out laughing. 'So does Mandy. She offered to take me to buy a suit. No, Guvnor, this'll have to do for the concert. I'll spend the fee on clothes if I'm that shabby.'

Charlie said, 'Here's you and me talking, and nobody'd think there was owt up with either of us. It's grand, is that.'

Ben considered, then he said, 'You can't go on minding about something every minute of the day – it isn't possible. Do you remember that Scottish handler giving an exhibition with a blind dog at York? It worked on commands, and its own hearing and scenting power. Animals have sense – they carry on with what they've got left. A blind dog works as best he can. He doesn't sit in his kennel and howl.'

'Or jump in sea,' said Charlie.

'I fell in,' said Ben, fairly calmly.

Charlie went away shortly afterwards, and returned around six o'clock with the Range Rover. They drove the ten miles to Hangleby in companionable silence, each thinking his own thoughts. Ben had no fears about the performance. He was going to sing in a group for the first time in public, joining Big Harry and the Dalesmen in a selection of old favourites. Afterwards, Big Harry was to sing alone, then Ben. Following Ben's spot, the schoolchildren were putting on a short Nativity play, and after that there was to be a grand finale, incorporating the Hangleby Ladies' Choir singing carols and popular songs.

Ben had approached his first session at the Hart Royal much like somebody heading for the dentist's chair – hoping not to disgrace himself. Ever since, his confidence had been growing. He knew he could hold an audience, make it listen, make it laugh, make it sing along. He controlled his listeners as once he had controlled fit racehorses, by knack rather than strength. Marvellous feeling of power.

'Penny for 'em,' said Charlie.

'I was thinking I might sing my own song tonight,' said Ben.

Lesley was growing used to living in a sort of limbo. She had gone to hear Ben sing more than once, but had not made herself known. She had seen him walk through the crowded bar confidently and quickly, Meg leading the way with what could only be called a smug air. Lesley had heard him silence a boisterous group with a softly sung lyric, she had heard him get the whole room singing along, fairly lifting the roof with *Blaydon Races* and *Ilkley Moor*, songs he had learned by ear.

Seeing Ben hit her hard. She didn't know which was worse, going or staying away.

Lesley worried in case the concert was a frost. It was less popular every year as more sophisticated entertainments were available. She sat with Owen and Henrietta who had recently returned from their honeymoon. Along with Phil Monk who was there too, they had done their best to promote the concert in the press and on local radio. At the hall, cold and musty and full of stack-a-bye chairs, they were the first arrivals.

The Boy Scouts had had a party the day before, and bedraggled homemade paper chains criss-crossed the ceiling. There was a smell of scorching paper and stewed tea. The stage was screened by limp curtains, of the sort which are drawn, not raised. Phil said, 'I almost hope Ronnie Hyde doesn't come.'

Ronnie was agent for many internationally famous pop groups. Slim Jim, Hellhounds, the Whatsits; all had been unknown until Ronnie took their affairs in hand. Now he was turning his attention to Country and Western. He had made Chuck Higgins a star. Henrietta had interviewed some of his discoveries, and it was to please her that he came, on a cold December night, to Hangleby Boy Scouts Hall.

The hall was filling up fast. Glancing back, Lesley saw Ben's great aunt Flora, looking like a giant balloon in a red plastic mac. With her was a scraggy little old woman, and a tall shaven-headed man, dressed in a cassock. Brother Sebastian and Daisy, no doubt. They must be kept away from Ben at all costs. Lesley had known they were coming, as Flora had written to enquire about the time. She had also sent through the post a pillowcase filled with dried roseleaves and instructions for making pot-pourri.

The rector and the school-teacher each made a speech. It was extraordinarily cold. Lesley shivered, not with cold, and Henrietta found her hand and squeezed it.

The Dalesmen were an assortment of musicians of varying quality. Their lead guitar, twenty-year-old Sefton Sykes, was good and going to be better. The others, much older men, were as good as they'd ever be.

Big Harry, a giant of a man in his forties, looked as if he might have a powerful bass voice locked up in his barrel chest. Actually, he was a light tenor. He had some of Ben's ability to hold an audience, but he did it with jokey asides and local allusions.

The curtains, jerkily drawn, revealed the Dalesmen, standing in a semicircle. Ben, with Meg at his feet, was perched on a stool. This was Big Harry's idea. They were greeted with tepid applause by the mainly local audience.

At the back of the hall, a latecomer was looking for a seat. 'Up here,' mouthed Phil. He'd been keeping the place between him and Henrietta for Ronnie Hyde, known to the media as Ronnie Hype. Ronnie, a loose limbed character, wrapped in a variety of scarves and cardigans, topped with a cape, sat down.

'God, what a circus,' he muttered.

The Dalesmen offered a selection guaranteed to offend nobody and please most people over fifty years old. When it was over, Ben got down from his stool and went to stand beside Big Harry. Together, they sang a hastily thrown together parody in which Hangleby Hall was made to rhyme with the Long and the Short and the Tall.

'I think I'm going to puke,' said Ronnie.

'Shut up,' whispered Henrietta savagely.

Ronnie turned to her in some surprise. 'I mean the set-up. Your guy can sing – as far as one can tell with that appalling backing.'

Next, the curtains were tweaked shut by more or less invisible Boy Scouts. Big Harry and Sefton Sykes appeared in the spotlight in front of them; the serious entertainment had begun.

Harry's songs were encored, especially *Riders in the Sky*, which had been his party piece for as long as most of them could remember. There was a fair amount of shouting and stamping, and his introduction of Ben was lost. Harry retreated, and Meg appeared in the gap in the curtains. She walked through, followed by Ben with his guitar. He looked preoccupied because he was counting his steps; the central spotlight was a fixture.

Half way through his opening song, the amplifier began to squeak and crackle. Ben retreated, leaving Meg sitting placidly in the spotlight, and an altercation was heard behind the curtains.

'Fix it in a minute –'

'Turn the thing off, I won't use it.'

'How do you expect to be heard at the back of the hall? You can't hope to fill it.'

'I could fill a ten acre field.'

'Okay, go ahead then. Be awkward.'

Ben reappeared, his expression stormy. His Napoleon look, thought Lesley. Meg turned her head and thumped her tail. He took the three even steps to the spot, bent, and just touched her head. Then he started the song again, without amplification. When it was over, there was fairly enthusiastic clapping. Nothing like as much as Big Harry's.

Ben turned his head this way and that, assessing the reaction, then he said, 'I hope you all have handkerchiefs with you, or a box of tissues. If not, they have them on sale at the door.'

One or two half hearted titters greeted this.

'He's nervous,' thought Lesley.

'This song is called *Girl in a Garden*,' said Ben briefly, and he began to sing. There was total silence in the hall as he ended.

> . . . *You slide away like a falling tear,*
> *The rain pours down and my arms hold air –*
> *Night in the garden.*

Ben sang the last words softly, with a wondering inflection, not sadly. He felt in his bones the reaction from the hall. A new song – was there another verse? They were hesitant, afraid of clapping too soon. He heard a myriad of sounds, and among them a stifled sob.

'That's it,' he shouted suddenly. 'That's all. Three verses are enough for anyone.' He struck a major chord. 'Do you know something? I was well rid of her, that girl in green – she wasn't worth feeding. And she hadn't that red hair for nothing – what a temper! God help the fellow that got her.'

The applause started and swelled. Ben began to feel reckless, thought he heard another sob, couldn't be sure, didn't much care. He broke into a chorus:

> *Let's not have a sniffle*
> *Let's have a bloody good cry,*
> *And always remember, the longer you live*
> *The sooner you'll bloody well die.*

There was shouting and stamping and whistling, while a few voices sang along. Ben's elation grew. Raising his voice, he told the audience, 'I've made you laugh and I've made you cry, and now I'm going to shock you.' A pause to allow this to sink in. 'Are you easily shocked?'

A roar of '*No!*' from the hall, while a scuffling behind him warned that the Hangleby Ladies' Committee was ready to muzzle him if he went too far.

'I'm going to sing you a song about a blind man whose wife tried to murder him,' said Ben, his voice deeply serious. The silence grew uneasy. But then he broke into the comic song, the *Old Woman from Wexford*, whose attempt to drown her 'oul man' resulted in her own demise.

> *So loudly did she screech and so loudly did she bawl;*
> *But, 'Hould your whisht oul woman,' said he, 'I can't*
> *see you at all –'*

Under cover of the applause afterwards, Ronnie Hyde said to Henrietta, 'You were right, he's a little winner – where's he been hiding?'

Henrietta didn't answer. On her other side, Lesley had just said, 'I don't know how much more of this I can stand.'

Henrietta whispered, 'He's singing for *you*. Can't you tell?'

'I wonder if he is.'

'Who else? Meg?'

'Perhaps.'

The clapping died away and Ben said, 'The play's due to start in a few minutes. Do you want another song first?'

'*Yes!*'

'I'll sing you a song I made up about friends. We know diamonds are a girl's best friend. Then there's the best friend who won't tell you about your bad breath, and the best friend who's sure to tell you if your favourite girl's got her eye on somebody else. My best friend is my dog Meg here. She keeps me out of mischief, don't you Meg? This is her song, and I call it *The Best Friend Game*.

He pulled the stool he'd sat on earlier towards him and patted it. Meg jumped onto it and sat beside him. Her expression was one of suffering bravely borne. The song had a swing and a beat and a neat punchy lyric. When it was over, Meg jumped down, Ben waved his hand, picked up her harness and followed her through the curtains to the accompaniment of clapping, shouting and cheers.

Lesley stood up with a muttered apology and went out.

It was dark outside, and a thin sleet was falling. She backed into a doorway. Steps behind her. She stood still, searching in her bag for a hanky; she didn't want to talk to Owen or Ronnie.

It was Geoff. He put a clumsy arm round her shoulders and she turned and pressed her face against his jacket.

In the hall, a spatter of clapping greeted the announcement of the play.

'Let me take you home,' said Geoff. He added gruffly, 'Ben doesn't deserve such devotion.'

Lesley said bitterly, her voice muffled by Harris tweed, 'Dog-like devotion. It's not enough.'

For a minute, he held her without speaking, feeling her

wretchedness as if it had been his own. Geoff was nearer sixty than fifty – he assured himself that his feelings were paternal and, wrongly, that his wife would sympathize and understand.

Lesley had cut her hair very short, the curls were gone. In the dim light, her fair head looked like a boy's. Geoff tried to find the words he needed.

'I know I've joked about you and Meg, Ben's two lady friends,' he said. 'It's no joke though, and I don't blame you for a minute for resenting her.'

'I'm a fool to be upset.'

'Ben looks to be starting out on a career which includes Meg, but not you – of course you're upset.'

Lesley blew her nose. She disengaged herself. 'With any luck I'll outlive my rival,' she said flippantly.

Geoff was shocked. 'I should hope so,' he said seriously. 'No, Lesley, you must try to think of Meg as a specially trained nurse-companion, tiding Ben over the rough patches. He doesn't want you as a nanny or a guide – he's too proud. He wants you on the same terms as before. Give him six months and he'll be making as much money as you are – maybe more. I was sitting behind that poofter in the cape. He wants to buy the performing rights of the song.'

'I thought,' Lesley said, her voice very small, 'Ben meant he was well rid of me. You heard how he went on after the garden song. And then he sang a song he'd made up for Meg.'

'Not he. I'm not musical, but I do know something about blind people. So do you when you're in your right mind. He was drunk with power, steering his audience this way and that – he can do it too. I tell you, it'll be the saving of him. Come back into the hall, or we'll have his old auntie and that monk bloke after us. Cheer up, lass, it's an all-male band,' he added with a gauche attempt at a joke.

They returned quietly to their seats in time to hear an aggressively Yorkshire angel telling the Christmas story to a class of infant shepherds.

Ronnie was missing from his seat. After the play, he returned from a speedy drink at the Cock and Lion, and went backstage for a word with Ben. A minute later he came back and asked Phil if a woman called Lesley Grant was in the audience or could be found.

'Here,' said Lesley.

'I can't get any sense out of Ben Glyn. He won't discuss his songs and says if there's anything to be signed he wants you to do it for him. We'll talk to him after the show.'

The amplifier had been put more or less to rights before the play. The grand finale, involving Dalesmen, shepherds, angels, Ben, Meg and the Hangleby Ladies' Choir, was voted a huge success. Phil was prodded by the mother of the angel Gabriel and asked to take another photograph.

'I saw you flashing when the blind man was on,' she said accusingly.

Henrietta giggled and drew a wrathful glare.

'Sorry, film's finished,' said Phil.

Afterwards, Ben went with Phil's party and Ronnie to the Cock and Lion, where they assembled in a private room. Lesley kept behind the others, but when Ronnie produced a document for signing they made way for her and she and Ben stood side by side.

Ben was still high on applause, but when he heard Lesley's voice, he knew that success was hollow without her. He told himself that one well received performance in a village hall was no guarantee for the future, even if he sold two songs. He must keep working at it.

'Lesley,' he said, 'will you do whatever you think best about the songs? I'd like to record them myself, and Sefton Sykes wants to leave the Dalesmen to join me. I can probably do my own horse-dealing, but I need somebody to sign things. Will you?'

'What does that make us, business partners?' asked Lesley.

'In a way. This may be a flash in the pan; don't do it if you'd rather not. Ask Phil.' He knew his words were brisk and

275

dismissive, and wondered if she sensed the depth of feeling behind them. 'Please, Lesley,' he said.

'I'll see to it,' she said. 'Of course I will.' Then she talked to Ronnie who wanted to act as Ben's agent, and it was decided that all three should visit a lawyer the next day.

They'd forgotten Charlie until they heard him out in the street, bellowing Ben's name. Lesley ran out to fetch him in, he thumped Ben's shoulder violently. 'Good lad, good lad,' he kept repeating.

Congratulations came from all sides. Ben felt bewildered and overwhelmingly sleepy. He sat on a hard settee with Meg lying at his feet, her chin on his instep. Ronnie wanted to talk about terms, but Ben said, 'Don't talk to me, talk to Lesley. Fix it up between you.'

'Do you want an agreement in your joint names?'

'No,' said Ben, 'not yet. I asked her because I trust her.'

Ronnie went away, and Ben sipped his beer, sleepily enjoying it.

Some strangers had overflowed into the room from the bar. He listened to fragments of conversation, and wondered again why people should assume that those who can't see can't hear either.

'A charismatic leader, blind or not,' said a female voice.

An unknown man said, 'That macho image won't go down with the feminists. They'll have hysterics.'

Lesley protested, 'He's not macho,' and Ben could tell she was remembering moments of tenderness and generosity and smiled to himself. He hadn't realized she was still there, standing close to him; hadn't noticed Meg quiver and raise her head.

'He need never worry about poverty or idleness again,' said Phil's voice, and there were murmurs of agreement.

Then Charlie said loudly, 'Haven't you folks no homes to go to? Time for bed, I reckon. Drink up, Ben.'

Ben emptied his glass obediently. He had made his mind up not to argue with Charlie, if possible. He was confused by a dozen voices saying goodnight.

276

'Goodnight Lesley,' he said.

As they went out through the saloon bar, somebody accosted Ben, standing in his path. Meg stopped.

'Kicked the door down, I see,' said Dr Strang.

'I suppose I did,' said Ben.

Charlie said, 'What brings you to Hangleby, Albert?'

'I came to hear Ben sing. Well done, lad. I enjoyed it.'

'God helps them that helps theirselves,' said Charlie, with the air of one who has just coined a telling phrase. 'Want a lift then?'

'What, half an hour before closing time?'

'Come to farm. Plenty of whisky there.'

Dr Strang struggled into his overcoat with a grunt of thanks. 'First time I've been out of Middlegarth this year,' he grumbled.

They all climbed into the Range Rover. 'What's the date?' Ben asked suddenly.

'Seventeenth,' said Charlie. 'Christmas tomorrow week, and eleven months to the day since you came to Yorkshire.'

Ben said, 'St Patrick's day's three months off. I'll know by then if I'm going to be any good.'

'You *are* good.' Charlie was almost shouting. 'What more do you want? Aren't you ever satisfied?'

'He wants recognition in Ireland, I should think,' remarked the doctor. 'That's it, isn't it, Ben?'

'You read my mind once before,' said Ben.

Ben sat in the back seat, the now familiar feeling of floating unreality, like having had one drink too many, invading him. He spoke to Meg, and she leaned her head against his leg. His hand smoothed her head, rubbed the backs of her ears. 'Meg,' he said, too softly for the others to overhear, 'you're a comfort to me.' He had thought that a dog would be a tedious responsibility; he couldn't imagine how he had been so mistaken. She was a support, a companion, filling much of his time, keeping him fit as he walked with her, even supplying some of his emotional needs.

Ben wished, with painful intensity, that Lesley was beside

277

him, driving back to their home with him. Meg whined, nosing his hand, trying with every nerve to communicate with him. Almost, he thought, as though she knew what he was thinking.

'What about a nightcap?' asked Charlie, whisky bottle poised.

'As long as you drive me home.'

Charlie poured a generous dollop of whisky for Dr Strang, and levered off the top of another bottle of grapefruit juice for himself. Ben had been invited in but had refused. He'd been half asleep anyway.

Dr Strang studied the grapefruit bottle with concentrated loathing. 'You'll poison yourself with that rubbish, Charlie. Acid muck.' He tipped a minute amount of water into his whisky and drank it off like medicine.

'He'll go far, will Ben,' he said suddenly.

'Don't see how he can, the way he is,' said Charlie. 'Oh, he'll try. Stubborn youth – always was. Got a temper too.'

Dr Strang's harsh chuckle surprised him. 'You'd be a sod yourself if you lost your sight, Charlie Thorpe,' he said.

'I would that. But what real future is there for him, blind?'

The doctor considered, absently holding out his glass as he did so. 'I used to have a patient, a lawyer,' he said, 'blind as a stone. Said he could tell if a man was telling the truth or not every time. Said looking at 'em used to influence him – pretty women especially. Then I've known teachers, parsons, lecturers, social workers, writers and journalists. . . . Trouble is, those are jobs for educated people. Ben deserved a good education, but he doesn't seem to have got it.'

Charlie filled the glass. 'Too late for poor lad now,' he said.

Dr Strang gulped, and set down the empty glass. 'Poor lad nothing,' he said. 'Ben's not a poor lad – never could be. He's too much character. He's fewer fixed notions than most; from being so much alone, I daresay. He'd never be one of the bunch.'

278

'He's treated that girl of his shameful,' said Charlie. 'Must make allowances, I suppose.'

'H'm. Probably knows what he's doing. Chances are he'll outgrow her and leave her behind. If fame's what he's after, he'll very likely get it – and the perks that go with it.' He finished his drink and thoughtfully rubbed his stomach. 'She'd best try to forget him if he makes the grade with this singing lark,' he said.

'Forget him? Bloody hell, you might as well tell sun to forget to rise.' Charlie stood up, steadying the old doctor's elbow.

'Poor lass,' muttered Dr Strang. 'Poor lass.'

Eighteen

The studio audience knew what to expect. The St Patrick's Day concert at the Gaiety Theatre in Dublin had been televised, and indeed some of them had been there. The name was being talked about all over Ireland; a new name and one with a lilt to it. Benedict Glyn.

Ben's appearance with Meg on television in the *Late Late Show* had been stage managed for the maximum impact. The first act was mediocre. The audience grew restive; they all wanted to see the blind singer and his guide dog; they wanted to hear him sing. Gay Byrne fed their impatience, playing them along.

The Best Friend Game had been an overnight success early in the new year. With its bouncy rhythm and singable tune, it was played at every party and wedding and in every pub. *Girl in a Garden* had taken longer to catch on. But almost everybody who heard Ben sing it at the Gaiety wanted to hear it again. Sales of the single were soaring, and both songs were included in a new album of current hits.

Ben's parents had been invited to appear on the *Late Late Show* too, and they were supposed to provide background for Ben. They had been well briefed beforehand, but both were overcome with stage fright and were tongue-tied. Gay Byrne did his professional best with Myles and Muriel, putting Muriel at her ease, and playing Myles along with questions about greyhound racing. On the subject of Ben, neither seemed to have anything to say.

'Yes, he used to play the guitar sometimes.'

'He wanted to be a jockey but he was too heavy.'

'He was good with sheep.'

They wore expressions of plaintive bewilderment, as if wondering how they'd got onto the show.

When it was Ben's turn, he played and sang *The Best Friend Game* as if he'd been performing all his life. Meg sat beside him on a sort of low pedestal, looking self-conscious.

When the applause had died away, Gay Byrne, smiling and gently clapping his hands, said, 'Wasn't that beautiful? Wasn't it? Thank you, Benedict.'

'I'm always called Ben.'

'Oh? But you like to be billed as Benedict. Why?'

'It's my name,' said Ben. If he'd said it was because his grandmother, now dead, would have wanted him to, they'd have thought he was crazy.

Gay Byrne didn't ask about girlfriends. In the circumstances, it seemed more tactful to talk about the dog. And Meg, handsome in her full coat, put on a demonstration, leading Ben round some obstacles on stage.

Sefton Sykes hadn't come to Ireland. He was organizing a concert in Yorkshire; Lesley was doing the paperwork. Ben had travelled to Ireland alone except for Meg.

When Ben stood up to sing *Girl in a Garden*, he felt supremely confident. Not happy exactly; happiness was left behind, somewhere along the line. Happiness would have to wait. The aggression, rooted in fear, which had bedevilled him for months had evaporated. Occupied to the limit of his ability, he had tried to fight his blindness. He knew he had won.

Ben was used to adulation now. He still loved to hear applause, still got high on it, but he could see that in time it might pall. What then? He felt he must continually drive himself to achieve more. Even as he acknowledged the cheers that greeted his song, the standing ovation he could only guess at, his mind was elsewhere. He had no intention of sitting back and living on his earnings. Now that he could perceive some object in it, he was learning Braille and how to use a home computer. The Guvnor had made a room in the farmhouse over to him. Already, Ben had grasped the basics; he listened to talking books half the night. He was educating himself.

Earlier in his Irish trip, there'd been a reception for him at Jury's Hotel. It had thrown him, in a way the concerts never had, because he had to meet family and friends without warning. They were eager to talk to him now – his new confidence was infectious.

'Take it easy – one at a time,' Ben protested, laughing, but they had taken no notice. He'd tried to disentangle the threads of three separate conversations without success.

'Four months old today – you'd take him for more, bless him . . .'

'Didn't try a yard after the last fence . . .'

'Engaged to a man with a hundred cows . . .'

'Won a packet at Phoenix Park . . .'

'Wish you could have seen her dress . . .'

'Wish you could see the foal . . .'

'Ran off with a cattle dealer from Navan . . .'

'Lost a few pounds on Jim's brindled bitch . . .'

Ben had been glad when dinner was announced and he was seated between the tour promoter and Muriel.

Being wined and dined in Dublin was great, he thought, but he was anxious to get back to Middlegarth. He had no wish to visit his old home, in spite of Muriel's urgings to settle at Cloninch.

'You'd never want to leave us again.'

Wouldn't I, thought Ben.

When he arrived back at Yeadon, the Press was there to meet him. He knew Lesley would be there and the Guvnor – he'd forgotten about reporters.

Meg led Ben off the small plane slowly and with great care. She gave the friendly stewardess a cold look. On level ground again, she stopped to show Ben that there were no more steps.

Ben's right hand was in his pocket. Meg knew that he

carried a small cube-shaped box in it. Sometimes when they were alone, he would open it and take out the ring inside, turning it round, almost as if he could see the pale blue stone in it. The corners of the box were scuffed from handling.

The reporters were taking photographs. Meg posed looking up, ears pricked, at Ben; then she stared intently straight ahead, then she sat down, her tongue lolling. She had learned to enjoy posing for the cameras. Ben just stood there, wearing his most wooden expression, waiting for the men to let him go.

One of them held out a microphone and said, 'Haven't you brought back an Irish colleen with you? I hear they mobbed you at your last concert.'

Ben said, 'No. I prefer Yorkshire lasses now.'

The reporter said, 'Oh, I see; lasses in the plural – not just one then?'

'No, two,' said Ben. 'The other one is my dog, Meg.' He added, 'Walk on, Meg,' and she steered him round and through the eager strangers.

As Ben spoke, Meg had seen the woman, Lesley, quite close. She must have heard, because she had that look on her face. She was pushing her way through the crowd towards Ben.

Meg gave one of her wide, yawning sighs. She had always known that one day she would have to share Ben with a human female, and that if she showed jealousy, Meg not Lesley would be sent away. But sharing love with a human is the lot of most men's dogs. Meg had hoped, by making herself indispensible, to postpone the woman's return. She knew, as she heard their voices and saw Ben's face light up, that she had failed.

Dog-like devotion had not been enough.